LEAVE NO CHILD BEHIND

A Novel

R. Overbeck

Heroic Teacher Press

For information on Reading Group guides, email publisher or go to the webpage.
www.heroicteacherpress.com
Email: info@heroicteacherpress.com

Library of Congress Cataloging-in-Publication Data

Overbeck, R.
Leave no child behind
ISBN 978-0-9842194-0-7
I. Title

Printed in the United States of America

DEDICATION

This story is dedicated to the hundreds of talented teachers I have had the privilege of working with over the years. Just like our heroine Dee Dee who put her life on the line to save her students, these teachers work tirelessly day after day to rescue their students from lives of illiteracy and poverty.

For all the times it was left unsaid and for all the students whose minds and lives were enriched by you—thanks.

I am especially grateful to the scores of colleagues and friends who served as critical readers of this work and whose insights enhance the final narrative.

--R. Overbeck

"In a rational world the best of us would become teachers and the rest of us would have to settle for something less."

--*Lee Iacocca*

Prologue
Chicago, Illinois

The Jihad soldier angled the car's side view mirror so that the image was perfectly centered. The top of the Sears Tower was captured precisely in the middle of the glass, the tip of the triangle neatly bisecting the glass. Turning and studying the end of the street, he noted the immense skyscraper appeared to rise out of the ground, jutting up into the azure July sky like some phallic monument to the material greed of Western culture. He counted down seven rows of windows from the top and found the targeted office. He allowed himself a small smile of triumph.

Asad Akadi glanced at his watch, 8:44. Two minutes. He picked up a small silver box and lovingly pawed the smooth metal sides. Gently he ran his fingers over the top of the red trigger, caressing it like the excited clitoris of one of the sacred women in the Cavern of Near Paradise. He got hard thinking about it, reveling in his power. Be patient. He reminded himself of the Sheik's warning. "Just as in our first battle with the Americans years ago, timing is critical."

Allah could wait.

It was amazing how simple it had been. Through the slimy little real estate agent, that Jew with the hooked nose, Asad had found several possible offices in the Sears Tower and selected one on the 103th floor as the target. It then took little effort to get his new "entertainment company" to land the job for a bachelor party, only a few flyers undercutting others' prices.

Asad scoffed, Americans were so predictable.

Fifteen minutes earlier, he had delivered the giant "cake"--complete with an almost nude stripper inside--to the bachelor party at the investment fund company in Room 10305. White icing covered the ten-tiered cake, with each layer meticulously decorated in leaves, figures, and ropes shaped into and throughout the icing. The Muslim baker had done a superb job of embellishing the walls of the "cake." Even for Asad, it was impossible to detect that more than one hundred pounds of plastique lay hidden beneath the intricate confectionery design. According to his source, that was enough to blow up at least the top ten floors of the building, adding more than two thousand new casualties to the great Jihad.

The security had been a joke. The rent-a-cops could not take their eyes off the whore curled up inside the cake shell. Each one just waved him on. Then, pasting a silly grin on his face, Asad stopped briefly in the office to make a few lewd jokes with the ignorant American partygoers, saying he had other "surprises" to deliver and would return for the party girl. **He simply drove out of the garage, down the street and into another parking spot saved by another believer, a maroon pick up exiting just as he pulled up.** *The location had been carefully researched and met the Sheik's criteria. "You must be within one-half mile for the signal to work and have a direct line of sight."*

He checked his watch again, 8:46. It had to be at the exact time. One minute. **He closed his eyes to whisper the traditional prayer of protection, his lips quietly pursing the syllables from the Koran.** *When he opened his eyes again, the red light on the silver box was pulsing, reminding him of the blinking monitor of his son's heart just before... It was time. His eyes focused on the Sears Tower in the side view mirror and he massaged the trigger once more. Then, using his thumb, he flipped the switch.*

He thought he saw an explosion, but he wasn't sure. He felt his door fly open and two huge hands dragged him out of the car and hurled him to the pavement. Asad's head collided with the cement, a large gash spreading crimson across his forehead, and his hands rushed to the cut. The device bounced and clattered on the sidewalk a few feet away. In agony, Asad gaped up at the tall figure looming above him. A dark baseball cap shadowed the attacker's eyes and nose. But that voice. As if falling through a tunnel, he could hear the cackling laugh dying away as the words were spat out, "I got ya' this time, you fucking Ahab!"

Chapter 1

I'm sure it was my fault. It must've been my own preoccupation that caused the collision. Either that or I just wasn't watching where I was going. Maybe I was pondering how many of my students failed the newest State graduation test, or was thinking about the National Guard soldiers stationed on every street corner.

You see, for me, a three-mile run through the quiet streets of Hammerville has become a Saturday morning ritual, one small part of my exercise regimen. I don't know if it was merely a phase or if I was actually getting serious about my fitness, but in the past two years I had begun running regularly, doing weight training and taking Tae Bo classes at the local Y, usually three times a week. Well, it's not like guys were ringing the phone off the hook and booking my social calendar. Besides, I had gotten to the point where I could feel my muscles strengthening and my stamina increasing. On good days, it was a rush-- and I didn't have enough of those feelings lately. Also, I knew the running was one of the only ways to keep the hips from collecting excess padding. I'm a teacher. And, you know with the huge salary I make, I find myself eating rich foods all the time, mostly macaroni and cheese from the school lunchroom. Just one of the great perks of the job.

Most days, I found that the fresh air of these runs freed my mind and allowed my feet to jettison the week's anxieties directly into the forgiving asphalt. My 5'4, 115-pound frame had run this route so often that my legs had the track memorized, my muscles automatically responding to each rise and hill, the aches and surges coming in predictable patterns.

But lately, it wasn't working.

The imminent execution of the terrorist Asad Akadi had transformed my beloved town of Hammerville into some grotesque three-ring circus, with the camouflaged National Guard soldiers in one ring, FBI agents in crewcuts guarding the second ring and a horde of reporters crowding the third. Of course, all the turmoil made my students more squirrelly than usual, causing my classes to be a challenge. And then, thanks largely to the lewd suggestions of my friend Christie, the image of a partially-nude figure of Jerod Thomas--the volunteer student mentor and sometime visitor to my class--was crowding my thoughts more than I wanted to admit.

In the final quarter mile, still at full speed, I rounded the blind curve on the park path bordered on both sides by tall hedges and crashed into the stranger. We both went down in a heap, legs and arms in a jumble. "I am so sorry," the man was saying, even before I was able to untangle my legs. "I did not see you and must have stepped into your path as I backed out of the bushes." Though I couldn't see a face, the voice used the careful pronunciation of a foreigner.

He jumped up first and reached out a hand to my prone figure. I took it. It was warm, a strong hand, and when I raised my glance, I saw that the hand was attached to the arm of one of the best looking men I had ever seen. I panted, trying to catch my breath but looking at this gorgeous stranger made that a little harder. His bronze skin and stunning green eyes reminded me of an actor, though I couldn't immediately remember whom. He smiled through his apology, teeth bright beneath a perfectly trimmed black mustache. I stared, dumbstruck, into his handsome face and couldn't get a word out. It would've been easy to just keep staring, but then I realized he was talking to me. After all, I'm a teacher; I couldn't let myself look too stupid.

"...I am so sorry. Please forgive me. It was all my fault," he was saying. "Are you... unharmed?"

I finally found my voice and managed, "Yeah, sure." I drew a shallow breath. "No...sweat," I huffed. Breath. Trying to regain some semblance of poise, I walked over to the nearby bench and started my cool-down exercises. When my fingers brushed some dirt off my spandex tights, I realized I was sweating through every pore in my body. It had been an especially intense run that morning and it showed. Lovely! I took one slow, long breath and let it out. "I was just about finished anyway," I said, glancing back at him in the middle of my first stretch.

He walked over to where I was. "How far do you run?"

"Three miles...well, almost three miles today," I said, turning my head and smiling back.

Black eyebrows rose. "That is quite good and you don't even look, uh-- winded?" he said, as if he were searching for the right word.

Right then, I should have been at least a little suspicious. There I was panting like an overheated collie and he said I didn't look winded? At the time,

I thought it was just an original pick up line. And, did I mention he was middling attractive?

I laughed nervously and switched legs. "I think you just knocked the wind out of me."

He tilted his head sideways and looked down at my figure and then, after a bit, chuckled. "Ah, knocked the wind out of you. It is a saying, no? Very good!"

His accent was Caribbean or maybe South American, I couldn't quite place it. My gaze strayed down the path as two oncoming joggers passed us single file, casting quick glances at us. When my eyes returned to him, my collision mate thrust a large hand at me. "My name is Jesus Ramirez and I am new to your town."

I rose from my stretching position on the park bench and shook the offered hand. Oh-h, my skin tingled from the warmth again. "I'm Danielle Sterber," I said, "but my friends just call me Dee Dee."

"I am glad to meet you...D. D.?" he said with some hesitation.

I nodded, releasing his hand. "Where are my manners? My mom would shoot me. Welcome to Hammerville." I paused a beat and then asked, "What brings you here?"

His face took on a quizzical look again; then I could see something flash behind his eyes. He took two strides back to where we had fallen and disappeared into the hedge; a second later, he emerged holding a red and gold plastic disc in his right hand. His shapely mouth twisted into a mustache-edged smile and he whistled. I turned to look but before I could react, a blur of blond rushed by. When I turned back, a golden retriever stood in front of the stranger, the dog's tail whipping vigorously back and forth like a metronome gone crazy. A dark-skinned hand held the Frisbee up and waved it erratically and the dog's quivering body pranced in anticipation. In one fluid motion, he released the disc and it sailed silently across the perfect blue sky in a large sweeping arc, the retriever in fierce pursuit.

He watched the dog for a bit and then turned back to me. "The fris--bee got stuck in the bush," he said, pointing to the spot on the path. "That is why I am here."

Chuckling, I shook my head. "No, I meant what brings you to Hammerville?" I asked.

He didn't seem to understand and he shrugged.

I tried another approach. "Are you with one of the news crews?" No response other than a squinting of one of his emerald eyes. "You know, a TV crew covering the execution?" There were national outlets from all over the globe in town and it was easy to see him as a handsome reporter. In fact, it was hard to go to a restaurant or store in Hammerville without running into a Saudi reporter or a cameraman from Brazil. Our merchants were ecstatic.

At first he nodded and then shook his head no. "I am sorry again. I did not understand. No, I am not with any news...crew? I have recently come to this country. I am teacher and am hoping to teach."

"Teach here?" I stifled a laugh. "In Hammerville? Why here?" When he didn't answer right away, I added, "And why now?"

He shrugged his shoulders.

I tried again. "Why does a guy from another country..." I stopped mid-sentence and asked. "You are from another country, aren't you?"

"I am from Ecuador, you know, small country in South America?" he asked.

"Yes, I know where Ecuador is," I said, smiling. "Okay, what brings a guy from Ecuador to Hammerville to teach? And in October? I mean, I don't know when the school year starts in Ecuador, but ours began two months ago."

"You are a teacher?" he asked. I nodded and his smile broadened. "Then this is lucky day for me."

"Yeah, I teach English at Hammerville High. What do you teach?"

"My field is science," he said, "as you say here, biology."

I nodded. "But there are no jobs now. At least I don't think there are. And besides, why would you come to Hammerville?"

At my last question, those green eyes flashed. "It is true, I come to your country too late and it is hard for an immigrant to get regular teaching job. So I respond to job listing for substitute teachers on district website and I come here. I arrived last night."

I know, you're thinking I should've seen through this improbable explanation. But back then, what did I know? And, did I mention he wasn't hard to look at?

The golden retriever was back, the Frisbee now properly slobbered in his mouth. Jesus bent down to dislodge it, not without some difficulty. The dog jumped as the stranger sent the disc flying again. The retriever did its thing. He jogged after the dog and called back to me, "It was good to meet you, Dee Dee Sterber. I hope I get to see you at Hammerville High School soon." "Good luck," I replied. "Glad I ran into you," I added and smiled. "Ran into you. Very good," he hollered back over his shoulder, laughing as he ran down the hill after his dog.

As I watched his figure descend the slope, I thought it actually was "nice running into you." Polite, considerate and handsome. All together not a bad package, I thought. Christie was right; Jerod is okay, but wait till she sees this guy. I could already predict the words out of her mouth, "Nice eye candy!"

After his figure disappeared, it suddenly dawned on me. "Ricardo!" I cried aloud like some excited game show contestant. A couple holding hands on a nearby bench threw me a curious look and then returned to staring into each others' eyes. The stranger I had just met reminded me of the Hollywood actor, the dashing character I remembered from one of my parents' favorite TV shows, "Fantasy Island." At that point I could almost have sworn that I had just run into a young Ricardo Montalban.

I headed back down the path, intent now only on getting back to my apartment to call Christie. She'd never believe this. In retrospect, you probably think this was all pretty naive, even stupid on my part. What did I know a few months ago? But this one scene has stayed with me, replayed time and again, like some video loop inside my head. Maybe, that's because it was just the first of my "collisions" with Jesus, and, ultimately, fate.

But I guess I should begin at the beginning.

As much as I could, I've struggled to be faithful to the truth, to tell things as they really happened. Or to rebuild the parts of this story I was only able to learn about later, after it all came down.

In my small-town, comfortably quiet existence, I collided with the rapacious beast of terrorism and it dragged me into its nest of deceit, violence and death. In the depth of this morass, I, a fledging "woman of letters" as one prof liked to call me in college, learned too much about the world, a lot about myself, and even a little about love.

Chapter 2
Baku Valley, Afganistan

The lean teenager stood outside the small hut, scratching at the soil with the toe of one worn sandal and shivering in his thin abaya, two scrawny arms slashing back and forth across his body. Unleashed from the shadowy valley below, the wind rushed around him and screamed a warning at him to flee. Rashid knew, once his trembling hand knocked on the door and he stepped through the dark portal, the decision was out of his hands.

He was terrified of what lay ahead, though he would never admit it. He had no idea of the particulars of the assignment, but he had been told how it must end. They had drilled that particular lesson often enough during his training. It could end only in his "glorious martyrdom."

A small, insistent voice inside him whispered, "But you are only sixteen. You haven't yet begun to live."

Immediately he cursed himself for his weakness, for allowing Satan to tempt him with any thought of quitting. Besides, the elders had made it clear that once in, quitting was never an option. Like many of his age, he had joined the training in the Baku Valley not out of any particular religious fervor, but because he was hungry. Not hungry for the truth, but hungry for bread ... or anything else to eat. His mother and his sister had been so poor that he remembered being famished almost all the time. Before joining Al Quaida, his most prevalent memory had been an aching belly, as if some tapeworm gnawed constantly at his insides, unrelenting for days on end.

As a child, the earliest lessons he could remember were those of trickery, deceit, and, when necessary, escape. He couldn't remember ever having enough to eat until he joined "the favored ones." In the two years since signing his pledge, they had filled his stomach, developed his body and honed his mind. In his lessons, between the morsels of precious food, he had learned that the hedonistic culture of the West was the cause of his people's suffering. Then, when he finally began to grasp the meaning of the great Jihad, they had altered his training. Much to his surprise, he was then taught English, the language of the infidels, and found he could pick it up quickly.

Now he was about to find out how he would serve Allah. So he "screwed up his courage"--he remembered learning that phrase in his English class and thought it amazingly appropriate now--and raised his hand to knock on the weathered door.

"Come in."

He was startled to hear a hoarse voice bark out in English and his hand jumped to the pitted metal handle. He tugged at the door but it wouldn't move. He strained but the warped boards refused to budge. For a moment Rashid was struck by the thought that Allah was conspiring with the screaming wind and the aged wooden door to warn him to stay out, to run away, to save himself. Then, abruptly, the door jerked free and almost rammed into his face. Reacting quickly, he dodged it and propelled his body though the opening, stumbling into the gloomy interior.

"Rashid, my young soldier, how are you?" the voice continued in English, oozing personal concern. As his eyes adjusted to the near darkness, Rashid was able to discern two flickering candles on the far side of the room. In the shadows cast by the licking flames he could barely distinguish the shapes of three figures. His pupils slowly dilating, he realized one of the men was Abu Zarif, his teacher, but the other two were little more than outlines. They were both tall men who towered over the short, fat teacher he had learned from over the past two years. Rashid could make out enough to see that both had lanky figures with long flowing beards and prominent ears, but the weak candlelight washed out the details, giving both almost featureless faces. They stood like stretched silhouettes, their faces little more than dark masks.

"Abu Zarif tells us that you are becoming a soldier of Allah and already are one of his star pupils, that you have learned your lessons from the Koran almost as well as your lessons in English." The voice seemed to emanate from the figure on the left, but Rashid could not see the lips move in the semidarkness.

Peering from one shadowy face to the next, Rashid stammered, "I-I-I have tried to learn what I can," uncertain of what was expected.

"Nonsense!" the voice from the other end of the room boomed. "What does the Koran teach us about false modesty?"

"That it is no less a sin than bragging," Rashid quickly answered, "but—"

"Don't be afraid, my boy," Abu Zarif said, laughing and stepping forward, placing a fleshy, discolored hand on the teen's arm. Rashid could detect the telltale, sweet smell of the pipe Zarif smoked incessantly in class. "I have already told them how hard you have worked on your studies and how you have

excelled. In fact, I have told them that you are by far d'best student in my entire group."

"I do what I can to serve Allah and use what gifts the Great One has given me," Rashid responded, finally finding his voice. "But, holy one, you addressed me as soldier. Surely, my teacher has told you that many other students surpass me in many lessons needed for the great Jihad."

"Allah has a plan for each of us, don't you agree?" the same voice asked quietly now.

"Yes, of course, you are right."

"We have sat in the mosque and prayed, and we believe Allah has revealed that your time has come, young one," the voice continued.

The voice's English was almost completely unaccented, as if it belonged to a CNN reporter, Rashid mused and then was terrified as he realized he was missing part of what was being spoken.

"... not your concern. Now come sit down so we can discuss the details of your assignment anointed by Allah," the voice said.

Rashid quickly sat on the hard, dirt floor and crossed his legs. The speaker did the same across the room, though when "the voice" settled himself, he managed to remain in the shadows, still only a silhouette to the teenager's eyes.

"Others will teach you the details, that is not my concern. I decided to come personally to meet you. I can tell Abu has chosen well," the speaker's darkened face turned toward the teacher, who beamed back. "Now that I have met you and can feel the faith flowing through you, I am certain Allah will bless you with success. Let me tell you this much. After you complete your training, which your teachers tell me will be soon, we wish to send you to America."

Noting Rashid's surprise, he went on, "Yes, you will go to the land of the infidels because that is where you can best serve Allah and the great Jihad. But I do not wish to deceive you. I also came here to share with you that this assignment is quite dangerous. Although your death is not certain, it is possible that you might be asked to give your young life in this effort. Do you believe you could do that?"

"My life belongs to Allah and if he wills that I must die, then I will gladly surrender my life," Rashid answered quickly as he had been taught and struggled to keep any doubt out of his tone.

"I am glad to hear the conviction in your voice," the speaker said. "It is critical that you not be seduced by the Great Satan. Because of their opulence and greed, Americans have it much easier than the faithful here. They have gone soft. The Westerners are a people who have no morals and are corrupting the world Allah has given us."

Rashid felt, but couldn't see, the penetrating stare of the two black eyes boring into him and tried to sit up straighter.

"Rashid, you would not be the first believer who succumbed to the temptations of the West. If we send you into the underbelly of the beast, we need to know that you will not be seduced."

"Whatever you ask, I will do," Rashid answered. "I will not disappoint you. I will carry out Allah's will."

"Good. Good. I was confident your teachers had chosen well." The silhouetted face glanced at the ground, one long finger drawing an imaginary figure on the ground. "When you begin to have those doubts--" a shadowy hand came up to silence Rashid's attempted objections, "and you will have doubts: after all, we are all only human." The speaker paused, turned his shadowy face toward Rashid and continued in a measured monotone, "Remember that we have your family with us and will ... take care of them."

The hair on the back of his neck stiffened and Rashid swallowed once. But--even at his young age--he had learned enough not to voice these thoughts. Unable to speak, he merely nodded.

"For them as well as for Allah," the speaker continued, "it is necessary that you do not fail in your mission. Do you understand?"

Rashid nodded in stunned obedience. Then the wind screamed again, rattling the shuttered windows like some wild animal trying to claw its way into the room through the slats. Struggling to contain his terror, he nodded again and said, "Honored Sheik, I understand. I will not fail."

"I know you will not." The speaker's voice took on a paternal tone. "Your teachers will train you in all the details, but I will tell you this much. You will travel to America and enroll in a high school in a part of their country called Ohio."

Rashid had no idea where such a place was.

As if reading the boy's thoughts, the speaker said, "This is an area in the interior of the country with small towns far from any of the major cities. While in Ohio, you will do there what you have done here -- become an excellent student. You will study hard and wait."

"That is all you want me to do? Study?" asked Rashid.

"Of course you will do more when the time comes," answered the speaker curtly. "As I said, you may even have the chance to achieve martyrdom in the Jihad. From your teachers you will learn the specifics of the important role Allah has planned for you."

The tall figure stood up and moved toward the door, seeming to Rashid to almost float across the ground. Rashid scrambled to his feet. The speaker's voice changed, this time again becoming paternal. "But if you are soon to face death, then we need to show you some of the fruits of rewards that Allah has bestowed on all faithful. First we will provide you with a glimpse of the glory that awaits those who die in His service." His bony finger gestured to the third figure in the small space. "Later Hassan will direct you to the Cavern of Near Paradise for your indulgence. Then you will pay a farewell visit to your family. Go with the blessing of Allah."

The three men emerged from the shadows, strode quickly past Rashid and pushed open the door. After a moment Rashid followed, stumbling out into the howling wind.

Chapter 3

I know what you're thinking; this is a strange tale for a teacher to tell. It certainly seems odd to me in the telling. I signed on to this job to open up students' minds to the best ideas of the best writers, and maybe help them discover something about themselves as well. The only things I expected to protect students from were the occasional dangling modifier and a classroom bully. Certainly not gun-toting terrorists.

It's been months since it ended, and even as my fingers hover over the keys and my memory replays every scene, I still can't keep from trembling.

On one level I really don't want to write this down, don't want to revisit even one horrifying moment. I've read the words others have used to describe their experiences in terrorist strikes--traumatic, harrowing, frightening, life-altering. These descriptors were all true but not nearly enough. Surviving this experience has consumed me. But I've decided that I really have no choice: I have to write this.

Oh, by the way, I'm a high school English teacher. To be more precise, or to "use better language" as I preach incessantly, I teach 11th and 12th grade English and journalism. My students would tell you I'm always after them to "write it down," to put their thoughts on paper. Actually they would call it "nagging," but I prefer to think of my exhortations as vigorous encouragement.

"That's the only way a writer can lay his thoughts bare for examination," I repeatedly urge my students. "In this fleeting world of impermanence, of deleted voice mails and erasable e-mails," I admonished in a recent lecture, "we are losing the records of the evolving thoughts of people, great and small. Thoughts captured in the papers such as the original drafts of Lincoln's Gettysburg Address and Martin Luther King's 'Letters from A Birmingham Jail.' Or even the simple letters with the anguished handwriting of the homesick soldiers from the Iraq War."

And to which my students would say, "Yada, yada, yada." Frankly, most of the time my "teacher words" fall on deaf ears. After all, these are teenagers we're talking about. Every once in a while, there is a glimmer of recognition, a ray of hope that my inspiration is taking root. But, to be honest, most of the time I only see the glazed eyes of teenage boredom staring back at me. What I wouldn't give to see a few of those empty stares right now. But I'm getting ahead of myself.

As long as I can remember, I wanted to be a teacher. You could say I'm here because of my dad. When I was born, I became his princess and he decided early on that I would have a better life than the one fate dealt him. He earned his living as a smelter mechanic working twelve-hour shifts for 33 interminable years in the Francis Foundry. Having exhausted himself in a filthy, often thankless job and trying to raise a family of five, he encouraged me, persuaded me, prodded me to get an education so I could have the chance he never had. Because of his vision for me, I was always going to college, no question about it. The teaching part, though, was my choice.

When I went away to college, I was only too anxious to shake the dust of this town from my shoes, or, rather back then it would have been my sandals. Anyway, I believed I needed to find new horizons, to strike out on my own, so I got a degree in English education with a minor in Mideastern languages of all things. What can I say? I had a great language prof and, as it turned out, a knack for Arabic and Farsi. When I graduated, I got my first teaching job in Cleveland.

But, in my third year of teaching, my father collapsed -- on the job, of course. When they raced him to the hospital, they found his whole body was riddled with cancer that had started in his pancreas. Typical of him, Dad had never said a word. The disease had progressed so far the doctors didn't even bother to operate on him. He died two months later.

You'd think that event alone would have propelled me as far away from home as possible. But, shortly after we interred his body in St. Simon's Cemetery, I received an "inspiration" that I'd like to think came from my father. I walked in and announced to my stunned mom and my sisters that I wanted to come home to teach. My inspiration convinced me that perhaps my mission-- that's a word I heard a lot from my dad--was to try to help other hometown kids realize that education can give them a chance for a better life.

I apologize for digressing. Maybe I stray because I fear what is to come and want to stave it off for as long as I can. I am only 29, certainly not old, but in the past few months have already lived enough of life to realize I need this catharsis. So, I force myself to stare at the monitor until these letters appear, like fanciful black etchings tripping across the white screen.

This story, or at least my part of it, begins in the small town of Hammerville. That's Ohio, the heart of the Midwest. When I returned home, I was fortunate enough to secure the position vacated by Mr. Downs, Dean of the English department and teacher for 32 years.

I guess the real reason I returned was because I truly loved my hometown, even though for a while I was too stubborn to admit it. Like lots of towns in the Midwest rust belt, 25 years ago Hammerville was humming along as a thriving, even fairly prosperous hamlet with plenty of well-paying jobs. Of course, this was changing as I grew up but I didn't realize it, or maybe didn't want to. But when the manufacturing jobs went south -- excuse the pun -- the town's prosperity took a permanent vacation as well. The factories have long since gone idle and been left to, well, rust. You get the picture. I finally did too, but not until after I took this job and returned to my hometown.

And yet here I sat in impoverished Hammerville using cutting-edge technology in a state-of-the-art facility the town named James Thurber High School. How's that for Americana? (Some of the townsfolk wanted to name it Mark Twain High School, but he's not an Ohio author. Thurber, of course, is as he grew up not sixty miles from Hammerville.) The building is a beautifully constructed, two-story structure with gleaming metal and glass slicing at sharp, perpendicular angles. It boasts a massive auditorium with a stage full of technological wonders, a cavernous gym to host the largest of crowds, and a stadium with a manicured field most towns like Hammerville can only dream of. (I know, I know I'm not supposed to end a sentence with a preposition.) A fully enhanced distance learning television studio with the latest in technology, in addition to top notch aquatic and fitness centers, place our school's facilities among the finest in the state. But the school feature the students appreciated most was Thurber Commons, a striking 200 ft. by 400 ft. crafted oak and brass deck attached to the cafeteria. In friendly weather students enjoy congregating in the gazebo, on the benches and at the tables that overlook the two thousand acre lake.

You're probably asking how a little town like Hammerville with meager resources, on the verge of destitution could ever land a school facility like James Thurber High School. I wish I could say that the townspeople realized that investing in their children was the best way to ensure their future and that of the town, but come on. We're talking about school funding in a state that holds a record for inadequacy. Just ask our Supreme Court. But that's another story. Our new school is really where my story begins.

In 2000, the recession that wouldn't hit the rest of the nation for a few years was already in full swing in Hammerville. The big automobile plants had closed after the UAW wouldn't agree to that round of concessions and, within eleven months, the steel mill and other heavy industry shops followed suit. So while "9/11" was only a sick dream in terrorists' warped minds and the next stock market plunge wasn't even dreamt of yet, Hammerville was running a full dress rehearsal of the nation's coming economic woes. There was little remaining industry in town and, without the cash infusion from those jobs, commercial businesses were descending swiftly along the same disastrous path. Years later, onto this field of financially scorched earth marched the polished, briefcase-toting representatives of Harold Barr Enterprises.

Harold Barr Enterprises was a company that in the late '90s had read the tea leaves and predicted that the country would need more space for housing the growing number of criminals, especially those in federal facilities. They had even guessed the conservatives would tighten their grip on Washington politics and would press their agenda for privatizing more government services, including prisons. As businessmen, they had done their homework carefully and chosen the town well. On a cold day in December, the HBE people paraded into the cash-starved town of Hammerville, Ohio, and approached the city fathers with a proposal to build a huge, federal maximum-security prison on the outskirts of town. It was a proposal the city officials couldn't refuse.

Of course, it's usually not easy to find a home for a prison, especially a maximum- security prison. According to Al Smith, editor of the weekly *Gazette*, "Just about everyone believes that it's important to put the bad guys behind bars, but they also believe that someone else's town should house them." Hammerville, Ohio could hardly afford to be choosy. The HBE reps who made the presentation to the Town Council were good, professional and--had I been there, I would have said--slick. They sold their vision for "the renaissance of Hammerville" with a lure of jobs. The prospectus for the proposed prison promised fairly well-paying jobs for about half the town. Of course, these new jobs wouldn't pay as well as the old UAW auto plant jobs, the reps apologized; the economy wouldn't allow it and the market was just too competitive. What they didn't have to say was that those old jobs were long gone and Hammerville stood little chance of attracting other new industry.

To sweeten the deal, they offered to build a state-of-the-art, comprehensive high school using the same construction firm, arguing that it made financial sense to strengthen the infrastructure of the town to support our new "business." (Of course, this was part of the proposal they had already pitched to their influential friends in Washington; they had even received matching funds from the feds for the school as well as the prison, but we didn't learn that until later.) Town Council members practically ran over each other to be the first in line to accept HBE's "generous offer." It was a regular political lovefest. Al Smith even ran an editorial endorsing the proposal, writing that "the prison project signals the dawning of a new day for Hammerville and it will put our small town on the map." He didn't know how prophetic his words were.

So, in three short years, on an extensive platte of land several miles outside of town--bought for pennies on the dollar, by the way--Harold Barr Enterprises built "the finest state-of-the-art maximum security prison in the world," according to their brochures, complete with a massive, man-made lake flanking one side. Directly across this two thousand acre lake sat the new James Thurber High, looking remarkably like an inferior metal and glass cousin to the imposing security facility. Of course, we had no bars or electrified razor wires, but the similarities in the modern architectural design are striking.

I don't believe for a moment that Harold Barr had a crystal ball. How could he possibly have foreseen just how much that the country would need highly secure prisons in remote locations to hold those convicted of the most vicious crimes? How could they have predicted that the federal government would desperately need a place to house the Guantanamo prisoners? Perhaps HBE was just at the right place at the right time. And perhaps there really is a tooth fairy. At any rate, HBE's friends inside the Beltway did pay handsomely for this "private" government service of incarcerating the especially incorrigible.

And thus Asad Akadi, the first terrorist to be executed on American soil, became the most famous resident of Hammerville.

Chapter 4

Barcelona, Spain

The cigarette smoke was so thick in the cramped room that Yassim had a difficult time discerning the features of the three other men sitting across the room. A haze hung like a charcoal gray Burqa, the traditional female Muslim garment, designed to obscure more than it reveals. Having met with these men before, Yassim knew what to expect and was confident he would be able to lead these "soldiers" when it was time. They were known only as the Baqir cell, a loose band of ruthless fighters blindly devoted to the Sheik. Yassim had to respect them for their unfettered devotion, though he gave that respect grudgingly.

He scratched his bare chin, which no longer held his black and gray beard, and studied the men in the cramped hotel room. He knew them and their lives and was repulsed by their often sinful ways. In his conversion he had learned anew that true followers of Allah did not smoke, imbibe alcohol or cavort with unclean women. It was true that he too was once like these men, before the Imam had shown him the errors of his old ways. Critics labeled him and others like him "born-again Muslims." It was intended as a slight, an effort to ridicule believers who had rediscovered the true meaning of the Koran and had taken a dramatic U-turn with their lives. But Yassim believed this title was exactly right. Since that day last year in the mosque in Frankfurt, the Imam's words had made him feel like a new person. He saw things differently, with such increased clarity. This newly discovered lucidity had given him a filter to see and judge all those around him. He now recognized the truth perfectly. He finally understood that his destiny was to bring down Allah's enemies.

But he realized that these men, precisely because they were skilled warriors, felt they were above the edicts of the Koran, and this sickened him. However, he had learned not to question the Sheik's orders and the Sheik had assigned these men to him. In the end he satisfied himself that it must be Allah's will that these would serve the great cause in their own ways.

He waved his hands in front of him in a vain attempt to disperse the darkening smoke. His slicing gesture caught the men's attention. "How many of you are up-to-date with the situation of our brother Akadi?" he asked in English, testing their knowledge of the language. The Sheik's rules for these meetings stated that all conversations were to be held in English--complete with idioms--to ascertain the soldiers' ability to use the foreign tongue. Watching their brows crease with the effort, Yassim could almost see their brains wrestling with the translation, like worn engines struggling against their gears. Mohammed was the first to respond. He was the tallest of the three, at 6'3, filling a thin, almost lanky frame. A crease of pink skin crawled down the right side of his face, like some elongated insect, the scar attesting to a long-ago knife fight. His angular nose was badly broken in two places, testimony of earlier humiliations. He did not smile. "Asad was sentenced by the woman judge to death. After that he was transported ... to new prison in O-hi-o to wait for execution." The English words came out in a deep, guttural voice as he puffed heavily on the Turkish cigarette he favored, any expression lost in the dark smoke.

Finally catching on to the meaning, the other two men jumped in quickly, trying to impress the cell leader. "How could only a mere woman show such, such...,uh, pride? Is that right word?" asked Hassan, the shortest of the group with an almost squeaky voice. At only 5' 6 he was built like a fireplug and, Yassim knew, was the fiercest fighter among them. With eyes the color of mahogany, he was an expert marksman, well trained in explosives and killed easily. Even though Hassan possessed many weaknesses including having sex with any willing--and many not so willing--females, Yassim knew him as the most dangerous in the cell. None dared ridicule his voice, which too was a reward from a knife fight. On the few occasions when the squat soldier smiled, his broken, decaying teeth also bore witness to earlier battles. When the cell leader gave a slight nod, Hassan continued somewhat haltingly. "Does this feeble-mind woman not know the Koran sets place for woman? She crosses over the stripe--?" he stopped and paused briefly, brow wrinkled again, then caught the idea and continued. "This fake woman judge crossed over d'line and should be ... should be ... er, taught a lesson."

"We know that Allah will punish the infidels, but we can be Allah's hands," added Fadi, brandishing two huge, calloused hands and strangling an imaginary neck. Standing an even six foot tall, the third soldier had shoulders as broad as a refrigerator and sprouted a menacing face, even when partially hidden behind an elongated gray beard. "Her death be example for nonbelievers, it .... it, will send"--he paused obviously searching for the right word and then found it--"send a message to others."

Unsmiling, Yassim stared at them. The satisfied glances the three men exchanged made them look like cocky adolescents, with the false bravado of those that think they know far more than they do. The cell leader's curt reply in Arabic wiped away the smirks instantly. "لتعلم الآن حتى الكثير لديك. الوقت من الكثير وليس لغتهم *You have much yet to learn in their language and not much time.*" *Yassim took a deep breath and continued more slowly in English, his fingers scratching the black stubble on his chin. "It is true the female judge deserves to be taught a lesson, but it appears Allah may choose others to perform that assignment. Allah has other designs for us and the Leader has informed us it is nearing the time to act."*

As one, the three cell members responded automatically in Arabic, creating a momentary cacophony in the room. With a harsh look, Yassim stopped them mid-sentence. Mohammed was the first to recover in English. "What honored responsibility has the Sheik given us?"

Yassim stared intently at all three men as they sat transfixed, their hard eyes appearing like colored slits in the gray fog. "It is Allah's will that we free our brother Asad from the American prison...or join him in Paradise trying."

The three soldiers yelled, "واشاد الل *Allah be praised!"*

"As always, the Leader has coordinated all preparations for us. We are to travel first to Canada, and arrangements have been made for our entry into North America. Mohammed and Hassan, you are to fly into Toronto Airport next Friday. Here are your documents." *The cell leader handed each man a bulging manila envelope with a name typed in black on a label across the top and continued. "Mohammed, you will be traveling as an oil executive from Saudi Arabia, negotiating sales with contacts from U.S. and Canadian companies. Hassan, you will be traveling as his bodyguard and personal assistant, so it will be easy for d' two of you to travel together. Do you understand?"*

Both Mohammed and Hassan were engrossed in reviewing the papers in their packets and gave a cursory nod. The cell leader then turned to Fadi and handed him a third envelope.

"Fadi, you will enter the continent as a rich Arab tourist, interested in viewing Niagara Falls. So as not to alert the authorities, your flight will originate from Turkey and you will also fly into Toronto four days later. Then you will drive to meet us in Montreal."

"Details of each of your identities have been carefully laid out in the packages, including Canadian and American money. Spend it wisely. Everything you will need is there. Review all the papers, then destroy them. There has been much work done by your brothers to make your role in Allah's plan possible. Act responsibly and do not call attention to yourselves." He paused and looked into the eyes of each man so they could read the resolve in his face, even in the murky haze.

Satisfied, he continued, *"One advantage for each of us is that we believe we have been able to stay below the Western radar"*--he noticed the puzzlement on their faces, so he searched mentally for a translation without idioms. *"The Sheik's sources believe we are not well known to the Americans so can travel under our own names. It should make the holy task one step easier. After today, we will not see or talk to each other, until we meet in Canada. Are there any questions?"*

The three exchanged glances and then looked back at Yassim, saying nothing. Finally, Fadi asked Yassim, *"And you? What identity will you use to travel to the land of the Great Satan?"* The three heads turned expectantly toward the cell leader. For the first time in the meeting, Yassim broke into a broad grin.

"In my case, the Sheik has outdone himself. He has decided that I am to visit Canada as a member of the Nigerian delegation to the World Peace Conference in Toronto. Truly poetic justice for a soldier in Allah's great army!" He allowed himself a laugh.

The other cell members joined him and shouted again through their laughter, *"Allah, be praised!"*

Chapter 5

The fate of Asad Akadi was never in much doubt to me or anyone else. Five years earlier he had attempted to blow up the top ten stories of the Sears Tower in Chicago. His bomb, concealed inside a large bachelor party cake, did detonate but only a tiny portion of the C-4 ignited. The resulting explosion blew out four windows on the 82nd floor and killed two, including the stripper hiding inside the cake. But these few deaths were more than enough to earn him a death sentence.

When CNN carried Federal Judge Cynthia Hopkins' sentencing of the first terrorist caught in the act on American soil and broadcast her words of "Hammerville, Ohio," I could feel the electricity ripple through the town. My fellow townspeople were so excited that they were dancing, if not in the streets, then at least in Slim's Bar and Grill with the jukebox playing "Proud to be an American." For a while, it even looked like Harold Barr Enterprises had delivered on their yellow-brick road promise. During those days, many of my colleagues like Mark "the Music Man" Bender and social studies teacher Robert Holden took pleasure in chiding me for my long-standing skepticism. Much to my amazement, it appeared then that the emperor did in fact have new clothes.

After the judge's pronouncement of Akadi's sentence, Al Smith, always one to twist a phrase, cited the mood of the town in his editorial as one of "delightful derision at the fate of the convicted terrorist and triumphant pride that Hammerville had been selected to carry out this just sentence." Eerily, it seemed to me that HBE had foreseen this precise set of consequences. The national spotlight focused suddenly on Hammerville and almost everyone in the town started strutting. Even I had to admit that it made a real difference.

Local merchants and shopkeepers were positively ecstatic about the additional business the entourage of newsmen, the gawking tourists and the extra security were bringing to town. The town fathers strutted around local hot spots like Linda's and The Corner Restaurant, proclaiming their excitement at the chance to showcase the new prison, along with their town of course. They even hired a PR firm to advise them on how best to market the town and, almost immediately, began a campaign to beautify common areas of the town, concentrating on those locations most likely to be filmed by the networks. The square in front of the courthouse went through such a transformation that it looked like it had been attacked by the "Extreme Makeover" team. Rather than being threatened by the possible danger this crazed terrorist zealot could bring to town, most Hammerville residents were seduced by the celebrity and hypnotized by the thinly veiled promise of a better future for the town.

As if on patriotic cue, the FBI arrived in force on the Fourth of July and began the preparations for Akadi's arrival in town. With their company-issue navy suits and crisp military haircuts, the special agents descended upon the town like a coordinated flock of sparrows. Usually they announced their presence and their intentions, patiently explaining the need for heightened security and vigilance, but they still ruffled feathers with the local constabulary and some town officials.

But something didn't sit right with me. I never quite shared the enthusiasm for our notoriety and the town's sudden transformation. It felt like an elaborate dress rehearsal for a major production, but I could never be sure if there was anything behind the sets and the props. Back then I felt alone, staring incredulously at the entire spectacle like Alice through the Looking Glass, my neighbors now characters in Wonderland.

What did I know that they did not? I possessed no special clairvoyance. But my own skeptical perspective did have one unique advantage. It was skewed by a new factor; his name was Jerod Thomas.

During that summer Harold Barr Enterprises launched a new corporate campaign to heighten the involvement of their employees in "various community endeavors," according to the HBE press release. And Jerod Thomas was one of those civic-minded HBE employees. In actuality, he was a third-shift correctional officer who volunteered as a mentor at the school and, by what I thought at the time was a giant cosmic misalignment, was assigned to a few young men in my third and seventh period classes. I sometimes have this vision of God as a great prankster, just looking for ways to have fun at our expense down here on earth. Perhaps that's why, at the start of the school year, Officer Thomas entered my classroom to play the antagonist in my little drama.

That didn't come out like I wanted. Now, even I'd have to admit Jerod was pleasant to look at, as several female students never tired of commenting. In fact, he was handsome in a hard-bitten way, with his short brown hair and deep-set green eyes perched over a squat nose with nostrils that flared slightly when he was angry. As a prison guard, he could have walked out of central casting; he was a well-kept 30ish, with delightfully broad shoulders, long, well-developed arms and a body of six feet one that seemed to exude hardness. All attributes that served him well in his chosen profession, no doubt. To the delight of my students, he was cocky, with an irreverent sense of humor that managed to stay just this side of antiauthoritarian.

When he strolled into my classroom for the first time, the details of the celebrity prisoner were all over the news. In fact, the plight of the condemned terrorist was one of the only adult topics the teens wanted to discuss. Because of the newfound notoriety of the prison, my students were in awe of the "kickin" job of correctional officer. For his part Jerod--he insisted he and I be on a first name basis, though it was strictly Officer Thomas to the kids--did what he could to downplay this celebrity to the students. "When Akadi arrives, I'll treat 'im like any other prisoner. No more or less," he said in his slow, Southern drawl in answer to their persistent questions. Head cocked slightly to one side, he went on. "He'll be just another con on death row. One of fourteen awaitin' execution here at Hammerville." His demeanor was one of calm confidence. "You realize, when you make a big deal about this guy, you give him just what he wants--fame and recognition."

After the bell rang and the students made their normal hasty exit, it was my free period--excuse me, planning period--and I decided to be hospitable; I invited Jerod to stay and chat a bit and he readily agreed.

In the small talk, he shared that he was from another small, rural town in Tennessee and had come to Hammerville because his grandmother who lived in Mayboro, a little town up the road, had told him the prison was hiring. He said he arrived in town on a Wednesday, filled out an application on Thursday, interviewed and was hired on Friday. (Some guys just have it made; it took me two months and four interviews to get this job.)

When I attempted to praise him for handling the students' questions about Akadi so sensibly, his only response to my compliment was a flippant remark, "I was lying to 'em."

"What?" I asked, not certain I had heard him correctly.

He didn't answer right away and instead leaned back on the student chair, lifting the front legs off the floor. He looked straight into my eyes. "You heard me right, I lied to 'em. No reason for them to get all hyped up, just because we got the most dangerous man in America about to take up residence just across that big lake. Teens got enough stress in their life, they don't need me adding to it."

That was it. That was all he was going to say and he flashed that smile of his at me, that smile that seemed to hang halfway between innocence and "I just got away with it."

Well, I couldn't let that stand. "Do you think there is any real chance of danger here in Hammerville?"

He latched his fingers behind his head, leaned back and yawned. "Lemme put it this way. The powers-that-be at HBE believe that this guy and his group are crazy enough to try anything. With the rantings and ravings of these fanatics, I wouldn't dismiss any possibility." He shook his head, but the sardonic smile never waned. "The scuttlebutt among the guards is that the security they're planning for Akadi is tighter than the skin on a dried-up rooster. Hell, it's tighter than the presidential Secret Service detail. Cameras, microphones, even extra guards on rotating shifts. According to the plan we're going to know any time Asad scratches his nose or his--"

I cut him off with a hard glance, but only briefly.

"Or any other bodily part," he finished with a grin and one raised eyebrow.

Lowering his chair to the floor, he extracted his bent, large frame from the student desk, not without some difficulty, and made his way toward the hall. Though I resented him for voicing them, his words only confirmed my own fears. I wasn't sure what to say. I asked, "Is there anything you think we should do?"

As his tall, broad body slipped through the doorway, he turned, cocky smile still intact. "Yep. Pray."

Chapter 6

Rashid could not believe that he was here, staring down at his calloused, bare feet perched on a perfect triangle rock. He had been told this stone marked the entrance to the Cavern of Near Paradise. Like most believers, he had thought this place was merely a myth, a legend told by bragging warriors, each one exaggerating the tale to the point of incredulity. Now that he was here to discover the truth for himself, he was trembling, anxious about all he had heard. How could there be such a place as "Near Paradise"? As a warrior in the great Jihad, he had been promised indescribable delights in the hereafter if he were to surrender his life on his holy mission. According to the stories told, this cavern was a small glimpse into that pleasure and glory. The stories were too fantastical to believe, and yet...he trembled at the possibility.

After what he had endured the past few months, his rational mind told him that there was little he should fear. After all, he was no longer that scared kid; he was now a man, a tested soldier. To get here, he had experienced the harshest, cruelest months of his life. And he had survived. His trainers and teachers had driven him, day and night, till he was completely spent. All he wanted was to quit, surrender and sleep. But he had not been allowed to rest. He had been pushed and marched through the freezing rain and snow in a fierce wind that mocked him endlessly. Relentlessly he was interrogated and drilled again until he could answer every question and follow every barked order, even in his sleep.

His command of English was now so extensive that he could dream in it, complete with idioms, on the few occasions he was permitted to sleep. Of course, he realized he still spoke the foreign tongue with a pronounced accent of a man from the "Mideast"--the American derogatory reference to his homeland since all Americans believed the world revolved around them and their geography. His teachers were satisfied. He needed only to pass as who he was--a humble, backward Arab student who wanted to learn the ways of the West.

Academic studies had always come easily to him, but Rashid had surprised himself with the speed with which he had learned how to incapacitate--he truly relished that English word that seemed to ooze with his newfound power--or even kill the enemies of Allah. It is true that, years ago when his belly was empty, he had beaten off other, stronger boys who had tried to take his recently stolen food. But this strength was different.

Like his more youthful violence, this new power was driven by desperation--he only had to call up the Sheik's message about his family as incentive--but this was also fueled by a growing hatred of Allah's enemies, a fire so fierce it threatened to consume all else. In his heart of hearts, he realized he had grown to enjoy, even revel in this new power he would hold over the lives of others.

He easily completed the short course on explosives and found that he enjoyed the direct, hands-on applications of his earlier science studies. With practice and some focused concentration, he had even learned to wield a homemade knife with enough precision to strike its target. He admitted to himself he was no expert in any of these skills, but he knew now he could hold his own.

It had been a grueling couple of months and he found he was more tired than he could ever remember. But it was the near pleasant exhaustion of accomplishment. Rashid had become a confident soldier, one now almost ready to serve Allah. He was scheduled to leave for America in just five days.

And yet with all this newfound assurance, he was still frightened. What powers did the frail creatures of the fantastic tales hold over him? What should the newest soldier of Allah's holy army have to fear from this cavern? And yet, try as he might, his mind could not win this battle of confidence. As he stood there outside the cavern, his bruised and beaten feet felt the grit of the rock against his skin, his gut tightened and his loins roared. Inhaling the fragrance of the moss and earth and moving water, Rashid took a deep breath and stepped through the almost invisible slit in the rock face.

Once through the opening, he panicked. For a moment he felt as if he had been swallowed by a vacuum with all his senses cut off. The darkness ahead of him was so complete that he jerked his head around to reassure himself by the tiny zipper of light in the rock face behind him. It seemed to be fading, but--he breathed an audible sigh--it was still there. Then, as he watched, his bare feet frozen to the spot and his body contorted backwards, the light appeared to flicker and slowly ebb before his eyes like some fading vision. His panic rose and he felt his heart beat heavily, its thumping sound like the footsteps of a predator.

A wild thought seized him; perhaps this was but another of the Sheik's cruel trials, some sensory deprivation to further test his stamina and resolve. Involuntarily, he railed against his trainers for tricking him again and submitting him to yet another of their ordeals. His cut and bruised hands clawed at the air in front of him, arms flailing like a desperate blind man and grasping nothing. He felt his heart rate spike again and he fought his alarm.

"Just breathe deeply," he heard a soft voice whisper in his own language ... or was it the wind, he wondered. He realized that he could feel some sort of warm breeze on his skin, was glad to experience something, any sensation.

"Please just close your eyes and take several deep breaths," the voice said. He twisted his head from side to side, eyes scanning, trying desperately to locate the source of the words in the darkness. He couldn't find it and his panic inched up.

"I know the darkness is disorienting at first, but please do as I request," the quiet voice continued, though more insistent. "Just stand where you are and close your eyes." Seeing little choice, Rashid surrendered and did as he was bid. "Yes. That is good. Now feel the warm breeze on your face."

With closed eyes, he could experience the gentle touch of air moving against his skin. He took one deep, slow breath and could even hear his heart rate slowing. The voice was soothing and he felt his anxiety start to drain away, found himself able to appreciate the experience of the soft breeze like the flutter of butterfly wings on his face.

"That's better," the voice whispered again. "Just breathe deeply for a moment and allow the sacred air to ease your concerns." Eyes still shut, he inhaled, a faint, aromatic scent that triggered a memory of expensive perfume from the market place. "It is the sweet breath of the holy ground on which you stand. After all the trials you have endured in recent weeks, its only purpose is to comfort you. In fact, this is but the first of Allah's gifts sent to assuage your hurts and sustain you for the fight ahead." The words flowed quietly across the space.

Rashid continued his rhythmic breathing. He thought, or sensed that the voice was slightly louder, but still could not quite place the direction. Just as he was deciding whether to open his eyes again, he felt the slightest touch on his forearm like the soft brush of fine silk.

"Now you may open your eyes, but slowly please," the female voice continued and Rashid complied. This time, as he lifted his eyelids, finding them incredibly heavy, his sight slowly returned, images coming into focus, much as he imagined that the blind men cured by the Prophet must have seen. The image

*of a beautiful woman seemed to shimmer in the air beside him as if wrapped in a
gauze of haze. His mind struggled to make sense out of the apparition.*

*As if reading his mind, she breathed rather than spoke. "Oh, I am real
enough, flesh and blood just like you, as you will learn soon enough. Please
follow me on the path and you need not worry, even with your bruised feet and
injured toe. The ground here is even and the path is clear, and Allah will guide
your every step."*

*How did she know of the injury to his toe? Then, noticing her insubstantial
form seeming to float ahead of him, disappearing into the vapor, he took up
behind her, eyes darting down and to the sides. As he moved, he studied the
ghostlike mist that now wrapped around him like a large white blanket. It
appeared to be mist rising from beside the path, probably from some warm
underwater spring.*

*She jarred him by reading his thoughts again. "The steam that floats
through this chamber is caused by the hot spring that bubbles up through the
floor of several chambers in the cavern."*

*He followed her on the wide path as it wound through a series of curves
and bends and as he went, he studied her form ahead of him. She was smaller
than he, about five four he would guess and was wearing only the thinnest of
tunics that seemed to cloak her body in translucent light as she glided lithely
over the stone path. Unlike the traditional Muslim garb for women, the clothing
did little to conceal the shape of her figure. As she rounded another corner in
front of him, he gazed at the sway of her slim hips, and as she turned at the next
corner, he caught a glimpse of two full breasts. He grew hard at the thought,
his loins reacting, but then worked to restrain himself, reacting as he had been
taught in the moral lessons at the camp. Before he could find his voice to utter
the traditional objection to her clothing, she stopped abruptly on the path,
turned to face him and spoke again. By the time he realized she had stopped,
Rashid was only a few inches from her and had to pull up short.*

*"I am sure you must wonder at my dress," she said quietly, her eyes first
looking into his and then demurely casting their gaze to the ground. "Like any
honorable man, you must wonder why I am not wearing the burqa."*

*How could she read his very thoughts before he can even voice them. In
his life of poverty and in the years of study and trials at the camp, he had
learned to keep his thoughts and feelings to himself, to keep his "poker face on,"*

as the Americans would say. And yet she breathed his every thought almost before his mind could fully form it. He wondered if she also knew his most intimate thoughts and feelings. She raised her face and, when he looked across at her, she nodded slightly.

Realizing she was waiting for his agreement, he nodded and she continued. "Because of our assigned role in Allah's plan, we have been granted special permission regarding the covering of our body, but only while in the Cavern of Near Paradise. I hope my appearance does not offend you?"

"No ... no ... no," he stammered, feeling again like an awkward schoolboy. "I am not offended," he said.

"Good."

In that second, facing her, he realized that she was much older than he-- perhaps ten years older--and quite beautiful. Because of her age and beauty, her tone of deference pleased him even more. Involuntarily, he felt his hard-on return. That sensation reminded him of the tales told of this place and he thought perhaps he understood her role. "Allah, be praised," he managed and his smile met hers.

"Yes, then let us continue," her soft voice whispered. "We are almost there." She turned and walked down a slight incline and then bent down to step through a low doorway.

Bending his body, Rashid followed her through the opening hollowed out of the rock and stepped into a large anteroom, the air filled with a pleasant mist rising from the ground. His eyes followed the vapor as it swirled upward. He noted the chamber was so high the rock face that formed the ceiling was not visible. It gave the room the sense of being infinite.

As his eyes adjusted, he could make out the center of the chamber. Several large gray rocks lined the perimeter, each one forming a smooth platform that sloped down into a pool of gently bubbling water. A narrow path circled the small crystal lake, weaving around the giant boulders. He peered into the water. It was remarkably clear and he could see the even stone bottom several feet below. At the edge, he dipped his toe into the surface, expecting to have to withdraw it quickly from the hot temperature. Instead he was surprised to find the water to be pleasantly warm to his touch.

When he looked up, she was standing beside him, watching him patiently. "Where am I? What is this place?" he said.

"This is called the Cavern of Near Paradise, though I suspect you have heard the name spoken before," the woman beside him said, "and I am called Jabirah. It is an unusual name and it means 'comforter' because that is my role in Allah's great plan."

Rashid shifted uncomfortably on his tired, aching feet. As if sensing his discomfort, Jabirah spoke again, her voice a balm to his nerves. "I forget myself. Your feet must surely hurt after your long, trying journey. We must get them into the healing waters. First you should remove your tunic so we can properly cleanse you."

Still uncertain, Rashid did not move.

"You may go behind that rock and disrobe and then slip into the holy water." Her hand indicated the boulder halfway around the room.

Nodding his ascent, he followed the path around the room. Halfway around the circular chamber, his ears detected a sound, laughter he thought, men and women's excited laughter. He strained to listen but the sound was gone and replaced by only the soft gurgle of the water. His eyes darted left and right but he saw no one. Yanking his torn abaya over his head, he dropped it onto the rock path and lowered his body into the water. It was warm and welcoming.

At the edge of the path, the water came up to his stomach, and as he waded further into the pool, the level became deeper till it was over his head. He allowed his body to drift under the water, all sound and sight cut off, enjoying the warm effervescence on his bruises and cuts, and then he resurfaced. He could not see Jabirah, but he heard her voice from beyond the rock.

"It gets deeper as you move to the center." Her words floated across the water to him like Allah's angel. "The rock in the center is perched on a ledge, so you may want to swim over to it."

He made his way to the boulder in clumsy strokes, his bruised body drinking in the liquid warmth. When his hand touched the smooth curve of the rock side, he pulled himself partially out of the water and onto the rock. He lay there a while, contented for the first time in months, his back against the cool rock and feet on the underwater ledge, water lapping at his waist. Staring into the warm water, he could make out the bottom half of his naked body beneath the misty surface, could see the muscles of his strong legs and his skin marked with the crisscross pattern of fresh cuts, and noted that his penis was in that pleasant state halfway between erection and softness.

As he was staring down at himself, he heard Jabirah emerge from the water behind him. She made little sound as she climbed onto the ledge and stood up straight along side him. When he turned toward the sound, he noticed that she too was now naked. Lying on the rock, he stared up at her standing form, now towering over him. Except for glances at stolen Western photos, he had never before seen a woman in the nude. He gaped at her, feeling suddenly like the hormone-driven adolescent he was. Tresses of black, shoulder-length hair framed her small face, the strands flattened against her scalp as the water dripped from the ends, glistening down onto her umber-colored skin. His gaze followed a droplet as it glided down her body like a slow-moving liquid diamond, curving around her bare hips. Her hips were wider and looked firmer than they had appeared under her garment. He took in her small, firm buttocks that curved gracefully out from her hips. Allah makes all beautiful creatures, he thought.

"With your approval, I have something for you," he heard her say, though it didn't register at first. He wasn't concentrating, at least not on her words. As his glance traveled back up her body, it passed over her breasts and stopped. He caught his breath and felt his organ stiffen. Though her body was slim and spare, her two breasts were generous mounds erupting from the lean frame with darker circles surrounding the tips and the nipples pointed up, now only inches from his face. Embarrassed, he forced his gaze to move up to her face. Her found two deep, black eyes ridged in dark lashes.

She studied the water below his waist. "I think perhaps Allah's newest soldier approves, yes?" She smiled, a gentle, understanding smile that allowed Rashid's embarrassment to ebb away. Only then did he notice that she held a small clear vial in her hand. A golden liquid swirled in the glass.

"This is a special mixture of herbal extracts created to cleanse your body, heal your pains and bring you pleasure. May I?" she asked indicating the vial.

Rashid nodded and watched as the amber fluid flowed onto her fingers like warm honey and she massaged it onto his skin. His skin tingled at the touch of the liquid and her fingertips. The flesh she touched radiated a comforting heat. She started with his shoulders and her fingers moved down his chest, working patiently across each of the cuts slashed into his flesh. She worked without saying a word, the comforting smile never leaving her face. He lay, mesmerized by her naked beauty and gentle touch. When she had covered his chest with the amber solution, he glanced down at his body and thought he could feel his skin actually healing the hundreds of cuts and gashes. When he looked up, she had moved around the rock till she stood in front of him, her trim legs between his on the rock ledge. Without saying a word, she placed both hands on his submerged hips and lifted him up onto the rock until only his knees were below the waterline. Rashid wondered at her remarkable strength.

His attention returned when Jabirah picked up the vial she had set on the rock and continued her ministrations. She swirled the liquid around both of his hips, massaging it into the flesh, his skin dancing at her touch. Then she poured another portion onto her hands and wrapped her fingers around his now uncomfortably stiff organ, massaging the tingling mixture onto the sensitive skin. Excited, inexperienced, Rashid could not control himself. He squealed "Oh!" and erupted, sending jets of milky white into the air. She stopped her massaging, allowing him to fully experience the sudden climax. Feeling an odd mixture of orgasmic delight and shame, he stared in disbelief as the streams landed on the rock beside him.

Without knowing why, his immediate response was an embarrassed, "I'm sorry."

A comforting smile greeted him. "You have no reason to be sorry. You are a great young warrior and I know this is all new for you. My role--and those of my sisters--is to help you, coax you, soothe you, even teach you. Is that acceptable to you?"

Rashid nodded and she continued. "I know that you must leave in only five days for your mission to fulfill Allah's will. It is his will now that you experience much healing and great pleasure. For the next few days we will pull back the veil so you can see the delights that Allah has waiting for you if you are to join him when your mission is completed. So you see, we have just begun." Glancing down at the liquid oozing down the rock like a small white snake, she continued, allowing the corners of her mouth to turn up into a slightly different grin, "Allah has made man so that you have much more where this came from. Our task is to help you experience some small portion of the pleasure he has planned for you."

"Our?" Rashid asked, finally catching her reference to plural.

"Oh, yes. Four of us have been selected to minister to you and prepare you, body and will for the task ahead. Husna, Farah, Basinah and myself of course." As she spoke, three beautiful, bronze-skinned women emerged naked out of the water and stood beside Jabirah, the four forming a semicircle surrounding his body.

"We are the consorts given to you by the Sheik. We have been entrusted with the task of opening avenues of overwhelming delight for you," Jabirah finished.

Then Jabirah picked up the vial and poured golden portions onto the hands of all four women. Rashid stared in awe at the four nude beauties surrounding him, his male fantasies indulging in eight, large rounded breasts and a veritable forest of brown pubic hair. He found the power between his legs stirring again. He whispered, *"So this is heaven. Allah, be praised!"* He laughed in joyous celebration of his new manhood and role as warrior. As the hands of three new women descended toward his body, they joined their laughter with his, their mutual pleasure echoing through the chamber. Amidst the squeals of her sacred sisters, Jabirah grinned at Rashid and said, *"I believe I can coax this brave soldier of Allah to attention again. What do you think?"* Then she puckered her mouth.

Chapter 7

"I just can't believe I'm going to my first real press conference to hear Harold Samson!" squealed Tess Esselmann, squirming on the passenger seat of my '02 Ford Focus. "You're the greatest teacher, Ms. S, you know that!" Her brown eyes flashed with excitement.

Tess was the senior I had selected as editor of the student newspaper, aptly named The Anvil for our town's heritage. At the time we were headed to an "Official Press Conference" concerning the scheduled execution of Asad Akadi. The press conference was being held at the HBE Prison and hosted by the warden, James Cromer, but the guest of honor was none other than Harold Samson, Director of Homeland Security. I had wangled an invitation for the two of us by trumpeting the educational benefits for my aspiring young journalist. In fact, it took a carefully orchestrated plan of groveling before the powers that be at both James Thurber High School and HBE to obtain the two coveted press passes. Jerod, of course, wanted to claim credit for getting the guest passes, but I didn't believe him.

"Just take a couple of deep breaths, Tess." I said and smiled, stealing a glance across the car seat. "We're just supposed to be there to observe and learn."

Tess was a petite girl with a slightly oversized nose and beautiful, brown eyes she hid behind large dark-framed glasses. Like a number of girls at school, she couldn't decide how to wear her hair. It was on the shortish side and some days she wore it ratty and unkempt and other days she would braid it in mini cornrows. I once asked her why she seemed to work at looking plain--or at least trying to disguise some of her best stuff. Her only answer was "What do you know, Ms. S? After all, you're 29." The way she pronounced the number made it sound like a synonym for "ancient."

Glancing across, I was pleased to see her auburn tresses were curled and pleasantly framed her rather pretty face. She had even spruced up in a dress of navy and white, further evidence of the importance she placed on our invitation. I don't believe I'd ever seen her in a dress before.

I pulled the visor down to do a quick self-assessment. Not bad, I decided. Sparkling hazel eyes stared back under my carefully done eyebrows. A small, straight nose--which I've inherited from my mom, thank heaven--sat in the center of smooth skin that wrapped two prominent cheeks. In the mirror, I noted pale pink lips that circled mostly straight teeth when I smiled. I had selected a pearl gray sculptured pant suit that I hoped would make me look professional and feminine and, glancing down, I was pleased with how it hugged my 115-pound figure. I flipped the visor back.

"Ms. S, have you ever met somebody big, like Harold Samson?" Tess asked as she looked at me, her legs folded under her like a lanky, female pretzel, no doubt creasing the newly ironed dress.

"Do you mean somebody important or somebody with a large stature?" I asked for language clarification, and to pull her chain a little.

"Com'on Ms. S, somebody important, you know, nationally famous like Harold Samson?" she returned. Her right hand tugged on a loose curl.

"At college, I met a few moderately famous authors, but no, no one of national status like Harold Samson."

"What do I say to him?" she asked, genuinely earnest.

"I don't believe you need to say anything." We pulled up and stopped and I turned to face her. "Look, Tess, when you're asked, simply introduce yourself and show them your press pass."

"Oh my God, my pass!" She began a frantic search through her tiny black purse, finally resorting to dumping the contents on the seat. "We have to turn around! I forgot my press pass!" Her fingers clawed desperately through the few items.

"Relax, Tess. I've got your pass with me."

She sighed and began shoveling items back into the small pocketbook.

"Let's go. Move the car!" I heard the words barked and realized that the sentry was motioning me to pull up in line to the checkpoint, his gestures exuding annoyance.

I threw the car into gear and hit the gas pedal, jackrabbitting forward. When I turned back to my window, the soldier was there, his face huge and close in the window. A pair of hard gray eyes stared at me above a sloping nose and a mouth that was a live caricature of the scribbled line from a "Peanuts" comic strip. He was dressed in full combat fatigues, complete with camouflage helmet above his stern face. Startled at first, I recovered after a bit and started to wind down the window, vowing to make certain my next automobile purchase includes at least a few "luxury" features, like windows you didn't have to crank.

Before I had the window all the way down, he was speaking. "Press passes, please!" It was more command than request. As I fumbled in my cavernous bag, searching for our coveted press credentials, he said nothing, his face a disembodied visage hovering inches outside my window. His stern silence only made me more anxious, escalating my fumbling efforts. When this didn't immediately produce the two badges, I lost all patience and dumped the contents on the seat in a harried imitation of my younger partner. Sure enough, the last two items out of the bag were our press passes. I handed them through the opening.

"Tess, could you scoop my junk back into my bag?" I turned back to the officer who was checking the info on our badges against a paper on a shiny metallic clipboard. Staring at the sentry, I mused he was so young, just a few years older than Tess, I guessed. Lately in our country there seemed to be an immense shift of responsibility toward youth. First with so many of them fighting in Iraq and Afganistan and now here on the home front. It seemed that we were foisting a tremendous burden onto kids who only months before had populated classrooms like mine.

The young soldier made a check on the sheet and extended both badges back through the window.

When Tess started to reinsert the passes into my bag, I called "Not in there." She looked over at me, puzzled. As I pulled into the parking space the next sentry directed me toward, I said without looking at her, "If you put them back in there, we might never find them again."

She passed me the badge with my name and image digitally embedded into it, her hand trembling a bit but her face beaming. We both clipped on the passes, each trying to find a spot on our outfits where the clasp wouldn't ruin the fabric. Obviously, a guy had designed these clips. We slid out of the car seat and I automatically reminded her to lock the door. I had absolutely nothing worth stealing, unless you count a used CD of Paula Abdul's first album and realized that locking the car was redundant in this heavily secured compound.

It took a few more minutes to pass through the metal detector and have another guard scan our badges with a digital baton. Once cleared, we were sent through a connecting corridor shaped like a long glass cylinder. As I stepped across the opaque walkway, the experience felt very much like passing through the glass tunnel in some of the modern aquariums I had visited, where the fish swim free and you're caged. At just about the time I expected to see a shark swim by at eye level, Tess and I stepped through the opening to the conference room. We found ourselves clogged in the middle of a group of about a dozen journalists, all moving inside together.

Tess grabbed my sleeve and out of the corner of her mouth said, "Ms. S, I just saw a badge that said 'Newsweek' ...and another that said 'Wall Street Journal'!"

I squeezed her arm and mouthed, "Big Time" and she giggled slightly.

Once inside, I forgot who was standing beside or in front of me. I couldn't help it. I just stared numbly at the HBE Reception Room on this, my first visit to the famous Hammerville Security Facility. I edged Tess over to the right side, almost against the wall, as the flood of reporters continued to stream through the opening. While Tess stood stupified, wide-eyed at the journalistic celebrities among the throng, I tried to take in the incredible space we now occupied.

Nearly square, the room's four walls were fashioned almost entirely of sparklingly clear glass, running at least twelve feet floor to ceiling. According to a reliable source, the glass was fully tempered, six-inches thick and bulletproof. Although the glass appeared to be clear, the building had used some new refractory technology so that the room was flooded with light, but the sun never appeared too bright. At every juncture in the room--floor, ceiling, corners where walls met--the huge plates of glass were joined by gleaming rectangular brass rods.

Standing back and taking in the whole scene, I noted that the room had the appearance of a gigantic crystal jewelry box, every surface sparkling in the light. More than anything else, the place screamed of money. As a building, James Thurber High School was nice, I had to admit, but compared to this architecture, it was clearly only a poor relation. And this was built to house convicts.

In front of the fourth wall, where the reception room met the front offices of the prison, stood a small square platform. This platform also was crafted of perfectly clear glass with beveled edges ending in brass corners. Sprouting from the center of the platform was a slender column of brass topped with expanding prongs that supported a clear glass lectern. In the front of this unusual glass and metal form sprouted a dozen microphones, their black sinewy cords running down and across the glass platform like elongated tentacles of some hidden giant octopus.

As I turned to share all this with Tess, she grabbed my arms and, her eyes darting toward her right, half-whispered, half-squealed, " Look Ms. S, there's Wolf Blitzer!" As I turned to look in the direction she indicated, my attention was instead diverted by the pair of doors opening behind the platform. After a beat, two figures emerged. Though I had never met either, I immediately recognized both men from the media coverage.

James Cromer, warden of the HBE Prison, strode first through the glass doors, onto the raised platform and stopped in front of the mikes. His movements were matched step for step by the Homeland Security Czar himself, Harold Samson. The space exploded with flashes from a hundred cameras, the brilliant points of light bouncing off the glass walls. At the same time the whir of digital cameras and the clicks of the 35mm's echoed off the confluence of glass and metal and seemed to fill the air, instantly extinguishing all conversation. Both figures remained still, waiting for the bursts of light and sound to subside. Fifteen feet away I stood, studying the briefly frozen tableau, and something nagged at the back of my brain. Something was odd, but I couldn't put my finger on it. Then a thought jumped, full blown, into my head.

Both men standing before us were, well, really small. I made some quick mental calculations, subtracting the height of the platform, and realized that both men were only five feet six or seven. The impression portrayed in the media, no doubt carefully orchestrated by the government, was that these leaders were taller, much taller, even giants in command, as if height were an apt male metaphor for leadership. Standing now on the foot high platform, they were able to look down at the reporters, from a position of strength.

Warden James Cromer was the first to speak. "On behalf of HBE, I'd like to welcome you to the Hammerville Security Facility." I noticed that his features matched his diminutive frame--eyes, nose and mouth scrunched close together in a small, oval face--but his head was topped with a large coiffure of jet black hair, looking like a fashion holdover from two decades earlier. I took the big hair to be a futile attempt to enhance his height and I kept waiting for him to stick his right hand inside his lapel. Looking polished and all business, he wore an immaculate, gray double-breasted suit with the letters HBE discreetly embroidered above the breast pocket. Beneath the suit, a crisp white shirt and black and blue striped tie were held captive.

"Mr. Samson will read a brief statement and then he and I will do our best to answer your questions." He sported a beatific media smile as more cameras flashed and shutters clicked away furiously.

I stole a look at my student partner who stood with her eyes fixed on the platform. "Tess?" I whispered and got no response. "Tess?" I repeated, barely louder and pinched her arm slightly. Her head jerked toward me with the obvious question and I mouthed, "Notes." She didn't understand, so I whispered the single word and gestured toward the dais with my head. Suddenly she came alive, took the small notebook from her purse and began scribbling furiously.

Cromer cast a quick glance toward his press partner, who nodded and stepped up to the podium as he moved aside, the two movements seemingly choreographed.

"Mr. Asad Akadi is a terrorist," Samson began without hesitation, looking at a slip of paper he extracted from a jacket pocket. Harold Samson's moniker could not have been more inappropriate. Not one attribute did he share with his Biblical counterpart. Rather than the famous long black curls sheared by Delilah, his hair was short, close-cropped and a mixture of ginger and gray, worn crew cut style. Two large, bulging eyes stared through bifocal lenses atop a pug nose. His face was creased with a firm, straight mouth. The skin on his face enveloping these facial features had a pale, almost pasty look. He was dressed in a navy suit with his trademark bow tie, this one gray and white. Briefly I tried to picture Samson of the Old Testament with a bow tie and almost laughed. I shook myself from my imaginings as the director continued.

"He has brashly admitted as much, proclaiming his 'mission' as one of no less than exterminating the American way of life. Though Akadi and his ilk cloak their acts in the guise of religion and call themselves anointed fighters, the truth is that he and other international criminals like him have been responsible for the slaughter of thousands of innocents around the globe, a rampage that must and will be stopped." Samson's tone grew strident and he made no attempt to mask his contempt.

"One lesson we have learned in the War on Terror is that Asad Akadi and his kind have an insatiable blood lust. Terrorists like Akadi are consumed by hatred of others who are different and driven by jealousy of what they do not possess. All they know is murder and vengeance against some wrong, real or imagined. So it is no surprise that he was captured attempting to inflict similar desolation and destruction upon innocent civilians in the Sears Tower in Chicago."

"Unlike the thousands of men, women and children he and his organization have massacred, Akadi was given the full benefit of the law," he continued. "He has been in our country for almost ten years now and has even become a US citizen. But rather than embrace our freedoms, he has lain in wait all this time, plotting with his fellow criminals to destroy our way of life. In spite of all this, as an American citizen, Akadi has been provided expert legal representation, tried in an open court and found guilty by a jury of his peers. Over the past five years, he has had the opportunity to avail himself of all legal appeals, a process he has now exhausted." He stopped and took a moment to stare into the camera lenses before continuing, his fingers feathering the edge of his bow tie.

"With his conviction, Asad Akadi and other terrorists like him have learned that they can no longer run and hide from the law. He has been sentenced to die, and he will be executed by lethal injection at six p.m. on October 30th. I take no pleasure in the death of any man." He stopped and took a breath. "But in all my years in law enforcement, I have never seen a man more deserving of death. With his death, other international criminals and members of his terrorist organization will get the message that America and all freedom-loving nations will not tolerate this cold-blooded massacre of innocent men, women and children. Unless the terrorists cease their murderous ways, we will hunt them down, capture them, and bring them to justice."

He indicated the end of his statement by stepping aside and allowing Cromer to share the microphone. Before they were in position, hands shot up around the room and reporters began shouting. The questions, when they came, were predictable. Who will be allowed to be present at the execution? Were the protesters disrupting the business of the prison? Is there any chance a last-ditch effort to put off the execution will succeed? Is it true the President is considering offering a pardon in exchange for information on Osama bin Ladin? Yeah, right. Both men took turns answering the reporters' questions, Samson tossing some to Cromer to allow him to share the spotlight.

As the high-profile journalists cast their queries, I noted that Tess was dutifully recording their exchanges. I'm not sure what I expected when I arrived, but as the press conference progressed, a distinct feeling of unease gripped me. The little tingle at the back of my neck began to spread when I heard what turned out to be the last exchange.

"Director Samson, are you concerned about the threat that has been made by Al Quaida that they will free Akadi?" This question was posed by none other than Geraldo Rivera, who, after being fired years before, had managed to get hooked up with a new foreign cable outlet, Star News. The reporter's right hand went to his mustache and he fingered a few black strands.

"I'm glad you asked that, Mr. Rivera," answered Samson, showing just the smallest of smiles. "Terrorists threaten a lot of things. That's where they get their perceived power, in threats that try to terrorize people. One reason for my visit here was to personally inspect the security arrangements here at HBE. And I can tell you this: I am very impressed. The safety and security features they have built into this prison are truly state-of-the art." The Homeland Security Czar let his smile blossom a bit further. "In a way, I hope that some of Akadi's friends come here because they are going to receive a very rude reception. If they make such a foolish attempt, I can assure you that all that will happen is that the United States of America will kill or capture a few more of these murdering lunatics."

Chapter 8

I can still recall that fateful day in October when I received another new student in one of my Junior English classes. There's nothing noteworthy about that; with the crumbling economy in nearly every town around, I gain or lose students just about every week. The class lists in my grade book look like a baseball manager's lineup card in a losing game. But this student was different. His name is Rashid Hermani and he said he was a foreign exchange student from, of all places, Pakistan. I did what I could to get the other students to accept him, but all they saw was his olive skin and his Arabic features. Besides, he was probably the first student from the Middle East that these students had ever met.

When I asked Rashid to share a little about where he's from, he didn't help himself. Mainly he was withdrawn and cryptic, which looking back makes sense. At first he volunteered nothing, responding with the monosyllabic utterances so typical of all teenagers, but then I put on my most encouraging smile and finally got him to share a few things. When I got him to speak more than a few words, his command of English surprised me; it was quite good. He said only that his family was from the Baluchistan region of Pakistan and that his parents were killed in the fighting with the Taliban and that he recently emigrated to the US with his uncle.

You probably think I should have been tipped off by the fact that he had even read a number of American classics. I wasn't. When he joined us, we were studying excerpts from Thoreau's <u>Walden Pond</u> and Rashid surprised me by telling he had already read much of it in class in Pakistan. Of course, this did nothing to endear him to my other students who think Thoreau is too outdated to be relevant and just plain "bo-o-oring."

But at the end of the class, I thought I'd made a little dent in their adolescent armor when I overheard Dante, one of the African-American students in the class, say, "At least, this guy had the decency to learn our language."

But even these small hopes were dashed when Ted, his buddy, smarted back. Just as they were headed out the door he said, loud enough for me to hear, but not so loud that he couldn't deny it, "My dad says you can't trust any raghead. Said we've pumped all kinda money into the Mideast and got nothing but grief for our efforts. He says we oughta nuke the whole region."

Glancing back into the classroom, I saw that Rashid was still there, and then realized Ted's comment was intended more for his benefit than for mine. Rashid gathered up his books and headed out the door. I apologized to him, made some feeble argument that it was just teenagers shooting off their mouths and promised I would take care of them tomorrow. He just gave me an indifferent shrug of his shoulders and muttered, "It is just what I had been told to expect."

But, the truth be told, with all that's gone on in America and Hammerville in particular, I could hardly blame my students. They were merely aping their parent values, as much as they might rankle at the suggestion. And most of their parents, the fine citizens of this town, were educated right here in the school system. And "the elders" had been acting like ignorant, racist fools. This bigotry of Americans against Arabs feeds the Arabs' own distrust and hatred of the West. And so the cycle goes on.

Of course, Rashid wasn't the only new male from the Mideast to arrive in town. I've never been one to believe in coincidence, but I have to admit I didn't give this one much thought, not at the time anyway. I know I should've seen the connection from the get-go, but then hindsight is usually 20/20. A few weeks before Rashid became a student at James Thurber High, the government moved Asad Akadi, "the number one terrorist in the country," to Hammerville. It was immediately apparent that Jerod had been dead on about the security surrounding the special convict. When he arrived at the HBE prison, he was delivered by what appeared to be the complement of a full army division. There were jeeps, troop carriers, humvees and even a tank or two that took up permanent residence around the prison. They turned the south side of town into a veritable parade ground of khaki and camouflage, enraging both the capital punishment protesters and pro-Arab demonstrators, although I think that was the idea.

What accompanied this security contingent into Hammerville was the swarming evidence of our nation's freedom of the press. I had heard the term "media circus" before, but had never fully understood the implications until our big event. Every conceivable news outlet known to man, and woman--CNN, ABC, MSNBC, CBS, FOX and a dozen local channels--planted satellite news trucks on the streets leading to "Justice Drive," as HBE dubbed the entrance to the prison. Packed tightly one after the other on the pavement with bodies frantically scurrying about, this procession of vehicles gave the impression of an uncoordinated circus train.

Of course, most of us poor Hammerville townsfolk never actually saw the terrorist, at least not in person. Like the rest of the nation, we watched him on the six o'clock news. Captured in vivid detail and color on the news broadcast-- and repeated endlessly on the web-- the heavily fortified motorcade, more than a half-mile of police, guards, and dignitaries surrounding the prisoner, sped down the long winding drive to the prison. Lights flashing and sirens bleating, the bulletproofed Highway Patrol cruiser with "the specially reinforced wire mesh separating the front seat from the prisoner," screeched to a halt in front of the receiving door of the prison, flanked by two army jeeps complete with mounted automatic weapons. As the world watched, Asad Akadi emerged from the rear seat, wearing a bright orange jumpsuit with "HBE Prison" stenciled across the back. The prisoner was manacled hand and foot and forced, by the silver chain connecting the two sets of cuffs, to bend over in a perpetually stooped position. Hunched over, he was forced to march up the sidewalk like a limping hunchback and stepped bowl-legged across the concrete.

In the few steps between vehicle and door, a reporter with more nerve than sense--though that doesn't narrow it down much--tried to jump into the cordoned off area and shove a microphone at our celebrity prisoner. Before he was even able to finish his query, he was efficiently manhandled by two guards in full army dress and hustled out of the camera's eye. In spite of the quick military maneuver, all the TV cameras were able to capture for the nation's viewing pleasure was the now-famous, insolent grin of Asad Akadi.

Mesmerized by the commotion and national news attention, my journalism students were in heaven, even Tyler and Charity--you know, the two who never care about anything. The journalism students peppered me with questions, speculations, and arguments about the exciting lives of tele-journalists.

In fact, there looked to be so many news journalists scurrying around town like forest animals foraging for food, they would interview just about anyone who stopped for a "Don't Walk" light. Most of what ended up on video was hardly the highest thoughts of our midwestern town. Comments of the townspeople, captured for all the world by the magic of digital video, satellite and the internet, included such wonderful tidbits as "I'm just glad they're going to fry his ass. Maybe teach a lesson to all those other Arabs who might have ideas about the old US of A" and "When they throw the switch, I'm planning to grab a front row seat. But the death penalty is just too good for him. I think maybe we oughta drop the bomb on his home town and see how they like it."

After all this country has been through in the past several years, their sentiments were certainly understandable. It was clear that our public school effort to teach the values of tolerance was no match for the nation's thirst for justice...or revenge, depending on your perspective. My students--and their parents and neighbors--had real trouble distinguishing between Akadi, the Arab terrorist caught in this despicable act, and all Arabs. I have to admit, after the past several weeks, I'm having trouble keeping this line from blurring myself.

I remember, in the middle of this national pageantry of justice and celebrity, sitting in my classroom after one of those incredibly exhausting days watching, or should I say staring at, the latest commentary on CNN. When my weary eyes glanced up to the open door, I caught a glimpse of Jose Cordons sauntering into my room. Jose was one of our day custodians and his slim, six-foot-four, 198-pound figure has been a familiar sight around Thurber for longer than I've been here. A head of long, stringy black hair, perpetually in need of a trim, framed an angular face and he sported a drooping mustache in a limp imitation of Pancho Villa. Some of the other custodians had a thing about keeping their appearance orderly, but Jose didn't do neat. His clothes always looked like he slept in them.

Even though he usually wore a wry smile complete with crooked teeth and was ever ready with the smart remark, his deep sockets carried two coal-black eyes that seemed perpetually sad. Jose had migrated from Mexico to the US almost twenty years ago, but he had never lost his accent. When he spoke, he often sounded like he had just washed up on our shores. "You know, it's all about zee money?" he said when he entered.

"What?" I responded, trying to rouse myself from my exhaustion.

Grabbing the garbage can with his left, he gestured at the TV with his right, "Zee execution. It brings boatload of money to Hammerville."

I watched as he deftly dumped the contents into his trash bag and then my eyes went back to the TV. The reporter was standing in front of the prison and recapping for the nth time the last ditch efforts Akadi's lawyers would make. Looking back at Jose, I didn't say anything, but he must have seen the question in my expression, because he tried to explain.

"This make the town famous. And for restaurants and stores, business is good, real good with army and reporters. " He shook his stringy hair.

Finally grasping his logic, I said, "Jose, I don't think it's quite that simple. This is about a lot more than money."

"Sure it ees, Ms. Dee Dee, money and fame!" He flashed me his crooked smile.

"Well, Jose, I can't even get into a restaurant without waiting. And don't you think this is about right and wrong…and the American system of justice?"

"I like you Ms. Dee Dee, but sometimes you are silly." Dropping that piece of wisdom, he was gone.

I gazed numbly at the now vacant doorframe for a while and went back to planning a lesson that would somehow use great American literature to teach universal human values to both my Arab Rashid and my redneck Ted. Back then I believed in miracles; after all, I'm a teacher.

Chapter 9

Yassim reached over and pushed the button again to change the radio station. Try as he might, he just couldn't get accustomed to what came out of the small speakers of the American car. Either the stations whined on with the sounds of shrill Western music with godless words or feeble-minded women screeched that their men were not "sensitive enough." It was little wonder that these Americans would fail. He hated opening his ears to such foolishness, but he had his orders.

He had been told to monitor the radio whenever he was traveling. Americans, he had learned in the Al Kim training camp, were so stupid that they announced all their security notices publicly on the radio and TV, so monitoring different stations was the best way to know if the team's mission had been compromised. So he listened and didn't like it. But he liked what he did not hear.

As he switched from one station to the other, he had heard no announcement, nothing about any "terrorist threat," as Americans liked to characterize the celebrated acts of martyrdom for the Great Jihad. There had been an occasional news story about the coming execution of Akadi, but even these seemed to be just the same repeated reports. And newsmen had routinely announced that the readiness level for the country was moderate, the "yellow level," but then nothing, no warning about any specific threat. It was exactly as the Sheik had predicted. They would strike and Americans would never suspect- -until it was once again too late. He half-closed his eyes and visualized the smoking debris of the World Trade Center, the scene replayed thousands of times on TV screens across the world.

Idly, he thought about the "yellow level" designation and pondered the Western preoccupation to label everything with a letter or number or color. Do these unbelievers feel that nothing could stand by itself, and every act, that every idea needed to be cataloged and ordered? He was pleased to have been chosen as Allah's instrument to disrupt their precious order and to avenge his family.

Yawning loudly, he stared in the rearview mirror to assure himself the others were still there. His eyes were tired and he had to squint to be sure. The sky was almost dark and there was just enough light to make out the colors of the cars behind him. He noted that the black Chevy Blazer carrying

Mohammed, Hassan and Patti, the American volunteer to their cause, was almost a quarter-mile back and separated by two cars.

He caught a glimpse of his own face in the rearview mirror. In the fading light, the black stubble on his chin, so different from the salt and pepper beard that had adorned his chin just a few weeks earlier, gave his face a dark, brooding look. In the brief flash of light from a passing car's high beams, he had just enough time to make out a long, sloping nose and the strong set of his jaw. The next car's headlights illuminated his eyes, once a deep olive green, now only two dark, haunted sockets, overhung by the black lines of dense eyebrows.

In the encroaching darkness there was little evidence of the handsome face and smug smile that had stolen so many maidens' hearts. His mother had often told him that, with his looks, he would be a heartbreaker and when he was young, he had been only too happy to prove the accuracy of her prophecy. At least, until Fatima. Beautiful, charming, sexy Fatima. At that thought, his heart leapt and then plummeted, his chest feeling as if he had been slammed with a hammer. He winced and then tried to move on the seat, to stir some life into his thighs, numbing against the cool vinyl.

He glanced across the seat toward the long, bulky form of Fadi curled uncomfortably against the door, snoring through a partially open, ugly mouth, his long beard dropping onto the seat below. Yassim could not blame him, he too was bone tired, but he resented Fadi grabbing the sleep denied him. Then he reminded himself that according to the Koran, the man who was able to deny himself the pleasures of this world would be rewarded with delights in the next. He realized, once again, that life had given him far too many opportunities to practice that denial and he groused a weary thanks to Allah.

Angling the visor mirror, he studied the small boy, lying quietly, his head of bristly brown hair sticking out from the edge of the tan blanket. They had said his name was Asim but Yassim did not know the boy. He was a lad who had volunteered--been volunteered, Yassim thought surely--to ride with two of Allah's soldiers. The Sheik had determined that two men from the Mideast with a young boy would draw less notice from the authorities. The boy, a clever prop in the drama, would be driven back to his home soon after they had reached Cleveland, so Yassim could not get attached to the boy.

Perhaps it was the nest of dark hair lying beyond the edge of the blanket or the whimpered sigh the boy made as he turned toward the seat. Or maybe it was a trick played by the light or even simple exhaustion, but just for a moment, when Yassim stared in the mirror at the boy on the backseat, he could have sworn the figure was Jamal.

Jamal and Fatima. His heart ached at the very thought of their names. He knew it could not be Jamal lying there on the back seat, but for a moment, Yassim wanted desperately to believe it was. He was seized by an almost uncontrollable desire to pull the car over, wake the sleeping boy and hold the small body in his arms. The desire gripped him like a sudden fever, and then it passed--he forced it to pass. He glanced out the window and forced his eyes to study the landscapes rushing past. As if reflecting his heart, all was darkness and shadows. Then a brightly lit driveway flew by and he caught sight of a spotlighted American flag. He spat on the floor of the car.

He stole another quick look at the backseat. More than two years ago, he had last held the burnt, blood-smeared body of his four-year-old son and cried. He wept so heavily that he had drenched the small, charred, rag-doll body with his tears as he cradled him that final time.

On that crisp fall morning, Jamal and Fatima had been walking down the Shuqba hill, heading home from the market with fresh fish for him. Johana, the toothless neighbor woman across the street, said she looked up from her sewing and watched Fatima and Jamal playing a counting game on the broken stones of the road. She told him afterwards she never even heard the Israeli gun ships until the helicopters had crested the rise. She heard the swoosh of the two rockets as they were released and sizzled through the cool autumn air. A second later, both missiles struck their target and the building Fatima and Jamal were passing exploded, sending fireballs into the air and raining debris below. After the rockets struck, the explosives inside the building echoed the initial blast with repeated volcanic eruptions of fire engulfing mother and son. Stunned neighbors tried to rush to help, using their own burqas to try to extinguish the burning bodies of the woman and child. But all they could do was drag the now lifeless bodies away from the blazing inferno.

By the time Yassim arrived, it was too late. He could only wail and grieve, and swear revenge. Standing on that scorching pavement, holding Jamal's limp body in his arms, he made an oath to Allah. American money and technology had built that gun ship, so American children would someday pay. One day American parents would feel his grief, his burning anger. Now he was honored to have been anointed by the Sheik as the instrument of Allah's revenge.

The sudden blaring of a horn jerked Yassim back to the present and he looked up in time to wrench the steering wheel, sending the car back into his own lane just in time, jostling both passengers. He cursed himself for indulging in such daydreaming. He had important work to do and he would need all his resources to achieve success. Both Fadi and the boy adjusted their positions and then returned to their slumber. Yassim himself took one long, deep breath, then another and began to regain his calm.

He could not believe how smoothly their plans had gone thus far. The Sheik's genius was in the meticulous planning and coordination. In spite of all the heightened "antiterrorist" efforts of the West, all four members of his team had entered Canada without a hitch. Arriving on different flights, the men had been met by different members of one of the Ontario cells--Yassim himself didn't know which one--and each had used the few days to effectively establish his identity in Canada.

Mohammed and Hassan joined other Arabs from the Saudi Oil Company and even participated in some of the negotiation talks with Western executives. Fadi, the fawning tourist, had excelled in his role. In his loud, boisterous manner, he made a dramatic fuss in public about the North American "Water Wonder of the World" at Niagara Falls. Yassim himself got to sit in on the opening talks on the World Peace Conference, all the time marveling at the fools and cowards in the gathering. Then each man had disappeared unnoticed and, with help from the Ontario cell, was delivered to the safe house outside Toronto.

From there it had been only a short ride to the marina at Crystal Springs. Just as the Leader had promised, a small boat and captain were waiting for the men and their gear. They boarded and after several rough hours on the choppy lake waters--Fadi got sick twice and vomited compulsively over the rail, all to the jeering of his traveling companions--they arrived at another nondescript marina in Dunkirk, New York. Just like that, they stepped off the deck of the battered cabin cruiser and onto American soil. No border guards, no customs, no searching, no questions.

At the dock the four soldiers had been met by their new "family members." He and Fadi were joined by the boy, and they were riding together to their next stop in a white Trans Am. The Western woman, Patti, joined Mohammed and Hassan as Mohammed's wife and the three were following at a discrete distance in a weathered black Chevy Blazer. They had been careful to travel on I-90 only briefly and then had stayed on the smaller state routes.

The entire process had gone so smoothly that, when little Asim had complained of being hungry, Yassim had agreed to stop and get something to eat. From the notes he had memorized, he had remembered that a half-hour down on Route 5 was a place called the Parkway Tavern. This out-of-the-way restaurant, in a small town named Northeast just across the state line in Pennsylvania, was known for its Mideastern menu and, since it was a favorite of many Arab Americans in the area, his group would likely go unnoticed. Even there, though, the two groups were careful not to sit together. Mohammed, Hassan, and the woman sat at stools at the bar eating and smoking, while he, Fadi and the boy took a table in the back. The food, especially the Fattush and the Kefta Skewers, was quite good and the men, who hadn't eaten since leaving the safe house, had their fill. No doubt the full stomachs were why Fadi and the boy had collapsed so quickly into slumber.

Sighing audibly, Yassim glanced back at the rearview mirror. After they had left the restaurant, the group had turned onto Route 89, a rural route, to travel south through part of Pennsylvania. This road was narrow and wound through the rolling hills, curling around bends like an endless serpent. He studied the headlights in the mirror again. He had memorized the configuration of the Blazer, so he could recognize it quickly. But because the direction of the road ahead kept shifting, Yassim had to alternate his gaze from the road to the mirror and back to the road again. Looking intently at the small mirror, he examined the sets of headlights as the two cars rounded the bend behind him. Suddenly he realized that neither matched the signature of the Blazer lights. The longer he studied the lights behind him, the more certain he became. He fought to control a rising apprehension and made an instant decision.

Sighting a wide driveway off to the left, he turned the wheel sharply and the sports car leaped from the paved road onto the gravel drive. He turned the car in a sharp arc, ignoring Fadi's muffled complaints and Asim's whimpered cries as they were tossed about by the sudden maneuver. Within seconds the car made the 180-degree turnaround. Yassim suppressed a desire to speed, alternately watching the road, the rearview mirror and the speedometer. He knew he couldn't allow a stupid mistake like being caught speeding to put his name and description into some police log. How long had he been traveling without keeping them within range? Yassim cursed himself for not knowing the answer. Like some lazy schoolboy, he had allowed his mind to wander.

He glanced at his odometer, watching the tenths roll by. One mile. Two miles. How far back had he lost them? Had they turned off for some reason? He pushed the car as much as he dared, cautioning himself about the winding road and possible police patrol. Three miles. As he drove, his eyes searched the shoulder of the road, darting back and forth, frantically scanning both sides. Adrenaline shot through his body instantly extinguishing his fatigue.

Just ahead, he noticed a turnoff to the right, heading west. Could they have turned there? He caught a sign with the words, "Findlay Lake, 3 miles" and an arrow pointing east. He hesitated just a second and made an instant decision not to turn off. Four miles, still no sign of them, but he had passed only two other cars on this back road. He thanked Allah for small blessings.

Then, as the "0" of the fifth mile crept past on the odometer, he spotted the Blazer just off the highway, its wheels sitting unevenly on the gravel and mud with a marked car of the Pennsylvania State Police behind it. As he passed, he was alarmed to see that the blue light atop the police cruiser was flashing, but he couldn't make out the silhouettes of the officer or his own men. Not yet daring to stop, he drove past and followed the road around the bend ahead until the blue strobe disappeared behind him. Checking to be sure there were no cars behind him, Yassim eased the Trans Am across both lanes and onto the left shoulder and beyond onto the soft soil between a pair of denuded trees. He extinguished the lights and barked to Fadi and the boy, "Stay here out of sight!"

Keeping just inside the second row of trees of what he now recognized was an apple orchard, he followed a path parallel to the road to get to where Mohammed and Hassan had been stopped. In the darkness, the flashing blue light made it easy to keep his destination in sight. As he crept through the small growth, a branch, invisible in the dark, almost stabbed his eye. He turned his face quickly and let out a quiet curse as the limb etched a red slice across his chin. He listened intently and at first heard nothing. Then a muffled sound hit his ears and he shuddered. A string of words were uttered in quick Arabic, though he was only able to make out some of what was said. This was followed by another voice in English and he at first thought it must be the policeman, but then heard the squelch of static and realized it was the squad car radio. From the sounds he figured he was in the orchard just opposite both cars and he began to approach, keeping low to the ground.

Before he was through the first row of trees, the shrill voice of Hassan, this time in English, bellowed, "Oh, I'm so sorry! I know we're supposed to speak in English. Okay, what do you think we should do?"

Mohammed said, "We had better ask Yassim," and then the satellite phone buzzed alive.

Hassan squealed, "We don't need--" and, before he could finish, Yassim came through the last of the trees and was upon both men.

"Ask me what?" Yassim asked even before he reached them. Suddenly his eyes stared wide at the large, squat figure of Hassan, one knee on the ground, as he wiped the long, curved blade of his knife on the clothes of the Pennsylvania State trooper. The body lay lifeless, blood pooling from his neck, staining the dirt and grass.

"Allah, save us!" Yassim said between gritted teeth.

Chapter 10

"You know, there are a good many adults who believe you shouldn't be allowed to read this book!" I announced to my 7th period students that dry autumn Tuesday, holding high a tattered copy of <u>Huckleberry Finn</u>. By the time these teenagers wandered into my room around one o'clock each afternoon, they were usually drowsy, apathetic or antagonistic. I was counting on the final, hoping my ploy might engage or even enrage them. "Several groups have even tried to have this book banned from schools," I continued, dangling the bait.

"I didn't know a book could be banned because it's boring," offered Brian, angling for laughter and agreement from his peers. He got both. Brian, a blond-haired, blue-eyed jokester, was one of the smartest students in the class but wore a feigned disdain for all things academic like a shield. I knew the truth anyway.

You might not know this but if high schoolers find a book or story too dated, too demanding, or just too far from their own experience, their automatic response is, "It's boring." However I've found that, with a combination of prodding and taunting, you can hook many adolescents into literature they would at first dismiss. And with this class I was desperate. I hoped I could pull off this little trick with *Huckleberry Finn* and reel them in.

My gaze wandered to the desk in the back corner of the classroom. Christie, my friend and teaching colleague, smiled at me. The two of us had volunteered to participate in the school's Peer Coaching program, and this was her first visit to my classroom. I stopped to introduce her briefly to the class and, it took a bit, but I managed to get the students past their visitor. You see, while I don't think I'm a slouch in the looks department, Christie has the kind of looks my male students delightfully refer to as "hot!" Last week I had overheard Brian claim "Ms. Ferguson looked like the May model in this year's <u>Sports Illustrated Swimsuit Edition</u>." So, after the introduction I had to wait a while till the stir passed and the guys put their tongues back in their mouths. Then, as Christie and I planned, I ignored her and carried on.

"Well, you've read about 150 pages so far..." I started again and spotted Heather leaning sideways, ready to mouth something to her neighbor, Kim. Heather and Kim were two female "buds" in the class, using their make-up and jewelry to create cosmetic twins, right down to the six earrings in their right ears. Even their hairdos were black and brown imitations of each other, or rather weak imitations of the latest teen sensation from *American Idol*, Athena something. And like most of my girls, they were about a hundred times more interested in the guys in class than in anything I'd say. I tolerated it all and even let them sit together because, well, I wasn't too old to remember what I was like then.

I met the gazes of both girls and went on, chuckling slightly at what they thought was going to be their private joke, "Well, most of us have read about 150 pages." Letting my glance drift back over the class, I then dropped the lure into the tepid water of Room 124. "Why do you think certain groups might believe you shouldn't be allowed to read <u>Huckleberry Finn</u>?"

This caught them off guard, just what I wanted. For a long moment my question hung in the air, like a slow bubble waiting to explode. Briefly the twenty-four teenagers were speechless, a beautiful thing when it happens.

"Well, maybe it's because it's about slavery?" James offered tentatively. I love James. With his ardent green eyes behind black-framed glasses, he is always ready to offer an answer in his soft-spoken voice. He's often not right and sometimes completely off base. But he recognized the awkward silence and was eager to fill it.

"That's a possibility," I returned, trying to dignify his answer before one of his peers could belittle it. "But I can tell you that these groups don't have any such concern with students reading other books about slavery, *Uncle Tom's Cabin*, for example. So I think their concern may be something else."

"It's 'cause it's about a white kid and a black man hangin' together," Ted offered more as an assertion than a suggestion. Ted had flaming red hair and a generous sprinkling of freckles across his face. He was from a redneck home and, even though he shared some of the same attitudes, he kept a few black friends mainly, I suspect, to antagonize his parents.

"Why do you think that, Ted?" I challenged.

"Because lots of people have big problems with black and white guys being together, especially when the black guy is the older one. You know, a black guy having 'influence' over a white kid." He winked at me to be sure I couldn't miss the innuendo.

I didn't dignify the insinuation with a response. Instead, I asked if anyone else had an idea why some may have wanted this book banned. I strolled down the center of the room and placed my hand on Ted's shoulder, a light touch with heavy implications, and waited. I was pleased when Jeremy rose to my challenge and lifted his hand hesitantly.

"Before we could say what they didn't like about the book, wouldn't it be important to know who wanted it banned?" he asked, absently brushing one long blond bang out of his eyes.

"Very good question, Jeremy," I said, rewarding him with a brief flash of teeth. "Any ideas who they might be?"

Kristen's carefully manicured hand came up for the first time. She was a sleepy, petite little thing with a brunette pageboy cut who had quite a good head atop her shapely shoulders. For a change, today she wore a jersey from the Indiana Fever, the women's professional basketball team. She and I had a silent, though understood, mutual compact. As long as she agreed to continue thinking, I agreed not to betray the secret of her intelligence to the boys. I too remembered what it was like to be smarter than some of the guys you liked. I edged around two clusters of desks till I stood directly in front of her. I read in her now-awake blue eyes a sight most teachers live for--the unmistakable evidence of inspiration. "Kristen?"

"I thought I remember reading somewhere," she started off haltingly as if she were unsure. Standing immediately in front of her, only I could see the thrill of certainty in her expression, as she realized she was the first to "get it."

A male voice from the other side of the room blurted out, "I believe you're talking about black activist groups like the National Association for the Advancement of Colored People and the National Urban League." I looked across the class to see the speaker, Rashid. I glanced back at Kristen just in time to see the anger flare in her eyes and replaced immediately by the ice of brittle disappointment.

I felt compelled to recognize one of few initiatives of my newest student, so I acknowledged Rashid's remarks but tried to maintain that elusive order of the classroom. "Good contribution, Rashid," I said simply. "I'm not sure what the protocol was in the schools in Pakistan, but in this country it is customary we take our turns and do not interrupt others when they are speaking." I tried to keep my tone even, hoping to make my response supportive and corrective at the same time. Probably achieved neither. "We were ready to hear what Kristen had to say. Kristen?"

When I looked back at Kristen, the earlier light in her cobalt eyes was now extinguished and her slender arms slowly folded in front of her. She glared back at me and said nothing. For her, the teachable moment had passed and I silently berated myself for letting it slip through my fingers. At the time I made a quick mental note to talk to her briefly as she left class, to compliment her and try to re-establish rapport. But as the class evolved, even that small good intention was swamped by a tide I couldn't control.

Studying the young faces before me, I could tell that Kristen's resentment was spreading quickly to the other students, ignited by a smoldering heat of bigotry. I wasn't sure I had made the right choice here, but I wanted to move the class on and scanned the class for possible allies and settled on Jeremy again. "What do you think groups like the NAACP might find offensive in a story like *Huckleberry Finn*, Jeremy?"

"Well, I don't rightly know, Miss Sterber," he began, now no longer sure if he wanted to take the risk. As he pondered my question, I watched an answer dawn on his handsome features. "If I were to guess, I would say it's because the story uses the 'N' word," he offered.

"By the 'N' word," I started, hoping to relieve him from having to say it. I was cut off before I could finish.

"He's talkin' 'bout 'NIGGER.' Ain't ya, Jeremy?" chortled Ted.

"Ted. I just reminded Rashid that we use a little common courtesy in this room. You're hardly new here. You shouldn't need to be reminded." I was more curt than necessary, but it was getting to be really hard to like Ted. I know, teachers are not supposed to admit to such preferences, but get real. We're not automatons and Ted was just plain obnoxious, a role I think he enjoyed. I struggled to get the class back on track. "Jeremy?" I simply said and looked at grey-green eyes.

"Well," he began hesitantly and I studied the room, my even stare commanding quiet and attention, I hoped. The other twenty-three students were quiet, studying Jeremy. "Well, I would expect that the way Twain has his characters use the word 'Nigger' regularly--" he looked down at the Formica desk top and almost swallowed the "N" word--"might offend some people, like maybe civil rights groups." He hesitated and glanced up at me for confirmation. I nodded my head once, my eyes rising slightly. Apparently he was encouraged.

"I dunno, maybe they thought kids reading <u>Huckleberry Finn</u> might get too used to seeing the 'N' word and might think it's okay to use it themselves."

There are times as a teacher that you just get blown away by the insight coming out of the mouth of what a few minutes ago was a raging mass of hormones.

"But isn't the black guy kinda a good guy for Twain?" suddenly Heather piped up from across the room, her two fingers caressing the fifth earring on her right lobe. "What's his name?"

Without waiting for my okay, three different students shouted more or less simultaneously, "Jim! His name's Jim, Heather. Get a clue!"

I was so surprised by the comment from Heather that I didn't have time to react to the outburst and instead directed my question back at Heather. "Why does it matter if you have a hero--the good guy--who is called a nigger in the book?" I asked, staring directly at her so no one else would jump in.

She looked briefly at Kim and munched on a nonexistent wad of gum--I hoped since gum was outlawed in school--and said, talking faster, "Well, if you have a good guy, a hero in a story and he gets called a dumb thing like, you know. Doesn't that mean the author is trying to say we shouldn't pay attention to a name like nigger?"

And this was coming from Heather, a comment that had nothing to do with boys, make-up or hip-hop. I stole a quick glance heavenward and then returned to reality. "Perhaps it would be best to ask how an African American might see this question." My glance roamed around the classroom. There were only three black students in the seventh period class and of course all three refused to meet my gaze. After a beat, I settled on Dante, a tall, thin handsome young black man with close-set brown eyes, a prominent nose and a winning smile. "Dante, what is your opinion on Twain's use of the word 'nigger' in the dialogue of the book?"

"Well that's pretty much how they talked back then, wasn't it?" he asked looking up at me. "That don't make it right or anything, but Twain couldn't hardly have them talk like they wuddnt real people, could he? I mean I kinda understand, but I gotta admit it still bothers me when I read the word 'nigger' in the book." He hesitated a few seconds and then continued as if he just had a thought. "But that don't mean we shouldn't read it. Sometimes you gotta read things that hurts ya."

I know what you're thinking. English teachers have a duty to correct our students' grammar. There are times when that'd be appropriate, but this day I wouldn't have done anything to intrude on Dante's honest self-expression. In fact, I could have kissed him. His ungrammatical words were far more eloquent than mine could ever be. So instead I pressed my luck. "How do feel about Heather's point?" I asked, wanting to give her the credit. "Does the fact that, even though Jim is called a nigger in the book, he is clearly at least one of the heroes in the book, does that mitigate your feelings at all?"

I'm always trying to squeeze in another new vocabulary word when I can. I'm not sure it worked in this case, as Dante just frowned at me. I tried to recover. "Did having Jim a hero in the book make you feel a little less bad about the use of the 'N' word describing him?"

"Maybe a little," Dante said and stopped. When I thought he wasn't going to say any more, he did. "Like maybe, how can he have this man who saves Huck's life and all and protects him and then Huck calls him such a lousy name like nigger? It does kinda show that Twain dudn't think he was just some 'nigger.'"

No one made any response to this, not even smart-mouthed Ted, and I let it be. Then I pushed my luck one more time. "Perhaps, it would be good to get the perspective of someone from a different culture than ours," I said and could just detect the barely audible groans from the other students, which I pretended to ignore. "Rashid, since you're from Pakistan, I'd like to hear your point of view."

His eyes looked up from the notebook in which he was always jotting notes. He spoke in a quiet, confident voice. "In my country, it is common that adults would determine what young people should read. It is their job to know better and to keep us from,.uh, sin, and if they thought reading a book might bring us to any such ....harm, they might tell us to read another, better book."

"That's quite interesting, Rashid," I answered, before one of the students could say "sissy wimp ass" under his breath and I'd have to pretend I didn't hear it. "Could you share with us your opinion on the issue we are discussing, about the use of the word 'nigger' in the novel?"

The olive-skinned youth stared back at me, his eyes two hard beads of black. His response carried a tone of razor-edged arrogance "I think this discussion illustrates that bigotry is still very much alive in your country. That race hatred is one of the central beliefs in this 'classless' society of America. That the face you try to show to the world of tolerance and understanding of others is pretty much a lie."

Rashid either had incredible timing or great luck because just as the other students were about to offer their angry retorts, the final bell of the day blared, blocking out all competing sounds, and the other 23 students jumped out of their seats and barreled out the door, looking ready to stone the foreigner. Rashid remained in his seat, his face a neutral mask and I waited till the commotion of the end-of-day stampede receded. Slowly I walked across the room and lowered myself into the curve of the desk next to him. He was staring, almost defiantly, back at me.

I said, "Your comments today about the book certainly raised some interesting points. It definitely gave everyone something to think about, even if you could have chosen your words a little more carefully."

"I apologize if I do not use your language correctly," he said, his voice sounding not at all apologetic.

"Oh, I've listened to your use of English in my class for the past several days and I think your command of the language is quite good. Probably better than some of my students who are native speakers." I gave him my best knowing smile. "At any rate it's a cinch no one left here today saying my class was 'bor-r-ring,' " I said, mimicking Ted.

He still did not smile back. "Thank you," he said.

"You know," I continued, searching for some way to connect to this strange young man, "my goal today was to find a way to get the students to delve into *Huckleberry Finn*. You certainly helped with that."

"Thank you." This time his voice carried a curious combination of deference and defiance.

"But I don't think you made yourself any friends today."

"I did not come to America to make friends," he said, his voice hard-edged.

"Why did you come to America?" I asked in all innocence. I saw something flash briefly in his eyes--surprise, alarm, fear--and then it disappeared just as quickly as it had appeared.

"I have come to learn about America and to make my fortune."

It sounded like he was reading from a script but at the time I wrote off my uneasiness to the fact that he was still adjusting to our culture and had probably learned much of his usage from TV and movies. At least that's what I told myself. I tried to switch subjects.

"I'd love to hear about your schooling in Pakistan."

That same strange look washed over his features again before he forced the earlier calm back into his eyes. Extricating himself from the desk, he murmured, "In my country, according to the Koran, women are not supposed to ask such personal questions of men."

I was caught a bit off guard at first and then said, "I thought you said that America is now your country."

Moving hastily through the aisle, he muttered, "Good day, Ms. Sterber."

It wasn't until he was out the door and the sounds of his hollow footfalls on the new tile floor died away that I pulled my contorted body out of the student desk, not without some effort.

"Not bad, kiddo," called my friend Christie from the back of the room.

Chapter 11

"Before you open that grinning mouth of yours, I need a drink," I said to my friend before she had even reached the front of the room. "How about you?"

"I will, if you're buying," Christie said, her wide smile showing off her set of pearly whites. She was taller than I by a good three inches and had the lean, sleek form of a supermodel. It took her only four strides to reach the front of the room. Watching her move, it wasn't hard to see where my male students got their fantasies. Her long blond hair hung perfectly across her shoulders and bounced slightly as she arrived at the front of the room. If she hadn't been my best friend, it would've been easy to hate that hair.

"Let's see, it's only been four days since we got paid. I suppose I can scrounge up another fifty cents, even on my paltry salary," I said and she smiled back at me. That slightly demented smile is what I remember most about the first time we met.

At the end of my first official day at James Thurber--after an interminable day of officious orientations, mandatory meetings and tedious training sessions-- she popped her head in my classroom as I sat at my desk, overwhelmed.

"Hi, my name is Christie Ferguson," she beamed and literally bounced into the room. Christie always seemed to be just a little bit this side of crazy and she carried a ready supply of smirks that screamed guilty pleasures. "Since you're the new girl on the block, I just wanted to say welcome to good old James Thurber."

I learned that we were about the same age but she had started teaching at Hammerville right out of college and was already in her sixth year here. She reminded me that gave her seniority <u>and</u> first dibs on all new hunks in the building.

"You settling in okay?" she asked after the preliminaries were out of the way.

"I'm exhausted, my brain is frizzled from information overload and my derriere is numb," I said, slumped in my chair.

"Yeah, first day here will do that to you," she responded. "But don't worry, it'll get a lot worse."

"Gee, thanks."

"You know what you need?" she said without changing expressions.

"Yeah, a cool fan, a long bubble bath and a good night's sleep."

"Nope," she said, that smirk reappearing, "a cold drink, a guy and a rousing night out."

"Christie, you've got to be kidding. Tomorrow is the first day of classes and I'm not ready yet."

"Girl, nobody can help you get better prepared for this place than yours truly. Tonight is your last night of freedom; we need to make the most of it."

Then she grabbed my arm and bodily dragged me to her car despite my weak protests. We spent the next several hours in "intense preparations" at a local watering hole called Nick's as she delivered on the cold drinks and, a few times, almost on the hot guys. Several Buds later, she had me laughing and matching her smirk for smirk.

Between the drinks and the passes, we talked about everything--the school, the administration, the students, our lives outside of school. In an alcohol-induced daze, we even swapped stories about our love lives, or rather hers and my lack thereof. She said she was dating one guy and I told her I "was looking." I shared with her that I had lost my dad recently and why I chose to return to Hammerville.

"At least, you had a dad worth missing," she said between sips. "My father deserted mom and me when I was ten. Never saw him again. Had to fight for everything myself."

"In this go-round," I still remember her saying--okay I don't remember a lot of details from that night, but I remember this--"you can't go through life always hedging your bets. If you don't take some risks, you're not really living."

The next day I had the worst hangover of my life, but somehow was relaxed, confident and able to teach through the day. After that night, we became inseparable.

Most days I found her good humor irresistibly contagious, and today was no exception. Together we headed out the door and down the hall to the lounge--oh, excuse me, teachers' workroom. Of course, Christie was just getting started.

"If I had the time and we could sneak out of here, I'd suggest we head to Nick's and I'd have you buy me something that'd cost more than fifty cents," she said, her eyebrows doing the Groucho Marx thing.

"Don't give me any ideas. I've got about a hundred papers to grade and I suspect a trip with you to Nicks would impair my professional judgment," I said.

"Yeah, but your students' grades might all improve in the process. I'm only suggesting it so I can help students bring up their grades in your class."

I smacked her on the shoulder and laughed. "Looks like my students will have to make their grades the old-fashioned way--they'll have to EARN them!" I continued, mimicking the old TV commercial that had been a favorite of my dad.

"Well, I'm glad to see you two are in a good mood today," said Hal Thompson, our principal, who suddenly materialized across the hallway from us. I always thought it was spooky how good administrators could sometimes just appear like that.

"Hey, Mr. Thompson," Christie jumped in, turning her smile on him. She was always faster than I on the draw. "I just finished an observation of Dee Dee's class and we're just getting ready to do a little R and R."

"R and R?" asked Thompson, his bass voice holding the question up, like a suspicious parent. He pushed his wire-rimmed glasses over his slightly crooked nose, letting his fingers brush his smallish black mustache. His deep gray eyes studied Christie with what he probably thought was a penetrating stare. But he was no match for her.

"Oh not that kind of R and R!" she slapped him playfully on the shoulder. "Don't we wish? I just observed Dee Dee teaching one of the best lessons I've seen and we were about to embark on the 'Review and Reflect' process. We thought we needed a drink before we start, but decided to settle for a couple of Diets."

"Oh, I get it! R & R. Great! I like that," he said, chuckling. "I'm really glad you two volunteered for the Peer Coaching Program. You have a lot to offer each other as coaches as well as friends. If you get the chance, talk it up. I'd like to see other teachers take advantage of the program and you can probably do more to convince them than I can. Anyway, I hope you have a good R & R session."

Right then, a student burst out of the next classroom door and started running down the corridor. In two seconds, Principal Thompson was in action. "Craig, hold it right there!" he called out and the guy stopped in his tracks.

"Where are you heading in such a hurry?" was the last we heard as the two disappeared around the corner.

I turned and looked at my coaching partner. "Quick thinking, oh great sneaky one," I said, when I was sure Thompson was out of earshot.

When we arrived at the glass door marked "Workroom," she pulled it open and I walked through. As I started across the small room to the single pop machine, I found my path blocked by another colleague, and I use that term loosely. Sprawled across two of the few chairs in the cramped room sat Rob Holden, social studies teacher. Two chubby hands held the sports section in front of him and all I could see was the shiny top of his head, but I knew whom that pate belonged to.

Believe it or not, Rob Holden had been my American History teacher when I attended high school more than twelve years before. I remember little from his classes except the many times he enjoyed pontificating on politics. Lately he had taken to reminding anyone who would listen that he had taught for thirty-three years, all at Hammerville. But, to be more precise, based on what I knew as both his student and his colleague, he had taught the same year--thirty-three times. Years ago Rob had been the football coach for Hammerville, and not a very good one at that from what I had heard. So he had been induced to resign from coaching, as they say, and decided to take up periodic residence in the lounge, er, workroom, occasionally giving the same lecture he had for thirty-some years.

Over the years his indolence had done his appearance few favors as he had developed a rotund pouch and chubby legs. He looked like an oversized elf who had amassed sufficient fat to survive several harsh winters. I doubt that he could walk the length of the football field any longer, much less jog it.

"Rob, don't you have something better to do than sitting here reading the sports page?" Christie asked with just enough edge to wrestle his attention from the award-winning journalism of The Sporting News.

"What?" he mumbled and glanced over the paper. He arched a pair of bushy black eyebrows that would've given Andy Rooney's serious competition.

"Well, some of us have some real teaching work to do," she said. "You know, little things like planning lessons, doing research for our classes and grading papers."

"Bite me, Christie," he snarled back, snapping the paper and retreating again behind the printed page.

"Only in that rich fantasy life of yours, Robert," she said.

Trying to regain some semblance of his dignity, he folded the paper in a show of defiance. "You ought to show a little respect for those of us with experience around here!" he blustered and was out the door. Before the door had shut all the way, Christie and I collapsed on the chairs in twin fits of laughter.

"Here, have a Diet," I said as I got two from the machine. Between laughs and sips, it took us a full three minutes before we were able to speak without giggling. We used the time to retrace our steps back to my room.

"Well," I finally managed, "give me your report. I can take it. What'd you really think of the class?"

Christie stopped her laughing and said, "Oh, that." She made a deal of having her eyes glance around my room. "I guess, I might as well give you the bad news." She opened the small notebook I had seen on her lap in my room and, flipping past a few pages, she studied her scribbled handwriting. Her eyes scanned her notes and her forehead wrinkled, but she didn't say anything, raising my anxiety.

"Come on, let's have it."

"Actually," Christie started and then made me wait a full five seconds before continuing. "I loved the hook."

"What?"

"The hook. You know the bit about adults trying to prohibit kids from reading Huckleberry Finn. That was brilliant. There's nothing these kids hate more than being told by adults 'you can't do that.' I wish I'd thought of it."

"Well, it's true," I said.

"I know it is, that's the beauty of it," she responded. "It actually woke them up. Not easy for this group during seventh period."

I squinted at her, waiting for the other shoe to drop.

"Stop looking at me that way. I meant what I said to Thompson. It really was a great lesson. Nearly all the students were engaged, from what I could see."

"Okay, give me the rest."

"Well, of course, you know, some of them still won't read the book, even with your great motivation," Christie said.

"I'm a teacher, not a magician."

"And there were three students in the back who were not on task most of the period." She pulled out the seating chart I had given her. "Tami, Jake Harton and Eli," she read from the chart. "You didn't seem to notice. Did you?"

"No, I didn't that much. Eli's mom is home dying of breast cancer and he's got all he can do to just show up. So I'm cutting him some slack. Tami and Jake sit in front of Eli and I guess I hadn't been looking that way enough." I paused and then went on. "Besides, Tami's pregnant and Jake is the father ... maybe. So in the back of my mind, I might've been thinking that they've got more to be concerned with than Huck and Jim, but you're right, I still should've been paying more attention to them."

She shook her head at me, her blond tresses flipping across her face. "Dee Dee, I don't know how you know so much about your students. I know I've been pretty preoccupied with all the wedding plans lately, but I've got all three of those guys in my biology classes and I didn't know any of that."

"I don't know," I replied. "I guess I got more time than you and I'm a pretty good listener. Sometimes they need someone to talk to."

"It's more than that. You seem to know all your students pretty well. You even handled that Rashid pretty well," Christie kept on. "I knew that we had a student from the Middle East, and I'd seen him in the halls, but today was the first time I really watched him. Have you talked with him? What's his story?"

"I've tried, but he hasn't talked much..."

As the door swung open, we heard Jose's unmistakable off-key singing. Once inside, he stopped in the middle of the second chorus of "Take This Job and Shove It."

" 'Cuse me, ladies. I just need to empty the trash." He moved to the side. In the middle of emptying the can, he turned and looked at Christie. "Did I overhear you mention Rasheed?"

Although a little surprised by the interruption, Christie said, "Yeah, Jose. I just observed Dee Dee's 7th period class and we were talking about some of her students."

"Well, if you ask me," Jose went on, " I think Rasheed is okay. I talk to him some and I think Arabs are getting bad rap. Rasheed not a bad boy." He grabbed the half full trashcan liner and replaced it with a new black one.

"What makes you say that?" I ventured.

"Oh, nothing. Just what I think," said Jose. "But what do I know? I'm just a janitor."

"What was that about?" Christie asked me after he left.

"I don't know," I responded, shaking my head. "He's been acting strange lately. Have you noticed?"

"Stranger than the normal Jose? Can't say that I have, but I haven't given it much thought." Christie looked around and said, "Okay, you were talking about Rashid?"

I settled back into my chair. "Well, he told me he's from Pakistan and his mother and dad died fighting against the Taliban," I said.

"His mom and dad?"

"That's what he told me. He said his father was in the Afgan police and was killed in a battle in Kabul. He also said his village was raided by the Taliban and every woman was taken out and shot. He was off with relatives when it happened. He also told me he came to this country only a few weeks ago and he's living here with his uncle."

"Have you met his uncle?"

"No, I haven't had any reason. He's been a good student. Knows the work as well as any of my students, better than most. Comes prepared. Heck, I wish my other students were half as studious."

Christie turned pensive. "I don't know, Dee Dee, but there's something about that guy that bothers me. While I was sitting in the back of the room, I found myself watching him. It wasn't planned or deliberate or anything, I was back there studying the class and would end up watching him. You know the rest of the kids were pretty well tuned into you and paying good attention."

"Rashid was contributing along with everyone else," I said.

"I know he was," she started back again and then paused a second. "And I thought you did a good job of both correcting him and allowing him to participate in the discussion."

"But?"

"Well, I never actually caught him doing it and I could've imagined it, but I could've sworn he was watching me. It was creepy."

"Maybe, my friend is letting her imagination get the best of her. Rashid is from a culture where women are second-class citizens and they are always covered. He's probably never seen a woman as attractive as you who wasn't being kept hidden behind a burqa. I'm sure all this is a little much for him. I'm probably a little much for him. It's obvious he's not used to forceful women."

"I don't know..."

"Besides, my rule of thumb is always give students the benefit of the doubt."

She raised her perfectly shaped eyebrows.

"At least, until they give me reason not to," I concluded.

"Maybe, I'm just being paranoid..."

"You think?"

"But don't you think it's a little coincidental," she argued, "that Asad, the super terrorist, is set to be executed here and the first Arab student in forever enrolls at our school?"

"Coincidences are some of life's little mysteries," I said, as if I had the answer.

Chapter 12

Yassim used the fingers of both hands to massage his temples, struggling to keep the encroaching headache at bay. The pain crawled relentlessly across his forehead like a desert scorpion, stinging a trail across his crown. He didn't have time for this, he told himself and tried to shake it off. He had to think and act quickly. Another car would be speeding by any second and then, because of the flashing blue light, would suddenly brake and see what? Three Arab men standing next to a police car!

The squawk of the cruiser's radio jerked him back. "Harry, come back.... Harry, are you there?" The high-pitched voice of the female dispatcher called out. Listening, he took some comfort in the fact that the woman's tone conveyed more annoyance than worry.

"Harry Birch, if you left your radio on again while you pulled over to take a leak, I'm going to kill you. I've got another call. I'm signing off. If you can hear my voice, Harry, you call me when you get back in your car. Vel, out."

Yassim yanked the front door open. As the last words were out of the speaker, he reached in and twisted the volume knob down. Then, his fingers probed the buttons and levers on the dash panel and found what he was seeking. He flipped the switch and the strobe sputtered one last blue burst and died. The push of one more knob extinguished the headlights, plunging the scene into darkness. Scowling at his men as he backed out of the car, he noticed their eyes, barely lit by the dome light of the cop car. Before he closed the door extinguishing all light, Yassim noted that both men's eyes were red, bloodshot.

Forcing a fierce calm upon himself and trying to drive the migraine from his consciousness, he assessed the situation. The men smelled of alcohol, but as he wheeled to face them, the sound of an approaching car came from around the bend. All three men crouched involuntarily. The car, a black outline behind a salvo of blinding white, sped around the curve, igniting the scene briefly like a white hot flare and then barreled down the road away from them. When he was certain it was gone and no immediate threat, Yassim barked his order, "Mohammed, tell me what happened!"

Before Mohammed could open his mouth to speak, the back door of the Blazer opened and the Western woman crawled out, nearly on all fours. The dome light outlined her silhouette and even thirty feet away, Yassim could make out the shape of a liquor bottle dangling in her right hand.

"Hassan, honey, is everything all right?" she said and giggled. When she was able to extricate herself from the seat, she took a wobbly step forward. "Say hi to the nice policeman for me and come back," she called in the direction of the men.

Even in the outline cast by the interior light, Yassim could see that the buttons of her dress were unbuttoned down the front. She took another unsteady step, as if the ground had shaken beneath her, and the bodice of her dress flapped open, revealing the clear shape of a naked breast. "Oh, hi, Yas-s-sim."

Yassim fought to control his anger. "Mohammed, tell me what happened. There is not much time."

"Hassan and I bought something to drink back at restaurant," Mohammed answered between puffs on the Turkish cigarette, "and he and Patti were sharing the..." he paused momentarily searching for the right word ... "liquid," he filled in. Both men glanced over at the woman who smiled childishly.

"Hassan, did you purchase the drink?" Yassim asked

"Yes."

"And the policeman?"

"He just appeared behind us with his lights flashing," said Mohammed. The sickle scar on his face seemed to pulse in the faint light, an angry purple slash.

"He was weaving," whined a squeaky voice from the ground.

"Hassan, get up!" hissed Yassim. Hassan used the blade of the jambiya to push himself up, his strong, compact body rising with ease. As he rose, he raised his knife so it was propped menacingly in front of Yassim. He took his time, wiping the glinting steel blade, and although the smile never left his mouth, his eyes were hard.

"He was weaving, and I was telling him to watch his driving. Before I could get him straightened out, the cop appeared behind us with that...that flashing light. Mohammed had to pull over."

"Then the cop came over to Mo's door and told him to get out," said Patti, who had stumbled over to where the men were standing. "Hassan and I scrunched down in the back seat," she looked over to the short man and smiled, "which wadn't too hard since we were pretty far down in the seat, anyway." She giggled once. "Then the cop started to ask a lot of questions so Hassan snuck out the other door quiet-like." She put her index finger to her lips and laughed *again.* "*He snuck around the car and the cop never even saw him.*" *Her finger slid crookedly across his throat.*

"*Patti, get back into the car,*" *Yassim said between clenched teeth.*

"*But...*"

"*Patti!*" *Yassim repeated.*

The woman stumbled across the distance back to the car, dragging the booze bottle. Time was slipping away and he had to deal with this godless woman. Yassim turned to the other two men, "*We must act now. I will address all this later. Mohammed, can you drive?*"

"*Yessir!*" *came the quick reply and Mohammed seemed to sober up and regain his tall, lanky stature again.*

"*Get back in and slowly turn the car around. We will head back the way we came. I'll drive the police car and you will follow me. Hassan, help me get the body of the policeman into the back seat of the patrol car.*"

Without comment, Hassan put his knife away. He and Yassim grabbed opposite ends of the limp body and slid it across the cushion.

"*Now, Hassan listen to me carefully,*" *Yassim said, his face inches from Hassan.* "*Follow this row of trees around the bend and you will find my car. Get into the back seat with the boy and tell Fadi he is to drive and follow me.*"

Hassan hesitated and then complied.

Forcing himself to focus only on the next step, Yassim climbed behind the wheel of the police cruiser and was relieved to find the keys still hanging from the ignition. As he turned the key and the massive engine roared to life, he thought that at least something was going right. He turned the car and angled it back around toward the pavement; he saw a car coasting around the bend and stop. He recognized the headlights of the Trans Am and edged the cruiser carefully onto the road and accelerated. When his scan of the rearview mirror convinced him that both cars were lined up behind him, he pressed the accelerator.

The immediate threat had passed, but he knew they had only a few minutes before "*Vel*"*--whoever she was--would be calling back to check on Harry. His concentration on a solution was almost stalled by his anger at Hassan and Mohammed. How could they be so stupid? To jeopardize everything because of alcohol and a woman!*

"*Do not concern yourself overmuch with future obstacles; solve the problem at hand,*" *the Sheik had taught them. Yassim tried not to think ahead and continued on autopilot, unsure of his next move when the sign came into view again.*

"*Findlay Lake, 3 miles.*"

He remembered and slammed on the brakes and turned the wheel furiously to make the ninety-degree turn. The tires squealed loudly in protest and the sound echoed off the rows of trees. Looking quickly in the rearview mirror, he was grateful the cars behind him made smooth turns around the corner and their headlights were again lined up behind him. Flipping on his bright beams, he peered at the road and, as far as he could make out, the ribbon of asphalt stretched ahead straight and flat. Aloud he gave thanks to Allah and pressed the accelerator. As he watched the speedometer needle slide to the right, he stole a quick glance at the odometer and made note of the mileage and calculated the distance to his destination. Then his eyes returned to the rearview mirror. He would not let the others out of his sight again

Yassim tried to assess their chances of success. They were not good, he decided. Even though he was furious with Hassan and Mohammed, he did not blame them. It was his own guilt that stung most. After the Sheik's meticulous planning, to have everything blown away by a moment of foolish distraction, all because he was indulging his memories. His Imam had been proven right again. "Alcohol and women mixed together are only for the weak of mind and will." He was the cell leader and knew of the men's weakness. Why hadn't he been more wary?

Just as he was becoming desperate, he saw the second sign and sighed with relief. He flicked on his turn signal and eased the big car onto the right fork of the road. The others followed.

Off the main road, the darkness of the wooded area quickly enveloped the three cars. It was at once chilling and reassuring. On the narrow side road, the only lights were from the police car and the two sets of headlights behind him. Leading the small procession, Yassim proceeded slowly and was soon rewarded. Another sign with the words "Findlay Lake" in script indicated a gravel lane little bigger than a driveway to the left. He slowed the cruiser almost to a crawl and turned the car carefully, aiming the headlights into the narrow lane. The bright lights of Mohammed's car struck his rearview mirror and blinded him momentarily and he turned the mirror down. Then his attention returned to the dark woods engulfing his car from both sides; immediately he saw what he was looking for. The lane opened up to a broader gravel area wide enough to turn around a boat and he slowed the vehicle to a stop. Thirty feet ahead he could see the lake. Letting the car engine run, he got out of the car, the door open.

He walked into the beams in front of the car and in a few steps he felt the sloping decline of a wooden boat ramp. With the headlights as illumination, he stepped forward carefully. In three steps the cold water was sloshing over his shoes. Continuing forward, he counted his steps until his right foot fell away into the deeper water ahead of him. He was at the end of the ramp. But how deep was the water? He had to find out. Standing there, the water chilling his feet, he made a decision. I am the leader; perhaps this is part of Allah's penance for my lack of discipline.

Yassim walked deeper into the cold, black water. Within two steps his entire body was submerged. His head below the water, he was blind and disoriented. He floundered, his hands grasping for purchase until he caught a slimy piece of wood that he guessed was one of the submerged supports of the ramp. He forced himself to turn 360 degrees until he could determine the exact direction of the headlights. He angled his body toward the light and paddled in that direction. He used his feet and hands to find the slope of the wooden ramp. A few more sluggish steps and he dragged his drenched, shivering body out of the water.

Still in the direct path of the car lights, he could see little but could make out the shape of a figure approaching. "Yassim, are you okay? Do you need my help?" It was Fadi's anxious voice.

"I am fine, Fadi. Get back to the car."

"Are you sure, Yassim? Do you need my help getting--"

"I am sure, Fadi," Yassim shot back. "Get to your car now. We will need to leave here in a minute."

As the cold night wind whipped through his soaked clothes, he shivered and his teeth began to chatter. He climbed quickly back inside the police cruiser and closed the door. He depressed the buttons at his fingertips and lowered both front windows, thinking how weak the Americans are that they must have a car that even opens its own windows. Then, he put the car into gear and eased it down the slope. He depressed the accelerator and the car glided into the water.

In a few seconds the water flowed over the hood of the car and into the open windows. It poured onto the car seat, immediately chilling his groin and legs again. Yassim stared ahead at the car's hood and what he could see of the lake quickly surrounding the vehicle. He panicked. What if he hadn't gotten the car far enough into the lake to submerge it? Just then, he thought of the light "bubble" atop the car and realized his mistake. If the car is not deep enough, the "bubble" will be the first thing showing. It will be recognized immediately as a police car.

Preoccupied with his doubts, he swallowed a mouthful of lake water. He spat it out and then turned his face toward the roof of the car and tried desperately to take a gulp of air. He had to repeat the effort three times before he was able to expel all the water, take a deep breath and hold it. Then, using both hands, he pushed himself out through the open driver's window.

Halfway out, looking into the path of light left by the headlights, he cursed himself silently. He forced his body partly back through the opening and he used his right hand to frantically search for the light switch. His body half in and half out, he felt the car sinking into the depths of the lake, pulling him down with it, like some dying beast, trying to drag its prey with it to its grave. Blindly he ran his fingers furiously across the panel but he couldn't find the right switch. As seconds ticked by, he struggled to hold his breath and his lungs burned. Although he had had a few rudimentary lessons, he was no swimmer. The vehicle descended farther and he realized he would have to give up the effort or risk being pulled down with the car. As he was pushed away, his hand bumped a button and the lights suddenly went out and all was black in the water.

With the blackness came disorientation and a new desperation raced through his mind. He struggled to regain his calm as he allowed his natural buoyancy to raise him in the water. Yassim searched through the dark water for the headlights of the other cars he knew must be there. Seconds before he broke the surface, he saw the lights. As he came up, his lungs expelled and then greedily gulped air. He forgot the cold, the fear, and panic as the fresh air flooded into his lungs. As soon as he could breathe clearly, he cried, "Allah, be praised!"

Treading water, he turned around in his position and searched for any sign of the police car. He heard a few bubbles break the surface but he saw nothing in the water. Satisfied that he had done what he could, he took slow, awkward strokes toward the beckoning headlights.

Chapter 13

You might not know this but good teachers use whatever's at hand to motivate students. The best government teacher I ever worked with, a talented veteran by the name of Doug Halpin, used current events to get his students excited, even arguing about issues like the latest Supreme Court ruling or the most recent battle in the UN, no small feat for a class of teenagers. He had the power that truly gifted teachers have; his room was seldom quiet and the students were the ones doing most of the talking. They were, as we say in this business, engaged.

I'm not in Doug's league by a long shot, but after working down the hall from him for three years, I had learned a few things. Since all of us in Hammerville were in the midst of the biggest current event that would ever directly involve us, I decided to make full use of it. At least that's what I had in mind at the time with my Journalism class. The next issue of The Anvil was coming up, and, as our sports teams weren't providing any stellar material lately, I had planned to do a theme issue for the student paper. I decided it might be a good idea to devote the edition to the issue of capital punishment. I knew I had struck gold--at least from a motivational perspective--thirty seconds after the announcement was out of my mouth.

"You mean we're going to write about how they're going to fry the Arab? Count me in!" said Keith, an athletic type with the build of a linebacker but who chose not to play any sports. His long, stringy, blond hair tended to fall down over his eyes when he talked and he had to constantly brush it off his forehead.

I didn't respond as I knew Tess would rise to the challenge. "Keith, you can really be a lightweight, you know that? Try to rein in your prejudice, would ya?" she called across the room, momentarily looking up from the computer screen. "This state doesn't 'fry' anybody. They haven't since 1963. They use lethal injection." Her voice took on the pedantic tone she adopted when she wanted to.

"Gimme a break, madame editor," Keith said. "I was just usin' a figure of speech or somethin'. Everybody knows the prison guys are goin' plug that drug into the IV and it will be lights out for old Asad."

I glanced around the room, scanning the students' faces and eventually landed on Ms. Christie Ferguson sitting again in a rear corner desk. My "peer coach" and friend was already jotting her notes on what was happening in my classroom. With her and my personal antagonist, Jerod, both visiting today, my room seemed over full. I nodded briefly at Christie but, with the discussion that was about to unfold, it was the last thought I would give to my peer coach. I wish I would've been that lucky with Jerod.

I started again. "Well, I thought *The Anvil* might take a little broader perspective than focusing on 'frying him,' as you so eloquently put it, Keith. Since we're a school newspaper, I thought maybe we should try something different than the tabloid approach."

"Whadda you mean, Ms. S?" asked Jake, a red-haired sophomore who was the youngest in the Journalism class and a decent writer. He's a likable kid with a good sense of humor and the older students in the class usually cut him some slack. Most of the time Jake wasn't afraid to ask the questions other students thought about but wouldn't voice.

"Well, this is supposed to be your newspaper. What do you guys think we ought to do?" I asked.

"What if we did the 'theme' not on Akadi?" said Tess. All the other students were quiet. Studying the faces of the teens in the room, I was reminded of what a good choice I had made in naming her student editor. She was smart and savvy about what other students think and when she spoke, the rest usually took heed. "What if we covered Akadi, but..." she paused, placing her index finger on her pursed lips, "but we did the edition on the whole issue of capital punishment."

"Yeah," piped up Goat, a tall, gangly kid nicknamed for the prized black goatee that adorned his pointed chin, "we could do something on the number of cons on death row and what crimes they're in for."

"Where?" I asked, breaking in but trying to make the question innocent.

"Whadda mean?" asked Goat.

"The number of cons on death row in Hammerville or in Ohio or...in the U.S.?"

"I dunno," said Goat, "I guess Hammerville...or Ohio? Does it matter?"

"Sure it does," said Tess. "The students here would be more interested in how many's at HBE, but we need to have a little context to make the numbers make sense."

Keith turned to Jerod. "Mr. Thomas, do you know how many cons are on death row at HBE?"

"As of to-day, HBE houses fourteen males awaitin' execution, eight African-Americans, three Hispanic-Americans, two whites 'n Asad, of course," Jerod twanged.

I know I shouldn't but I couldn't help it. I just found that drawl irritating.

"Does it bother anybody else that more than half of the cons on death row here at HBE are black, while only 12% of the population of the state is black?" asked Tyrone, the sole African-American member of the journalism class, and one of a small minority in the whole high school.

"If you do the crime, you better be ready to do the time...or get fried as the case may be," quipped Keith. I was relieved when no one laughed.

"Keith, that ain't funny," Tyrone shot back, "or at least you wouldn't think so if your face wadn't so white."

Of course, Keith took exception to this and was quickly pulling his long legs from inside the desk when I thought it might be the appropriate time for a little instructional intervention.

"Mr. Thomas, do you know how the racial composition of the death row convicts at HBE compare with other prisons in Ohio?" I asked, looking for an ally.

"Naw, Miss Sterber, I dunno. Do you?" He flashed that baby boy smile at me. I could've strangled him.

But his slow pronunciation gave me enough time to cross the room and lay my "teacher" hand on Keith's right shoulder.

Editor Tess recognized my dilemma and jumped in. "According to the flyer that was given to me by the protester at the prison," Tess hastily pulled the red and white sheet from her book bag, "85% of all those on death row are minority, mainly black and Hispanic. Now, I don't know if their figures are right, and as journalists we have to consider the source. But, Tyrone, you have a good point and I think it's significant that none of us know the answer to Ms. Sterber's question. Not even Mr. Thomas, who works there."

She went on. "Maybe, if we want to do a real theme issue dealing with capital punishment, we ought to do more than just rehash the story on Akadi. Heck, everybody's already done that." She got nods of agreement all around the room. "We ought to find a way to use all this attention to grab a new angle, to do something that hasn't been done. Any ideas, anybody?"

"Why don't we start by asking the other students?" Goat offered, like a young child eager to please a parent.

"Ask them what?" I asked and the answers came flying from every student in the room.

"We could ask 'em if they're in favor of capital punishment."

"Do they agree that we should fry Akadi?"

"What crimes do they think are serious enough to get death?"

"Why are there more minorities on death row?"

"Do they have any idea of how many convicts are on death row?"

"Do they know how many states still have the death penalty?"

"How many countries have the death penalty?"

"Do they believe the death penalty is a deterrent to crime?"

The ideas sprang from one mouth after the other, some full with shiny, silver braces, others naturally bright white. The room was abuzz with real questions about a real issue from real teenagers. I was impressed, or just lucky. But I knew it wouldn't be long until it spiraled into bedlam or an argument, so I intervened again.

"Okay, wait," I said and then a little louder, "Everybody...everybody, wait, wait! Wait just a second. Goat, make a list of everyone's questions and then we can decide which ones we want to use."

In the middle of the excited exchange, Tyrone pulled away from the group now ganged up around Goat's desk and directed a question at me. "Ms. S, could we ask questions of anybody else?"

"Who'd you have in mind, the teachers?" I asked back.

"Naw," he said and paused, as if contemplating his options, and then, "What if we interviewed some protesters?" At his question, all the other students stopped, the chaotic cacophony suddenly silenced, and they turned as one to hear my response.

I hesitated and the students interpreted my pause as reluctance--correctly, as a matter of fact. Before I could formulate a reasonable response, they all jumped on me.

"Some of these questions would work real well with the protesters, I think," said Goat.

"I think those people have a right to be heard, even if their opinions aren't particularly popular," suggested Jake, his bright green eyes making his red hair more prominent.

Zoë, a pimply-faced junior with bleached blonde hair, usually too shy to say much, even wanted to add her argument, "I believe," she said so softly that I wouldn't have heard her if the room wasn't completely still, "that they have a right to tell their story, at least the way they see it."

Tess added the final blow. "Ms. S, we've been to the prison. It'd be no big deal. You saw the protesters up close with me. We saw how committed some of them are, staying at the prison through the rain, the cold, and the bad weather. If we're serious about doing an issue, aren't we obligated as journalists to tell all sides of a story, including theirs?"

"Well, Tess, I'm not sure it's possible or practical to tell all sides to a story," I responded, "but any journalist worth her salt needs to get alternate views to make sure the reporting is as balanced and unbiased as possible. After we get the student survey part down, we can take a look at some of the questions to see if any might be appropriate to ask the protesters."

"Hey, I got a great idea!" cried Keith, waving one long arm in the air, looking like one of the persistent reporters at the press conference. By the excited look in his eyes, I knew I was not going to like what came out of his mouth. But, I asked anyway, trying not to sound anxious.

"What, Keith?"

"I think we ought to see if we can interview some of the convicts on death row," he offered.

"I don't know about that--"

He cut me off. "Or maybe they'd let us interview Akadi! Maybe Mr. Thomas could help arrange it with the suits over at HBE?" The whole class turned to look at Jerod who sat in the back of the room.

"Keith, I appreciate your enthusiasm," I said, "but I'm sure Mr. Thomas could tell us that it's far too dangerous to have students enter into a maximum security prison, even for such a lofty goal as interviewing death row inmates for a student newspaper." I glared at Jerod, my arched eyebrows telegraphing my message.

"Wel-l-l, I'm not sure 'bout that. The HBE execs might be interested, for PR purposes, of course. They're always talkin' about how they want to show the whole town just how safe our facility is. And it certainly would be a true learning experience, that's for sure. I can't make any promises, but I'll be glad to check with the powers that be. That is, if it's aw right with Miss Sterber?" He said all this and turned to look squarely at me. And then smiled, dammit. And of course, every adolescent eye in the room turned back to gauge my response.

"Well, um, well," I stumbled for an answer, dumbfounded. "I, uh, I, uh...I'm not sure about this. I don't think Central Office will allow us to go...probably for liability purposes." When in doubt, blame the administrators.

"Could you at least check and ask for us?" pleaded Jake, his youthful face beaming naive anticipation.

"I--" was all I got out and the bell intervened. To my surprise, not one student moved to the door, not even Keith--who I think started all this just for fun. Even he was engaged. Amazing! All of them sat there and I realized they weren't going to move till I said something. So I said, "Okay, I'll check on it and get back to you tomorrow."

In seconds, chaos ruled again and the room was evacuated faster than a fire drill, leaving Jerod and me in the center of the room. Since I couldn't be certain what might come out of my mouth, I was silent. I shot a quick glance to Christie still in the back of the room and commenced my "busy teacher" routine, collecting papers to be taken home and graded, picking up leftover student debris, straightening the bookshelf and hoped he would take the hint. He didn't.

"What a fascinatin' class," he said, breaking the silence. "I could tell the students were really excited, ... ya know, about the idea to do a theme issue of the newspaper." His words weren't as glib as normal and I suspected something was up. "I hope I was helpful," he said, his eyes looking at the floor.

"Are you kidding?"

"Well, I could tell they were really excited 'bout the assignment and I didn't want to discourage 'em."

"You just told a bunch of naïve teenagers that you think it'd be a good idea if they strutted into the prison and conduct interviews with death row inmates." I deigned to look at him for the first time. "For God's sake, are you out of your correctional officer mind?"

"No sweat," he said. "I figgered the principal wouldn't allow 'em to go anyway." He flashed that damn pretty boy smile at me again. "Besides, we want the kids to think we take them seriously, don't we?"

"Well, Mr. Mentor! The problem with your flawless logic is that you can never tell what an administrator's going to do. They can be downright unpredictable at times. What happens if Mr. Thompson and the Super decide it's good for the school image and they say yes? What do you suggest then?"

"I'm not sure," he said, still grinning. "Perhaps, I could suggest that we discuss it further over dinner. That is, if you're free tonight?"

After the 47 minutes I had just endured, I was only too happy to respond. I finished assembling all my student papers and other junk and stuffing them fiercely into my Hilton Head tote bag. As I slung it over my shoulder, I called, "Thanks anyway. I'm busy," and flashed him my own version of that "pretty boy" smile. I gave a quick nod to Christie and headed out the door, leaving them both behind.

Chapter 14

"Mr. Samson, they are ready for you now," said the Secret Service agent in a tone that managed to convey both service and authority. Harold Samson, Director of Homeland Security, nodded at the young man in the nondescript black suit and, glancing down through his bifocals, gathered up the folder of papers for his report. Samson's right hand moved to his bow tie, his fingers doing a final tactile inspection and, satisfied, made a brief pass across his crew cut. He took up alongside the young agent as they proceeded down the hallway.

"Son, how old are you?" Samson asked, partly out of interest and partly to fill the awkward moments of silence as they made the brief trip to the Oval Office.

"Twenty-eight, sir."

"Jeez!"

"Something wrong, sir?" The agent paused and looked at the director for the first time, as he held open the door into the office.

"Oh, nothing much, son," said Samson. "I was just pondering the fruits of my ill-spent youth."

"Sir?"

Standing in the doorway, Samson placed a small hand on the agent's large arm. "Son, I was just wondering where the time has gone. When I was twenty-eight, I was a maverick cop, chasing perps and the ladies, not necessarily in that order. Here you are at the same age guarding the President."

The agent smiled. "That doesn't mean I'm not chasing the ladies."

The Director chuckled. "Anyway, now I'm 55 and I'm wondering what I did with all that time. I guess it's true that the young will inherit the earth. I just hope it's our young."

Samson stepped through the doorway into the President's office. Even though he had been in this office numerous times, he was again struck by the impressive appearance of the room. Glancing around, he recalled his first visit to the Oval Office. That was more than ten years ago, he mused, when President Clinton recognized him for his conviction rate as the District Attorney for Seattle as one of America's "Law Enforcement Heroes." Samson kept that certificate and a photo of him shaking hands with the President, both preserved in fine cherry wood frames, on his wall to this day. Those mementos had not escaped the notice of his new boss, he had been told once at a briefing. But he had not removed them.

Though he had had considerable success in another political world--not much was more political than the public work of the district attorney--he had only tolerated the politics, not relished it like so many of his colleagues. He had been good enough to succeed, in spite of the politics, not because of it, at least that's what he told himself. Now that he was in DC, the maelstrom of political fury, he often questioned his decision to come to Washington. He had attended enough of these security "team" meetings with this president to know the landscape. Yet, it still bothered him that his knowledge of the law and the criminal mind counted for so little. He had learned the hard way that at these meetings any argument not seen as politically expedient was often dismissed. He had to come to each session over-prepared, or his advice to the President was likely to be drowned out by a chorus of concerns from the latest poll results.

But he had to admit he loved the Oval Office. The unusual rounded room, he knew, had been designed by William Howard Taft a century earlier. Legend gave two explanations for the special design. According to historical myth, it was either a metaphor for the democratic concept of equality by making sure no one was at the foot or head of the room, or the design was created to indicate the President as the center of the government with his aides encircling him.

Samson strolled across to the chair indicated by Dean Settler, the President's Chief of Staff. Settler was a tall rail of a man, standing a full ten inches above Samson, but weighing no more than 175. His bony hands hung at the end of his sleeves as if they were attached to his skinny arms by Velcro. His long, gaunt, fiercely pockmarked face reminded Samson of the photos of the moon surface.

Taking his seat, Samson noticed his two colleagues were already there. Tommy Dickson, Director of the FBI, sat on the couch nearest to his chair. Still possessing the physique of his youth when he played for the NFL, his huge frame flattened the tan cushion into an oversized pancake. He nodded, "Hey, Harold," and a smile creased his ruggedly handsome features. Even at 48, Dickson looked like he should be out on the street, crushing perps, which of course was how he made his bones at the FBI.

In an opposite chair, CIA Director Jerry Garcia (who, Harry had quickly learned, didn't like being kidded about his name's connection to the Grateful

Dead) sat quietly, his eyes closed. The first time they had been introduced, Samson thought he had never met a man more "average." Average height, average build, average hair, and average, almost forgettable features. Samson thought whimsically that Garcia, despite his name, could be a poster child for WASP success. Hearing Dickson's greeting, he abruptly opened his eyes and nodded at Samson.

President Ryan Gregory came from behind his desk and collapsed onto the couch next to Garcia, facing Samson. When he wanted to, Gregory was one of the most photogenic men Samson had ever met, an attribute that had no doubt boosted his elect-ability, or perhaps even made it possible. Partly because of his own "idiosyncratic" looks--Samson had read this description of him in a favorable column and held onto it ever since--Samson did not put much stock in appearances, but clearly the voting American public did.

In the media-crazed world politics had become, the only viable national candidates were those with great teeth and a sharp profile, Samson realized. Gregory met all those qualifications and then some. With his slightly graying blonde hair and patrician features, he looked like the consummate American leader of the 21st century. Any time there was a camera on, President Gregory had the ability to instantly project, with his trademark smile, intense blue eyes and long straight nose, a complete sense of affable competence. Without a word, his thoughtful gaze into the lens seemed to convey, "Everything was okay. The nation is in good hands."

At least that's how it had been when he was elected several years before. But now the honeymoon was long over and President Gregory, having had to make some tough decisions, had seen his approval rating decline recently. And off-camera, the stress showed.

Samson had never quite understood why he had been tapped by President Gregory as the Director of Homeland Security. Although he had garnered national attention for himself and his department for a startlingly high percentage of convictions, he had not met President Gregory or donated to his campaign before he had been asked to take the cabinet spot. In the interview, the President had said that he expected Samson to replicate the kind of successful work he had engineered in the office of District Attorney. Honored, Samson had accepted on the spot and moved his family across the country. So far though, he had found the federal bureaucracy much more resistant to his "engineering" and had had to fight constantly against competing special interests to keep from being sucked into the political vortex.

"Well Czar Samson, how was your trip to Ohio?" asked the President, settling back against the rich cushions of the sofa. The fingers of his right hand wrapped around a ballpoint pen as if he were about to trigger a detonator.

"Very well, Mr. President," answered Harold Samson. "I was truly impressed with all the security arrangements of the HBE prison. No prison is impregnable but HBE has built redundancy on top of redundancy into its security system. They are prepared to handle pretty much any eventuality."

"Pretty much any eventuality?" President Gregory clicked the pen twice.

"No place is 100 percent secure and there is no way to prepare for everything."

Garcia spoke up. "Not the impression I got from your comments at the press conference."

"Jerry, I think you know better than to confuse media hype with reality," said Samson.

"Personally, I liked the part where you called the terrorists murdering lunatics," commented Settler. "The phrase played well with the media too."

"You certainly have the ability to cut to the chase, Harold," commented the President. "That's one of the reasons I placed you in that spot." He paused briefly. "Seriously, what is your assessment of the threats by Al Quaida to rescue him? Not what you fed the media. The real deal."

Samson opened his folder and pulled a few sheets of paper and handed a copy to each of the men. "Mr. President, I meant what I said about the security of the Hammerville prison. It is about as close as you can get to an impenetrable fortress in the middle of Ohio."

"But--" interrupted the President.

"But, I don't expect Akadi's old pals to just sit and take it. I expect them to do something. That's why I was goading them at the press conference to attack the prison. I believe we would stop them cold there."

The President pointed impatiently to the paper in his hand, the pen clicked once in the silence.

Samson continued, "This is a translation of a 'letter to the American people' on an underground Syrian website, titled roughly 'Allah's Voice.' From what we can tell, it was released yesterday and Jerry's people at Langley uncovered it." Samson had learned the importance of sharing the credit with other agencies.

"If the Leaders of the Great Satan..." intoned President Gregory, examining the small print on the paper with the black reading glasses he had pulled from his pocket. "If the Leaders of the Great Satan choose to execute the freedom fighter, Asad Akadi, it will only hasten his journey to martyrdom and Allah will welcome him to paradise." The President didn't attempt to hide his disdain. "But Allah will release his full wrath upon the children of America and families will weep when they are taken from them. Blah-blah-blah. Is this legit?" he asked, pointing with the glasses removed from his head.

"I don't believe we can dismiss this," Samson said.

"Jerry, have your people detected any unusual activity, anything that might be construed as a specific threat?" the President asked, glancing over at the CIA Director.

"Pretty much the usual, Mr. President," answered Garcia. "Since Afghanistan and Iraq have been partially stabilized, the terrorists have had to go further underground, but you know that, Mr. President. Our people are watching all the major players in their organization, but nothing yet."

"Tommy, anything unusual within our borders?" President Gregory asked.

"Depends on what you mean by unusual. There are several cases that are out of the ordinary we're working on," the Director of the FBI said, ticking items off on the massive fingers of his right hand. "The disappearance of a freighter from the harbor in New Orleans, a nuclear engineer at the Ozark Power Plant caught trying to sell some enriched uranium and an undercover DEA agent found slain in a lake in Louisiana--nothing too much out of the ordinary." The President nodded. "Oh, and I have sent additional agents to Hammerville. If anyone so much as blows his nose there, we'll know it."

"So, you three gentlemen," said the President, looking at all three directors, "are telling me you know of no reason to change Akadi's execution?"

"None that I can see," answered Garcia first.

"I concur," added Dickson.

"And Mr. Samson, what about the crystal ball at Homeland Security?"

"We clearly don't have a crystal ball. If we did, I'd bet a bundle at the Preakness and pack it in." The other men chuckled briefly at his jest. "I'm still concerned about their threats, but no, sir, I can give no specific reason to advise you otherwise."

"And we should not forget, Mr. President," put in the chief of staff in a hollow voice that matched his gaunt frame, "that the pollsters predict that Akadi's execution five days before the election will cause your rating to jump several points. According to their argument, the American people will sleep better at night with Akadi dead. To them, it will be a tangible sign that we are winning the war on terrorism."

When none of the directors felt the need to respond, or perhaps didn't know how to, President Gregory broke the silence. "Let's go ahead with it then. Keep me informed."

Chapter 15

Christie Ferguson caught up with me in the hall a few minutes after my uneremonious departure from my classroom. Grabbing my arm, she dragged me two doors down into the teachers' restroom and then closed and locked the door. Within a few seconds, I was grateful for the privacy.

"Are you crazy, girl?" were the first words out of her mouth.

The two of us stood there by the sink, in front of the half-length mirror. I glanced at the reflection of my side profile. My brunette hair, though not exactly disheveled, was no longer in the neat tresses I had styled that morning. My right hand brushed it distractedly. One hazel eye, watching me from the glass, sat atop a sloping nose that was slightly too large and a small half mouth. A hint of red bloomed on my curved cheek and I fought to contain it. "Look, I'm sorry. I just had to get out of that room."

Nonplussed, Christie repeated, her eyes like two blue lasers, "Are you out-of-your-mind crazy, girl?"

"Maybe," I said shaking my head.

Christie's perfectly trimmed eyebrows did a quick up-and-down dance on her forehead, but she said nothing.

"Well, that's not how I planned the class," I said. "I figured they'd come up with the idea of doing more research on capital punishment or maybe think about interviewing a victim or collecting some statistics on the death penalty. I never dreamt they'd want to interview the inmates at the prison. Things just got out of control. I know I should've cut them off, but I didn't want to stifle their discussion..."

"Whoa, slow down, girl," Christie broke in, chuckling.

"It's not funny," I protested, but her delight was too contagious and I couldn't help myself. In seconds, I found myself laughing too. "I guess I can really get myself into it when I want to. I can't wait to see Thompson's face when I ask him. He's going to say, 'You've really lost it this time, Ms. Sterber.'"

The grin departed from Christie's face as if yanked by an unseen hand. "Dee Dee, sometimes you are just clueless, you know that. Look, from a coaching perspective, I thought the class went fine. In fact, I thought it was the best class I've observed so far. You created an authentic learning assignment and, from what I could tell, every single one of your students was on board. Hell, I wish half my classes were anywhere near that engaging."

"But..."

She cut me off. "Oh, the conversation with Hard-Ass Thompson's going to be a little interesting, but nothing you can't handle, girl. He'll probably say no and you can tell your students how much you advocated for them. Besides, it sounds like whichever way it goes, it's going to be a really good edition of the paper, one people might actually read, and probably a great learning experience for the students. I don't have enough time now, but we can go over all my notes later."

"But you just said I was crazy."

She shook her head at me, the styled blond waves doing that slow, delayed dance.

I said, "Oh, I apologize, I didn't mean to walk out on you and just leave you there in the classroom."

"Hey, that's all right. I didn't mind," she said.

"Okay, I give up," I responded, throwing my hands in the air. "Why am I so crazy then?" Her only answer was that devilish smile. "What?"

"Well, let me put it to you this way," Christie began, tilting her head. "You haven't had a date in, what, four months and you haven't had hot steamy sex in God knows how long?"

"I don't really want to get into that---"

"...and you turn down that great invitation."

"Do you mean...Jerod?" I asked, incredulous.

"Girl," she took up, "I just don't understand you. You tore out of your room like Satan was chasing you. I hung around and talked with Jerod for a while, you know, about his volunteering as a mentor and some of the kids he's working with. He seems like a really nice guy."

"You've got to be kidding."

"Then he wanted to know about you ... all about you."

"What did he want to know?" I demanded.

She grinned at me.

"What did you tell him?" I asked, slapping her arm.

"Not much. You're not that interesting."

"Christie!"

"Relax. I only told him the good stuff."

"Like?"

This time she laughed out loud. "Okay, I just told him what a great teacher you are and how you came back to your hometown to teach these students when you could've gotten a job at a lot better schools and been paid a lot more money. I told him that one reason you're so good at your job is because you care so much about your students."

I started feeling embarrassed and Christie stared across to make sure her point was delivered. Some friend, huh?

"In fact, I tried to ask about him and his job but all he wanted to talk about was you. If we weren't such good friends, it might give a girl a complex. I told him you were funny... and interesting..." she said, finger to her lips in that thoughtful pose of hers. "Oh, and I told him the reason you were such a great teacher is because you are so, uh ... passionate."

She made me wait for the last word because she knew how I'd react. I tried to open my mouth but she was not to be stopped. "Look, Dee Dee, I was just trying to help you. Lord knows you need the help, and besides, he's gorgeous."

"Maybe I don't want that kind of help."

Like the friend who knows me too well, she answered with one of my favorite sayings. "Methinks the woman protests too much! Dee Dee, don't be stupid. This guy seems interested in you. Lord knows why when all you do is brush him off. Reality check, gal! You live in Hammerville and it's not exactly as if you had guys lined up outside your door."

I said, "I think Jerod is a jerk. Sometimes I think he works at being exasperating."

"Well, what guy isn't?" she countered. "It's what guys do best." She smiled at me and then corrected herself. "Well, it's one of two things guys do best. Come on, Dee Dee, with that guy sitting in your room almost every day, you can't tell me you haven't done a little fantasizing about him?"

"Gimme a break."

"I was only talking to him for about ten minutes," she said, her blue eyes glazing over, "and before I was done, I was already building one major fantasy project. You know, clothes on the floor, his hands on my body, our breathing shallow." She closed her eyes and was gone.

"Hey! Earth to Christie!" I said. "Aren't you forgetting something?"

"What?" She opened just one blue eye.

"Oh, a little thing like the fact that...you're engaged to get married in two months! I'm not sure Kurt would be too crazy about your fantasy project."

"Who says my fiancé has to know?" she snapped back. "Anyway, according to this book I'm reading, The Passionate Marriage, fantasizing can be a boost to a healthy sexual relationship. Besides, in our vows, we promise to love, honor and cherish. Nowhere does it say a word about halting my fantasy indulgences."

"You are something else, girlfriend. You know that?" I said.

"Yeah, I am, aren't I?" she chuckled. "Are you going to sit there and tell me you have never designed your own little fantasy scenario with Jerod the hunk?"

"Well, I-I-I..." I stammered.

She took this as a sign that I was weakening--which I was--and took full advantage of it. "Look me in the eye and tell me, Ms. Danielle Sterber, that when you're standing there, having one of your intellectual discussions with Jerod the hunk that you're not secretly peeling away his clothes."

"Th-that's ridiculous," I protested, unable to keep the stammering out of my voice. In the mirror I caught a glimpse of scarlet blossoming up my neck.

"Ah-ha!" she said.

"Christie, I wouldn't make love to him if I was about to die and he was the only male around!"

"Really."

"Besides, I-I-I think he's crazy...and maybe dangerous. You heard what he told the kids. What if he actually arranges for them to interview Asad?"

"Oh, that. It was probably just what he told you," she answered. "Anyway, they're supposed to have all this super tight security at HBE. I'd be surprised if they'd do anything to endanger that."

" I don't know. That Asad is one really nasty dude, as my guys would say. I've got this really bad feeling about the whole execution." I said. "I'll just be glad when it's over."

But Christie couldn't stay serious for long. "Dee Dee, you worry way too much," she said, smiling. "Whatever's going to happen will happen. That's why you've got to take advantage of opportunities when they come along ... or when they walk into your classroom."

"Christie, you know you are exasperating!" I said, but returned her smile.

"Girlfriend, I'm outta here. I got a class to catch. I'll see you tomorrow." She was out the restroom door before I could open my mouth again.

Chapter 16

No matter what he did, Yassim couldn't shake the numbing chill from his body. After climbing out of the water, he had stripped and grabbed some clothes out of his sports bag in the trunk, his breath frosty puffs in the night air. Then he had Fadi drive the Trans Am so he could call the Sheik to report what had happened. He took three slow breaths, using the oxygen to cleanse his mind and steady his nerves. But as he punched in the ten digits, his hand still trembled. He spoke slowly and deliberately in measured Arabic for two minutes into the satellite phone he had received in Canada. When he was finished, he listened for the next ninety seconds, the color slowly ebbing from his features.

His body shivered again, but he couldn't be sure if it was from the icy water clinging to his skin or from the Sheik's new directives. He would follow them of course; in Allah's army there was no room for questioning orders. Besides, he believed fervently in the Jihad and was convinced it was the only way to purge his people of the Great Satan in their midst. His devotion to the Sheik was total. But that didn't mean he enjoyed killing. After the savage murder of his wife and son, all he had wanted was revenge, or so he thought. Now, after he himself had inflicted death several times, he hadn't found it. He had found only that the hole left by the death of his wife and son was still a ragged, open wound gnawed constantly by some parasite inside him. The longing and desperation lingered, and festered.

He glanced up and spied the exit marker on the side of the highway. "That's our exit, three miles ahead!" he called at Fadi so loudly that he woke the boy.

"It's okay, Asim," he said more gently. "It's all right. Everything's going to be all right."

The boy gazed into the half darkness with red swollen eyes. The boy slowed his crying and sniffed back the snot in his nose. Yassim reached into his pocket to pull out a handkerchief and realized it was with the rest of his soaked clothes in the trunk. "Give me a handkerchief," he growled to Fadi.

As Fadi reached into his back pocket, the car veered onto the shoulder of the road.

"Watch what you're doing!" Yassim screamed as Fadi regained control of the car. "There, there, Asim," Yassim said in a more soothing voice, handing the boy the large white cloth. "Blow your nose and you'll feel better." The

youth gave a loud honk and then reduced his crying to a few sniffles. "Isn't that better?" The boy nodded.

Ever since Yassim had spoken with the Sheik, Fadi had said nothing. The driver's massive hands choked the leather around the steering wheel, his knuckles white from the tension. His broad shoulders were stiff and the cords in his neck stood out. But he asked no questions.

"Put your blinker on for Hassan and exit here," Yassim said.

The Trans Am rolled down the exit ramp and stopped, its big engine rumbling at the light. "At the second light, turn right and then another right directly into the parking garage."

Yassim turned again to check, for the thousandth time, on the Blazer behind them and was satisfied to see that the SUV matched every move of their car. As they stopped at the ticketing machine, the SUV pulled up behind them, headlights brightly illuminating the interior of the Trans Am. Yassim glanced back through the glare but could make out nothing. He hoped that the hour drive into Cleveland had given them ample time to think. Not that it mattered now.

"Follow the ramp to the bottom floor," Yassim said, "and pull to the rear of the building. There will be four cars there. Pull behind the first car."

Fadi nodded but kept his eyes on the twisting ramp ahead. In the narrow passage, the whine of the car's engine reverberated off the concrete walls like some wounded animal. Fadi twisted the Trans Am down the spiral as the floors went by in a dizzying procession until they arrived at the bottom level, the Blazer close behind. The headlights of both cars probed the darkness of the underground chamber, their beams swallowed up by the damp mist. In the limited space illuminated by the lights, they could see nothing. Yassim began to second-guess himself and thought for a moment he had misunderstood the Sheik's directions.

Just then a pair of lights blinked twice in the distance and then went black. Fadi said, "Did you see that?"

"Of course," replied Yassim. "Drive toward those lights."

Both cars rolled across the floor of the garage, their engine noises still audible, but more subdued in the open space. As they neared the parked automobiles, Yassim noticed that they were quite different than the cars they were driving. The first was a white panel van with writing on the side. Parked *next to it was an aged, tan Dodge Minivan, probably '98 or '99, he couldn't tell. The final two cars were identical, late model Honda Civics. The Trans Am pulled to a stop and Yassim got out. As he approached the cars, the door of the white van slid open and two men stepped out.*

"Cut d' lights," Yassim heard the first man say. Before the lights were extinguished, Yassim caught a glimpse of two dark-skinned men with sharp Arab features and clean-shaven faces. Light spilled feebly out from the interior of the van and the Trans Am, barely outlining the figures standing between the cars.

"Where are the boy and the woman?" the same voice said. "I will take care of them."

Yassim opened the back door of the Trans Am and coaxed the boy out. "It's okay, Asim. We're here." He worked to keep his voice light. "This man will take you to your Uncle Nazir. Come on."

The boy crawled out of the back seat, a small brown blanket clutched tightly in his right fist. Yassim took his other hand and led him to the stranger. The man caught the boy's hand, a little too roughly, thought Yassim as he turned and went back to the Blazer and opened the passenger door.

"Patti, go with this man." She slid out of the seat and strutted past him without a word. Her eyes were defiant, but, with her lipstick smudged and her curls disobediently flopping down across her forehead, her earlier bravado had evaporated. Motionless, Yassim stood next to the SUV and watched as the trio got into the first Honda and drove away. In ten seconds the car disappeared up the ramp.

"Hassan and Mohammed," he called out without glancing inside the car, "the Sheik says that before you can take your next step you need to face Mecca on your knees. He has directed that you do penance for your sins. Allah demands it."

"Here?" said Hassan, his voice squeaking.

"The Sheik says that for this penance, the place does not matter. It is what is in your heart that Allah sees."

While they exited the Blazer, Yassim walked over to the other stranger and spoke quietly. "Do you have it?" Without speaking, the man produced an object from a cavernous pants pocket and handed it over to Yassim, its steel briefly catching the faint light from the car's interior.

"What are we to do?" asked Hassan, his tone petulant.

"The Sheik says you must face east, kneel and touch your head to the ground and recite the traditional prayer for forgiveness," the cell leader answered.

"Which way is east?" asked Mohammed, looking around anxiously. Without thinking, Yassim pointed to the back wall of the garage.

"Come on, Mohammed," Hassan whined as the two moved a little away from the parked cars, trying to locate an unsoiled spot on the concrete floor. The two knelt down, lowering their foreheads to the cement. Together they began intoning the required prayer, reciting the words aloud in Arabic in a monotone.

Yassim followed them and stopped a few feet behind the prone figures. Taking a deep breath, he whispered, *"May Allah have mercy on your souls."* Both men rattled on, unhearing, loudly reciting the lengthy prayers. Yassim bent over their figures. He raised the small revolver to the back of the heads of the two praying men. The gun spit fire twice, the sound deafening as it bounced off the concrete wall.

He lowered his hand and slowly walked back to where the stranger was standing. Handing him back the weapon, he said, *"You will clean up."* The man nodded. Yassim shouted back toward the Trans Am. *"Come, Fadi, we take the minivan."* Fadi jumped out of the car and ran to catch up, visibly shaking.

"Isn't this great, Fadi?" Yassim said, pointing at the car. *"We'll be touring America in a Caravan. How Arab. Allah would approve of the irony."* His laugh, when it came, was hollow. *"You drive. The keys are in it."* They both climbed in and the two car doors shut in unison, sending an echo through the darkened garage.

Chapter 17

Yassim adjusted his position on the uncomfortable folding chair and studied the screen of the laptop. He still could not believe what he read. He reread the decoded text in Arabic and translated the words aloud into English, unconsciously mimicking the staccato cadence of the Sheik in his voice. "This mission is of vital importance. The present trouble must not be allowed to be an impediment to your progress. There is no soldier I trust more than you. I place the next decision in your anointed hands. I am certain that Allah will guide your actions. The files of the recruits to replace your fallen men are below. Follow these simple directions. Study this information carefully, then destroy it. To expedite the process, these men have been flown nearby. Like true disciples of Allah, they only await your call. Call and interview those you wish. Select the two men Allah tells you to choose. Then swiftly deliver the others to their reward in Paradise. Until it is too late for the Americans, your mission must not be discovered."

He stopped reading and raised his eyes, his glance darting around the empty room, searching for fresh demons. But Yassim knew he was alone. Fadi had dropped him here at this dilapidated apartment building a half hour ago. Yassim had retrieved the key and a slip of paper, the only contents of the stunted glove compartment. The white sheet contained an address and a single word in English and Yassim had barked curt directions to his remaining soldier. As instructed, Fadi had delivered him here, then driven the minivan to a different, more secluded location, and registered at a seedy hotel nearby.

Ignoring the two drug-crazed Hispanics on the stoop, Yassim had climbed the crumbling concrete steps leading up to the aged brownstone. Slowly he made his way up five flights of darkened, urine-stained stairs, as if he were ascending into some special hell. Now, examining the peeling, faded wallpaper of this ugly bedroom, he realized that they had been directed here, somewhere in the ethnic neighborhood of Parma just outside of Cleveland, because he and Fadi would never be noticed. A look at the Mideastern man and woman he had passed, shamelessly groping each other on the second floor landing, had confirmed this. At least, he thought with relief, he was close, the objective of the mission less than a two-hour drive away.

Once inside the apartment, the door locked and bolted behind him, Yassim had entered the rear bedroom and found the black laptop sitting, as promised, atop a blond fiberboard desk, its cable snaking down across the top. It took him only a few seconds to open the case and turn it on, watching as the screen brightened with color and the short message scrolled slowly down the screen.

Yassim read the message again, this time to himself, needing to distill its meaning and weigh the consequences. The fingers of his right hand pinched the stubble that had replaced his long beard. So many senseless deaths, he thought and heard himself whisper her name, "Fatima" aloud in the bare room. Then, without willing it, he was back home, sailing on the Mediterranean Sea, a warm breeze on his face. She was smiling up at him, those beautiful brown eyes beaming, both graceful arms encircling the small body of Jamal. It had been their son's first sail and his body bounced with the excitement. In his reverie, Yassim could hear the snap of the sail in the wind and smell the salty sea air.

Dragging his attention back to the laptop, he opened the message and scanned the files, studying the brief bios of the new recruits. When he had finished reading, he flipped open the phone and punched in the first number, beginning the process of exercising control over life and death.

It took only three hours and three interviews for Yassim to make his decision. The first was easy. Mustafa was a monster of a man, 6'4" and 260 pounds. He had massive hands and biceps to match. Beardless, his face had a harsh, rugged look with a nose that had been broken and reset badly. The fractured nose was perched between steely gray eyes that looked like two bb's floating in pools of white. His dossier revealed an expertise with handguns and knives, knowledge and experience with several different types of explosives as well as a radical devotion to the Jihad. From the few words he has spoken, his English was excellent and, when told of his selection, he said aloud, "Allah, be praised," though without much feeling. He would serve as an apt replacement for Hassan. In fifteen minutes, Yassim had sketched out only the barest details of the mission and dispatched him to the motel where Fadi waited.

The second interview was shorter and less productive. Yassim only needed a few minutes to recognize the young black-bearded firebrand as a powder keg of hatred. The recruit's hazel eyes glazed when he spoke of his devotion and his willingness to die to punish Allah's enemies. The cell leader decided that even with the young man's considerable skills, his temperament was too much of a liability. Yassim ended the interview, not even bothering to remember his name. It would be easier that way, he told himself. He sent the recruit into the bedroom for the traditional prayers, following a few feet behind him. As the recruit bent low to the ground, Yassim retrieved the silenced Makarov from a side pocket and pulled the trigger, hearing the spit of the silencer. The cell leader stood over the limp body as blood flowed into a crimson pool. He whispered, "May Allah give you sweet reward," hoping he believed it. Then, summoning up control he did not know he possessed, he closed the door and moved back to the front room. He called the next name.

The third interview was the one that surprised the cell leader. According to the file, the soldier's name was Jesus, and when he walked through the doorway, Yassim could not help but glare. Like many of al Quaida's soldiers, this soldier was tall and muscular, but this one was not an Arab. Instead he was an incredibly handsome Latino. No more than 25, he carried himself with an uncommon confidence and had a carefree, almost disarming air. With his small black mustache, crystal green eyes and broad smile, this one had broken the hearts of many women, Yassim guessed. Studying the man in front of him, he was reminded of a Hollywood actor, but at first he couldn't remember which one.

At first, Yassim was put off by the man's appearance, willing to dismiss his handsome looks as a lack of substance or, worse yet, a sign of weakness. However, examining the man's dossier again, Yassim reappraised the new recruit and was met with an inspiration so powerful that it could only have come from Allah himself. Looking into the new face, he smiled at the idea. Clearly the Americans would never suspect such a man.

With a powerful handshake, he welcomed Jesus and then briefed him on the general outlines of the mission. Giving the new soldier the address for papers and funds, he got down to specifics. "Jesus, I have a very specific task for you, one I think you will enjoy," began Yassim. "I want you to leave today and head to Hammerville. Once there, I want you to charm your way into the school district office and get hired as a substitute teacher. We will follow in a few weeks, but in the meantime I want you to learn the high school inside and out. Get to know the teachers and learn the layout. Though we have already made arrangements to secure the blueprints from an inside source, anything you can learn may prove helpful when we arrive."

Jesus sported a dazzling smile, his teeth white and perfectly straight beneath his black mustache. A mischievous gleam in his emerald eyes, he asked, "Are there beautiful women at this Hammerville school?"

"I'm sure there are," answered Yassim, his features now lined with anxiety, "but our mission will leave little time for what Americans call 'fraternizing.'"

Jesus' grin never dimmed. "Do not misunderstand, Leader Yassim. My heart and soul belong to Allah and I will carry out my responsibilities as promised. But the job is more enjoyable when the scenery is beautiful. With your permission, I'll be off to Hammerville ... and beautiful women."

As he shook the recruit's hand, Yassim could not help but smile himself. When the door closed behind Jesus, his first thought was that the team was intact again. He could succeed with these men. He picked up the phone one last time. "It is done," he said into the receiver. Then after a brief wait, he said only, "Mustafa and Jesus," and flipped the phone closed.

Chapter 18

Harold Samson stood in the Oval Office, waiting. He was alone and he fiddled with his brown and gold bow tie and looked down at his watch for the fifth time, 11:39 P. M. Even as many times as he had been to this room, he still couldn't help but be intimidated. Just pondering the decisions made in this room made him feel smaller. Woodrow Wilson's argument for the US to join the League of Nations. FDR's decision to go to war with the Allies. Kennedy's determination to blockade Cuba. Nixon's resignation. He must have still been daydreaming about the history of this place because he didn't hear the door.

"Well, Mr. Director of Homeland Security, you said it was important and so I am here," announced Ryan Gregory, looking regal in a black dinner jacket complete with ribbed vest.

"Mr. President, I apologize." His eyes flitted to the packet he was holding and then back to the President, "When I called, I did not mean to interrupt your schedule. I told your secretary that I could wait till you were finished for the evening."

"Nonsense, Harold," President Gregory responded and slapped Samson on the back. "I'm afraid that I will not be 'free' until well into the wee morning hours. To tell you the truth, this dinner was so boring I was delighted to have the excuse to leave. You would not believe this woman they had me seated beside, the wife of the Spanish Ambassador." He gestured to the green couch, "So forget the intrusion and tell me what brings you out so late this evening. Not good news, I suspect."

"No sir," said Samson, "I wouldn't call it an emergency, but it is definitely not good news." Sitting, he pulled out several sheets of paper. He handed a grainy, black and white photograph to the President. "This photo was taken at a toll booth on I-90 near the New York/Pennsylvania border a few miles from Lake Erie. As I'm sure you remember, Mr. President, one of the changes I made last year was to install cameras at the toll booths near any of our borders, and we included a number of places along the Great Lakes as well."

When President Gregory nodded, Samson continued, "Admittedly, it's not the best picture, but we are pretty sure this is Mohammed Armdi, one of the terrorists on our international watch list." He handed the President the second picture and paused as Gregory, pulling glasses from his breast pocket, compared the two photos. " We believe he belongs to a cell of Islamic terrorists operating out of Syria. This group is known to have ties to the group that made 'The Voice of Allah' announcement I shared yesterday."

"You are certain that these two are of the same man?"

"No sir, we are not certain. The resolution on the second photo is not distinct enough and we believe he may have been aware of the camera and made sure we could only get a shadowed profile. In fact, the examiners didn't even see the connection upon their first analysis and the computers only flagged it when they ran the digital analogy software." Pulling a pen from his pocket, Harold used it as a pointer to highlight an area on the recent photo. "The face is not completely clear, but see this scar down the right side of his face? That matches the description and photo we have on file for this man."

"Can you tell what car he is driving?"

"The cameras are designed primarily to capture faces, but analysts believe the contours match either a Chevrolet Blazer or GMC Tahoe."

"When was this new photo taken?"

"About 30 hours ago. It took about a day for the computers to analyze every photo taken at all the border security cameras."

The President moved over to the lamp on the end table and turning it on, held the two photos under the light, one in each hand. After a few seconds he returned his attention to his visitor. "Assuming this is the same man, have there been any further sightings?"

"No, sir, we have not had any further reports of the man but I've issued a BOLO to all the offices in the Midwest and Northeast states," admitted Samson.

"I can see why you might be concerned, Harold, but this doesn't seem to be very much. I don't see why you thought you needed to see me tonight. Couldn't this wait till our regular briefing on Tuesday? Or do you have something else?"

"Perhaps, Mr. President."

"Perhaps?"

"I'll let you decide after I share the second piece of information with you. This report was turned in less than 50 miles from the toll booth where the second photo was taken." Samson took back the photos and handed the president the next sheet of paper.

He gave the President time to scan the brief report. Then Samson pulled a map of the Great Lakes states from his briefcase and continued. "That was called in from a Pennsylvania State Trooper at this location. Right here," he indicated a yellow dot on the map. "Also this red dot indicates the location where the surveillance photo was taken." He pointed to the second spot on the map. "The time on the call was 22:09, approximately two hours after the photo at the toll booth."

"How long would it take to drive from here to here?" Gregory said, tapping the two dots with the pen.

"I'm not familiar with the roads in that area but they tell me about an hour."

The President's attention went back to the police report, his finger tapping the paper. "It says he was stopping a car for a suspected DUI," Gregory began. "No report from him after that?"

"No sir. No one has seen or heard from Officer Birch since then."

"What about his cruiser? Any report of a stolen or abandoned police cruiser in the area?"

"None, sir. Both the local and state authorities are looking for the police car, but so far nothing has turned up."

"This officer," Gregory tapped the report again, "Officer Jeffrey Birch called in a make and plate number," he glanced again at the paper, "Black Chevrolet Blazer, 235DTZ—PA. Any luck on tracing the car?"

"The plate was stolen a week ago off a car in Erie." Samson pointed back at the map, indicating the city near the two colored dots.

"I assume the agencies have had an APB for the car?"

"Yessir, that's what prompted my visit. Thirty minutes ago a mud-splattered dark blue Chevy Blazer was found abandoned in a parking garage right here in Parma, a suburb of Cleveland." Samson raised the map again from the couch and pointed out a third dot on the east end of Cleveland. "The SUV bore no plates, but a search of a dumpster in an alley a few blocks away turned up that plate. Crime scene techs are examining the car now." He stopped to let his boss process.

"So you believe this fellow," the President's eyes strayed briefly to the first photo, "this Mohammed Armdi was the driver of the car stopped by Officer Birch?" He clicked his pen once.

"It looks like it may have happened that way, sir."

"And you are saying that this terrorist," the President glanced again at the grainy photograph, "this Mohammed Armdi was confronted by this Officer Birch, and he somehow managed to dispose of him and his car. He then drove the Chevy Blazer to Cleveland and abandoned it. Is that it?"

"Obviously, we don't know but, yes, sir, we believe it is certainly a real possibility. Also, the photo experts believe there may have been a second person in the car. In one of the photos taken as the Blazer passed through the toll booth, the camera caught what appears to be a shadow of at least one more person." Samson handed the third photo to the President. "It's possible the person may have ducked down to avoid the camera, but when they examined the shots they believe this," he pointed to a darkened area on the photo, "is the shadow caused by another person."

The President got up and carried the new photo over to the lighted lamp and examined it. "Boy, that smudge isn't much to go on."

"No, sir."

"When do you expect the crime techs to be done with their analysis of the car? Will that tell you if there were other passengers?"

"We hope so sir, but in their initial inspection, they thought the car had been wiped clean," Samson said. "At any rate, they should be completing their analysis within the next few hours and I will let you know immediately if anything turns up."

"And you've picked up no other notice of either Armdi or this other one since these photos were taken?"

"No sir. We have alerted all the appropriate agencies, but so far nothing."

"Thank you for bringing this to my attention, Harold. Anything else?" President Gregory asked, rising from the couch. The pen clicked twice and disappeared into a jacket pocket. Then he brushed imaginary crumbs off his black vest.

"Yes sir. I think it may be time to raise the threat level and notify the public of the terrorist."

The President looked at him sharply. "Didn't you tell me you've already alerted all the agencies?"

"Yes, sir, we have and we've sent each agency photos of Armdi and a list of his known associates along with any photos we have."

"Don't jump the gun on me, Harold," the President said and turned his head to the closed door and called, "I'm ready, Bradley." Immediately the Secret Service agent stepped back into the room and held the door open for his boss. Gregory turned and beamed his best smile back toward Samson. "I do not want to get the people of this country stirred up unnecessarily." He clasped his Director of Homeland Security on the shoulder and finished, "Besides, we have an election in less than two weeks. We can't have the voters of this fine country thinking I can't protect them, can we? Come back and see me if the examination of the car turns up anything solid or if we get a hit on Armdi. Okay, Bradley, I believe we've kept the beautiful women waiting long enough, don't you?"

"Yes, sir," answered the agent, returning the President's smile.

President Gregory stopped at the door and turned back to the room. "Thanks again, Harold. Get me some hard intel. A definitive sighting of Armdi. Find me that state trooper. Stay on it and get back to me. I'll feel better just knowing you're on top of this."

Samson stood there for a full minute, staring at the now closed door. His hand tugged on the right end of his brown and gold bow tie, pulling the knot free and then yanked the tie off his neck.

Chapter 19

Rashid raised his hand to rap on the steel door with "260" in black raised numbers on the center panel. Standing in the hallway, his eyes jerked left, then right. He studied the doors that lined both sides of the narrow corridor of the Red Roof Inn. He was hot and trickles of sweat stained his underarms and under the straps of the backpack. As his knuckles rapped the cold, metal surface, his memory flashed back to another door, a worn, weather-beaten wooden one he had knocked on, more than three months ago.

Had it been just three months? he asked himself, unbelieving. Then I was just a scared kid, he thought. Now here I am, in the belly of Satan, a soldier in the great Jihad, with a mission direct from Allah's anointed Leader. His lips moving, he quietly voiced the mantra memorized in the camp, nodding his head with the effort. He mumbled the three words in the hallway, repeating them again and again.

This practice usually helped him, but somehow the mental exercise did little to assure him this time. The old fears began to claw their way back, the image of his family suddenly hovering before him. On the pale green surface of the door, the emaciated face of his mother and young sister suddenly materialized, both weeping.

A voice called from beyond the closed door, interrupting his thoughts. "Yes?"

The voice jolted Rashid and it took him a bit to respond. "God, uh...is good to all who believe." There was a pause, long enough for Rashid to doubt himself again. In the excruciating seconds his fear flooded back. Had he gotten it wrong? Was this the right room? The right hotel? Seconds ticked by and his heart raced as an enlarged olive eye appeared in the peephole. Then the dead bolt clicked and the lock was thrown open.

"Come in, quickly," the same voice said quietly. Rashid stepped through the opening and the door was closed behind him. He heard the lock being set. Turning to face his contact, he studied his cell leader. The man was tall, towering a good six inches over Rashid and outweighing him by at least a hundred pounds. Broad shoulders. Strong arms. A pair of fierce olive-green eyes stared out from under heavy brows, appraising his visitor. The face bore no emotion and Rashid's anxiety spiked again. Then, the man slowly extended his right hand. "I am called Yassim."

The teenager grasped the extended hand and noticed that the man's arm was striped with burn scars. When they shook hands, he winced inwardly at the cell leader's strong grip but gave away nothing. "I am Rashid," he said, "the humble servant of Allah and the Sheik."

"Come and we will talk," said Yassim. He led the way over to the small oval table in the cramped hotel room and sat at one of the hard back chairs. Rashid followed him and, sliding the backpack off, took the seat opposite the cell leader. "Give your report," the man commanded.

"Where would you like me to start?"

"Tell me about the school."

Opening his worn blue vinyl and brown suede knapsack, Rashid pulled out some wrinkled sheets of paper. He laid them on the flat Formica surface and, using both hands, worked to smooth them out. The graph paper contained several rough sketches, some scribbled dimensions and directions. His index finger pointing to different places on the drawings, the youth began to explain. "The building is a basic two-story structure in the shape of a T." He indicated the simple diagram he had made as he sat in the classes, "idly doodling" as one teacher had called it. "At the end of each point on the T is one of the common areas." He slid his fingers to the top right point of the diagram. "This is the large gymnasium and this," his finger slid to the other top point of the T, "is what is called an auditorium, basically a large theater."

"I know what an auditorium is," Yassim chided. "How many individuals can this auditorium hold?"

"I am not sure, about 500, I thin...."

"Can the area hold all the students?" the older man asked without waiting.

"Yes. Last week all the students were sent there to hear a speaker."

"Go on."

The teenager's hand returned to the drawing. "This section of the building holds the classrooms and offices for the principal and counselors."

"What about this space marked with a C?" Yassim's finger pointed to the bottom of the diagram.

When the man gestured, Rashid noticed for the first time that the forefinger of Yassim's left hand was an ugly stump, cut off at the knuckle. He inhaled sharply and a wild memory flooded back.

In the camp he had witnessed a similar amputation, made with the curved jambiya, of the right hand of a trainee who had challenged an order of the guards. It had been Yemel, with the flaming red hair and the temper to match, who had argued with one of the guards about something small. After the short argument, Yemel and the rest of the other recruits were on the way back to their tent when two guards grabbed the redheaded teen. In front of the other boys, two guards slammed the loudly protesting Yemel spread-eagle against a training wall. A third guard sliced off the tip of the boy's left forefinger, spurting blood on the wall. Unbelieving, Yemel had stared at the stump and begun screaming. The third guard slapped him once. He said, "There is no room for disagreement here. The devotion to Allah's cause must be total." It had all taken less than fifteen seconds and Rashid and the other trainees stared in disbelief as the three guards sauntered away. Then the youths grabbed their friend and, without speaking, led him to his cot in the tent. Rashid remembered trying to stem the bleeding of his hand and could still picture the gushing blood staining his own fingers red.

"Well?"

Not knowing how long he had been distracted, Rashid stuttered, "Uh-umm-that is..uh..." Then as quickly as he could, the teen recovered and responded, finally aware of the area of the diagram the man was indicating. "That end of the building is the cafeteria, where the students eat lunch."

"Where do the teachers eat?"

"They have a room next to the cafeteria," *the youth said, his finger on a space next to the rectangular block with the C.*

"When do the students go to the cafeteria?"

"Uh...I don't know," *the teen faltered and then went on,* "we get sent to lunch in two groups. The first around 11:15 and the second about twenty minutes later, I think."

"Are all the students in this eating area at the same time?" *Yassim asked.*

"Well, like I said, we come in at different times, but yes, for a few minutes, around 11:30 I think, Group A is just moving out as my group gets in line."

For a while, the cell leader said nothing, pondering the answer. "Okay...and this area with these x's?" *the older man continued, indicating the pie-shaped area attached to the end of the building design.*

"That's a balcony that is connected to the cafeteria," Rashid explained, " and I drew the x's to represent the benches and chairs on the balcony."

"Benches and chairs?"

"I have been told that students sit out there at lunch and after school in good weather."

For a moment, Yassim stopped again as if considering options, then he asked, "And beyond this balcony?"

"There is the water they call Lake Harold," Rashid replied. "And at the other end of the water is the HBE prison."

"Very good." The cell leader nodded. Glancing up from the diagrams for the first time, his eyes bored into the teenager's. "Tell me about these people."

"Who?" answered Rashid, his voice faltering for the first time.

"The teachers, the students, those in charge. What are they like? How will they respond?"

"Uh, I'm not sure how to describe them." Seeing the impatience in his leader's face, he continued. "The teenagers are quite spoiled. They all have places to live and plenty to eat, but all they do is complain."

"Complain?"

"Yes, complain about the food and their school work. They do not respect their parents or other elders."

"And the teachers and others in charge tolerate this disrespect?"

"Most of the time the students complain when the elders cannot hear. But, yes, sometimes the elders hear it and ignore them."

"Do you think they will be brave when the time comes?" Yassim scratched his stubble. "Do you think the young men will show courage?"

"No, I don't think so. Some of the students talk tough. I have been threatened several times. But I found that most of their threats are just empty bragging. Most of the time the teachers hide behind the principal and threaten to throw out any offending student. They are not allowed to use violence on their students."

"They do not beat the students for misbehavior or disrespect?"

"No. They cannot put a hand on a student. I have learned that it is against their law."

"The cowardice of this society is incredible. How have you been treated?" Yassim asked.

"About as I was told to expect. Most of the students either ignore me or treat me with contempt. They often whisper as I walk by. They think I cannot hear but many times I do." Rashid waited a beat and went on. *"I can tell that most teachers seem to harbor some kind of suspicion toward me."*

"You think the teachers may suspect something?"

"No, it's not that," Rashid started again. *"Even though they talk about accepting all students, deep down the teachers are all racist and prejudiced against me and as a result don't trust me ... all except one teacher."*

"One?"

"Yeah, I haven't figured her out. Her name is Danielle Sterber. She is my English teacher and she has treated me better. She seems different from the others."

Rashid watched as the inside edge of Yassim's eyebrows climbed the cell leader's forehead forming a brown arch. *"Different. How?"*

"Well, first of all, she knows the Koran."

"She what?" Yassim said sharply.

"She even knows much about our culture and speaks some Arabic. And, she seems to treat me with respect."

"It sounds like you favor this American woman?"

Catching the disapproval in the leader's glance, Rashid responded quickly. *"That is not true. I serve no one but Allah and our cause!"*

"Perhaps this woman bears watching," Yassim said.

"Yes. I will do that."

"That is not your concern."

"What is it you want me to do?" the teenager asked.

"Continue what you are doing and wait. You will be notified when it is time." The leader paused and then went on. *"And Rashid?"*

"Yes?"

"Allah will not keep you waiting long."

"I will be ready," the teenager responded immediately.

Rashid thought the cell leader was about to extend his hand when they heard a hard knock on the hotel door. In three seconds, the cell leader's right hand moved to his side and reappeared with a Makarov pointed directly at the teen's chest. Rashid gaped at the cell leader and then at the gun in his hand. In *that split-second, he studied the polished wood handle and steel barrel aimed at his rapidly beating heart. His breathing stopped.*

Chapter 20

"Into the bathroom!" hissed Yassim.

"What?" Rashid suddenly pictured his body lying in a pool of his blood on the bathroom tile.

The hand with the gun jerked toward the closed door. "Now. Hurry!" The heavy knock echoed through the metal door again. Yassim swiveled his head toward the door and he noticed the backpack lying on the floor. Grabbing it, he threw it to Rashid. "Take this!"

When Rashid caught the hard toss, he staggered backward, realizing he was physically out of his league. Before he could get another word out, Yassim shoved him roughly through the now open bathroom door.

"And say nothing," spat out the cell leader, just before the door closed.

Rashid stood frozen. He released his breath, trying to get his heart to slow its racing. He told himself he was safe, at least for now. The adrenaline rushed out of him like a liquid through an open drain. He exhaled a third time and collapsed on the tiled floor. His fear dissipating slightly, his mind edged back to normal and he became aware of voices he could make out from the other side of the door. Ear to the door, he listened intently.

Two voices, both male. The first was Yassim and the second Rashid thought he knew.

"I told you three o'clock," Yassim said, his voice tense with anger.

"Sorry, Sayeeb. I think it good to be early," the second voice responded.

"Sit down."

Rashid listened and heard the rustling of papers and then more conversation.

"Hey, thees look like the layout of Thurber. I thought you said I was inside man."

"That is not your concern."

"Where did you get these?"

"Also, not your concern. You will learn that Allah provides all to those who believe," Yassim responded. "You are being well paid. Do you have the information we need?"

"Right here," the second voice responded with a short laugh.

It was the quick laugh that gave it away to Rashid. "Jose!" he said aloud in the small space and his glance darted to the door. When he heard the voices continue, he relaxed a bit.

"...not like that screebled paper. I bring you real building plans," Jose announced.

"Where will we enter the building?"

"You come in through the delivery entrance, right here. I will be there to make certain that you are not seen. No one else goes there except me. I am your ace in the hole." Rashid could hear the broken tooth smile in Jose's words.

"That will work for us."

"When will you be in need of my services?" Jose asked.

"We will let you know when the time is decided. It will be soon. You must be ready."

"I will be ready. You said you had sometheeg for me."

"Here." Rashid could hear nothing for a bit. And then, "Do not count it here! Now you must leave and I will contact you in the normal manner."

Straining, Rashid heard footfalls and the hotel room door open and close. Realizing that Yassim would be coming soon, he scooted quickly away from the door and started to rise from the floor. Before he was up all the way, the door flung open and he caught his breath. Yassim was standing directly in front, but the pistol was nowhere in sight.

"Come out." Yassim's voice was neither harsh nor angry. "I assume you heard?"

Rashid somehow knew that to try to deceive this man would likely cost him his life. He said, "Yes."

"It would be better if you did not." The cell leader paused, studying the youth.

For a few torturous seconds, neither man spoke and Rashid could feel his heart rate accelerate again. He struggled to keep the terror from his eyes.

"It would have been better if you had not," repeated Yassim, "but it could not be helped. Perhaps it is Allah's will. We will not speak of it and you must forget it."

Rashid's mouth was so dry he could force no words out, so he simply nodded again, this time more slowly to indicate his submission.

"It is time for you to return. Do you have anything else to report?"

"Perhaps, one more item, leader," said Rashid, his confidence slowly returning. "This teacher I told you about, Ms. Sterber?"

"What about her?"

"She has asked permission for her students to interview Asad."

"You will go and interview Asad?" Yassim asked.

"No, I am not one of these students."

"I thought you said she was one of your teachers."

"I am but I am not in the Journalism class. Those students are the ones who have asked to go to the prison to talk with Asad. I have heard the students say it is not likely that they will receive permission this close to the execution."

The cell leader scratched his chin with his thumb. "I think this can work for us. I will arrange it so the students are permitted to come and I want you to be among the visitors."

"How can you do that?" Rashid was unable to hide his incredulity.

"You have only been in the land of the infidels a short time and you have forgotten your lessons already. Allah makes all things possible for those who are faithful."

Finally the second part of Yassim's statement sunk in with Rashid. "How am I supposed to become one of the student visitors? I do not even take that class."

A small smile crossed Yassim's lips. "Allah cannot do everything. We must all do our small part, and this is yours."

"Leader, I will do whatever I can, but I am not sure that this is possible," Rashid said, looking tentatively at Yassim.

The older man did not speak but his eyes never left the young soldier. Then he went on, "I was told to deliver a message to you. The Sheik says to tell you your family is doing well and being cared for. Your brother has joined the camp at Baku Valley. The Sheik said that you should rest easy at night knowing that your family are in his hands, and he will keep all harm from them if you are faithful."

The terror returned to the teen's eyes and he managed, "What do you wish me to do?"

Yassim nodded. He stepped across the room and grabbed a small pad from the nightstand. He said, "Give Asad this message," and scribbled six words on a small piece of paper. "Memorize this and then burn it."

The teenager accepted the piece of paper and nodded, not even bothering to look at the words.

"Now you must leave," Yassim said and walked across the room.

"May Allah bless you," the teen said as he stepped into the corridor.

"And keep those you love safe," Yassim responded and closed the door.

Chapter 21

Days later I sat at the Formica lunchroom table, my gaze alternating between the scrawny piece of pizza in front of me and the slashing sleet on the windows. As if foretelling the upcoming events, the weather had turned suddenly bitter, beautiful autumn days mutating into the cold misery that northern Ohio often became in late October. The wind whipped the water off the lake and drove it onto the Commons. The massive oaken deck that was such a student haven in friendlier weather had been glazed into an 80,000 square foot sheet of ice. Under the onslaught of the hostile weather, the tranquil lake had metamorphosed into an angry, frothing monster.

On the soundless TV mounted in the corner, the weatherman seemed to take delight in endlessly warning of approaching doom as a cold front muscled its way down from Canada. As if to demonstrate his point, the accompanying live footage featured some shivering demonstrators outside the HBE prison, slashed by wind and freezing rain even as they tried feebly to use their water-logged placards as makeshift umbrellas. Several teachers in the room took notice of the TV report, probably hoping for a snow day. I pulled my glance from the window and TV and focused my concentration back on my plate. "They call this pizza?" I asked Christie, who sat across from me, fork in hand poised over a wilted salad of mixed greens.

"Well, this 'fresh special' looks like it was probably rejected by Mickie D's three days ago," she said. The tines of her fork speared the concoction of darkened greens on the plate in front of her. We huddled in the last two chairs at the small table in the teachers' lunchroom. We were at the end of the L-shaped room, as far away as possible from the door and the throng of five hundred boisterous teenagers. Although we were hardly alone--several other teachers sat at the long table or in the few worn chairs in the room--we had tried to place a little distance between the teens and us. Even in this relative peace, we had to endure the pontifications of Rob Holden, his bald head glistening in the fluorescent lights as he espoused the latest right-wing tripe he had lapped up on Fox the night before. We could hear the low rumble of the students next door in the cafeteria.

"At least your lunch looks like it might have had some nutritional value, at one time. I wouldn't swear to it, but this," I held up the limp rectangle for demonstration, "I believe may once have been a piece of tag board that they smeared with ketchup and some imitation cheese." I took a bite and continued talking with my mouth full. "I know kids' tastes aren't very discriminating, but I don't get what they see in these things." I chewed and tried to swallow.

"Beats me," Christie returned, "it just goes to show you that I was right."

"About what?" I washed downed the red cardboard with a swig from my water bottle.

"I told you we should've snuck out and grabbed something at Nicks," she said with a grin.

"Oh yeah," I lowered my voice, "not only would we get killed if we were caught, we probably couldn't even get anything to eat in our measly 37 minutes."

"Maybe not," she said, her eyes glancing around then meeting mine conspiratorially, "but I bet we could've gotten a drink." Her smile widened and I laughed. "Anyway, this," she pointed to the drooping salad, "is just one more concession to the big event. Gotta fit into that white dress."

I nodded and we were quiet for a bit while our eyes wandered back to the precipitation freezing against the window and we chewed without taste. I was able to manage only about three more bites and threw down the tattered remains of my school lunch. "I'm going to head back to my room to see if I have something more edible stashed in my bag, like maybe a piece of used sandpaper." I picked up my tray.

"Might as well join you." Christie dropped her fork on her plate.

We pitched the garbage, stowed the trays and headed back out into the melee of the lunchroom. In the lead, I opened the door and was met, face-to-face, with a broad, mustached smile perched beneath a pair of gorgeous green eyes. Staring, I stopped short and Christie ran smack into me. I ignored her muffled cry of "Hey!"

When he saw me, Jesus Ramirez's eyes brightened in recognition and he tried to say something, but his words were drowned out by the hubbub of the adjoining student cafeteria. Shoving Christie behind me, I stepped back into the teachers' lunchroom, inviting him to follow.

"So we meet again, Miss Sterber," the visitor said in that crisp, learned English of a foreigner, with only the slightest Latin accent.

"Dee Dee. I'm surprised you remembered."

"After such a pleasant collision, I could hardly forget," Jesus said and smiled. I smiled in return.

"It didn't take you long to get a sub job," I said.

"Today is my first day, but I think I will be working much. At the personnel office, they said they are always in need of good subs."

Christie pushed past me and thrust her hand at Jesus. "Excuse the bad manners of my friend," she said with a brisk nod at me. "My name is Christie Ferguson and I teach science here."

"I am pleased to meet you, Miss Christie Ferguson," Jesus grasped her extended hand. "I am called Jesus Ramirez, a science teacher also, an itinerant science teacher, recently from Ecaudor." Then, looking from me to Christie, he added, "But I am surprised that such a beautiful woman as Miss Sterber would have an equally attractive friend."

I know, I should have suspected something, but what can I say? I didn't. Christie and I exchanged a quick glance, mine telling her, "See, I told you!"

"So who are you today?" I asked, a bit playfully.

"Pardon?" Jesus responded, perplexed.

"What teacher are you subbing for?" I said.

"Oh, I understand. Who am I today? Christie Ferguson, your friend has sense of humor."

"Thank you," I said, smiling, before Christie could say anything. "Well, who are you?"

"Ah, today, I am," he glanced at a paper in a folder he carried, "Janet Striker, Family and Consumer Science. I'm not sure I know what it is I am teaching."

"We used to call it Home Economics," I said.

"Miss Sterber, I have a favor to ask, if I could," said Jesus. "This is beautiful school. We have nothing like this in my country. I wondered if you could give me a tour of the building, that is, if you have time after we are done with our classes."

Christie started to answer and I elbowed her hard and she stopped mid-sentence. "Jesus, I could...."

"Jesus, I'd be glad to show you around," I got in before Christie caught her breath.

I was enjoying this too much, so of course the bell had to ring, cutting off any further conversation. When the obnoxious tone concluded, Christie spoke first, "We'd like to chat more, but if we don't get going, we're going to be late for our next class."

"Glad you were able to start here at Thurber. I'll meet you at 3:00 outside the office," I said as Christie dragged me by the arm through the door into the swirling throng of high school students moving to their next period's classes.

"I didn't want to leave yet," I hollered, barely audible above the student din as we were swept away from the teachers' lunchroom.

"I could tell," she said back, "but I knew that unless we got out, you were about to make a fool of yourself. I thought I was going to have to wipe the drool off your lips."

Wrenching my arm away, I hustled ahead and slid across into a side hallway where students weren't allowed during lunch and the noise subsided some. When Christie pulled up beside me, I was ready. "Jealous?"

"Of course not. I've got Kurt almost to the altar," she replied as we kept on walking to our classrooms. "Okay, maybe a little bit."

I stopped. "Didn't I tell you he was drop-dead gorgeous?"

Christie stopped alongside of me. "Okay, I admit, you were right." She stole a glance around the emptying hallway. "I wouldn't have minded colliding with that body one bit. And you were right about one more thing."

"What's that?"

"Nice butt," she said.

"How could you tell?"

"I looked before the door closed."

I laughed. "Christie, I have just two words for you."

"What?" she said, wary.

"Kurt Sanders."

"Oh, yeah! But I still want to know how do you do it?"

"Do what?" I asked.

"You have all the luck. First Jerod drops into your lap and then you literally run into that hunk. How long do I have to wait before you can tell me juicy stories of their naked bodies?"

"Christie, you are incorrigible."

"Yeah, don't you just love that about me?"

We traveled to the end of the side hallway, our feet making slapping sounds on the new vinyl floor like hands clapping, and turned into the central corridor. Although the groups of kids talked animatedly, the noise was nothing like the Babel that had filled the cafeteria and we were still able to hear each other. "I need to split," she said and pointed toward the floor and then down the hall, our secret sign for restroom break.

I was laughing as I turned to enter my classroom and stepped into a tightly bunched clique of ninth grade girls. As I made it through the throng with my eyes taking note of one girl's ten piercings--I counted them quickly-- I retrieved my key from my Disney bag. Without looking I raised it toward my locked door and found myself pushing the point into Rashid's stomach.

"Sorry, Rashid, I didn't see you there," I said, wondering how he had suddenly materialized in my path.

"I wanted to know if I could speak with you, Ms. Sterber," he said, his hard brown pupils staring straight at me, remindng me of the wary eyes of the owl I passed during the last night's jog.

"I've got a couple of things I need to do before class, but I can give you a few minutes," I said.

He lowered his gaze and spoke with his eyes focused on the gray and red pattern on the vinyl. "I have heard that you are planning to accompany some students to interview Asad Akadi at HBE Prison. Is that the truth?" His eyes rose to meet mine.

I said, "It's possible that one or two Journalism students and I may be granted an interview with some death row inmates for an article in The Anvil. We have not received word from HBE, and I'm not sure I will agree even if they do."

"Why?" he blurted out.

His hasty response surprised me. "Because I haven't decided if it may be too dangerous for my students. I'm not sure about Pakistan, but teenagers in this country think they're immortal and I have no death wish."

Rashid asked, "You fear for your life?"

"No, just being cautious." When he didn't respond, I went on. "Rashid, why are you asking? Do you distrust Americans interviewing another Arab? Are you afraid the famous American bigotry you talk about will raise its ugly head?"

Rashid looked taken aback for a bit and then he responded, his words tumbling out. "Oh, oh, no, Ms. Sterber. I would not worry about that with you. I did not say you show bigotry. In fact, you seem very fair in class."

"Okay, Rashid, I give up. What is it? Why did you ask me about the interview then?"

"I would like to help." His reply was, uncharacteristically for him, solicitous, even humble. "I thought I could help as a translator," he said and immediately went on. "I know something about Asad Akadi. He is from Peshawa, the same region of Pakistan where I grew up." When I didn't respond immediately, he went on, "And he speaks Western Farsi, the same dialect as me."

At this point my face must have registered my confusion. "I understand that Akadi speaks English quite well and there wasn't going to be any need for a translator."

"Yes, Ms. Sterber, he can speak English if he chooses to," Rashid responded. "I just thought that if he chooses to be uncooperative and only mutters in Western Farsi, I would be able to translate what he says."

I paused. This was the first initiative I had seen from Rashid and didn't want to blow him off. "I am very grateful for your offer, but I'd need to think about it. You are not in the Journalism class and a number of students asked to go to the prison for the interview and I already have to tell most of them no."

"I do not want to make trouble for you as our teacher. That is why I did not want to speak of this in front of other students," he said. "I just believe I could help with this."

"Rashid, like I said, this interview could be dangerous," I placed my hand on his arm. "Let me think about your offer and I'll let you know."

At this he brightened and smiled. "Thank you, Ms. Sterber. And I am sorry for taking up your time."

"That's all right, Rashid, but I have to get going."

"Thank you, Ms. Sterber," he repeated.

Chapter 22

"Our questions rock, guys!" declared Jake, after the Journalism class had finally decided on the questions for the interviews at the prison.

To my surprise and disbelief, HBE officials had agreed to our request for two students from The Anvil to conduct prisoner interviews, and Principal Thompson had even granted his reluctant approval for the trip. Three death row inmates, including Asad Akadi, had agreed to be interviewed and the prison warden concurred. The class had worked for over a week to come up with the questions for the inmates awaiting execution. After a great deal of argument and lobbying, the class had narrowed them down to the "Final Four," as Keith dubbed them. In the end, I had let them decide. Now, it seemed they were pleased with their work.

"And thanks, Mr. Thomas, for helping get us into the prison." As the youngest student in the class, Jake knew he'd never be selected but was grateful for his chance to contribute to the whole process. "Man, I can't wait to see how they answer the question about advice to their sister," he said excitedly.

"If your sister came to you and confided that she was planning on committing a crime similar to the one you're going to be executed for, what would you tell her?" Keith read the handwriting off the white board as he stood and flexed his muscles. "I bet we'll get some interesting stuff, all right."

"I'll bet Asad'll say he will urge her on," commented Goat, his brown eyes glancing up from the science test notes he was studying. "He'll probably tell her it's her duty to carry on the Jihad, to annihilate the Great Satan of America," he added, scratching the short black whiskers lining his chin.

"I'm not so sure," added Tess. "Traditional Muslims have a very different view of women, believe they should be guarded, cared for, and placed on a pedestal. If he's truthful, I can't see him wanting to send her to exposure and certain death."

"The only thing Akadi cares about is destroying America," Keith countered, shaking his blonde hair out of his eyes again and casting a glance at Tess. "His mission is not about being Muslim, it's about hating America."

"I suppose we'll have to wait and see," I broke in and slid off the top of my desk where I had perched and moved into the center aisle.

"Ms. S, isn't it about time you told us who you selected to conduct the prison interview?" asked Tyrone in his deep voice. "Of course, I should mention that since two of the three prisoners have dark skin, you would want to have a brother with you," he continued, his grin showing a set of bright white teeth.

"Thank you for that helpful hint, Mr. Tyrone Bates," I peered across the room at the only black face in the room. "The truth is, I had a very difficult time trying to decide who should participate in this interview. You know, I've had some concerns about any of you going into the lion's den over at HBE. I was afraid it was going to be dangerous, but Mr. Thomas assures me it will be okay." I cast a glance at Jerod, slouching in a student desk off to the left.

"Way to go, Mr. Thomas!" cheered Jake, shaking his uncombed mop of red hair.

Jerod raised both hands over his head, clenched in a victory clasp. "Glad to be of some help."

I wrestled their attention away from Jerod. "The truth is that many of you have made good contributions to what we are going to finally use for the interview. So in a way, you will all be part of the interviewing team."

"Blah-blah-blah," said Goat. "I know we're all wonderful and you love us all, Ms. S and don't want to leave any of your children behind. Just dish all the nicey crap and cut to the chase."

I should say, Goat was not a bad kid, but like too many adolescents today, he had a smart tongue and wasn't afraid to use it. I guess if I had to admit it, my dad might've said that at sixteen I was a smart mouth too at times. The difference is I would never 've used "that tone," as my father called it, with a teacher. Today, a number of students think nothing of smarting off to a teacher, or more accurately, many of today's teens have no one like my dad to rein them in when they get out of line. I knew that was the case with Goat.

I had met his mom, who was only 36, but bore the creased face and gray-streaked hair of a 50-year-old. From our one parent-teacher conference it was obvious she was overmatched with her son. Goat was one of Jerod's mentees and was the ostensible reason for the prison guard's presence often in my Journalism class. Even I had to admit, Jerod had a decent chance to get through to Goat--it was a macho, male thing.

"Goat?" I arched my brows and returned his stare. I caught a hard glance from Jerod in the corner of the room.

"As Goat so aptly put it, though he should have been more careful with his language, you all are great and if I had a choice, I'd take all of you." I paused, letting my gaze roam around the room until my eyes found every student and then settled back on Goat. "But before I tell you my decision, I have a question for Goat."

Goat looked up, more wary and his fingers twirled the steel post embedded in his right earlobe.

"Do you trust me to make the right decision, Goat?" When he didn't answer, I added, "What about it, Mr. Edward Manor?" using his given name.

His brown eyes studied me carefully, trying to appraise his options. Finally he said, "Yeah, I guess so."

I wasn't going to let him off so easy. "You guess what, Goat?"

His eyes read my challenge and rose to it. "Yeah, I trust ya to make the right decision, Miss S."

"What about the rest of you?" My eyes met every glance in the classroom.

"Sure, Miss S!" chimed in Jake, his freckled face beaming.

"Yes, Miss S," said an earnest Tess, the round frames of her glasses reflecting in duplicate the image on the computer screen.

"Yeah, I guess so," added Keith, his large body still slouched against the white board in the front of the room, his posture radiating the indolence he wore like a badge of honor.

"Sure." "Of course." "Okay, yeah. Just tell us already!" came the replies from the rest of the students. The eyes of all fourteen students were trained on me. Even Jerod leaned forward in his chair.

"Okay, then here goes," I began. "As you heard, HBE will let us bring a two-student interviewing team."

"We already know that, Ms. S," Goat's voice rose with exaggerated impatience.

I shot him another quick "teacher" look and continued. "My first choice was obvious. I've selected Tess, our student editor."

"Duh, that was a 'no-brainer,' Ms. S," declared Tyrone. "We all knew that. What about the second student?"

"Well, that was a bit harder," I admitted. "I know, some of you are going to be surprised by my choice, but I have given it a lot of thought." I studied all the expectant faces and continued.

"I know that we are all looking for some major results from our interview with Akadi, right? Something even the other news people haven't gotten from him?" All fourteen heads nodded in unison. "Knowing that Asad is a clever, devious terrorist, I think we'll need all the help we can get, including help with his language." I stopped again, studying them. They all waited, no one uttering a word. I went on, "After giving it much thought, I have decided to have Rashid Hermani be the second member of the student team."

I held my breath and waited. I didn't have to wait long.

"What! That raghead!" exploded Keith, finally pulling himself off the white board and slamming his large frame into his seat.

"When I said a dark face, I didn't mean his, Ms. S!" said Tyrone.

Tess looked up from her computer and stared at me, her brilliant hazel eyes enlarged inside the horn-rimmed frames. "I think what my prejudiced classmates mean," casting a quick glance, "is that we don't understand why you would select a new student, even if he is from the Mideast, when you have good students right here who have put in the time and earned the right to go."

"You are quite right, Tess. I do have a number of students who have worked hard in this class and, all things being equal, deserve a chance to participate in the interview."

Needing some think time to be sure my answer was phrased correctly, I retreated to the front of the room and sat on the edge of my desk again, turning to face them again. "Before I give my explanation, I have a question for all of you."

The teens were perfectly silent, waiting to hear what I had to say. I didn't flinch.

"Kind of a quiz," I said, working to keep my voice light.

"Jeez, Ms. S! Now? Don't you ever quit?" blurted out Goat.

"Not if I can help it. Now, what did we learn about how an editor decides which reporters he--or she--sends on an assignment?"

At first, no one answered, even though I knew most knew the answer.

Then Jake raised his hand, of course.

My student editor did not respond, but I called on her anyway. "Tess?"

"The reporters best qualified to get the story," she said, her voice heavy with reluctance. Then she asked, "Okay, what makes Rashid more qualified than any other student in here."

"He's not. You're the most qualified," I said simply.

"Besides me, then?" Her voice was almost peevish now, unusual for Tess.

"Because he has something no one else has, including me."

"You mean because he's an A-rab?" Keith bellowed.

"Cool it, Keith," Tess shot back.

"Of course, the fact that he's from the Mideast is a help, but the big difference is that he's fluent in the same dialect of Farsi as Akadi."

"But I watched him on TV. He spoke English fine," declared a now-confused Jake.

"That's true, Jake," I said, "he understands English quite well. He probably couldn't have carried out his terrorist acts if he didn't. But what if he decides to be an uncooperative interviewee? Don't you think it might be helpful to have someone along who can draw him out, in his own language?"

"Yeah, I guess that makes some sense," Tyrone admitted.

"And maybe it'll help to have the perspective of another Arab to help interpret the answers. You know, the connotations behind the words," said Tess.

"An Arab who is not intent on blowing up the U. S. of A." I added. "Plus, I've asked Rashid to do an opinion piece on how the terrorists pervert the teachings of Islam for their own ends."

"Hey, that could add something to the edition," volunteered Jake. I thought, thank God for Jake.

His emotions still boiling, Keith sat hunched over his desk and Tyrone remained equally unconvinced, arms stiffly crossed across his chest. But I could tell the others were coming around. I was considering other possible strategies when the bell rescued me from having to further defend myself.

"Tomorrow, we'll talk about the remaining assignments for the edition, so be thinking about what you can do," I called above the din of the movement of student chairs, mostly to the backs of teens headed for the door.

When the kids were gone, Jerod climbed out of the student chair in the corner and, of course, immediately began to drawl. "It looks like your choices for the interviewin' team didn't go over all that well." He leaned against the desk where I sat, flashing that damn grin of his.

"Well, I didn't expect it'd be easy," I said, hoping to dismiss him.

"A little surprised you decided to bring along Rashid."

"Yeah?"

"Jus' a little curious, that's all," Jerod said.

"Why?"

"It's just who he is, where he's from."

"That's the point, Mr. Thomas," I pointed my finger at him. "He's from the same region, speaks the same dialect as Asad."

"Mebbe," he said, shaking his head.

"Are you prejudiced like some of my red-necked students?" I asked.

"Let's just say I'm the naturally suspicious type," Jerod said, his grin returning.

"Well it's a little late for all this concern now. And I'd like to remind you, Officer Thomas, that you're the one who got me into this situation."

"Excuse me?" Jerod said, surprised.

"Well, until you piped up, the idea of interviewing death row inmates was just a crazy teenage fantasy."

"So, what d'ya want me to do now? Have HBE cancel the permission for your interview?"

"You could do that?" I said, incredulous. "It doesn't matter now. It's usually too late to close Pandora's box. The demons have already escaped."

"Pandora's what? Is that some kind of sexual reference?"

"Oh, stop!" I pulled myself from the desk, and began the never-ending process of organizing the stacks of student papers to drag them home for the night.

"When are you coming to HBE for the interviews?" he asked, his tone serious again.

"In two days, Thursday afternoon." My eyes met his. "Why?"

"Thursday afternoon. Not my shift." He paused. "Jus' be careful, okay?" He seemed suddenly anxious.

"Great!" I announced, "**Now** you're concerned. When the students cooked up this idea, I said it was <u>way</u> too dangerous. But you tell my students that there is no place around here more secure than HBE. Now that we're on the brink, getting ready to jump into that dark hole, you get cold feet. Why?"

"I'm concerned for you, that's all," he said. "Don't want anything to happen to ya."

He wouldn't meet my gaze, not typical for him.

"Is there some danger about this trip that I should know about? Is there something specific? After all, I'm taking two kids over there."

"Naw." Pause. "I guess not. Some of the guards were just talkin'."

"About?"

"Well, it's just that there's a lotta talk about Asad trying to use the interview to pass messages to the outside."

"So what. The man's a few days away from being executed. What message is he going to try to get out, 'Send Allah to rescue me!'"

At first he didn't answer and only shook his head. "Jus' don't forget who this guy is," Jerod said.

Chapter 23

"Mr. Samson, you said you couldn't wait till our regular briefing, so you have my undivided attention. Get on with it. I still have three campaign stops to make," began President Gregory.

Harold Samson glanced nervously around the Oval Office. The gang's all here, he sighed inwardly. When he called the President's secretary a half hour ago, arguing that he urgently needed to see him ASAP, he hoped he'd get a chance to speak to President Gregory alone as he had during his evening meeting.

Jerry Garcia peered suspiciously across the room and Tom Dickson looked just as apprehensive. Only a few feet to the side of the seat Harold had been given, Dean Settler sat erect and soldier-like in the straight-backed Queen Anne chair that he preferred, as if keeping guard over Samson. Overshadowing all four men, President Gregory stood and stared, his tall figure slouched back against the front of the famous cherry desk.

Adjusting his bifocals, Samson began. "Mr. President, thank you for taking time from your busy schedule to speak with me."

"Yes, Harold," the President said, " the voters in Virginia are waiting." The ballpoint pen in his hand clicked.

The Homeland Security Director continued, his confidence suddenly ebbing. "I received this report in my office an hour ago." Rising from the couch, he handed the President the two sheets of paper filled with single-spaced typing. "After I read the report, I knew you would want to be apprised."

Chief of Staff Settler leaned over to study the document in Samson's hand and Samson added, "Sorry, I didn't know you would be here or I would've brought additional copies."

"Would you like me to make copies, Mr. President?" Settler asked.

"Not just yet. " Holding the papers at arm's length, Gregory squinted his famous blue eyes, trying to read the small print and, giving up, edged around to the front of the desk to retrieve his reading glasses. Putting them on, he scanned the pages quickly. "Am I supposed to understand this? What am I reading, Harold?"

"An autopsy, sir..."

"Anyone I know, Harold?"

"Yes, sir, Mr. President. The deceased, a Jeffrey Birch, is the missing Pennsylvania State Trooper that we discussed the other night." Samson paused, studying the President and seeing confusion there, went on quickly. "He was the State Trooper who went missing last week after pulling over a GMC Tahoe, the vehicle we believe may have been connected to the suspected terrorist, Mohammed Armdi."

When the President nodded, Samson continued, "Yesterday, they pulled his cruiser out of a small lake..." he looked down at his notes and continued, " a Findlay Lake, less than six miles from the last location Trooper Birch had radioed in. The body of the officer was still in the car."

"Do they think he was driving when the car went in? Was there any sign of an accident?"

"No, sir. From indications at the scene it looks as if the car was driven into the lake, but not by Trooper Birch. His body was found lying on the floor in the back seat. His throat had been slit and he was dead before he was placed back into the car, according to the medical examiner."

"I am deeply saddened by the officer's death, but I still don't see the urgency."

With more courtesy than he felt, Samson said, "Mr. President, if you would please read the second-last paragraph on the next page. I've highlighted the passage on your copy."

Gregory flipped the paper over, went silent and studied the paragraph. The office was so quiet Samson could hear the breathing of the other men near him. Twenty seconds ticked by, punctuated by two pen clicks, and the President asked, "What's a jambiya?"

"A jambiya?" responded CIA Director Garcia, surprised. "Sir, that is a long curved knife favored by Yemeni fighters." He held his hands apart, demonstrating the length for everyone. "Why?"

"Because, according to this autopsy report," the President indicated the paper in his hand, "the Trooper's neck was slit with a jambiya or something like it." Turning his attention back to Samson, he asked, "How competent is this guy, Harold?"

"More than competent, Mr. President. I've been concerned about this from the start and made a call to Tom Widman, two days ago. He's the Chief Medical Examiner for Pennsylvania and a friend of mine." Samson took a quick look around at his cabinet colleagues and noted their earlier irritation was gone. "As soon as they pulled the car from the lake he flew up and performed the autopsy. He took several hours and was very thorough. Those are just his preliminary conclusions you have. I expect to have the full report in my hands tomorrow morning."

Gregory shook his head, pondering the report.

"Mr. President, may I see the report?" Garcia asked. Without responding, Gregory handed him the two sheets. Tom Dickson leaned in next to Garcia. "Harold, let's see if I got this right. This Pennsylvania State Trooper …" the President said and looked to Samson.

"Jeffrey Birch," Samson supplied.

"You believe Officer Birch may have stopped a car in which one of the terrorists on our watch list--"

"Mohammed Armdi."

"Yes, this Mohammed Armdi was driving," Gregory continued, "and killed Trooper Birch on a back highway in Pennsylvania when he was stopped. Then you believe Armdi drove the cruiser with the officer's body into a nearby lake, hoping to hide it."

"Yes sir. And this attack took place two days ago at a location only a five-hour drive from Hammerville," added Samson.

The President nodded and asked, "This jambiya? If it turns out it was used on the officer, you believe it was an Arab terrorist who used it?"

"Sir, we do not know anything for sure," answered Samson, "but we are trying to put the pieces together. And Jerry is correct in his description," he continued, nodding at the CIA Director. Harold realized it was expedient--both practically and politically--to give credit to the others whenever possible. "The jambiya is a very conspicuous weapon. Outside of collectors, it's hard to imagine anyone else carrying around this extended knife." He held his hands eighteen inches apart. "It's just not a very efficient weapon."

The President nodded again and asked, "Anything else, Harold?"

"One more item I thought I should bring to your attention. We have received an unconfirmed report of a theft of a considerable quantity of C-4 explosives out of a storage warehouse in Cleveland, Ohio. We're working with the local authorities to confirm the extent and nature of the theft."

"And I'm sure that in the past twenty-four hours there were probably many more such thefts," the President said. "Obviously you believe this theft may also be connected?"

"Yes, sir. You realize that Cleveland is less than 100 miles from both the site of Trooper Birch's death and from the HBE prison. Also, it is what this particular explosive is used for, that I believe may tie in."

"And that would be?" asked the President.

"Well sir, it seems the army developed this particular C-4 with some peculiar qualities and for very specific uses. I'm told it has been used in several successful attempts to free hostages overseas. Most recently in Iraq and Afghanistan."

The President leaned forward, his blue eyes bright, as Samson continued. "It looks almost like the clothesline that your mom used to use. It's called tensile rope explosive compound or TREC. But I've also been told by some Army Ranger friends of mine who have used this particular composition that they've given it a new name. They call it 'the prison break.'"

Chapter 24

I couldn't believe the difference in our surroundings. The interview room we had been sitting in for almost three hours was dark, smelly, and bleak. The immaculate steel and glass appearance of the lobby we had passed through, the same one used for the press conference with Harold Samson, was but a dim memory. In fact, I would have been hard pressed to say we were even in the same building.

After a brief handshake and commemorative photo of our group with the egg-shaped face of Warden Cromer in the shining lobby, we had left the photographers and officials behind and passed through three impressive electronic security gates. As the third steel lock clicked loudly behind us, the final massive door seemed to add an oppressiveness, silencing even the usually chatty Tess. As a layman--okay, I recognize the sexism but I like the term anyway--I thought the prison did seem virtually impregnable. Perhaps, all the cocky assurance by Director Samson and Warden Cromer about their secure correctional facility was not male braggadocio after all.

Once the security checks were cleared, the guards led our little band snaking through the maze of the prison hallways. As we walked, our footfalls clattering down stark concrete and steel hallways, our lead escort informed us that we would conduct our interviews in the room reserved for conferences between inmates and their lawyers. At first, I was surprised that the warden hadn't chosen to accompany us. Once we arrived at our grimy destination though, I realized that he was probably only too happy to watch the whole affair on closed circuit from the plush chair in his office and let the guards babysit the visitors.

The interview room looked like a poor imitation of an interrogation room from Law and Order. The walls had been painted an ugly green-gray and were stained with browns and dingy reds in what I thought was intended as deliberate distress. Some smears looked as if someone had doused coffee or other fluids onto the dry wall, letting them ooze down in staggered streaks. I knew the prison was less than four years old, but the ambiance of the room made it appear as if it suffered from decades of abuse and neglect. Buried, as we were, in the bowels of the building, with no windows and only the one narrow door, the close walls seemed to crowd upon our space. And the obvious camera in the corner above the door added the perfect touch of Big Brother, but I was glad for it anyway.

Waiting nervously, my party of three shifted for the nth time on the worn metal folding chairs with uneven legs, made deliberately uncomfortable, no doubt. I looked again at Tess and Rashid and then stole another glance at the blinking red light on the camera in the upper right corner of the room. Hunched over the scarred wooden table, Tess sat forward on her chair, reviewing the notes I knew she had committed to memory two days ago. Unconsciously, she rocked back and forth and I placed a hand on her shoulder to ease her fidgeting. Rashid sat next to her, impassive, not moving, his olive face, framed by dark brown hair, an impenetrable mask. His stare was severe and stoic, his eyes narrow slits inside hard brown circles, and I could read no expression in his face.

Although we spent most of our time at the prison waiting, once started, the first two interviews had gone smoothly. After the perfunctory introductions, Tess, the thorough professional, led the questioning, with Rashid and me as silent partners. For each "guest," she delivered the questions the class had agreed on, but followed up and pressed when the convict tried to evade or she felt we could use clarification. The manner she had adopted alternated between interested adolescent and skeptical reporter, depending on which she thought would work better at the time. Her big eyes, enlarged by the round brown frames, gave her a look of innocence that I watched her use to her advantage more than once.

As each interviewee spoke, Tess took copious notes, the pen in her small fingers etching black scratches furiously down the pages in her reporter's notepad. Perched on a precarious folding chair beside her, I jotted down an occasional quote, trying to capture a few memorable comments in the prisoners' own words. Sitting on the other side, Rashid sat with a blue binder open, but, while I noticed, I never saw him lift the pen and write. All the while, the light on the digital recorder blinked green.

Both of the first two prisoners had been convicted of brutal murders and, though not protesting their innocence, they still claimed to be victims of the system. As we listened, they told similar stories, though one was black and the other white, one from inner city Cleveland and the second from an Irish family farm in Pennsylvania. But once we got past differences in race and geography, Reggie Horn and Gerri Fitzpatrick could have told the same tale.

Both men argued they were products of abusive homes, Reggie the victim of an abusive stepfather ("I ain't never known my real father, and my step dad screwed my mom then beat the shit out of me") and Gerri "the easy punching bag for my old man." Neither finished school, both dropping out in high school because as Reggie put it, "it was boring and nobody gave a damn anyway." After years in the system, they had both finally gotten around to completing their GED, though according to Gerri, "I only did that crap cause I thought it might help me with the parole board."

Staring at his auburn hair and handsome, slightly freckled face, I was reminded of Christie's parting words. Just before I left to collect Tess and Rashid for our interview trip, she had caught me in the hall outside my room.

"Okay, I have one request for my best friend," she said staring at me, solemn-faced.

"Christie, I'm late already. What is it?"

"I need you to check out one thing for me at HBE."

"And that would be?" My impatience was showing.

"I just need to know," she said seriously, "if he's as hot as I've heard."

"Who? Asad?"

Christie choked trying to answer. "NO. Oh, God no, Dee Dee. I'm talking about Gerri."

"Gerri?"

"You know, Gerald Fitzpatrick, Jr., inmate interviewee number two," she answered grinning at me.

"Christie, have you totally lost it?" I shot back. "The man is scheduled to be executed in two months for beating a man to death with his fists! And you want to know if he's hot!"

She glanced conspiratorially up and down the deserted corridor and turned her gaze on me. "I know, I know but word is that the prison photos don't do him justice," she said. "They say he is quite the hot bad boy and I just want to know if it's true." Looking at my stunned face, she added, "Well, you may not know it, but before I met Kurt, I had quite a thing for bad boys."

As she looked at me, I couldn't say a word and just stared back. Finally, she relented and said, "Anyway, I don't think that's too much to ask my best friend." Then she laughed out loud. "Gotcha!"

In the gritty interview room, I found myself grinning, thinking of her but made sure the students, and Big Brother couldn't see it. Watching Gerri's self-confident smirk, I thought, yeah, Christie, the word was right. She had known how uptight I had been about the interviews and tried to get me to laugh a bit. It worked.

Tess's question brought me back to the present. "Now that you are facing execution, who do you blame for your fate?"

Both men admitted to having a quick temper, though they said something like they "only gave it to those who asked for it." The single time I noticed Tess falter with both men, her hand stopping its relentless path down the notebook page, was when she asked if either was sorry for what he did. Both men expressed little remorse for the act--"he had it coming" (Reggie) and "he was comin' after me and I jus' got him before he got me" (Gerri).

The time reserved for each interview had been twenty minutes, but with Tess's probing, each session went a few minutes over. When Gerri Fitzpatrick was led back out, the chain between his wrists and ankles dangling against the metal door, we got out of the uncomfortable chairs to stretch and I turned to talk to my students.

"Well, Rashid, what do you think of the first two interviews?" I asked.

"I must admit I am impressed," he said. "Miss Esselmann has handled our questioning quite well."

"I agree. Tess has done a remarkable job," I said and smiled at Tess, who blushed at the compliments. "It looks like we'll have lots of quotes to sift through for our special edition. How many pages of notes have you taken, Tess?"

Licking her thumb, she rifled her way back through the scribbled pages of the notebook. "Seventeen. ... No eighteen."

"Great job, Tess. I've only taken down a few comments that struck me so I only have a couple of pages." I asked, "What about you, Rashid?" even though I knew his answer.

I studied the youth. He squirmed slightly at the question. Then, the hardened, young Mideastern man reemerged. "I do not take notes. I do not believe you asked me to take notes, Ms. Sterber." He paused and then gave me a cold stare. "I have very strong memory. In my country, where it is not possible to waste the luxury of paper and pen on children, students must learn to remember without such aids." His voice even held an edge of rebuke. "And besides, you have the recorder." He pointed to the table.

Out of the corner of my eye I saw the slightest flare in Tess' face and I intervened. "Okay, Rashid, I selected you, so please don't make me regret it. When you get home tonight, put down on paper as much as you can remember fom that great memory and turn in your notes to me tomorrow. That way, we'll have them to compare with the notes that Tess and I took. Plus we are going to need your perspective as an Arab, especially for Akadi, to provide another perspective for our story."

As the electronic lock clanged open again, both students glanced at me quizzically. I nodded, smiling. "Let's go."

We took our places again as Akadi, shackled hand and foot, was led clumsily to the empty chair at the table. Without a word, the guard stepped back and stood, his back against the wall beside the door, his hand on his gun, a parallel form to the guard who never moved. I noticed for the first time that both figures would be just beyond the view of the camera. I shot a quick look over at Tess and she began.

"Thank you, Mr. Akadi, for agreeing to speak with us," she began. "My name is Tess Esselmann and I am the editor for <u>The Anvil</u>, the student newspaper for James Thurber High School." She looked straight at the prisoner. Pointing to her left, she indicated me and continued, "And this is our advisor, Miss Sterber." She pointed to her right, "And this is Rashid Hermani, who is a student like me and who has agreed to assist in translating, if needed."

I was studying the prisoner and saw what I took to be a flicker of recognition in his eyes. His words erupted in a flurry, Arab syllables snapping out in furious cadence like automatic gunfire. I managed to catch a few snatches of words and was trying desperately to translate them in my head. Something about "what is going on here" and "I swear by Allah" was all I could decipher. Before Tess or I could get a word out, Rashid answered back in another rapid sequence in what I took to be the same dialect.

There was a pause and when Rashid started to say something again, I interrupted him. "Rashid, it's Tess' responsibility to conduct the interview." And then I turned to the prisoner, "Mr. Akadi, I have asked Miss Esselmann to conduct the interview. Mr. Hermani is here to assist to be certain we get any translation issues correct." I stared directly at Akadi who would not meet my gaze and instead continued to peer at Rashid.

Asad emitted another quick string of words. This time I didn't have the chance to intervene because Tess beat me to it. "Mr. Akadi," she said firmly, staring at the prisoner directly across from her. "I have watched you on TV and I know you speak quite good English. As editor of this paper, it's my responsibility to ask the questions, and that's what I plan to do." Her gaze was intense and she waited until at last his stare moved from Rashid and met hers.

His initial reaction--one of angry defiance, I saw explode in his eyes like a pair of quick, mirrored flares. Then his look softened, and a small smile broke across his face and he spoke, this time in English. "My apologies, Miss ... Esselmann, for my bad manners," he said. His voice was not the shrill call of the accused Islamic terrorist we had heard on TV, but had a soft, almost warm tone. "It is true that I speak English, though not as well as you may think. Much of what you see and hear on the news are words I have...how do you say, practiced?"

"Rehearsed?" Tess offered.

"Yes, I think that is it, rehearsed," Asad continued, his smile broadening. "So, what I am trying to say is dat it is harder for me to think and talk in English." His voice was now soft, a humble entreaty. "This may be last time I have chance to give my story. I would like to speak in my language and boy," he nodded to Rashid, "could translate for me."

"Mr. Akadi," Tess interrupted before I could interject. "This is not an interview with The New York Times or The Washington Post. We're just talking about a school newspaper. I believe your English is probably good enough for The Anvil." I had to admit, she was going to make a hell of a journalist in a few years.

Akadi seemed to be caught off guard and he regained his composure and went on. "Miss, you may be from small school paper, but you are here interviewing international terrorist. And you have come wanting terrorist story, no?"

"Yes, but..." Tess began, but Asad cut her off.

"If I am to speak to you about my life, I wish to speak in my own tongue so nothing is lost," the prisoner continued.

Tess turned to me, the question in her eyes. I looked across at Rashid and noticed that he was staring back at me. "Rashid, what do you think?"

"I will do whatever you ask, Miss Sterber," the Mideast teen responded, keeping his dark eyes level on mine. Glancing between the two Arabs, I realized I was out of my depth, and so was Tess.

I decided. "Okay, Tess will read each question and Rashid, you will translate them as precisely as you can. When Mr. Akadi answers, you will translate back to English so Tess and I can record his answers. Is that clear?"

"Yes, Miss Sterber," Rashid said. After a moment's hesitation, Tess nodded in agreement and picked up her pen to begin her notes.

"Okay, Rashid, let's begin by making it clear to Mr. Akadi how we are going to handle the interview," I turned toward the terrorist whose stare was now fixed on me.

Rashid began slowly at first, gesturing to the prisoner who in turn nodded his understanding. His explanation went on for a while and I labored my way through my own rusty command of the Arabic language. Forcing my left side of my brain to comply, I was able to make out some phrases and one or two complete sentences, always well behind the exchange between Rashid and Asad.

Even as I struggled to process the first exchange, Rashid nodded to Tess to ask the first question.

"Now that you are faced with inevitable death and condemnation from most of the world, you must see things differently than before. If your sister confided to you she was planning …"

I was hearing Tess's words, but wasn't able to concentrate on them because something of the earlier exchange between Rashid and Asad still nagged at me. I tried to replay the missing part of the conversation in Farsi. "Tess will ask...she is careful to get it right...she comprehends," Rashid was saying. What does that word mean? I struggled, willing my brain to remember.

Rashid's translation of the question completed, Akadi was already part way through his answer, an answer I hadn't even heard. I tried to tell myself to let it go, that it would come back to me later, but I couldn't.

Two sentences in Farsi, three sentences in English to translate. A follow-up question from Tess, all the while her hand writing furiously, recording everything. Another sentence in Farsi, this time from Rashid and then no response from Akadi. The terrorist seemed to be stunned. Then, for Tess' benefit, two more translated English sentences. No matter how hard I concentrated, I couldn't keep up.

When, a few moments later, the answer came barreling through my consciousness, I gasped. I couldn't help myself. As one, Asad and Rashid turned to me, ceasing both answer and translation simultaneously. Even Tess looked up from her notebook, perplexed.

"Sorry," I said, trying to cover my gaffe. "Please continue."

For a long moment, no one said anything and the silence hung heavy in the small room. Then Akadi started again, the Farsi phrases began flowing again. As the terrorist spoke, he appeared to grow more confident again with each sentence and Rashid translated effortlessly. The process of turning response into translation became almost fluid, the two working easily together.

While I fought to display nothing on my face, my brain silently screamed the sentences it had struggled to translate: "Be careful what you say. She understands our language."

Chapter 25

By the time Rashid arrived at the second floor of the Red Roof Inn and was admitted into the room, the rest of the men had already gathered. The massive frames of the three Arab men were crowded tightly around the small circular table, their faces hunched over papers on the surface. Yassim returned to the far end of the room and gestured for Rashid to join the others at the table.

"It is good that we are all here," began the leader, standing over the three seated men. "This is Rashid, the youngest member of our team."

"Fadi," said the first man with broad shoulders and a long gray beard.

The next man was even larger, with huge muscles on both arms. "Mustafa," he grunted.

The fourth man said without waiting, "The name is Jesus and we have already met in the halls of James Thurber, I believe."

Rashid remembered passing Jesus in the hallway at school and had wondered about him. He knew the Sheik had men everywhere. But seeing him here, with this group, Rashid thought Jesus looked strangely out of place, like a beautiful koi in an ugly pond.

"I am glad that we are together," Yassim said, "though this will be the only time all the members of the Baqir cell will meet ... until we execute our assignment. This meeting will be short."

Yassim gestured to the papers spread out on the table and Rashid realized they were his rough drawings of the school. "The young one has provided us with good maps of the school building. Although Allah has found a way to provide us with actual blueprints of the building, they are too complicated for our plans."

Rashid knew where the original blueprints had come from, even though he wasn't supposed to. He mused that it was interesting that Yassim had attributed them to Allah, but he was not about to contradict the cell leader.

"Fadi, have you committed the boy's maps to memory?" the leader was saying.

"Yes."

"Mustafa?"

The man with the huge arms said, " Of course, and these are sufficient for knowledge of the building, but I will need the blueprints for my work."

"You will have them when you leave," the cell leader replied. *"Jesus, what have you learned about the building?"*

"I have learned much already," the handsome man responded, smiling. *"I was given a full tour of the building."*

"How did that happen?" Yassim asked, concern in his voice.

"I simply asked," Jesus said.

"Did you not think that would appear strange?"

"No, not at all. I was new to building and asked a teacher if she could show me their new building, explaining we have nothing like this in my country."

"Which teacher?"

"The one we talked about, Miss Sterber," Jesus said.

Rashid looked up sharply at the mention of the name and then lowered his head, hoping he hadn't been noticed.

"She seemed quite happy to help. I think she may have thought I had secret reason for the request."

"What would that be?" Yassim asked.

"Romance!" Jesus said, sporting his bright smile. The other men laughed, showing rows of stained and decaying teeth.

"Let us go over the preparations again," the leader said. *"Mustafa and Fadi, you will arrive with the delivery of janitorial supplies. I have made arrangements with the Stark driver and he says delivery will be about 5:00 a.m. He will leave the panel door unlocked overnight and you will need to find a good time in the night to get inside. You will be in the back of van and will come out after contact comes to get you."*

"Who is our contact?" asked Mustafa.

"A building janitor by the name of Jose," Yassim replied. *"Also, the weapons and explosives will be hidden in one of the delivery drums, the one marked degreaser. The contact is to take you and weapons to a safe place, a storage closet off the cafeteria. There you will wait for me. Do you understand?"*

Both men nodded.

"Rashid," Yassim said, *"you will be there, at school?"*

"I am there every day," Rashid answered, *"as instructed."*

"Good," the cell leader said. "And Jesus, do you have more substitute teaching jobs?"

"Yes, I have already received calls for the next several days," he replied, "and I expect more calls. They like me."

"What about you?" Fadi asked and everyone turned toward Yassim.

"Did you not know," the cell leader answered, a smile now in his voice, "that I am the milkman? The school uses Silver Dairy products and we have contacts in the company. I will deliver milk on the appointed day ... as well as Allah's justice." The men grinned at this.

"Any other questions?"

"Yes," said Mustafa, "when do we strike?"

"Soon, quite soon. Allah will let us know. You must now wait, pray, and make sure you are ready. You will keep your phones on you always?"

The other three men nodded, but Rashid looked puzzled. The cell leader said, "Not you Rashid. You do not have a cell phone because you are not permitted to have one in school. And you will be there every day, yes?"

Rashid nodded.

Yassim looked into the faces of all the men and said, "Allah be praised!" The others answered in unison, "Allah be praised!"

"It is time to leave. Fadi, you shall leave first."

Fadi rose immediately, his beard sliding off the edge of the table as he stood.

"Mustafa, come here." Yassim went over to the bottom drawer in the small dresser. The cell leader moved some sweaters and pulled a legal-sized manila envelope from the drawer. "Since you cannot memorize such a document, keep it safe at all times."

"Yes, of course." When Mustafa reached for the envelope with his large right hand, Rashid noted a "c" shaped scar on his rippling biceps. Mustafa took the package and went out the door.

"Jesus," the cell leader said, "you may go now."

Jesus grabbed Yassim's hand and shook it Western style. "May Allah give us good hunting!" he said, still grasping the cell leader's hand.

Finally Rashid was alone again with Yassim. A familiar tremor of fear rippled through his body.

Yassim turned. "You have a question?"

Rashid suddenly felt the need to clear his throat. "Is there any reason I will not know ahead of time the day of our strike?"

"I thought it best you not be burdened with that knowledge," Yassim answered quickly. "You are young yet and the task ahead will be hard enough for those of us hardened in battle. Jesus will inform you when the day is upon us."

Rashid nodded and turned toward the door. The cell leader asked coolly, "Do you have a message for your family?"

Rashid stopped at the door, the handle half way through its turn. He did not look back. "May Allah keep them safe."

Chapter 26

"I think today is the day!" Christie whispered to me in full conspiratorial mode.

We stood in the lunch line in the cafeteria, studying the day's "gourmet" offerings. You see, teachers--at least at our school--get to cut in line, so we don't spend half our generous lunch period waiting behind bored teenagers and can actually use most of our 37 minutes to enjoy the fabulous cuisine of "Chez Thurber." Just one of the great perks of our job, like grading a hundred papers a night and chaperoning the prom.

Struggling with the difficult choice of lard-fried chicken patty or chili fries, I hadn't realized Christie was talking to me.

"I just know today is going to be the day. Last night when I was making out the final invitations, I stole a glance at the horoscopes. Yours said, 'You will receive an unexpected invite. Accept it.'"

I knew I'd be sorry, but I asked, "What are you talking about?"

She leaned closer to me and said in my ear, "Jesus is subbing again today and this is the day he's going to ask you out!" she practically squealed into my eardrum, like a six year old telling a secret.

I looked at her, shook my head. "You're certifiable, girl." I grabbed a bowl of almost fresh fruit and moved down the line.

"No, I'm tellin' you, Dee Dee, this guy's hot for you. I can tell the way he looks at you. Besides, he saw me in the hallway and asked if you were here today."

When I fought my natural urge to ask a hundred questions, she pressed the matter, a little more quietly this time. Fishing money out of her purse, she said "Don't you act like you don't care either!"

We stepped back out into the cafeteria and into the constant din of an adolescent lunch period. I turned and said loud enough for her to hear, "Let's just say I wouldn't say no."

As we walked through the chaos, I glanced down to see a student deep in thought reading a novel. I was again amazed how anyone could hear, much less be able to read in the lunchroom. From where we stood, the cafeteria stretched out like an elongated square with doors to hallways that spun off like the arms of some monstrous octopus. The rear wall of the lunchroom was lined with glass doors, which led to the deck overlooking the lake. The kitchen and chow line, complete with obligatory swinging aluminum doors, was nestled in one rear corner and the teachers' lunchroom was stuck in the opposite corner, so we had to navigate across the entire cafeteria, trays in hand. The seats around every table were filled with teenagers who were doing more talking than eating and the result was raucous pandemonium. We weaved our way through the teenage crowd to the door of the teacher's lunchroom.

As we entered, I noticed that Jesus was already sitting on the other side of the table, facing the door. He looked up and smiled. I smiled back.

The small room was nearly full. On one side of my would-be date sat Hal Thompson, our fearless principal, and across the table from them was Bob Holden. Hal was talking to Jesus and Bob, except that Bob was stuffing his face behind this week's copy of <u>Sports Illustrated</u>. Janet Striker, the matron of Home Ec, overflowed the one seat with her large bulk and Brian Foley, our young, new, wet-behind-the-ears, French teacher slouched in the other.

Jesus turned to Thompson and said, "Excuse me, Mr. Thompson," and then to us, "Ladies, won't you brighten our dreary table and join us?"

Holden flapped his magazine loudly on the table and, through a full mouth of ketchup-drenched French Fries said, "Give it a rest, Jesus. Some of us are eating."

"We can see that, Robert. In fact, we can see, I think, a little too much of that," Jesus said.

Everyone in the room laughed, everyone except Bob of course, who slapped the magazine back up in place.

Christie, as usual, was quicker than I. "Thank you, Jesus. I do believe we will," she said and we took the two remaining unoccupied chairs. Christie grabbed hers first, making sure I had to take the only seat left, the one next to Jesus.

"You were saying, Jesus, what you thought was one of the biggest differences between American schools and schools in your country. What country was that again?" asked Hal Thompson, as he absently checked the state of his comb over.

"Ecaudor," said Jesus and smiled at me again.

I glanced across at Christie and she was brandishing her "See I told you" smirk. Then my eyes roamed past her to the deck and lake outside. The slashing rain that I had waded through this morning in my leather boots had turned to snow and the flakes were beginning to cover the surface of the wood on the deck like tiny white leaves. Seeing the frigid weather, I shivered.

Hal Thompson looked across at me and then followed my glance to the window behind him. "I didn't know it had started to snow. This could get nasty," he said, snatching up his tray from the table. "Sorry, we'll have to pick this up later," he nodded to Jesus. "I better get up to the office and talk to Jim, that's our superintendent, about an early dismissal." With that he was out the door, releasing another brief sound wave of the student cacophony.

"Boy, it'd be great to get out early today. I'm so tired," said Bob from behind his magazine to no one in particular.

"Yeah, I'm sure holding up that magazine all day can really tire a guy like you out," said Christie.

"Shut up, Ferguson!"

Jesus interrupted before Christie could say anymore. "Good to see you again, Miss Sterber," Jesus began, turning to me. And then, almost as an afterthought, "You too, Miss Ferguson."

"I'm glad to see that you got another sub job," I said. "Who are you today?"

"Can you not tell? Today I am Carl Bernard, algebra expert. And before I forget it," he added, "I want to tell you I am quite grateful for the tour of the school you gave me last week. It has helped me in ways you cannot guess."

"Jesus," Christie piped up, her voice bubbling, "if you need somebody to show you around town, Dee Dee can handle that, too."

"That would be very nice," responded Jesus, as if he and my best friend had scripted this part. "Is there an evening that would be convenient for you, Miss Sterber?"

"Dee Dee, please."

Just then Jerod burst through the door and, as soon as he saw me, started babbling. "Oh good, here ya are, Dee Dee. I've been lookin' everywhere for you. I need to talk to you."

"Jerod, I'm eating now." I said firmly without looking up. "I'll catch you after lunch." I kept my eyes on Jesus--no trouble doing that.

But Jerod doesn't get subtlety. "I don't think it can wait," he said. He leaned close and said in a whisper, "It's about Rashid." But the whisper was so loud, that instead of keeping the comment between us, everyone started up from their eating.

Still looking across at Jesus' face, I saw a flash of recognition in his eyes. I asked, "Do you know Rashid?"

Jesus looked flustered at first and then said, "I met him in one class I subbed in last week."

Before I could even think, Jerod butted in again. "Dee Dee, I need to show ya something in your room!"

"Can I at least finish my measly bowl of fruit?" I said.

"Bring it with you," Jerod insisted.

Before I could object, Jesus was up and moving. "It sounds important, Miss Sterber," he said, "and I need to get to my 5th period Algebra class. We can continue our discussion of possible sightseeing later ... I hope."

With that, he was out the door before I could even voice an objection. Jerod just stood there, holding the door open as Jesus walked out. I got up and exited too.

Stomping across the cafeteria, I walked ahead of Jerod and cut over to the side hallway. I heard Jerod's rapid footsteps pounding the tile behind me and then he pulled up beside me and grabbed my arm. I stopped and turned to face him, now a few feet from my classroom door.

"Sorry, that I interrupted your lunch," he started. "I found out somethin' important and thought you'd want to know."

I studied the geometric pattern on the floor and refused to look at him.

He sighed and said, "Oh, excu-use me, Ms. Sterber, I didn' know lunch was such a big deal."

"Never mind!" Then I turned, forcing him to let go of my arm, and unlocked the door to my classroom. "What did you have to show me about Rashid that couldn't wait?"

He ignored my peevish tone, "What was the reason Rashid gave for offerin' to accompany you on your interview with Akadi?"

"Jerod," I said, "I really don't feel like playing Twenty Questions!"

"Humor me, Dee Dee. Why?"

"He said he could help with the translation," I said.

"You told him you knew Farsi, right?"

"Yes, but he said he could speak the same dialect as Akadi because he grew up in the same province in Pakistan. But I told you all this before we went to HBE."

"Dee Dee, I checked with a friend a' mine at the FBI and he said that Akadi's not from Pakistan."

"You have friends in the FBI?"

"Yeah, a'course. Anyway, he said that Akadi is not from Pakistan and his primary language is Dari Persian-Afghan."

"That's not what Rashid said. Are you sure?"

"John seemed pretty damn sure of himself. He knew the army translator who worked with Asad when he was captured."

"That can't be right. I was there," I protested. "Jerod, I heard them talking. Rashid used the same dialect as Asad. Remember, I told you that I thought Rashid told Asad to watch what he said because I knew Farsi."

"I know, you told me that when you got back. I thought there might be more to it. That's why I went to John. Dee Dee, I believe you heard what you said you did," he said. "But John said you had trouble translating because they were not speaking West Farsi. He thinks Rashid and Akadi were both talkin' in Dari Persian-Afghan part of the time," he began.

"Could be. Maybe that's why I had so much trouble following. So what?"

"They don't speak Dari Persian-Afgan in Pakistan," he said. "According to the FBI translator, it's only spoken in certain remote parts of Afghanistan. The same parts that some of al Quaida training camps have been found."

"How can that be right? Rashid said he lived in Pakistan. There's got to be some mistake. Maybe some parts of Pakistan speak that dialect. I'll ask Rashid when he comes in."

"I'm not sure asking Rashid is such a good idear just yet. Here, look at this," he said as he handed me a manila folder. I recognized it as a cumulative student folder from the office and read the name typed across the top, "Rashid Hermani."

"How did you get this?" I asked, holding the folder and looking at him. "Only authorized staff are supposed to have access to these files."

He grinned and said, "That Lisa who works the office is a nice gal. I just told her that ya needed to see Rashid's folder and sent me to get it."

"You mean, you schmoozed her."

Jerod shrugged his shoulders. "You didn' know it, but I knew you needed t' see it." Leaning over my desk, we flipped open the folder and I ran my finger down the entries to find the listings for previous school and previous address. I read aloud. "See, it's right here. He put down that his home and his last school was in Bannu, Pakistan."

"And we all know everythin' in these folders are checked out thoroughly." He let that hang. "Have you had an opportunity to talk with Rashid's uncle?" He looked down and read the name from the file, "Jamal Serstani?"

"No, I haven't."

He grabbed the phone off my desk, handed it to me and said, "No time like the present. Let's call right now." He read the phone number out loud and punched in the numbers, "793-2665."

"What am I going to say?"

"You'll think of something."

After the third ring, I heard the line pick up and opened my mouth to speak. Then an electronic voice informed me that the number had been disconnected. Not trusting Jerod's dialing, I checked the number myself and punched it in again. After the obligatory three rings, the non-human voice went through the routine again.

After the second attempt, I looked across at Jerod. "You knew it was going to do that, didn't you?"

He shrugged those big shoulders and said, "Mebbe."

I picked the phone back up and punched in 411. When Jerod started to say something, I put up my palm to stop him and at the same time, I heard another disembodied phone voice ask, "City and state, please?"

I said, "Hammerville, Ohio," trying hard to enunciate clearly for the telephone computer. My words must have registered because a human voice came on the line and stated in a flat tone, "What listing?" I glanced down at the folder again. "Could I have the newest listing for a Jamal Serstani at 5644 Copeland Ct., Hammerville?" I asked, spelling the last name for the operator.

"One moment," the voice said and I waited. The pause seemed interminable but was probably only about ten seconds. I stole a glance at the clock and then at the small window in the door. The students would be here in two minutes. Then I heard the operator in my ear again. "Ma'am?"

"Yes, I'm here."

"We have no listing for a Jamal Serstani in Hammerville or anywhere in Ohio," she said. "Do you want me to check another state?"

"No, thank you." I was just about to let her go when I thought of another question. "What if he has an unlisted number?"

"Ma'am, if he had an unlisted number, I couldn't give it to you," the operator responded. "But I can tell you that I do not have a number for your party, listed or unlisted, in the area."

"Thank you."

"Well?"

"The operator said there is no one like that listed around here."

The door slammed open and the students began to pour in. We both watched the teens flooding into the room. Then Jerod said to me, "I think you were right, though."

I closed the folder and slid it under a stack of papers and asked "About what?"

"I think we need t' talk to Rashid and soon, especially since there's only one day before Akadi is scheduled to be executed," he said above the noise of the entering students. "I'll see if I can find him." Then he moved from behind my desk, turned and said, "I'll be in touch."

Chapter 27

"Okay, Harold, your update," said President Gregory.

This team meeting was in the Situation Room in the White House. The five men sat at one end of a large, polished cherry conference table and Samson noted that all the King's men were again here. Around them large-screen monitors flashed images and menus and bright, interactive maps of the regions of the world stretched across two entire walls. Another set of massive monitors projected the real-time images of national security satellites, small dots blinking red and blue on the screens. At the far end of the room, beyond the large oval table were several smaller tables and trays, with phones, laptop computers and other communication devices, ready to be pressed into use.

Samson gathered his breath and tried to take it all in, this room, this team, his responsibility. "Mr. President, we have received two important reports in the last 24 hours." Handing each man a manila folder stamped "Top Secret" across the top, he removed the first sheet from his own. "We received the lab report on the State Trooper car pulled from Lake Findlay in Pennsylvania. The CSI team was able to isolate several fingerprints as well as several fibers and hairs in the vehicle, though most matched Jeffrey Birch, the slain officer. There were a few others, but we could not find a match for them in any national or international database."

He glanced around the table, studying the faces of his colleagues. The distinct features of the large oval face of Tom Dickson were hard, unmoving, his brown eyes focused intently on Harold. Next to Dickson, Jerry Garcia stared absent-mindedly at Samson, the gray eyes blank as slate. Harold could not tell if Garcia was unconcerned or even paying attention. Sitting across the table in the chair next to the president perched Dean Settler, White House Chief of Staff, his tall, emaciated frame looked like it could slide right out of the chair. Settler's scowl seemed permanently etched--at least whenever Harold was present--and he wondered idly how President Gregory could stand to have him around all the time.

Harold brushed the folds of his bow tie and then unconsciously pushed his glasses higher on the bridge of his nose. "Yesterday, the Cleveland Police pulled two bodies from the Cuyahoga River." He pulled two black and white photos from the folder. "What you have are faxed copies of the photos of the two bodies. The color originals will arrive later this morning. Although we're not sure--the water had affected the condition of the corpses and the faxed copies are not the best--we believe the body in this first photo," he held up the one to illustrate, "is, or rather was, Mohammed Armdi."

Samson stared directly at the President. "You will remember, Mr. President, that this is the man we captured on camera, at the tollbooth on I-90."

"The man your analysts thought the cameras caught," corrected Gregory.

"Yes, sir."

"What happened to him?" the President asked.

"Sir?"

"How did he die, this man you believe to be Mohammed Armdi?"

"He was shot in the back of the head, execution-style." Samson pulled the next page out of the folder.

"What about the other man?" This was from Dickson, his body leaning forward. "Do you have an ID on the second body?"

"No, Tom, not yet," Harold turned toward the FBI Director and then read from the sheet he was holding. "Unidentified Mideastern man, dark skin, brown eyes, age approximately 27, medium height but strong build and weight about 250."

"Same manner of death?" President Gregory asked.

"Yes, sir. One shot to the back of the head," answered Samson. "Based on the trajectory of both fatal bullets, we assume both were executed in the same manner."

"Executed," Gregory said aloud.

With that comment, the posture of the other three men at the table shifted, all three now leaned forward, arms sliding slightly forward on the polished wood.

Harold continued, "We isolated DNA markers from both bodies-- Mohammed and the second Arab--and found that we could still get a decent set of prints from them. We were able to match the prints and the hairs found in the Pennsylvania police car. So we can place these two," he pointed to the two faxed photos, "one a confirmed terrorist and the other likely one as well, inside the police car of a slain Pennsylvania State Trooper." He waited to see the President's reaction before going on.

All four men looked to President Gregory, who studied the photos in his hand. He let the pictures drop to the polished surface of the table and pulled a ballpoint pen from his pocket. Without looking up, he said, "Your assessment, Harold?"

"Sir, as a prosecutor, I would need more solid evidence than this to convict, but this certainly looks like these two were members of a Mideast terrorist cell that has entered the US. I would speculate that these two encountered Officer Birch and killed him as I described to you last week."

"How did this encounter take place?" asked Garcia

"We obviously don't know, but according to the dispatcher, Officer Birch radioed in that he was pulling over a driver who was driving erratically and he suspected was DUI." He selected another paper from the report. "According to the preliminary autopsy results, the digestive systems of both men contained traces of alcohol. So we suspect Armdi--or the other man--was the driver Officer Birch pulled over. We also suspect that they overpowered and murdered the officer."

In unison, all four men leaned forward. He had seen the same reaction numerous times at trials when he had unveiled the right evidence. He knew what it meant and pressed on. He rose from his chair and moved over to the lighted map of the Midwestern US.

"It would appear that an unidentified number of foreign terrorists entered the US somewhere in this region." With the pointer on the tray below the map, Harold indicated the area bordering Canada, western New York state and western Pennsylvania. "Two of these terrorists encountered Officer Birch on a state highway here." His pointer tapped a spot on the lighted map of western Pennsylvania and a white dot bloomed on the map and started blinking. The four men all stared intently at the visual display. Samson was grateful he had taken the time to work up the program with the Situation Room computer expert earlier this morning.

Studying their reactions, he continued his explanation, drawing on delivery skills he had honed as a prosecutor in the courtroom. "At least these two men, and probably more, continued south across Pennsylvania and traveled into Ohio to Cleveland." Sliding the pointer along the described route, he tapped again and this time a blue dot glowed and began blinking in time with the white spot. "There I would further speculate, these two men, Mohammed Armdi and his partner, were executed by the leader of the cell, probably for allowing themselves to be discovered.

"Likely then, based on what we have learned from other captured terrorists, these two men have been replaced. Now we believe this cell is on its way to here, Hammerville, Ohio." The pointer moved to a spot a scant two inches below the blue dot on the huge map and Harold tapped the screen again. A larger red dot exploded, pulsing like a heart beat.

"Given the time frame of these events and the information we have pieced together, it is my assessment that we can expect some kind of terrorist activity in this area to correspond with the scheduled execution of Asad Akadi."

"Which is?" Gregory's pen clicked relentlessly.

"In thirty hours, at 6:00 p.m., tomorrow," answered Samson. The eyes of all four men were focused on the red dot, flashing on and off in the map of northeastern Ohio.

"What steps have you taken?" asked the President.

"We have sent alerts to all law enforcement agencies in this area and asked them to increase their already high vigilance. We have informed them that a terrorist cell may be planning an operation within the next thirty hours."

"I still hear a 'but' in your explanation, Mr. Samson." Gregory leaned his head down so his eyes over the top of his glasses would have an unobstructed view of the Director of Homeland Security.

"Yes, sir, I am still very concerned." As Samson watched the other men, he saw their faces harden and knew he was in for a debate. He plunged ahead. "Mr. President, it is the best judgment of my team that we should postpone the execution by four days and move the site to the nearby maximum-security prison at Lucasville, Ohio. This would give us time to set up additional precautions and establish a net to capture the terrorist cell when it moves with Akadi."

"And what reason would I give for this move?" asked the president, arching one eyebrow.

"Technical problems," Samson responded. "Since Akadi is the first prisoner to be executed at HBE, we could say that we have discovered an error in the injection system. But since it is critical that Akadi suffer the consequences of his actions, you are ordering him moved to the prison in Lucasville for execution on Tuesday evening."

President Gregory nodded his head slowly. Two slow clicks of the ballpoint pen. Samson took his chair again and everyone was silent, awaiting the President. Finally, Gregory asked, "Thoughts anyone?"

"I can't fault Harold's analysis. This is critical information his team has uncovered," began Garcia, nodding to his colleague.

Samson was immediately on alert. In his years as a prosecutor, he had learned that when opposing counsel started with a compliment, they were usually getting ready to unleash a frontal attack. Of course, the CIA Director was supposed to be on the same team, but Samson wasn't sure.

"But it's possible that his assessment is flawed," said Garcia. "For example, if these two were terrorists as Harold believes, it's just as likely they are acting alone and were killed in some dispute over a drug deal." When Samson started to object, Garcia held his hand up. "Almost always, when these terrorists are preparing for an attack, there is considerable chatter. Look at the reports of talk in the month before 9/11.

"Aside from that obscure comment on the one Syrian website, 'Allah's Voice,' my people have picked up nothing. These guys like to proclaim their victories in advance, at least to each other. If they were really planning such an operation, I think we certainly would have heard something by now."

"What's your take, Tom?" President Gregory turned to the FBI Director.

Dickson didn't hesitate. "My people received Homeland Security's call to arms this morning and I only learned the details about a half hour before we started. Jerry has a point; we should've heard more about any such operation by now. We've learned no more than the CIA guys."

"But--" the president said.

"But," the FBI Director continued, his massive body alone commanding attention, "Harold makes a pretty strong case out of the circumstantial evidence he has collected. Besides, if I were these guys and I got it into my head I was going to spring my guy, I'd go about it pretty much as Harold described. Maybe the cell got in under our radar and are in place right now."

Samson admired Dickson's courage in his admission. If the terrorists have gotten in, it would have been on his watch and everyone in the room knew it.

"Okay, thanks," said the president.

Ryan Gregory turned to his Chief of Staff. "Any thoughts, Dean?"

Settler raised one bony finger to his forehead and slowly massaged a point in the center of his temple. "I don't know, Mr. President. While Harold makes a good argument, we need to remember that it is mostly speculation. There's not a lot we know for sure. I tend to agree with Jerry. We would likely have heard something, anything by now if there was an effort to spring Akadi. As Harold said himself, the prison's virtually impregnable. And besides, I have every confidence in our people and in HBE's staff."

Samson remembered that Harold Barr, the Harold Barr of Harold Barr Enterprises, is an old friend of Settler, and a major contributor to Gregory's election campaign. Alarm bells went off in his head.

"I assume Homeland Security is coordinating with the administration at HBE?" Settler turned and looked at Samson.

Gregory interjected, "What have you told Warden Cromer, Harold?"

"I've worked very closely with James Cromer and have tried to keep him informed. But the full scenario I presented to you this morning only took shape in the last three hours. I didn't think I should brief him until I had a chance to present the information to you, sir."

"I concur, Harold," responded the president. "Let's call him now and you can review the possible threat and I can get his assessment as well. Do you have the number here or should we get it?"

"Yes sir, I have it." Samson pulled his IPhone from his jacket pocket, scrolled through some numbers and slid the device across the table to Gregory.

Settler intercepted it and said, "I'll take care of that, Mr. President." He read the screen and punched in the numbers on the pad on one of the three speakerphones.

It took less than thirty seconds.

"James Cromer here."

"Good morning, James. This is President Gregory. I'm calling from the Situation Room and I'm here with Jerry Garcia, Tom Dickson, and Harold Samson. And of course, Dean Settler."

"Hey James," Samson said aloud and the others followed suit.

"James," the President broke in, cutting off the greetings. "We called to discuss some developments concerning Akadi's execution. We all just received an update from Harold on some new intel and I wanted you to hear it."

"Thank you, Mr. President," came the response through the speakers.

"I'm going to have Harold brief you much the same as he did us, a few minutes ago and then I want to know your assessment of the situation."

"Certainly."

Four minutes later Samson was finished and the President asked, "James, did you get that?"

"I believe so," said Cromer.

"What do you think, James?"

"Obviously, we are concerned about the threat," the warden said.

"Possible threat," corrected Garcia.

"Possible threat," acknowledged Cromer. "I've got to be honest with you, Mr. President. Around here we've always worked from the assumption that these boys would try to mount some kind of threat. It's the only way to keep my people on their toes and safe. Now that we have some credible intel, we'll take some specific measures; we'll double the outside patrols and change the internal lock codes on a random basis, at least for the next two days, until this thing is done."

"So I take it that you don't agree with Harold's recommendation that we should move Akadi to a new location?" asked the president.

"Sir, I have great respect for his assessment, but in all humility, Akadi is a lot more secure inside this facility than he will be in transport, at least in my opinion."

"Thank you, James," said President Gregory. "For now this specific intel is for your ears only."

"Of course, Mr. President."

Settler reached over and switched the speakerphone off. The president asked, "Any final thoughts, gentlemen?"

"Just one, sir," said Settler. "If you do decide to move Akadi and postpone his execution, it may set off a firestorm. With all the trouble we had in closing Guantanamo and housing these terrorists on US soil, there'll likely be a good deal of criticism and finger-pointing if we postpone and move him. Your critics in the media are going to have a field day, not to mention our 'friends' in the Senate."

"I doubt that anyone would make that case," countered President Gregory.

"Sir, you know we can't control what the media will say, especially this close to the election." Settler's hollow eyes studied the President. "Sir, the polls say that Akadi's execution will give you a reasonable margin to win the election. Harold's plan would move the execution to election day. Who knows what postponing it will do to that margin?"

President Gregory looked first at Settler and then let his glance move around the table and land on Samson. Harold could read the body language and knew he had lost before the president uttered another word.

"For now, we stay the course. Harold, if anything changes in the next 24 hours, I want us all back in here and we will reassess."

"Yes, Mr. President."

"Keep me apprised. I have three more rallies yet today."

Chapter 28

"No one has seen 'im since fifth period yesterday," Jerod said, as we walked down the steps on our way to lunch the following day. "I talked to Lisa in the counselor's office and she said that Rashid didn't sign out yesterday."

We turned the corner and headed down the main corridor. Straight ahead loomed the huge picture window that overlooked Lake Harold. On good days the view was an incredible sight with the sun glistening off the pristine lake, the crystal clear water lapping gently at the shoreline. But over the past 24 hours the weather had worsened and the snow dropped out of a brooding, dark sky and turned the cold-whipped waters into a frothy monster.

We were still about a hundred feet away from the student cafeteria, but already the sound of teens jabbering at lunch barreled down the corridor. Jerod stopped and said, "While you were teachin' yesterday afternoon, I tried to track him down and found out Rashid wasn't in his classes all afternoon."

"Maybe there's a logical explanation. He'll probably be in my class sixth period and we can talk to him then," I said with more conviction than I felt.

"I don't think so," Jerod said, shaking his head. He grabbed my arms with both hands, forcing me to stop and looked directly at him. His face was only a few inches from mine. Okay, I had to admit, standing there staring at his aqua blue eyes, this wasn't all bad and just then, a strange thought occurred to me. Had a group of my students happened upon us there in the hall--not likely as it's off-limits to students at that time of the day--if they'd had seen us, face to face, whispering and glancing furtively around they would have assumed we were clandestine lovers.

Studying his face there in that vacant hall, I noticed how his eyes were swollen and drooped with fatigue. His chin was edged with what would have passed for a double five o'clock shadow. Jerod usually liked to exude the rumpled-guy look, but today his shirt looked like it had been on the floor of his apartment for a week. Even his southern boy smile was vacant and that worried me more than anything else.

"Jerod, you look terrible," I said.

"Gee, thanks," he replied, his lopsided grin back momentarily. "You don' look so hot yourself."

"I'm serious. You looked like you haven't slept."

"I haven't. After I took most of the afternoon to try to find Rashid, my boss called me and told me I had t' come back to work. When I got off this morning, I came straight here."

"Was something at HBE wrong?"

"I dunno. With Asad's execution coming up, everybody's jumpy. The talk among the guards is that they think somethin's up. Rumor is that the warden got a call from the president."

"Of HBE?" I asked, confused.

"Naw. You know, Ryan Gregory, president of the US of A."

"Really? Why would the president call your warden?"

"I dunno! They don't tell us peons," he answered irritably, the exhaustion leaking through his words. "But my guess would be two words."

"Asad Akadi."

"Three stars for the lit'l lady. My supervisors had everybody pull double shifts, so as soon as I left here, I got the call and went straight back to work. Just got off a few minutes ago."

"Jerod, you need to go home and go to bed," I said, allowing concern into my voice.

He nodded his head. "I plan to, as soon as I get something t' eat." Then his grin was back briefly. "Unless you want to join me?" he asked quickly, breaking the tension.

"You're impossible!"

"Yeah, and you love it," he said and then just that quickly the grin disappeared. "I just wanted to tell you what I found out."

"I thought you said you never found Rashid."

"I didn', but I got his schedule from Lisa and checked with all his afternoon teachers. The only teacher I could find who saw him at all was Bruce Airhart, you know him?"

I nodded. "Yeah, math. Kids call him Mr. Airhead."

"That's him. Anyway, he said Rashid showed up in his fiftth-period class, just like normal. Then in the middle of the class, a guy comes to the door and ask'd to see Rashid. He said he let Rashid go out in the hallway to talk and forgot about him. It wasn't till the period had ended and he saw Rashid's backpack under his desk that he realized Rashid never came back in."

"Did he say who the guy was?" I asked.

"Said he didn' know 'm but said he was some older guy."

"Maybe Rashid's uncle?" I asked, sounding a little too hopeful.

"You mean the one who has no listing in the four-state area?"

I said mostly to myself, "I hope Rashid's not in trouble."

"I hope we're not in trouble," he mumbled.

"What?"

"Nothin'. I'm just tired. I just came over to tell ya about Rashid...oh, and for the great food. I just wanted to make sure you knew. Let's get somethin' to eat and then I'm heading for a bed, even if I have to go alone."

He started walking down the hall, his gait loping. Still, with the difference in our strides, I had to hurry to catch up and we walked in silence for a while. Then I asked, "Did he tell you what he looked like?"

"Airhead said he didn' get much of a look at him. He was too busy explainin' the beauty of the Pythagorean theorem. Said he was about my height, dark skin, black hair and he thought a trimmed black mustache. Sound like anybody we know?"

We rounded the bend to the cafeteria and came face to face with the teen lunch crowd. I glanced over at Jerod but he was peering straight ahead. I figured he was surveying the clusters of students, trying to locate Rashid. Then I felt his body tense. I followed the direction of his stare, hoping he had found Rashid. I turned to look at the far wall, where one set of vending machines stood waiting for students' eager quarters.

Right then, at the end table nearest me, I was distracted by two students arguing loudly and facing off, spoons in hand, apparently ready for a good old-fashioned food fight. Pondering for only a moment the likely impact upon my new red sweater, I stepped in front of Jerod to block the airborne mashed potatoes and flying macaroni and cheese. Just before I reached the two squabbling teens, I felt my arm yanked hard and I was pulled roughly to the floor. I tried to turn to look, even as I was falling to the floor, but then all hell broke loose.

My head slammed against the linoleum and Jerod's body landed on top of mine. Crushed, I had the wind knocked out of me. Jerod used his other hand to shove the two arguing freshmen aside and turned the table on its side. In the haze of time frozen, I tried to grasp what he was doing.

Then I heard several loud pops and saw the edge of the overturned table splinter as a fusillade of bullets hit the Formica. Then I heard a man with an Arab accent shout, "Everyone, down on the ground!"

I tried to look up. I could hear Jerod's ragged breathing above me. Around me, I sensed several hundred students and a scattering of adults stop in mid-conversation and mid-step.

The voice I didn't recognize screamed again, "Everyone on the floor, now!" To make his point, he let off another round from the automatic weapon. This time the bullets struck the ceiling fluorescent, shattering the fixture, the split electrical lines raining down a shower of sparks. The entire line of lights down the center of the cafeteria went black, dimming the room and throwing grotesque shadows. From where I lay, still squashed, I heard the sound of chaos--students diving for the floor, plastic chairs scraping the vinyl, flying books hitting the surface and the screams of hundreds of terrified teens.

The gun erupted again and this time the glass of the vending machines behind us shattered, glass fragments exploding onto the teens huddled on the floor nearby. I heard a student cry out, "I'm hit!" and managed to turn my head to see. Blood poured down Keith's face, the side of his head and blond hair now turning bright red. From my huddled position, I strained, but couldn't tell if he had been hit by a bullet or had caught some of the flying glass. Keith began to cuss loudly and then cry.

As it quieted again, I could hear others whimpering around me. My only thought was I've got to help them.

Before I could move, the Arab voice screamed, "Where is the principal?"

Squirming beneath Jerod's weight, I tried to turn toward the voice and peer around the end of the overturned table. Jerod pulled me back roughly, placing his body atop me. "Stay down!" he commanded in a hushed tone. Then he shifted and leaned around the table edge, trying to see the intruder himself. As he edged forward above me, his heart thumped furiously in my ears.

I heard a door open from the side and then a few quick footsteps. "I am the principal," said Hal Thompson. Even across the room, his fear was palpable in those few words, but I could detect remnants of his hard-ass resolve as well.

"Come with me," shouted the Arab voice. "Fadi, they are yours. You know what to do."

"Yes," a second Arab voice said. I realized that there was more than one intruder and my panic ratcheted up another notch.

I turned my head to the side and was just able to take in two pairs of legs striding down the hall behind us, one pair of black suited pants and the second a pair of worn jeans.

God, I wanted to see what was going on! I realized I was safer pinned under Jerod but I just couldn't lie there and do nothing. I never was very good at playing it safe. Growing up, I was always the first in the middle of the fray and still have a few scars to prove it. If I had known what my impetuous nature would get me into, I might've held back. But I doubt it.

Before I could decide on a course of action, the second man screamed. "Everyone, stand up! Everyone, on your feet!"

Still stunned and not knowing what to expect, students and teachers were slow to react. It was as if the entire room was awakening from some horrible nightmare, people moving slowly, awkwardly. Teens and adults struggled to get to their feet. All around me I heard the sound of chairs being pushed and tables skidding as teachers and students braced themselves and rose on shaky legs. Jerod slid off me, stood up, then reached a hand down to help me up. I took it and rose, noting for the first time the throbbing in my head from my collision with the floor. I massaged my temple, feeling the mushrooming knot. I scanned the faces and bodies, trying to locate who had been hurt. I could see only a few who were bloodied, like Keith Dettmer. I tried to recall where the first aid supplies were. The kit was probably in the kitchen, at the other end of the room. Before I could form a plan to get to it, the man with the gun was yelling again.

"Everyone who has cell phone, bring it here," the Arab called Fadi shouted, producing a large canvas bag. At first no one moved, perhaps still in shock or remembering stories of the passengers with cell phones on Flight 93 that crashed in Pennsylvania. The intruder seemed to expect the hesitation. "This AK-47 has very touchy trigger," he grinned and held up the rifle for all to see, "and if I hear one cell phone go off with one of those stupid ringers, I am going to fire in that direction." He aimed at the ceiling and let loose another burst as a demonstration.

A few teachers needed no more encouragement and began walking slowly up to the front of the room. Still apparently unsatisfied, the terrorist shouted, "I know there are hundreds of cell phones in this room and if I don't see d'em being tossed into this bag, I'll start shooting." He looked around to the crowd of teenagers huddling together. "And I think I'll start with her." With one huge hand, he grabbed the hair of the girl closest to him, a pretty brunette whose face turned ashen. She screamed and this caused the intruder to laugh. Staring across the room at her terrified face, I remember thinking her name is Michelle and she had run for Homecoming Queen. Last week she was worried about which outfit might get her the most votes and now she thought she was going to die. I wondered if we were all going to die.

The terrorist--I allowed my brain to formulate the unthinkable--threw the gray bag to a jock at the first table with his right hand without letting go of the gun while his left yanked Michelle's hair again. Even from across the room, I could tell the terrorist was an incredibly strong man. Atop massive shoulders stood an ugly, threatening face with a long gray beard. He said, "Here, you collect the phones!" Nervous and scared, the teen missed the tossed bag. "I hope you do not play for d' baseball team!" the Arab jeered as the teen bent down to pick up the limp sack. Then to the crowd, "Come! Drop your phones in ... or perhaps you want to sacrifice this pretty young thing!" Yanking on the brown hair with one huge hand, he wrenched the head of his captive and she cried out again.

A few of the teachers moved out of the adjoining room and filed up to the student holding the sack. One by one, they lowered their cell phones into the bag. Glen Miller lowered his teal phone into the bag and gently placed his hand on the quivering arms of the student athlete. As Janet Striker dropped her phone in the bag, she announced to the gunman, "You know, students aren't allowed to have cell phones in the building."

The terrorist squealed with delight and shot two rapids bullets into the ceiling. Striker shrank in terror. "Only one as foolish as you would believe that these," he gestured at the teens with the gun barrel, "would follow your stupid rules." Then to the students, "Show this foolish teacher I am right! Come!"

Obeying this command, students joined the teachers and made their way slowly, fearfully to the front of the room where the terrorist and sack waited. Their eyes locked on the automatic rifle, girls pulled petite, colorful cell phones out of small purses and guys took sleek black Iphones from pants pockets. Even from our position at the back of the room, I could hear the occasional ring tone as the phones hit the bottom.

Jerod didn't believe in cell phones and my phone was locked in my car, so we didn't move. But as we watched this somber procession proceed, the entire cafeteria quieted, a pall of dread settling over the large group. My glance darted around the room searching out the eyes of teenagers, trying to read their minds, to decipher their thoughts. Fear was etched on their faces, girls whimpering and guys trying to hold them, to comfort them. I just hoped that some male testosterone was not getting ready to test their fate by rushing the gunman. Some of the guys wore hardened looks and as I studied them, I was afraid they were plotting just that. I glanced over to Jerod to see if he was following my thoughts.

I eyed a group of students to the left of the terrorist. The four guys exchanged quick looks and one, a tall, red-headed teenager flipped open a slim phone and his fingers began tapping the keys in furious repetition. Text messaging. I had caught a kid doing the same in my class last week and had confiscated the phone. Now I was just hoping he would get something out.

My glance shifted to the terrorist, hoping he hadn't noticed, fearing he had. Almost, as if he read my thoughts, he turned to the knots of students. His eyes flashed recognition. In one second, the gun came up and fired once. The phone exploded in the boy's hand and blood spurted. The students started screaming again.

"Quiet!" he yelled and fired the AK-47 into the ceiling. Silence returned, except for the whimpering of the red-headed teen. "Anyone else want to try something?" the terrorist jeered. The rest of the students complied, dropping the cell phones into the bag.

Then behind me, I heard the shuffle of footsteps and turned. I caught a glimpse of the plump form of Rob Holden. He loped around the corner, grasping a cell phone and huffing from the effort. In the eerie quiet that had fallen over the room, the soles of his shoes pounded on the linoleum, loudly announcing his hasty exit. His terrified shouts echoed down the hallway, "Hello? Hello? 911!! Help! Help! We're under attack. At Thurber High School! Help! Hello? Hello?!"

I turned, expecting to see Fadi burst for the hallway and aim his weapon. Fearing the worst, I got ready to crouch again behind the overturned table. But as I watched him, the terrorist did not move from his watch. As he stood there motionless, another spray of bullets shattered the uneasy quiet down the hallway. I heard Rob Holden cry out and the thud of a body hitting the ground.

Then, in weird contrast to the sudden violence, the calm, deep voice of Principal Thompson came over the loudspeaker. "Attention, all students and teachers. Please report to the cafeteria now. This is a new safety drill and we need everyone's cooperation. It's important that everyone stop what they are doing and report to the cafeteria. Remember to walk, not run. This is a safety drill." The audible click of the PA.

I looked to Jerod, who whispered, "They want us all together. Why? To kill us?"

"Probably to hold us as hostages," he whispered. Looking at him, I couldn't tell if he was saying this to make me feel good or he really believed it. I didn't have time to ask.

Before we could say anymore, we watched as a familiar form emerged from the hall where Rob had run by only seconds before. Cradling a steel gray automatic rifle in his left arm, Jesus Ramirez strode into the cafeteria, caught sight of me and smiled. Behind the perfectly trimmed black mustache, he announced, "It is a shame that cell phones do not work inside the center of this building. But at least, Ms. Sterber, you will not have to put up with any more snide comments from Mr. Holden."

Chapter 29

I stared, speechless, struggling to process it. I was looking at the man I was trying to date yesterday, and he was holding a machine gun pointed directly at me. How could the handsome, smiling Jesus, whom I befriended and who I gave a tour of the school just last week, how could he have just gunned down Rob Holden in cold blood? And here he was, seconds later, strutting up the hallway wearing an ugly smirk. I couldn't take my eyes off his figure as he strode up around the scene of the terrified hostages and joined the other terrorist at the front of the room.

"Dee Dee!" Jerod's harsh whisper and his hand on her shoulder forced her to take her eyes off of Jesus.

"How could he do that?" I called at Jerod, tears fighting their way out. "Oh my God! I helped him. I tried to be his friend, I showed him around. I helped him to learn the layout of the school."

"Dee Dee!" he repeated.

"I helped them. I helped kill Rob!" I sobbed.

"Dee Dee!" Jerod called again, more intensely.

"Oh my God, what have I done?"

"Dee Dee, it's not your fault," he said between clenched teeth. He glanced around, obviously worried that my words would draw attention. "Dee Dee, ya can't do this right now. The students are going t' need us."

I suddenly felt so soiled, so manipulated that I couldn't let it go. I know I was going into shock but didn't care. More than anything else, I wanted to curl up on the floor and die. Let them put a bullet in my head.

Then Jerod grabbed both my arms and his fingers pinched hard, forcing me to look at him. He moved his face down so it was only millimeters from mine. His deep blue eyes, fierce, angry eyes bored into mine, willing me to stare back. He still kept his voice at a whisper, but in the intimate space between us, the words came out as shouted commands.

"If we don't help the kids, a lot of them are going t' die!"

"This doesn't make any sense, Jerod," I said, shaking my head. "Why would they do that?"

"I'm sure it's all about Akadi." He was so close I could smell his breath on my face, the stale, sour odor from not eating. "These men are psychotic, Dee

Dee. They'll hurt or kill whoever gets in their way. We have t' help the students so they don't do something stupid, like try to play a hero."

I fought to focus. I looked around the room, scanning for knots of students that I knew. I saw then that some of the teachers, who had to cross the room earlier to surrender their cell phones, had moved back into the middle of the students instead of returning to where they had stood on the side.

Jerod and I were still at the rear of the cafeteria where we had entered, next to the area where freshmen were usually consigned. We were still 50 feet from the teachers on the east side of the room and almost 75 feet the other way from where the two terrorists, Fadi and Jesus, kept watch in the northwest corner. In the weakened light, I surveyed the scene, searching for some of my own students and keeping an eye on the intruders. I watched both terrorists jeer at the frightened teens nearest them, brandishing their automatic weapons like proud trophies, jabbing the rifles at the students and laughing at them when they jumped.

Bunched in two's or three's, the students crouched together, quivering, crying, whispering, praying. I could see that a few brave kids were trying to comfort others, but it wasn't working. There was just too much fear in the room, like an evil plague spreading across the space. Even the tough, macho guys weren't immune. In the dim cafeteria, I could still see the terror in the guys' eyes, in the whimpering of the girls, in how the students stood closely bunched together, hoping desperately for safety in numbers, even though they knew there was none. As my eyes scanned the room, I saw Brian Foley, the new French teacher, standing against the wall on the other side of the room, almost by himself. Brian, with his long, shoulder-length, black hair and young handsome face, could pass for one of the students and this no doubt helped his popularity with many of the teens. Today, like most days, he wore a navy chamois shirt and his tan Dockers. His fear was even more obvious than most; it showed in the growing, dark stain on his pants by his groin but Brian seemed too terrified to notice, or care.

Looking around the partially darkened room, I could tell the intruders had done their job, at least their first job--spreading terror.

I again tried to focus on the immediate task. I heard Jerod say quietly, "There!" and I followed his eyes to the left side of the room. At first, I could not see what he was staring at and then I recognized them. Most of the journalism crowd--Tess, Goat, James, Zoë, and Tyler--stood together. As I studied them, I could see their lips moving and watched as their glances switched from the terrorists up front to Tess. Knowing how gutsy she was, I was afraid my student editor was cooking up some heroic stunt.

"I've got to get over there," I said to Jerod and turned to edge my way over to my students. His hand held my forearm and I couldn't move.

"Everyone listen up!" yelled the man the leader called Fadi, letting off another short burst of gunfire into the ceiling. The mumbles and whispers were cut off in mid-sentence and the room got quiet again. He turned to his partner and nodded.

"Good afternoon," Jesus announced, sprouting a broad smile beneath the mustache. "Many of you know me. I am Mr. Ramirez. I have substituted in a number of your classes. My friends and I need to use this school for only a short while. When we are finished, you can have it back, at least what's left of it." He grinned broadly and his comrade found this particularly funny, laughing out loud. "If you do what we tell you, there is no need for anyone to die." And then, as if remembering some minor slip of the tongue, he added, "No one else, that is."

Two girls in the group on his left clung desperately to each other and began to cry. He called, "Come now. Mr. Holden was an overbearing idiot and you cannot possibly be sorry he is dead." At this, the two girls only cried more loudly.

Studying Jesus, Jesus the terrorist, with the charming smile and Hollywood face, somehow made the terror all the worse. Standing next to him, Fadi, with his broad shoulders and long gray beard, looked like a stereotype of the FBI's wanted poster of a Mideastern terrorist. With a small turban, he could have been a stand-in for Osama Bin Laden or one of the others on the terrorist watch list. But, Jesus was handsome and virile, by any standard. If behind that handsome face lurked the rabid hatred of a terrorist, then somehow we were all doomed.

Ignoring the students' whimpering, Jesus went on, "I think what we need is a change in scenery," he announced brightly. "Many of you have told me how much you like to hang out on the balcony and it's such a beautiful day today. Let's all move outside to the balcony."

Stunned, no one moved immediately. Automatically, every face in the room turned from the terrorists to the slate gray lake and sky behind them.

Outside, the large snowflakes jumped and swirled endlessly in the wind, as if dancing and laughing at our fates. Not knowing what to do, the teens' frightened eyes darted to the adults around them, looking for some kind of answer. The teachers, I, had no answers.

Fadi fired his weapon again, this time into the floor, sending chunks of the linoleum and concrete onto the legs of nearby students. They jumped and then fell on the floor, grabbing their legs, and crying out. Then he yelled, "Let's go!" and pointed to the glass doors at the north end of the cafeteria. Jesus strode over to the door and held it open, grinning, like some demented doorman. A blast of freezing air sliced into the cafeteria immediately plummeting the room temperature. Every person in the room turned back and looked ominously at Fadi, cradling the AK-47, and began to make their way slowly toward the open doors.

Jerod placed his hand on my arm, lightly this time, and urged me forward and we joined the throng. As we took our places near the back of the large group, he leaned down and whispered to me, "When we get out there, we need to find your gang." I nodded.

Even with his touch light on my arm, I could feel his tension, a spring ready to uncoil. I said quietly without even turning my head, "You're not going to try anything crazy, are you?"

Taking my cue, he kept his face straight ahead and whispered just loud enough for me to hear, "Just trying t' keep us alive."

We made the rest of our way out into the freezing wind and snow along with the other five hundred captives. Thurber, like most school buildings, even newer buildings, can't seem to get the temperature right. It's either too hot and we all suffocate or it's way too cold and we have to walk around bundled up like Eskimos--okay Inuits--all day. Today was one of the too hot days and, since coats and wraps were securely stored in lockers and closets, no one, student or teacher, wore more than a sweater, a sweatshirt or blazer. In addition, huddling together in the cafeteria, we had been too terrified to notice, but the cafeteria had been even warmer, the additional heat generated by hundreds of bodies, adrenalin pumping and metabolism burning, the heat showing in the beads of perspiration on our faces.

But, when forced through the open doors and out onto the deck, we were immediately buffeted by the freezing temperatures--I thought I remembered hearing that the thermometer was supposed to stay in the teens--along with the whipping wind off the lake. The horrendous shift in temperatures leached our reserves. As I searched for the journalism group in the crowd, I noticed every person--teen and adult--had begun to shiver, exposed on the deck. Some of the students tried to bunch up even more tightly together and others knelt and curled down on the floor of the deck, trying to avoid the angry wind.

Jerod and I were two of the last ones through the glass doors. When Jesus recognized us moving through the opening, he flashed that smirk again and I tried to ignore it, to show nothing. The last of the group came through a few seconds after us and I heard Jesus and Fadi slam the doors so hard the glass rattled. Then Jesus left Fadi at the doors and he strutted to the edge of the deck near the water. Peering across the lake, through the mist of the gray cloud cover, I could just make out the outlines of HBE prison, its lights blinking in the winter dimness. Looking from the prison to Jesus, it became clear he too was staring at the compound. I could make out no figures and doubted that he could; it was too far and the haziness further obscured the view. That didn't mean a prison guard standing watch with binoculars couldn't see us.

Both hands on the AK-47, Jesus raised it high over his head and swung the weapon from side to side. Then he lowered it and fired a burst into the water and the sound died over the waves of the lake. Then he raised the gun over his head again in the pose of domination.

I'd seen that pose. I remembered on September 11th, watching CNN in my apartment for hours on end, the same tapes playing over and over. Though the footage of the planes striking the towers were horrendous, what I remember most was the image of those delighting in the massive deaths of the innocents, images of Palestinians and other Arabs dancing with rifles raised overhead, celebrating the demise of Americans. Standing in front of us was the same celebratory pose. I shuddered.

Jerod nudged my arm and I forced my attention away from Jesus and back to the students. With their heads bowed and hundreds of students and teachers in knotted groups, Jerod and I found it hard locating the journalism students. We made our way around the overcrowded deck, edging from group to group. As we moved, we checked on students and I tried to give some reassuring touches, mumbling false assurances. It took several minutes for us to find my group. I recognized their urgent whispering before we were able to see them.

When we did, we found they were almost to the very front of the deck, quite near where Jesus stood.

"We can't just stand here and do nothing!" I heard Tyler say as we approached the group.

"What the hell do you think we can do?" demanded Goat, stamping from one foot to the other, one hand absently brushing his goatee.

"I think we should just stay together and keep our heads down," said Zoë, her whole face reddened the color of her pimples.

"Well, I'm not going to stand around, doing nothing," declared Tess, her arms flapping repeatedly across her body. "Does anybody have a notebook?"

"I do. W-w-what are you going to do?" asked James, his voice shaking from the cold and fear. He pulled a reporter's spiral notebook from his back pocket,

"Maybe, one thing they want is a forum. We're a newspaper. Maybe if we give them a forum, they won't kill us," I heard her argue just as I worked my way around the last group of students. When I got to the group, I saw her take off toward Jesus.

I turned to Jerod. "Can you stay with them? I'm going to try to head off Tess." I didn't wait for his answer. By the time I caught up with her, she was already in conversation with Jesus.

"I was the student who interviewed Asad," Tess was saying. "I thought you might be interested in going on the record with me."

"On the record?" Jesus was skeptical.

"Mr. Ramirez," replied Tess in her journalist's patient voice, "when all this goes down, don't you want your side of the story to be told?"

"Americans do not want anyone's side of the story other than their own!" Jesus responded, displaying anger for the first time.

"Mr. Ramirez, I'm a journalist. I will tell your side," Tess began.

Jesus laughed at her and said, "You...you are a student."

"Okay, I'm studying to be a journalist," Tess continued, undaunted. "We are taught to cover different sides of a story."

I came up behind her and placed my hand on her shoulder and she jumped at the touch. Recognizing me, she turned and saw me, hugging me briefly. Then she turned back to Jesus. I noticed for the first time that he was wearing a blue sleeveless ski jacket which no doubt kept him comfortably snug even in the freezing temperatures. As I stared at him, up close, he flashed that smile of his that now seemed much more like a sneer and suddenly I was worried about what he had in mind. Without thinking, I intervened.

Stepping in front of her, I faced Jesus and asked, "Maybe you can't make any case for your actions. Are you man enough to go on the record?" When confronted with an alpha male, I have found it usually works when you challenge their manhood. I didn't expect it to work this well, like poking a rabid bear.

I saw the anger flash in his eyes and then he caught himself and said, "But Miss?" he looked politely to Tess.

Immediately she replied, "Esselmann. Tess Esselmann."

"Yes," he smiled again, turning on the charm, "Miss Esselmann has asked for the interview. No?"

Without looking back at Tess, I replied, "It doesn't matter. I'm the advisor." When he hesitated, I pressed my luck. "How about this? I'll ask the questions and Miss Esselmann will do the recording."

I waited for his answer. I really didn't care if he said yes or no. My real goal was to get Tess out of harm's way. But as another frigid wind sliced through me, I shivered.

AK-47 slung in front of his chest, Jesus raised his eyes upward, looking into the darkening clouds and falling snow. Then his glance swept across the deck as if checking his hostages. He returned his stare to me and faced me, fierce green eyes ablaze with condescension. Then he announced with a derisive laugh, "Why not! It will be an interesting, uh...ah, yes, diversion!"

Chapter 30

Okay, it was not a very smart thing to do, especially for someone that was at the top of her class. Well, near the top. To engage in an intellectual battle with a psychotic--I knew by this time Jerod was right about that--who was using an AK-47 to wield power over life and death, this was perhaps not the smartest thing I ever did. But seeing the abject terror in the students' faces, I was seized by a fury so fierce, it controlled me, not the other way around. Even though a part of me wanted to, I refused to allow myself to cower there on the cold, wooden slats of the deck even as these two insane criminals leered at us, laughing at us, preparing to execute us.

"Fadi, in the spirit of true American journalism, they wish to *interview* us," Jesus called to his compatriot across the deck. They laughed and Jesus proclaimed, "Who knows, Fadi? Perhaps we will help them win a Pulitzer Prize, although it may have to be awarded posthumously." He laughed again. "Very well then, Miss Sterber, ask away!" Relaxing his body, he leaned back against the three-foot high wood railing that edged the deck, elbows on the top rail and one leg on the bottom rung.

I tried to ignore his threat and stared past him into the frigid waters of Lake Harold. My body chilled by the biting wind, my mind conjured up visions of tiny icebergs in the waves of the lake below. Now that I got what I sought and Tess was out of harm's way, at least for now, I wasn't sure where to begin. So I started with the obvious. "Okay, Jesus, who are you?"

"You already know that, Miss Sterber," he said, smug smile firmly in place. "I am Jesus Ramirez, poor itinerant teacher." He lifted his hands from the railing, stood up and turned slightly in a mock modeling pose.

"Jesus, I doubt that you are either poor or a teacher," I said dismissively. He feigned hurt, but I ignored it. "Why are you doing this?"

"Ah, yes," he said, grinning again. "I guess you could put down that we are soldiers in Allah's sacred army fighting the great Jihad. That's J-I-H-A-D, Miss Esselmann."

"No, Jesus, I'm not talking about the whole band. I mean you. Why are you doing this?" I asked.

"Oh, you mean me personally," Jesus responded, nodding to his companion who shot a toothy grin back. "You mean what's a nice Hispanic boy like me doing with a group of Arab terrorists?"

When I stared back but didn't say anything, he went on, as I knew he would.

"There is much you do not know about me, Miss Sterber," he said, the smile vanishing. "For instance, you probably don't know that my mother was Muslim, a Palestinian in fact, married to a Ecuadorian businessman who had come to Lebanon to make his fortune, as you say in America. And you do not know that," he gritted his teeth, "when I was four years old, I watched my mother being raped and killed by Lebanese Christian militia. I watched her die in front of me and swore revenge…in the name of Allah, of course," he added.

I was stung by his admission and didn't know what to say. I cast a quick glance back to Tess and the crowd of students behind her. In the middle of the students, I saw Jerod put an arm around a terrified Goat and whisper something into his ear. Then he shot a warning look at me and I nodded slightly. To cover myself, I asked Tess, "You getting all this?" She shook her head and I went on, trying a new tact.

"Jesus, the death of your mother must have been horrible and I'm truly sorry. That would drive anyone to do desperate things, but you surely know these children had nothing to do with those events. Why are the students of James Thurber High School such a threat to Allah's army that they need to be held at gunpoint?" I asked.

"No one is a threat to Allah's army, as you and your country will soon find out," he said with icy coldness.

"If we are no threat, then why would your army want to terrorize several hundred innocent children?"

"You and your readers will learn that as long as Muslim children all over the world are massacred by American bombs, there can be NO innocent American children."

I studied our captor. It was as if his personal revelation had altered him. I could see Jesus darkening. Staring at him, watching him as he spoke, I could see a transformation spread over his whole face, the polite, handsome facade peeling away, like badly sunburned skin. His handsome features didn't change exactly, but I could see the rage flare in his green eyes, making them cold and distant. With each exchange I could watch harshness etching into the lines of his face and his charming smile morph into a fatalistic sneer.

I tried a different tact. "Would you be willing to give us an explanation of your grievances so our readers can understand all this?"

"Grievances, Fadi!" he bellowed. "She wants to know our grievances. How about a thousand years of oppression and persecution of Muslims at the hands of Christians? How about decades of attacks, conquest and rape of Muslim people and lands by the West? How about the murder of thousands of Muslims, children and adults, caused by American bullets and bombs?" His foot slid off the lower railing and he faced me.

"I admit the world can be a terrible place, loaded with injustice and cruelty. I even admit that there is much that America has done wrong. But that is not us and certainly not these children." My arms swept the crowd of students behind me. "Why are you here at Thurber?"

"I would have thought that that would be obvious," and then he added, "even to a simple high school teacher. We have the glorious duty to free another member of Allah's sacred army."

"Would this be the same member of Allah's sacred army who murdered other innocent Americans?"

"Miss Sterber, you really are more dense than I had thought," he said with an evil chuckle. "You have already forgotten. There are no innocent Americans."

Shaking from the chill, another icy blast ripping through me, I crossed my arms tightly across my chest, but it did little good. I was losing my body's fading warmth and any empathy. "I would think that even a simple soldier in Allah's sacred army," I mimicked, "would know that it is not possible to free Akadi from the most secure prison in the country."

"That is because you do not have faith, Miss Sterber," he announced pedantically. "As the prophet, peace be to him, said, if he cannot go to the mountain, then the mountain will come to him."

"I believe you are mistaken, I don't believe the prophet ever said that," I said, automatically drawing on my knowledge of the Koran. "It is a common enough mistake. Can you tell me, where is it written that the prophet uttered those words?"

"What do you know of these things?" Jesus demanded.

"Perhaps more than you might think, Jesus. I too am a person of faith and I have spent many hours studying the writings of the prophet."

"What you think, woman, is of no consequence." This assertion was said with barely disguised contempt and he stiffened his back. "This mountain will decide to come to Mohammed, peace be upon him, because if it does not," he stared at me coldly and announced, "then Allah's soldiers will begin sacrificing students and teachers!"

Out of the corner of my eye, I saw the students close enough to hear the exchange cower at his threat. It's what I wanted to do as well, but I was too far in now to back out. "And you claim the mission of your army is a holy one?"

"Of course," Jesus snapped, "this mission has been blessed by Allah and commissioned by the Sheik himself! If your American eyes were not so blind, you would see, this is just one part of the great Jihad sweeping the world." The transformation now complete, Jesus' green eyes held the rabid fervor of the crazed zealot.

The fierce wind howled and slapped at me and I lost my temper. "Hey, Jesus! If you and these Arab thugs want to break a criminal buddy out of prison, go right ahead. But do not use the holy Koran as a cover for such unholy acts. Nowhere in the Koran does it sanction the murder of innocents, for your cause or any other."

"Stupid woman, what do you know of such things?"

"Obviously more than you if you believe the great prophet Mohammed sanctioned the killing of innocent men, women and children."

Then Jesus spat at me, but the wind, that whipped my body and tormented my flesh, halted the phlegm inches before it could reach my face. The spittle hung there for a second and then was flung out to the water. With unbridled anger, he sprouted at me a memorized verse from the Koran in Arabic.

"أنّ الله قد فصل الخبيث من الطيب ، ووضع شرير على آخر ، ثم كومة معا ،
ثم يلقي بها في جهنم . هذه في الحقيقة هي الخاسرة. سورتا 8:37"

Even as freezing and petrified as I was, I held myself still and did not flinch. I returned his stare and then calmly translated his quote. "That Allah may separate the wicked from the good, and put the wicked one upon another, then heap them together, then cast them into hell. These indeed are the losers. Sutra 8:37." His surprise registered briefly in his features. "Like many with only hate in their hearts, you quote from Koran only to suit your own murderous purposes. If you had paid more attention to your lessons, your Imam would have taught you that that verse reveals what Allah will do, not what man is to do. If you were a true man of faith, you would also know the next verse of that chapter," I said and then uttered the remaining passage, first in Arabic and then in English. "أو قتل جريمة لارتكابه ذلك كان سواء -- شخص أي بذبح واضافاذا شخص أي كان واذا : كله الشعب بذبح أنه لو كما سيكون -- الأرض في الإفساد أنقذت حياة ، سيكون كما لو أنه أنقذ حياة شعب بألكمله If anyone slew a person — be it for murder or for spreading mischief in the land — it would be as if he slew the whole people: And if anyone saved a life, it would be as if he saved the life of the whole people."

Jesus moved away from the railing and strode toward me, but I did not budge. Eyes on fire and eyebrows raised, he screamed, "Woman, that is enough! I do not have to put up with such insolence from you."

He approached me and stopped, his angry face inches from mine. Standing directly in front of me, finger on the trigger of the rifle, he was so close that all else was blotted from my view. I had passed the point of no return and decided if I was going to die, I would not do so cowering and begging for my life. Behind me, I felt hands trying to pull me back away from the terrorist, but I shook them off, held my ground and glared, unflinching, back at my captor. Jesus broke the stare first, turned away, took a step back and I released a small breath.

Then I saw him whirl back and raise the AK-47 at my face. Finger on the trigger, he yelled, "I will teach you how insolent women are to be treated!"

Chapter 31

"Mr. Samson, I'm sorry to disturb you, sir, but you have a call on line one," said the Director's secretary. "It's James Cromer."

Samson glanced though the glass at the huge windows at the dome of the Capitol. He noticed the rain was back, slashing against the pane. It choked the air, darkening the sky and his mood. Within five seconds, his phone rang and he picked it up.

"Harold Samson."

"Well, Harry, old buddy!" called the voice on the other end of the line. "It's Jim Cromer."

Samson didn't detect any anxiety in his greeting and he relaxed a bit. "Well, Jim, how are things at HBE?"

"A little tense, Director. A little tense," answered Cromer, four hundred miles away. "I can tell you this. I'll be glad when this son-of-a-bitch is juiced!"

"I'm sure you will, Jim," Harold said. "Are the natives unusually restless?"

"About what you'd expect," said James Cromer. "After I got that call from the President, I talked to my bosses. They gave the okay to use as much overtime as I needed, so I've put all the guards on double shifts. It's probably overkill, but better safe than sorry."

"Probably a smart move. Jim, I have to keep this short. I'm due at the White House in a few minutes." Samson gathered up the folder his assistant had dated and organized, and slid it inside his briefcase. "Is everything okay? Any particular reason you called?"

"Oh, yeah. Well, you told me to keep you personally informed if anything happened, anything at all. Right?"

"Yeah, what do you got?"

"I just got a call from the Hammerville Police Chief, Jeff Barker. He called to check to make sure everything was all right out here at the prison. He said he'd gotten a prank 911 call for help from the high school and wanted to make sure we were okay here at the prison."

Harold stopped his preparations. "What did the caller say? Was he sure it was just a prank?"

"The caller yelled something about an attack on the high school. Apparently, they get a couple of these calls a year, you know when students want to get out of a test or something," Jim Cromer explained. "So before they roll a unit, they have a procedure that they call the school to double-check."

"And everything checked out?"

"I guess so," continued the HBE Warden. "He said Marie, that's the 911 operator, called the school and one of the janitors answered the phone. He said it had been a prank call from a student and the kid was getting grilled in the principal's office."

"Did you say the janitor answered the phone?" Harold's fingers reached behind the black and beige bow tie and tugged at it.

"Yeah, it was lunch time and I guess everybody else was in the cafeteria." Neither one spoke for a few seconds and then Cromer said, "Harold, are you there?"

"Yeah, I'm here. Did they run a squad car out to the high school?"

"Not yet. He said they were going to make a stop on their regular patrol route, in about an hour, I think." When Samson didn't respond, Cromer said, "Harold?"

"Okay. Follow up and have them make sure everything is okay at the high school."

"Sure."

"And then get back to me."

"Can do, Harold. In the meantime, don't let the big guys push you around too much."

"I'm not worried about the big guys. I'm worried about the bad guys," Samson said. "Gotta go. Call Joyce if anything breaks. She'll catch up with me. I'm due at the big house."

Chapter 33

"Strip off your clothes!" Jesus screamed at me.

Expecting a bullet, I was so stunned at his incredible demand that I couldn't move. "What?" I got out.

"Teacher, are you stupid <u>and</u> hard of hearing? I said take off all your clothes! Now!" A burst of gunfire exploded at my feet. I jumped back and fell into Jerod, who caught me. When he helped me to my feet, Jesus screamed, "Take off your clothes or I will rip them off in front of all these students! I will educate these children how insolent whores are to be treated!"

I looked helplessly at the students and teachers staring at me, mouths agape. Even though I tried to control it, embarrassment flooded my face and seeing the red in my cheeks resurrected the sneer on my captor's face. He nudged his partner and smiled in smug victory.

Here! my mind raced, outside, in the freezing cold? He must be crazy! In front of the students and my friends? I cannot do that! I will not do that! I shrieked inside my head.

Then, staring into the gray gun barrel, I quickly recognized that I had no choice. I fought to regain some composure. I figured that if I did not comply immediately, Jesus might begin firing again, this time maybe into the crowd, and take pleasure doing it. I had already resigned myself to the fact my death might well be imminent, but I was not about to allow my modesty to rush that fate onto my students.

Slowly I unwrapped my arms from my body. My grip around my middle had been so tight that I had bruised my ribs. The bracing cold wind struck me again, like a giant taunting hand. Up to that point, I had been locked in a battle so fierce, that I had been almost immune to the freezing temperatures, or at least hadn't noticed them. The instant I took my arms away, the cold invaded again and my whole body began to shake. I reached down and slowly removed my black shoes, one by one, and laid them next to me on the soaked deck. Then I tugged at each black sock, pulling them off my feet with a sharp yank and set them inside the shoes. I set my bare feet down on the sleet-covered wood. The biting cold invaded through my exposed soles and began crawling up my legs like a poisonous snake. On shaky feet, I straightened back up.

The two terrorists were both leering at my embarrassment. Each was taking turns elbowing the other and rubbing his groin. Allah's sacred army, my ass!

It took little imagination to envision what they had planned for me, in front of these students. I tried to steel myself. I glanced back and noticed all the students and teachers were still watching me, eyes glued in horrid fascination. I wanted to tell them look away. Don't you know this is what he wants, for you to watch me being humiliated? But I said nothing. I tried to keep my movements calm and controlled, fighting to hold on to some semblance of composure, even as I was shaking from the frigid temperatures and icy fear.

I pulled the new red sweater over my head and dropped it onto the shoes, exposing my rapidly numbing flesh and the pink-flowered bra I had bought at Victoria's Secret the previous week. Strangely, standing there half-naked, it flitted through my mind that I had purchased the bra with amorous intentions. I remembered standing there in front of the mirror in the fitting room, turning and modeling the bra, imagining how it might look to a lover. Did I pretend that to be Jerod, or God forbid, Jesus? Shame made me shiver at the thought.

Now detached, surrealism and numbness replaced my earlier embarrassment and I watched as tiny snowflakes drifted onto my bare arm, beautifully white, settling against my skin before they melted. I saw Tess and Zoë turn away, refusing to look at my exposed body, pity and fear mingled in their eyes. Then, I sighted Rashid, standing in the back of the huddled students, or at least I thought I saw him. Surprised, I stopped.

"Hurry up!" yelled Jesus. "We do not have all day," and then both men laughed again.

I unzipped the front of my pants, and using both hands, slowly pulled down my black slacks and stepped out of the legs, one at a time. Then I deposited them on top of the other clothes. The two terrorists elbowed each other again, pointing at me and shouting derisive phrases in Arabic. I looked down at my own partially exposed body for the first time, at the goose bumps erupting everywhere on my skin, like angry blisters. Impatient, Jesus motioned with his automatic weapon, indicating for me to finish.

My glance darted back to the crowd of students. Rashid was no longer there, or maybe never was. The students turned away and shielded their eyes, refusing to look.

Reaching behind my back, I unhooked my bra and slid the straps off my shoulders and gathered the top together in my right hand. I let it drop from my hand, without watching it fall to the wood. Woodenly, like I've done a thousand times before, I repeated the process with my panties, idly recalling that they matched the floral bra. Then I raised myself up and stood naked, facing the terrorists.

Within seconds, my composure began slipping and my body shook violently. Instinctually, I reached my arms back around in front of me, not concerned with modesty, searching only for any protection from the freezing wind. Another blast struck my face, forcing tears down my cheeks. I could feel the goose bumps spread from my torso down both my legs and I crossed them in another vain attempt to retain some body heat. Feeling my body temperature dropping, I was getting faint as the seconds ticked by. Oddly, at that moment I remembered hearing the weatherman predict the "wind-chill" temperatures would be in the single digits for the day and I shivered more, silently cursing the guy who invented "wind chill."

As I stood there alone, my whole body trembling now, I felt a hand touch my shoulder. Dazed, it took me a moment to respond and when I looked up, I saw Jerod slipping his jacket around my shoulders. He patted my arm and I gave him a weak smile and tried to say "Thank you," but no sound came out.

"No!" Jesus yelled and burst from his position by the rail. His boots clamored across the wet slats and he was upon us in seconds. In an instant, he pulled the rifle off his shoulder and swung the butt. It connected with Jerod's skull. Stunned, I watched in horror as Jerod fell, his hands flying to his sides before he collapsed onto the wooden deck.

I screamed his name, but he lay motionless, face up on the wood. Trembling, I bent over, reaching down to check his breathing. My tears rolled from my face to his, and I watched them, in a slow motion free fall, splash onto his lips. But before I could place my hand on his chest, Jesus yanked me up by my hair and tore the jacket off my shoulders, throwing it down. My body shuddered again as the frigid air knifed against my exposed skin.

I don't know that much about the effect of freezing temperatures upon a body, but I knew enough to know that my body was slipping into hypothermia. I knew I didn't have long.

I heard some pushing and shoving behind me, but was too spent now to turn around. Then I heard a familiar voice. "Okay, Jesus, we get it. We're sorry," Christie said and I saw her come up beside me, trying weakly to smile. "We're sorry for everything. You win. We are the bad guys, who have sinned against your people. Now please let her get her clothes back on."

"No," Jesus yelled again, whipping around to both of us. He fired two quick bursts, the pop sounds lost in the wind. I cringed and waited, but didn't feel anything. Perhaps, I'm just too numb, I thought. Then I looked over at Christie, who stood next to me with eyes wide and her lips open in a red circle. Her head tilted down and I followed her gaze. When I did, I saw a red bloom spreading in the center of her white sweater. Her hands flew to her stomach and she looked over to me, confused. Then I watched as her body crumpled onto the deck next to Jerod's motionless form.

"Oh, my god! Christie!" I cried and fell to my knees clutching at her head. "Christie! Christie!" I screamed again and began weeping uncontrollably.

Jesus strutted back to his position by the rail. "Come over here!" he commanded, gesturing with the AK-47 for effect. I refused to move. He stomped back and grabbed me by the hair again, forcing me to stand, and he pointed the rifle at my bare chest. "Over there!" he shouted, indicating the railing, "or I will begin shooting them!" The automatic weapon jerked toward the huddled students.

I edged across the deck slowly, covering the distance with difficulty, my feet and legs numbing. Anticipating I was about to get what he gave Jerod or Christie, I tried to keep my body poised to react, but it was little use. The freezing was spreading and I couldn't make myself care any more. Expecting a rape or the rifle butt or a bullet, I was caught off guard by what he said.

"Get up on the railing!"

I stared at him, listless.

"You heard me. Get up on top of that railing!" He shoved the gun roughly into my half-frozen breasts.

Whatever defiance I had was gone, eliminated by the unbearable cold and the horror of the violence. He had won. I climbed unsteadily onto the top flat rail, trying to keep an eye on the gray, freezing waters of Lake Harold and on the guns of the two terrorists. With no post to balance myself against and with little feeling left in my feet and legs, it was almost impossible to stand up, but somehow I managed. I stared down at Jesus.

"You see, Miss Sterber, as Muslims," Jesus shouted into the wind, "we hold our women in high esteem." He turned to Fadi and with his gun pointed to my exposed vulva, which was now at his eye level. "I believe the American idiom is 'to keep them on a pedestal.' " He laughed and Fadi joined in. "In exchange for such loving treatment, women know their place and perform their duties as expected."

I peered at him, no longer caring. I simply wanted it to end. Tears flooded my eyes and dripped off my face.

"But obviously, you deserve no such treatment. Now kneel down and I will show you what women like you are good for in my country."

I shuddered as I realized what he had in mind, but it didn't matter. My body refused to respond to threat or will. When I didn't move, Jesus reached up and yanked me down and I grabbed the rail to try to keep my balance. I do not know how, but with him forcing me to my knees, I managed to stay atop the top rail.

Kneeling there, wood splinters pressing into my flesh, I lowered my head, awaiting the final indignity he had planned. He bent his head down to mine. His fetid breath spread across my face and, as he spoke, the white puffs of his expelled breaths materialized like some poisonous gas. "Now where is that American insolence, Miss Sterber?" he snarled.

Thinking of Christie and Jerod, I managed to raise up my head and stared at him, eyes burning and tears dropping from my cheeks. In the only voice I could muster, a hoarse whisper, I said, "Fuck you, Jesus!"

I saw the anger explode in his eyes and the rifle butt came up so fast, I never even saw it move. The metal slammed into my head and I felt my consciousness slipping away. I must have lost my balance and fallen backwards, my body sprawling through space, my hands flailing at nothing. The last sensation I remembered was the angry slap of the freezing water against my back. Then blackness.

Chapter 33

"Tom, you worry about the interdiction efforts and you let me worry about the Congressional oversight committee!" bellowed President Gregory.

"Yes, sir," was the sheepish reply from Thomas Dickson. The reproach seemed even more dramatic because the FBI Director had almost eight inches and eighty pounds of muscle on the President.

They had been at the weekly Executive Briefing in the Situation Room for about twenty minutes and Harold Samson was already wishing he were back in his office. At least there he felt he was connected to what was going on, not sealed off in this sterile chamber. Of course, he knew he wouldn't breathe easy again until the execution of Asad Akadi, the first Islamic terrorist caught on American soil, was just a minor story on NPR's "All Things Considered." He realized it would be months and even years before it dropped off the radar of Fox News and the like. The talking heads, who masqueraded as journalists, would be milking every sensational detail out of this story for as long as they thought it would gild their ratings, or their agenda.

"Harold, what about your corner of my empire?" the President asked. "Is everything still on track for the Akadi execution?"

"Mr. President, I spoke with Warden Cromer just a few minutes before I came here," Harold Samson said. "And he told me that everyone is pretty jumpy, but his staff is fully prepared and waiting."

"Okay, that's what I want to hear."

"Of course, Mr. President, I'll feel a lot better after the execution is history and we've moved on to our next crisis."

"Harold, in today's world, we never seem to be short on those." The President rapped the top of the table with the cheap pen in his right hand. "Tom, your boys picked up anything on the two dead Arabs...?" He turned to the FBI Director for the names.

"Mohammed Armdi and the second vic still unknown," replied Tom Dickson, his big form shifting uncomfortably in his chair, not anxious to endure a second thrashing from his boss, "No, sir--"

His answer was cut off by the insistent beep of the intercom on the table.

"Forgive me, Mr. President," the voice of Marilyn Cook, the president's secretary filled the room. "I have a call for Mr. Samson and I think he--and you-

-might need to hear this." "MC," as she was known, had served four presidents before Ryan Gregory and had heard it all. Her voice was measured and calm.

"Okay, Marilyn, who is it?" said the President.

"Sir, it's Joyce Caster, Mr. Samson's secretary," she began and Harold felt every eye in the room on him. "She says that she has Warden Cromer on the line..."

"Put Joyce through," Samson called, louder than he meant to.

"Mr. Samson, Warden Cromer has called twice before and now he is on the line and is insisting on talking with you right now," the Homeland Security secretary said.

"Patch him through then." In the brief seconds that followed, Samson's eyes met the questioning glances around the table.

"Harry?" The voice of James Cromer came through. The one word was tinged with anxiety.

Harold said quickly. "Jim, I'm here with President Gregory, Tom Dickson and Dean Settler, and you're on speaker."

"Good afternoon, Mr. President."

"Warden, what's happening at HBE?" asked the President without preamble.

"Yes, Mr. President, well, I'm not really sure, sir."

"What the hell does that mean?" yelled Settler.

Samson broke in. "Jim, what is it? Just tell me why you called."

"Okay, Harry. I got a call from John Tupes, he's the guard on the west watchtower. He called in a few minutes ago and he said that he saw what looks like hundreds of people, students, I guess, on the deck at the school in the snow," started Jim Cromer.

"What are they doing?"

"He can't tell. Harry, he's almost half a mile away, and even with those powerful binoculars he can't make out that much. John said he thought he saw one or two of the students with guns, but he said he wasn't sure."

"You know this guy. Is he reliable?"

"He's been with us from the start and yes, he's been reliable."

"Jim, I hear a but in your voice."

"Well, I went up to his station in the watchtower and looked myself, but I couldn't make anything out that far away. But my eyesight's a whole lot worse than John's."

"What did they say at the school?" Samson said.

"That's the problem. We've called a couple of times and all we get is a busy signal."

"Did Chief Barker get a car out there yet?"

"He was going to, but I don't know if that's happened yet," responded the warden.

"Have him get a car out there now and then get back to me," ordered Samson without waiting for confirmation.

"Can do, Harry."

"I've got a better idea." Dickson spoke up for the first time, his voice strong. "You got an Agency copter on the helipad, a Bell Jet Ranger, don't you."

"Yes, we do, until the execution," said Cromer.

"Fire it up and fly it over there and get right back to us!" Dickson ordered.

"Yessir, Mr. Dickson," Cromer said.

"Okay, Jim, as soon as the pilot has a look, call us back," said Gregory, his tone softer. "Just keep everybody calm down there, okay?"

"We'll do our best, Mr. President."

Chapter 34

Yassim spoke little as he and Mustafa left the main hallway and turned the corner to the main office, their steps brisk. Yassim's stride was strong and purposeful as befits a man in charge, in control. Now, he was here, he thought, finally to the destiny Allah had called him to. He thought again of Fatima and Jamal and the long, tortuous road that had brought him here and he sighed with resignation. His heart ached anew as he realized his son, with those searching, brown eyes, would never reach the age of the youngest of these spoiled American teenagers. Today though, it was Allah's wish that Jamal's death, and the deaths of thousands of other Muslim children whose final vision in this life was of some fiery American bomb, be avenged and the Sheik had chosen Yassim as the instrument of that revenge.

As the empty rooms flashed by in quick succession, he again scanned the open doorways, ensuring that everyone had been rousted into the cafeteria. In the classrooms they passed, he noticed a few possessions of the students, no doubt left behind in the rush to comply with the principal's order. An expensive book bag strewn on the floor, a tattered camouflaged jacket hanging over a chair, a crumpled hat with a sports logo--all reminders of the students and adults whose fate was now in his hands. If it was Allah's plan that these American children were to be sacrificed to avenge Jamal and his Muslim brothers, so be it, thought Yassim.

The two terrorists went through the office door and Mustafa removed the chair wedged against the door handle. Yassim flung open the door. They found Principal Thompson at his computer, typing furiously at the keys. The tall, thin man halted suddenly as the terrorists came in through the doorway and his gaunt face went ashen at the sight of the two guns. Without a word, Yassim opened fire and a stream of bullets shattered the monitor. Thompson screamed "No!" and dove to the floor, hands to his face. The shooting stopped as abruptly as it began and the room got deathly quiet. Smoke hung visibly in the air pungent with cordite. Flying shards from the disintegrating computer had cut holes in Thompson's sleeve and lashed his right arm. Blood stained his shirt cuffs crimson. The principal grabbed his wrist and winced.

"Get up! We must go!" shouted Yassim.

Still holding one wrist, the principal struggled to lift himself up and Yassim motioned with a shake of his head to Mustafa. With one massive hand, the second terrorist grabbed Thompson's good arm and yanked the thin man up into a standing position. Startled, the principal threw a quick, terrified glance at Mustafa and started moving toward the door. Both terrorists followed.

None of the men spoke as they traversed the empty corridors, the only noise the sound of their shoes on the linoleum and the slap of the automatic weapons against the terrorists' bodies. As the threesome turned into the hallway to the cafeteria, Yassim asked, "Do you hear that?"

"Hear what? I don't hear anything," explained Mustafa.

"That's what I mean." The cell leader accelerated his pace to a trot. Mustafa, pushing the principal, had to speed up to make sure they both kept up. In seconds, they had covered the distance and arrived at the rear of the lunchroom. The room was empty now, partially darkened and eerily quiet. Yassim's eyes darted around the room, taking in the overturned tables and chairs, the shattered glass littering the floor and the splattered drops of blood.

"Where are they?" Yassim shouted, his question aimed at his partner, his eyes on fire.

"What have you done with my students?" demanded a startled Thompson.

Yassim raised his rifle butt to silence the principal and Mustafa yelled "There!" as he pointed to the glass doors at the other end of the large, rectangular-shaped room. Yassim peered in the direction of the second terrorist's outstretched hand. At first he could make out nothing in the gray light outside the glass and then he saw some movement. He marched across the cafeteria toward the glass doors. His right hand on the weapon, he used his left forearm to push the bar and force the door open and stepped out onto the deck.

Immediately the howling wind struck his face and he had to briefly shut his eyes against it. When he opened them again, partially shielding them with a hand, he could make out clumps of students and teachers huddled together everywhere across the large wooden expanse. Even though he couldn't see him through the crowd, over the wind he could hear Jesus' voice somewhere at the opposite end of the deck. He stomped in that direction, shoving groups of teens and their teachers out of his way.

Guns raised, Jesus and Fadi were standing next to the rail bordering the water. Next to them were two large male students, one on each end of a tall, limp body. Yassim strode toward the other terrorists and yelled, his words lost in the wind. Obviously, his fighters did not see or hear him, their attentions fixed on the students next to them. As the cell leader approached, he saw the two male students, pale with fear or effort, swing the body toward the building and then back. As the body came up in the swing, Yassim could see it was a large, adult man with brown hair and blood on his temple. Before he could reach the group, the two students used their momentum to swing the body back over the railing and, at the highest point in the arc, released him. The cell leader came up to the edge of the railing just in time to see the body slap the freezing water.

"What is going on here?" Yassim barked at Jesus.

Jesus slid his foot off the railing and stood upright. "Yassim, you are back. Great!" he exclaimed.

"Jesus, what is going on here?" The cell leader's hard green eyes indicated the water, where the bubbles were just subsiding from the splash.

"Oh, that," said Jesus. "That, that is nothing. That was a man who tried to interfere in our plan and will do so no more." He grinned and waited.

"And this?" Yassim pointed to a pool of red on the wooden slats.

"That was an impertinent woman who also tried to stop us. I have taken care of her as well."

Yassim's glance went back to the water and then to the crowds of students and teachers standing, shivering on the deck. He looked at Jesus again and asked, "What are you doing out here?"

Jesus smiled broadly. "It was such a beautiful day!"

"Jesus!"

"Well, to be honest, leader, I thought I needed to teach these arrogant young Americans a lesson."

Yassim glanced around the deck, taking in the students and adults cowering together closer to the building and shouted above the wind, "The lesson is over. They could die out here. They are no good to us dead, at least not yet." The cell leader turned and stared through the gray mist rising over the white-capped waters. He knew precisely where the prison that held another of Allah's soldiers was, but he could see nothing of it in this weather. "Besides, if anything happens, we are all too exposed out here."

Yassim gestured over to the huddled crowd, "Let's start moving this crowd back into the building." Glancing around again, he asked, "Where is Rashid?"

"He is over there, cowering with the rest of them," said Jesus, pointing to the left side of the crowd. "I spoke with him and he said you wanted him to remain among the students."

Yassim nodded and looked in the direction Jesus had indicated, but couldn't locate Rashid among the huddled students. He turned back and his steel gray eyes met the gazes of Jesus and Fadi. "Get these students and teachers back into the building."

Jesus and Fadi yelled into the wind, "Okay, get moving! Everybody inside!"

The freezing Americans needed little encouragement as the crowd immediately turned toward the doors and tried to hurry, though with cold, numbing limbs, it was difficult for many. Then he turned back to Mustafa and his prisoner.

"What about him?" Mustafa called above the wind, indicating Thompson.

"Take him back inside..." Yassim stopped, his ears cocked in the direction of the lake.

"What is it?" Mustafa asked loudly, seeing the sudden shift in the cell leader.

"Quiet!" screamed Yassim, straining to hear the noise over the movement of the hostages back inside. Then recognition dawned on his face and he shouted at the top of his lungs, "Everyone inside now!" and he fired several shots into the air. The crowd lurched forward, knocking each other down, cramming into the doorways.

Yassim scanned the sky over the lake and then shouted, "Mustafa, get the RPG! Quickly!"

Mustafa bolted for the doors, forcing students out of his way and disappeared inside. Yassim's gaze alternated impatiently between the sky above the waters and the doors where Mustafa had gone. In less than sixty seconds, Mustafa was bursting back through the doors. A large metal cylinder in hand, he ran to the edge of the deck where Yassim still stood. He pulled up alongside Yassim, knelt and then lifted the rocket launcher to his shoulder.

"Not yet, my friend," Yassim placed his hand on the man's shoulder. "Let's wait to see who our visitors are."

Eyes to the sky, both men remained motionless. Behind them the students struggled through the open doors, the collected bodies like moving streams into *an open drain. The sound from the sky grew louder and more distinct, though they could still see nothing because of the cloud cover. Yassim was sure what it was. A helicopter, probably a Bell, he thought, and no doubt from the prison. The sheriff wouldn't have anything like that. As they stared at the sky, the blue shape of the helicopter materialized out of the gray mist. The first thing visible was the large letters "FBI" on the side.*

Yassim smiled and said, "Mustafa, as soon as you get a sure shot."

Mustafa nodded, adjusted the long, black cylinder on his shoulder and focused through the eyepiece, studying his target. The flame shot from the barrel. His eyes quickly shifted to the sky where the helicopter was hovering over the water still several hundred yards from the deck. In a few seconds, a fiery ball exploded in the gray sky where the copter had been. Still fascinated, he watched as it hung briefly in the air.

Then, just as suddenly, it dropped from the sky and slammed into the water, the fires releasing steam as the shell of the helicopter descended into the lake. Mustafa stood up from his crouch and let the end of the launcher lean on the deck and together they watched the water. No figures emerged from the water where the wreckage disappeared.

"Now it has begun," Yassim announced.

Chapter 35

Rashid clutched the sweater of the small girl in front of him, as the student throng shoved through the too narrow opening. Freezing and terrified, they had bolted for the three sets of doors as soon as Yassim had given the order, stampeding out of the cold like a herd of terrified animals. That was what they had become, Rashid realized. He held tightly to the other student because he wanted, needed to stay on his feet and get into the lunchroom. In the wilds of Afghanistan he had witnessed what could happen to animals that didn't move with the herd in a stampede and he wasn't about to let himself be trampled by these cowardly American children.

So he held onto her, he thought her name was Brittany. He wasn't sure; there were so many girls named Brittany, he got them confused. She was a skinny rail of a girl, and he held on until they were through the doors and into the surprising warmth of the cafeteria. Rashid didn't know if Brittany, or whatever her name was, noticed that he had a hold of the back of her sweater, but she helped to get him through the frightened, pulsing throng. He let go and walked a little way off by himself, trying to edge into the partial darkness of the huge pillar on the side of the room.

Surreptitiously he tried to keep an eye on the students and the only teacher nearby. Obviously anxious and nervous, the fat American teacher--he thought her name was Mrs. Striker--and the scared students were whispering quietly to each other. They seemed concerned with consoling each other and didn't seem to even notice him. Dressed in a pair of faded jeans and a "No Fear" shirt, Rashid looked like just any other teen, except for his olive skin. But the students and teachers around seemed both relieved and terrified and they all were too self-absorbed to even give Rashid a thought. He was glad; that was as he had planned it.

When Rashid received his orders, the cell leader had been clear. "You are to stay hidden among the students. Go to school and do not call attention to yourself."

Rashid sighed. He realized that he had gotten lucky yesterday. If Jesus had not warned him, Jerod would have found him and he would have had to answer some difficult questions. That could have led to problems just a day before the exercise, though he hadn't known the day then.

Why had Yassim not thought he could tell him the day? Was he not to be trusted? He bent down and picked up the backpack he had hidden behind the pillar and checked to make sure it had not been bothered. Looking around to be sure he wasn't being watched, he made a quick inspection of the contents. Satisfied, he zipped it back up and laid it back next to the pillar again.

"On the day of the delivery, you will be treated like all the rest of the students," Yassim had said in that hotel room.

When he did not go on, Rashid had asked, "What do you want me to do?"

"Stay among them. Watch them. Listen to their talk. You will know if you need to contact one of us."

"Is that all?" Rashid had asked.

"No!" the cell leader said. "You have been trained like the rest of us. We will need you...when the time comes."

"How will I know when you want me to act?"

"Watch for my signal."

The young fighter knew better than to ask more.

Rashid moved around the pillar so he had a clear view of Yassim and the other terrorists who had reentered the cafeteria. The four men, the AK-47 automatic rifles draped across the front of their bodies, stood like sentries across the front of the lunchroom. His eyes roamed the crowd of teachers and students and noted, with some satisfaction, the paralyzing fear etched into the faces of the hostages. His stare landed on Yassim's face and he thought he noticed the slightest of recognition, a brief flash in the eyes. Surely the cell leader had not given the signal, Rashid assured himself.

In his head he repeated the names of his fellow fighters, a mental exercise, in case he would need to pull them up quickly. Yassim, Fadi, uh, Mustafa, yes, and, of course, Jesus.

He did not understand Jesus. Even though Miss Sterber, like all Americans, was an enemy, what he did to her was not necessary. Jesus' treatment of her was not what he had been taught in his lessons in the camps.

Of course, Jesus had been right, it is not a woman's place to correct a man and it is true that she attempted to demean him in front of these captives. Yes, she did twist the words of the prophet from the Koran to fit her meaning, trying even in this to better Jesus. But Allah would not approve of demeaning any woman so, Rashid thought. He had been taught that if your enemies embarrass or ridicule you, you may take the sword to them, but you do not humiliate them. At one point, it even looked like Jesus was going to force her to commit an obscene act, right there in front of the students. If he intended to execute her all along, her humiliation was not necessary, he thought. Since Miss Sterber was so strong and would not yield, it only made Jesus look to be the weak one.

Or, Rashid pondered, perhaps he felt this way because Miss Sterber was one of the only teachers who seemed to actually take an interest in him. He got the feeling that he was not simply a curiosity to her, that when she was asking about him, she was truly concerned. Of course, he could not have anyone asking about his family or his background so he had dismissed her questions, but he had to admit it was comforting to have someone interested in you just as you are, not for what they can get from you.

She did correct him also in class, he remembered, but even then she did not allow the other students to abuse him, at least when she could control it. And she had even allowed him to accompany her for the interview of Asad. He knew that Miss Sterber was suspicious of why he wanted to go to the prison and surely the others students must have been very upset with her selecting him over them, but still she allowed him to go to HBE to deliver his message.

Rashid shrugged his shoulders, not knowing what to think. Besides, his concern is too late; she was dead now.

The detour of his thoughts was jolted back to the front of the crowded, noisy lunchroom. In one of the few remaining bright lights, automatic weapon ready to fire, Yassim was yelling again. "Everyone listen!" Rashid did.

Chapter 36

"Dad, why do you like it so much here?" I asked, looking up at him with wide eyes.

"Let's see if you can guess, pumpkin," my father responded as we strolled, hand in hand, on the well-worn trail inside Mohican State Forest. We had visited this spot several times before and he called it "our secret hideaway." With its tall pillars of pine, the little clearing deep in the woods was tranquil and incredibly beautiful, like some sacred forest cathedral. I loved the quiet time with my dad. No doubt, my love for the outdoors was given birth in that little patch of forest.

"Tell me what you see and that may tell you why I like it here," he said to me when we arrived at "our spot."

"Well," I stared up at the green ceiling of our private woodland sanctuary. "I can see the sunlight and it looks like it's searching for cracks in the tree tops to sneak through."

"Very good, pumpkin. I couldn't 've said it better myself. Now, what do you hear?"

I crooked my head in one direction, cupping my ear with one small hand, and waited a beat before I spoke. "I hear the singing of birds and some crickets chirping, and--" I stared at my dad and lowered my head closer to the ground, "and some snakes crawling along the ground."

"You have very good hearing, Dee Dee," my dad said. He never made fun of my make-believes, just one more reason why I loved him. "If you're going to be a writer, you need to use your senses. Now here's a harder one. What do you smell?"

I wrinkled my nose at him and sniffed, testing the air. My eyes studied his figure with a question in them. "Dad, I smell...I smell something bad?" I said. "I smell stink, like Jimmy smells when he's been out playing basketball all day." I wrinkled my nose some more.

"Dad, what is that?" I asked, but got no response. "Dad? What is it that I smell?" I asked again, suddenly frightened. I shut my eyes in an effort to focus on the smell.

I opened my eyes again and it suddenly looked darker, now with only faint light everywhere I looked. When my eyes adjusted, all I could make out was gray, layers and layers of gray, as if all the colors had been washed out of my vision. And, instead of standing, I was surprised to find I was lying on my side with my head buried in something so that I could only see out of my left eye. Still half dreaming, I sniffed and the smell of human sweat permeated my nostrils. I tried to turn to free my head and look around, but when I moved, my body screamed in pain. I gasped and then heard a voice say, "It's okay. You're going to be all right."

The voice wasn't my dad. When I tried to see who was behind me speaking, an arm held me tight around my stomach, restraining my movement. When I attempted to shift, to turn over, the pain that shot through me was so intense I almost passed out. Struggling to focus, I forced my one free eye to glance down my own body. I was suddenly aware I had no clothes on. As if this realization shocked me, I began to shake uncontrollably all over.

"W-w-where am-m-m I?" I managed to get out between chattering teeth.

My mind labored to figure out where I was. I couldn't make sense of it. With all the willpower I could muster, I tried to concentrate, to force my mind to make out my surroundings. My one eye scanning wildly, I studied the gray surrounding my body, tried to take it all in. It didn't make any sense, but I recognized some clothing that looked like gray sweatshirts and sweatpants. Though it hurt to move, I was able to turn my head slightly and see a little sideways. My eyes were also able to make out the outline of a double door, a sliver of light marking the crease between the two door panels. The semidarkness enveloped me and it dawned on me that I must be on the floor, lying inside some closet.

"It's okay, you're safe. You're alive," I heard the voice behind me say quietly into my ear.

Lying there, my body aching from pain all over, I began to remember, a few flashes at a time streaking back like broken frames of a deteriorating movie. Awash in my disorientation, I fought to regain some hold on sanity, to decipher just what was going on. As soon as the memories started returning, each new one raw and angry, clawing the previous one out of the way, my fear returned. I didn't want to remember, but once the floodgates were open, it was no use. Without willing or now wanting it, I felt all over again the blast of bitter wind against my exposed flesh, the crushing blow to my head and the freezing water. And my trembling shame in front of the students. And Bob Holden, Jerod and Christie gone now! As it all came back, my eyes flooded with tears and I sobbed audibly, the sound magnified in the confined space. Then, as if the biting wind and the freezing water engulfed my exposed body all over again, my shaking became violent, my body quivering, as if the chill was permanently embedded in my bones.

I cried in a hoarse whisper, "I-I-I'm so c-c-c-cold."

I felt a strong arm wrap around my middle a little more tightly and I heard the now familiar voice. "It's goin' to be okay. You're safe now. I'll take care of ya." I realized then that I recognized the voice, and somehow that comforted me, but I couldn't quite place it. Then I felt his arm release the hand from beneath my breasts and lay it flat against my naked stomach. My modesty argued I should've been embarrassed, but I wasn't. Some part of me wanted to object, to protest, but I didn't, because the skin of the hand felt so warm against my flesh. I didn't want whoever it was to ever move his hand.

"You're freezin'!" the voice said. Then the warm hand was gone, the wonderful warmth lost and I opened my mouth to protest, but nothing came out. "I'm sorry, Dee Dee, I don' know what else t' do." It was Jerod's voice. How could that be? I saw Jesus hit him.

But it was Jerod. Through my hazy vision, I could make out his dim figure--I recognized him. He edged slightly away from me and knelt over my shivering body in the cramped quarters. I lay shivering in the pile of crumpled clothes, and it looked like Jerod, whose tall figure knelt over me, was taking off his clothes. That didn't make any sense. Why would he be getting undressed?

I turned to look, edging my head up even as the twist of my neck reignited the blazing pain. He was removing his own clothes. My confusion growing, I watched as he stripped completely and lay back down and settled his large body in next to me. He pulled a sweatshirt and pants out from underneath me and my body bumped against the floor. I winced. Then he used the clothes to spread over top of us. I tried to look at him, to catch his eyes, but his body was too long in that cramped space and all I could bring into focus was his neck. My senses dulled and my aches throbbing, I felt his naked body slide against my exposed flesh.

The incredible warmth of his flesh started to blossom onto my frigid skin. At least he's warm, wonderfully warm, was the last thought I remembered, as I felt the heat of his body radiating onto mine.

Then I was gone again.

Chapter 37

"Sir, this is James Cromer again, sir. I'm sorry, sir, I don't know how to tell you this,"

"What is it, Cromer?" snapped President Gregory.

"Sir," began the hesitant voice through the phone line. All eyes in the room stared at the speaker sitting in the center on the polished wood. "Sir, it's, it's gone."

"What? What's gone, Jim?" This time Tom Dickson fired the question, his large body leaning forward.

"The helicopter, sir," the Warden said, incredulity evident in each syllable. "I climbed up to the watchtower so I could get a better look at the helicopter. I was following it with my binoculars." He stopped and Harold could almost see his friend shaking his head in disbelief.

"And?" Dickson shouted back.

"Sir, the chopper's gone. One moment it was flying straight across the lake toward the high school, just like you directed." He took an audible breath and continued. "The next moment there was a huge explosion and then the chopper dropped into the water."

There was a pause and then the Warden said quietly, "I watched with the binoculars and I didn't see anyone get out of the helicopter."

"What the hell happened to it?" demanded the president.

"Mr. President, sir," Cromer said, "I don't know. It just exploded."

"Well, was it a bomb? Mechanical failure? Was it shot down?" President Gregory fired questions one after the other.

"It was too far away to tell for sure, but I doubt it was mechanical failure."

"There may be a way to find out, Mr. President," offered Samson. "Where are you now, Jim?"

"I'm in my office," answered the warden. "I thought we might need a secure land line for this conversation, so I came back here."

"Good thinking, Jim," said Samson, trying to settle the warden down.

"Do you want me to go to code red, Harry?" Cromer asked. "I've got the protocols ready."

"Hold on that for the moment, Jim," responded Samson. "First, patch me through to communications, will you?"

Samson looked up from the speaker and caught the gaze of the other three men at the table. They did not have a chance to raise any questions. A few seconds later, another, obviously younger voice came through the speakerphone. "This is David Wise, IT."

"David, this is Harold Samson in Washington. David, you're on the speaker with President Gregory, Director Dickson and Chief of Staff Dean Settler."

"Yes, sir, Mr. President. What can I do for you?"

"David, you're aware that we may have a situation out there at HBE?" Samson asked.

"Yes, sir, Mr. Samson, but we're not exactly sure what we have."

"That's what we're trying to find out, David," Harold replied coolly. "You have the feed from all the cameras there video-streamed into your archives, don't you?"

"Yes, sir, Mr. Samson. We archive an entire week from all one hundred forty-eight cameras around the prison."

"What about the camera from the FBI helicopter?"

"Yes sir, we have that as well, but the video's not as clear because it's bounced back to us."

"Okay, David, here's what I want you to do." Harold pulled out his PDA and turned it on. "I want you to isolate the video from the helicopter for today and stream it to the address I'm going to give you. You ready?"

"Yes sir, give me a chance to download it and send it. With this equipment, it shouldn't take but a few minutes," explained Wise.

Samson rattled off the address and said, "Thank you, son." He got up from the table and walked to a computer console at the rear of the room and began striking keys, explaining as he went. "Mr. President, if you will watch that monitor," he pointed to the third large screen display, "the video should come up there. The camera on the helicopter is automatically activated when the engine is started, so you should be able to see the film from the beginning of the flight. On the Bell, I believe the camera is mounted front right, just below the windshield, but there's no sound as the blades would drown everything out."

He returned to his seat at the table and, as all four men watched, the screen brightened. No one spoke as the projected image came alive on the monitor and then the picture bounced with the take off of the helicopter. The video swooped over the prison compound as the pilot banked and turned. The camera's view captured the water, the wind from the blades blowing up small whitecaps, as the helicopter skimmed not far off the surface. Then the water fell away as the Bell climbed to a higher altitude and there was little visible in the picture but gray mist.

For ten seconds, it was as if someone had drawn gauze over the camera lens. All four men squinted toward the display, straining to make out anything in the gray fog. Finally, the dim outlines of a building emerged from the mist and they were able to make out the rear of the high school.

The camera lens captured the deck at the rear of the building and they could make out a large number of individuals on the deck. Samson rose from his chair and edged nearer to the screen to get a better look, trying to stay out of the others' view. He peered at the display and was able to make out scores of people scurrying into the building, moving away from the camera. Then two men emerged from the throng and came toward the camera. One of the men raised something on his shoulder, something that looked like a pipe. After a beat, a flash erupted from just behind the man. A split second later, the picture jumped and turned away from the school. Two seconds later, the screen went blank.

"God dammit! That son-of-a-bitch just shot down our Bell helicopter," Tom Dickson screamed at the now blank screen, breaking the silence of the room. "That helicopter cost my budget $3.5 million dollars and they just blew it out of the sky!" He paused a second and then added, "To say nothing of the two good men who were piloting the chopper."

"Well, Harold, I think we just found your terrorists," muttered President Gregory. "Looks like you knew what you were talking about. Dean, get Garcia in here. I don't care if it is his daughter's birthday, tell him to get his ass in here."

"Will do, Mr. President," replied Dean Settler.

"Obviously, we need a better assessment of the situation," the President said. "Tom, what do you recommend?"

Wresting his gaze from the blank display, the FBI Director said, "Maybe, we should move some of the troops from the prison to put them in place by the high school."

"Harold?" President Ryan asked.

"Tom's idea has merit, sir," Harold said, "and we need to have a better idea of exactly what's going on at the high school. But, Mr. President, it's possible that's exactly what the terrorists want us to do. To move troops away from the prison."

As soon as Samson finished, the intercom phone beeped.

"Yes, Marilyn?"

"Joyce Caster, Mr. Samson's secretary, sir."

"Put her through," Ryan Gregory snapped.

"Mr. Samson?"

"Go ahead, Joyce," Samson said.

"Sir, we just received a fax that I think you and the President will want to see. May I send it there?"

"Do it now, Joyce."

Five seconds later, Harold jumped out of his chair and retrieved the fax. He slid the single sheet across the polished cherry surface of the table. Dickson rose and stood behind the President, peering at the fax.

President Gregory picked up the fax and read it carefully, taking his time but did not utter a word. The he set the single sheet of paper down and read aloud the few words printed in huge letters.

FREE ASAD, FEARLESS SOLDIER OF ALLAH OR SEND YOUR CHILDREN TO MEET HIM IN PARADISE TONIGHT
   --ALLAH'S FAVORED SONS

He slapped his hand down on the white sheet of paper. "God damn it!"

Chapter 39

I lay there, my eyes shut, and basked in the feel of the sun beaming on my face, radiating its life-giving heat. My body felt so much better, no longer frozen but warmer, wonderfully warmer. I could even sense a warm breeze on my hair. I curled my body and nuzzled closer into something comfortable. Perhaps this was heaven, I thought. Content and willing to chance it, I opened my eyes slowly.

It took a few seconds for my vision to focus and I was dragged sluggishly back to reality. I was not sunning myself on any sandy beach--and this sure as hell wasn't heaven--but instead I lay in some dark closet, staring up at Jerod's neck and feeling his hot breath on the top of my head. As consciousness ebbed back, I noticed our naked bodies were wrapped around one another. The embrace, if you could call it that, was anything but erotic. It was more like a desperate, protective clasp. His arms encircled my chest and his legs wrapped around my butt and legs, pulling me tight into him. And as reality dawned, unlike the fantasy of my recent dream, I realized I wasn't exactly warm. In fact, I was still chilled, but I was no longer freezing and could feel my body temperature rising. My body was sore and my head pounded where I had been hit. But, after a rest and some warming, the pains were more subdued, as if God had dialed the pangs back a notch.

I glanced across at Jerod; my rescuer was still asleep. Secretly, I hoped he wouldn't awake, at least not just yet. The touch of his skin on mine emanated such incredible warmth and comfort, that I didn't want it to end. I tried to tell myself that it was just the assurance of his body safely enfolding mine. Just that I was lying here alive and for the moment safe.. Okay, who was I kidding? Lying there naked, pore to pore, next to a man that I didn't know all that well, I should've been embarrassed. I'm usually pretty modest and would've thought I'd at least be uncomfortable. But I wasn't. Coming face to face with your imminent death can alter your perspective on a few things. To tell you the truth, right then what I really wanted was to just lie there and let him take care of me. I didn't want to play the heroine any more. Instead, I was the damsel in distress. A day earlier, I would've objected loudly; right then, it felt perfectly natural.

Tentatively, I stretched out my index finger to touch Jerod's upper arm and noticed that his skin had cooled considerably. Lying there, in that odd but comfortable embrace, I remembered the lesson taught in those required first aid classes.

"If you are outdoors in the freezing cold and you come upon a body whose temperature is dropping rapidly," explained Nurse Hedges to our group of teachers, "you need to find some way to raise the body temperature quickly or the person can go into hypothermia, shock or even die. If you don't have any other way--blankets, fire or warm shelter--one way you can save a freezing person is to lie close to them, your naked body against theirs, allowing the heat from your body to literally transfer from your skin to theirs."

Jerod had just saved my life.

He stirred then. "Are ya' awake?" he whispered.

"Yes," I tried to say, but all that came out was a single croaked syllable, my voice hoarse beyond recognition.

"You okay?" he asked.

"Yeah. I think so," I managed.

"Good," he said and pulled his arms tighter around my body. "Good."

One part of my brain recognized that this was a strange, forced intimacy. But at the same time I realized that this was the closest I've been to a man for a long time, and it felt good.

"Are you still cold?" Jerod asked faintly and I realized he wasn't merely whispering. He was hoarse as well.

I started to reassure him that I was better, was going to be all right, but then stopped. It occurred to me that he was probably being considerate and trying to respect my modesty. I figured he wanted to know if he should move his body away from mine. Fearing the sudden loss of his intimate warmth, I desperately didn't want him to move. I needed his protective embrace.

"I'm still pretty cold," I said, which was true enough. I was relieved when he shifted his naked body, wrapping his arms and legs a little more tightly around mine, and then adjusted the makeshift cover of sweats around us both.

I lay there, in his arms, desperate to know his thoughts. Without looking at him, I asked, "Why did you do that?"

"You were freezin' and shivering' something awful," Jerod said, "and I didn't know what else to do. From the EMT classes I took, I knew you were suffering from hypothermia and shock."

"Thank you. I realize that now. I meant up on the deck. You had to know you could get killed trying to help me." I turned my face up toward his.

"I dunno, I didn't think," he responded, looking down at my eyes. "I just saw what Jesus was tryin' to do and just couldn't stand by. I couldn't let that sadistic asshole get away with humiliating you."

"But, Jerod, you don't even know me that well. And besides, I haven't always been nice to you." Right there, in the vulnerability of my nakedness, it dawned on me that Jerod may not be the self-absorbed jerk that I originally thought.

"I think I know you pretty well. I've been in your classroom for a couple of months now and I've seen ya work with kids," he answered. "Besides, I saw what you were tryin' to do. You were trying to protect your students and keep them from getting killed. Perhaps you forgot that our Arab brothers don't have as high a regard for women as the all-American male."

I glanced around, trying to puzzle out where we were. "Jerod, what happened? How did we get here? I don't remember anything after I hit the water."

"I don't exactly know. I'd guess the collision with the freezin' water knocked you unconscious, but I didn't see that." He took a breath and relaxed his grip on me a bit. "I was knocked out after Jesus hit me with his rifle and I didn't come to till I was in the water. I woke up swallowin' half the lake and got myself to the surface, spittin' and coughing up water, that's when I saw you going under. I swam down but the water was so dark, I couldn't find you." He looked at me, tension in his face. "I grabbed a quick breath and went down two more times, but still couldn't find any sign of ya. Could feel my body numbing from the cold and knew I couldn't hold out much longer."

"How did you get to me?"

"Dumb luck, I think. I was pretty sure I knew where you went down, so I took another deep breath and dove as deep as I could. I couldn't see much of anything in the water so, as I swam down, I waved my hands back and forth, just tryin' to bump into you. Just when my lungs were ready to bust, I felt your arm. I grabbed it and held on for dear life and headed to the surface."

"How did you get us out of the water without them seeing us?"

"I dunno. When I surfaced with you, I glanced up at the deck, but couldn't see anythin'. I tried to listen, but I couldn't hear a damn thing. So I dragged you out of the water under the deck, all the while expectin' to see bullets exploding around me. Didn't happen and by the time I got you up on the mud, you weren't breathin'. Then I didn't think of anything else and gave you mouth to mouth until you spit out some water, coughed a few times and started breathin' again."

We were so close in that tight space that the vision of his intent mouth on mine flooded my brain. "Yeah, but where are we?" I asked, my glance wandering around our small space.

"Well, I crawled and dragged you all the way under the deck and found a narrow window that opened into the downstairs locker room," Jerod explained. "I forced it open. The damn opening was a little tight, but I managed t' get through it and then pulled you inside. I didn't know where the terrorists were or if they'd come down here. Hell, I dunno how many there are. So I figured I had to find some place for us to hide. I found this big closet in Coach Baumer's office and thought we could hide here, at least temporarily.

"I cleared out some old football equipment, just threw it in the corner, and then found some old sweat suits and covered you with them. But I guess your body temperature had dropped too much by then, and, well..." he stumbled in his explanation for the first time. "I didn't know what else to do." Embarrassed, he lowered his chin.

With one finger, I raised his face so he was looking at me again, his eyes two round question marks. I said, "You did great," and I nuzzled up closer to him. I scooted up a little, so that our faces were even and our gazes locked. "Thanks," I said and kissed him. Nothing major, mind you, just a simple brief kiss, my lips on his for just a few seconds.

"Dee Dee, wait, Dee Dee..." he protested, but I cut him off with another kiss.

I think it was the second, more insistent kiss that did it.

Chapter 39

"Mr. President, you must act now!" Dean Settler was up at the front of the room, gesturing at the monitor that held the frozen photo of the terrorist firing at the helicopter. "This man just declared war on the United States!" He poked a bony finger at the screen.

"Obviously, we can't give Akadi up," said Garcia. "We'd be the laughingstock of the free world."

"Aside from that brilliant observation, Jerry, what do you advise?" demanded an irate Gregory. His right hand massaged his temple and then ran absently through his once perfectly styled hair. "Harold?"

Sometime in the past thirty minutes, Samson's beige and black bow tie had been released from its knot and hung, dangling down the front of his shirt. "Sir, I think we need a plan. I don't think a show of force will do much right now. Anyone who's been anywhere near Hammerville knows we have enough troops there to start a war in a small third world country." Harold let his glance move from the President to the other cabinet members. "But that didn't stop the terrorists from dropping right into the middle of those troops. Hell, we don't even know how many terrorists there are or how heavily armed they are."

"How many children are in the school?" Gregory asked.

"From the best estimates that my people can get from the locals, approximately 500, counting both students and teachers," answered Samson.

"Jesus H. Christ," said the President.

"That's exactly why we can't wait around until these lunatics start executing children," bellowed Settler, throwing a fist at the huge computer monitor again.

"Tom, any issues deploying one of your units from HBE to the school? What do you have there?" Gregory asked.

"No sir, Mr. President." Dickson looked up from the report he was studying. "I have three units in Hammerville. Two are SWAT teams and one's an Urban Assault Team. I am concerned that we don't have a Hostage Rescue Team in the vicinity and I've ordered one to be flown there from Pittsburgh. It's the closest one on alert and the HRT should arrive within the hour. We can have one of the deployed units at the school site in ten minutes, without sacrificing necessary security at the prison." He shifted his massive frame uncomfortably in the upholstered wooden chair. "Right now we're coordinating with local law enforcement. The chief's been informed of an incident at the school, but no more. He and his deputy are stationed a half-mile away on the only road to the high school, keeping the media and any others away."

"Christ, the damn media!" Gregory declared. "That's all we need." His thumb tapped furiously on the top of the pen.

"Yes, sir," shot back Dickson, "but I don't know how long we can keep the lid on this thing. If nothing else, word of the attack on our chopper has spread around the prison by now. Something's going to leak soon."

"What do you propose, Tom?" asked the President.

"I think we need a stealth frontal assault by one of the SWAT teams, who could then sweep around the back. That might give us the eyes we need as well as possibly our best chance at getting to the terrorists."

"Harold, you've been the closest to these guys all along. What do you think they will do?" asked Gregory.

"Sir, I think Tom's plan is sound but a little premature," Samson answered. "We don't know what we're dealing with yet. They know we have all these troops. We could just as easily be walking into a trap."

The President shook his head slowly. "Any response from our fax, Harry?"

"Not yet, Mr. President. We faxed it three different times already to the number we got off the first fax. We know they were transmitted successfully, all three times. But we've gotten no response back. The phone company says that fax number is in the principal's office in the north end of the school."

Samson slid his chair back, rose and walked to the shelves in the rear of the Situation Room. He retrieved a set of computer blueprints and spread the printouts on the table. "When we saw the two terrorists," he pointed to a drawing of the deck, "they were at the south end of the building with the hostages. It's possible they haven't even seen the faxes, which were sent to this part of the building, right here. But they could have just as easily seen the faxes and ignored them. Maybe they never intended to pay them any attention."

"What about any other communication? I can't believe there isn't any way to get them to pick up the phone?" Gregory asked.

Harold shook his head. "We've checked it out, sir. It doesn't look like it. The school was built with the new 'Voice Over IP' technology and someone who knows what they're doing has gotten in there and fixed it so the whole system is tied up."

"What about cell phones?"

"My people thought of this as well, and we've gotten the numbers of many of the staff and students in the building," continued Samson. "They've been calling them, but so far haven't gotten an answer on any of the lines."

President Gregory rubbed his hand across his temple again. "We need to get some communication inside that school. We're blind without it."

"Yes sir, we'll keep trying."

There was an extended pause in the Situation Room, and then Dean Settler broke the silence. "Sir, I realize this is not about politics, but we should not forget what happened in Russia."

"Your point, Dean?" asked the President, turning toward his Chief of Staff.

"Well, sir," began Settler hesitantly, "the election is in four days and we can't pretend that the timing of this attack is coincidental."

"We're talking about hundreds of children and adults! I'll worry about the political fallout when this crisis is over."

"You're right, Mr. President." The Chief of Staff walked over from the bank of monitors to the conference table. "I understand, sir. But please remember that Putin held back and hesitated with the Chechen rebels. Many believe that his hesitation cost hundreds of lives."

When no one responded, Settler pressed his point. "I'm just saying that inaction on our part may cost students' lives as well as costing you the election."

The silence in the room that followed Settler's challenge stretched into sixty seconds, the only sounds from the TV's and internet screens and the persistent clicking of the President's pen. All eyes turned toward Ryan Gregory, who continued to study the pages in front of him. As the powerful men around the table watched, the President's eyes drifted to the monitor, which captured the blurred image of the attacking terrorists and settled there. When his gaze returned to his team, he had made a decision.

"Tom, I want you to get one of the SWAT teams to the checkpoint and coordinate with the chief. If this thing gets out, there's going to be a veritable mob trying to get to that school--parents, journalists, nosy neighbors. The police chief's going to need all the help he can get. But I want the unit to stay there and wait until the HRT arrives. I don't want them to approach the school yet. Do you understand?"

"Yes sir, Mr. President. With your leave, sir." Tom Dickson bounded for the door.

The President turned back to Garcia. "Get your people on these two!" He pointed to the blurred figures frozen on the computer monitor. "I want to know everything about them, where they're from, who they're with! And I want it now!"

"Yes sir!" Garcia said. "We'll do everything we can, sir."

"Okay, Harold, you need to find some way to communicate with someone inside the school. It's going to be hell to know what to do, if we don't have any idea what's going on inside."

"Yes Mr. President, we'll keep at it. There's got to be something. In my experience, these guys always screw up some place. We just have to find it."

"God help us, I hope you're right, Harold," responded the President.

Chapter 40

I think it was the second, insistent kiss that did it. The first was innocent, instinctual, you know, a "thanks for saving my life" kiss. The second though was deliberate, longer, tinged with desperation. As we huddled together, naked bodies already touching, as my lips met the smoothness of his, I felt something inside me stir.

I know you probably think I was crazy. Here we were about to be killed with the building under siege and we were acting like a couple of horny teenagers. I was aching all over and terrified for us and for the students, but I wanted to shut everything else out, at least for a moment. I desperately needed to feel alive.

Jerod's southern manners tried to assert themselves and he said, "Dee Dee, you just came through a horrible shock."

But his deep-set, emerald eyes betrayed another story, so I kissed him again. This time I felt him stir at the kiss and his hands slowly unlocked their tight grip and began drifting down my back. Then, coming out of our third, even longer kiss, I shifted my body against him, easing away just an inch or so. That's what gave it away. Without looking, I felt the organ between his legs, now released from its constricted space, rise up, skittering across the flesh of my tender thighs and stiffen.

Actually, I'm glad God arranged it so a guy can't ever fake it. I looked down and said, "It's good to know that we're both alive."

Jerod's almost embarrassed smile met mine. "I'd apologize, but when I'm naked with a beautiful woman, some things are jus' beyond my control." His fingers crawled a little further down my back and he pulled me closer to him again. I shifted slightly again and somehow his fingers found their way to my behind, pulling my body toward him again.

As if aware of his warm hands cradling my bottom, my own fingers suddenly felt cold, as if caught in the icy water again. I pulled them from behind him and flexed them. "Man, my hands are still freezing." I breathed into them.

"Well, I think I can help." He started to withdraw his hands from my behind, but I stopped him.

"You put those back, they feel quite good there." I tilted my head up toward his face, the quick movement of my head making me feel faint. I waited for the dizziness to pass.

By the time I could think clearly again, I was pleased that he immediately did as he was told. Maybe this guy had possibilities. I cupped both hands together and blew into them again, warming them slightly, and a mischievous idea struck me. By this time we were both a little crazy. Before Jerod could react, I wrapped both hands around his now hard arousal.

He flinched at first, backing away slightly in the small space and uttering a sharp "Oh-oh-oh!" and I could feel it slightly deflating, but I didn't relent. I did as we had been taught to warm something up; I rubbed both hands vigorously around and around. Although I couldn't see that well in the semidarkness, my hands could feel the stiffness return...with a noticeable increase in the warmth as well. "Oh-okay," he said and the fingers kneaded the skin on my butt a little more vigorously.

I realized that my body and head were aching and I was reeling from fear and grief, but for those long moments in that closet, I didn't care. I didn't care about my pain, about what the world would think. I was desperate and only wanted to feel alive. I was anxious to keep the terror at bay, and so was Jerod, I think.

Keeping one hand extended across my rear, he moved his other to the front of me and began a slow, vigorous massage on my left breast, caressing the tender skin and rubbing the nipple back and forth between his thumb and forefinger. As much as I could in that tight space, I lay back and let him, though my hands never lost their attentive grasp. Then, in an acrobatic feat I would have thought impossible in our cramped quarters, he somehow maneuvered his head around so his mouth was devouring my right breast.

"Jerod," I said quietly, "this is hardly how I pictured it, but we may be dead in the next few hours. I want you to make love to me!"

"Dee Dee, you sure this is what you want?"

I could see the yearning in his eyes and could feel his desire pulsing hard against my now, very busy fingers. I knew what he wanted, so I tried to make it easy for him. "Jerod, just stop trying to be the southern gentleman. Well, you've been trying to get into my pants since you met me, haven't you?"

He started to deny it and I said, "It's not nice to lie when you're this vulnerable." I gave a little squeeze on his arousal.

"If you insist," he whispered into my ear. Abruptly he stopped.

To be honest, in that moment of passion I hadn't thought about the small space of our cramped quarters or anything else for that matter. Driven by desperation, I wanted to feel Jerod inside me, to remind me that we were both alive and I didn't think of much else.

He placed both hands around my middle again and I felt him adjust the alignment of our two very horny bodies so I was a little ahead of him. Then, with a gentleness that surprised me, he lifted me, tilted my frame a bit and slid me back toward him. As he slid in, I heard him utter his whispered gasp of pleasure. "Oh, God, Dee Dee!"

"Not bad from this side, either," I answered, smiling even though he couldn't see it.

Then, both hands gripping my middle, Jerod lifted me in a soft, gentle motion up and slid me down. I felt my vagina slide on up and down on his erection again and again. Whether he was uncertain or just being gentle, I don't know, but he started tentatively, almost tenderly, and then slowly increased his pace. Up and down, up and down, his steady rhythm built and crescendoed as both our passions arced higher. Even before it erupted, I could feel his orgasm coming in the tightening of his grasp around my middle, and then he pounded me against his flesh and held me fiercely in place. He came first, exploding inside me--I could tell from his anguished cry, deliberately muffled in my hair. Then, unlike any of the men I had known before--in the biblical sense, that is-- he didn't just quit once his need was satisfied. After a brief pause while he savored his own climax, his strong arms continued this relentless locomotion unchecked. Though spent, he still propelled his motion and I was released a minute later. I started to scream my delight and his hand came around to stifle my cry.

God, until that moment, I forgot how long it had been. I'm not sure whether it was my woozy head, my emotional state, the perilous conditions of our confinement or the strange, cramped position of our lovemaking, but I can say I have never FELT like that before. Overcome with this indescribable delight, I started to quiver slightly and weep. This time not from fear or cold, but from my own, newly unleashed passion. By then, some of the aches began to resurface, but I was too numb with pleasure to notice much. He kissed me this time and held me in his warm, perspiring arms. Exquisitely spent, I laid my head against his body and drifted off to sleep again.

I slept contentedly in his arms and I think he fell asleep as well. The world briefly forgotten, we were both blissfully peaceful in that awkward embrace and we slept for I don't know how long.

Then, somewhere in that fog of slumber, we were jerked awake. A huge explosion roared outside and rocked the building, hammering both of us hard against the back wall.

Chapter 41

Yassim pulled the three sheets of paper from the fax tray, giving them a cursory examination. Realizing they were repeat copies, he handed one to each of the men with him. "Let us see what the Leader of the Free World has to say," he said, chuckling. He read aloud, "Asad Akadi is a criminal, convicted of murder and espionage by a jury of his peers. His release, then, is no simple matter. If your demand is to be granted, much will need to be arranged."

"Use the phone in the principal's office and call me so we can talk, one on one. You can reach me directly at 202-310-1112. I have arranged for a secure line so we can speak in confidence. When we talk, I will discuss what is possible with Akadi."--President Ryan Gregory." He held up the sheet. "What do you think of your president's words, Jose?"

"He's not my president, Yassim," Jose shook his head vigorously, making the disheveled black curls dance. "Hell, I didn't even vote for him."

"What do you think of his request to speak in confidence, Mustafa?" the cell leader asked.

"Yassim, I am but a poor soldier of Allah," the terrorist responded. "I am not knowledgeable about such things. But our experience has taught us that we can never trust the word of an American president."

"Did you see that?" Something outside drew Yassim's gaze toward the front of the school.

"No. What was it?" Mustafa said.

Yassim studied the scene outside the window of the office, but could detect no change, no movement. He could have sworn his eyes had caught something. His stare remained fixed on the curved parking drive that swept past the front sidewalk of the school. The circular driveway was lined with the yellow school buses that formed a half circle around the single flagpole. Atop the flagpole hung the American flag, the wind whipping the colors viciously. He could find nothing out of place, but still he stared.

"What is it, leader?" asked Mustafa. "Does something concern you?"

"I am not sure." Yassim did not take his eyes from the scene. "Hand me the binoculars."

Mustafa pulled a set of binoculars from the knapsack and handed them to his leader. Yassim grabbed them and, raising them to his eyes, continued his examination of the scene in front of the school, sweeping the glasses slowly left to right.

"Yassim?" Mustafa asked, concern in his voice.

"It appears we have company."

Mustafa cupped his massive hands around his eyes and peered out the window alongside his leader. Even Jose sauntered to the window, curious now, leaning his tall, rail frame forward against the pane. "I do not see anything, Yassim," Mustafa said uncertainly and turned toward the leader.

Yassim took the glasses down from his eyes and handed them to Mustafa. "Look carefully behind the tires of the fifth bus in line and you will see one of them. These soldiers are good to have gotten this far without us spotting them."

"Yes, now I see the one...and another behind the wheel of the next bus, and I see one more. How many do you think are there, leader?"

"It does not matter. You have the charges placed along the drive?"

"Yes, all along the approach, just as you said," Mustafa said.

"Good. Now hand me the detonator," Yassim held out his palm.

Mustafa removed the knapsack and pulled out a small silver box. His huge hand held it out to Yassim. "It is not turned on. You need only to flip the switch and then push the button."

The cell leader held the electronic box in his left palm and, using the index finger of his right hand, he flipped the switch. No sound was emitted but a red light blinked in a slow, repetitive pattern as the box came alive. He glanced out the window again and then back to the silver device, where his finger rested on the green button. He closed his eyes and whispered, "This is for you, Fatima and Jamal." His finger depressed the button.

For one second, nothing happened. Then the world rocked. As Yassim raised his eyes to look, the shock waves from the explosion struck the building, shattering the large office window. The three men dove to the floor as glass shards rained down on them. Just before he dropped down, Yassim saw the chassis of one of the buses hurled into the air by the explosion. For a full minute, the men lay on the gray carpet of the office, arms covering their heads, as they heard secondary explosions and fires erupt from the blast.

Convinced that the worst had passed, Yassim raised himself up and listened to the screams of men outside and the continued tinkling of cracking glass. Peering through the opening where the window had been, he could barely see through the smoke. Several fires roared where the yellow school buses had sat seconds earlier.

"Allah, be praised!" Yassim intoned.

"Allah, be praised," Mustafa echoed, getting to his feet.

"Me too," Jose added, struggling to pull himself up. With one powerful arm, Mustafa reached down and lifted the tall custodian as if he were weightless. Standing together, the three men stared out through the broken glass, transfixed at the scene of the carnage. Patches of grass around the flagpole were on fire, burning the green to ugly black cinders. The sidewalk and driveway wore great holes, as if some angry giant had ripped apart the concrete and asphalt and tossed it haphazardly around. Fragments of the bus chassis were strewn everywhere, the metal stretched and misshaped, the yellow paint charred. Among the ruins several bodies lay splayed on the ground, bloodied, and lifeless. The body closest to them, a boy of about eighteen, Yassim would have guessed, lay still. The body--although it would be hard to call it that after the explosion--was burned, blackened, with one arm and leg ripped off in the explosion. The body lay lifeless like some huge, desiccated doll in a garbage heap. Blood no longer pumped, but oozed slowly out from both ugly stumps, the two pools running together and staining the sun-bleached concrete bright crimson. Idly, Yassim looked around for the missing body parts, but could not see them.

Yassim studied the scene, looking for survivors that would have to be dealt with. No one moved. "Mustafa, go make a sweep to see if any survived. If you find any, kill them."

Yassim returned his attention to the inside of the office, deciding what he should do about the fax. His glance strayed to a panel of lights above the fax machine and he noticed that one light was on. He peered more closely at the light and read aloud the small number typed below. "015?" He turned with a question to Jose. "Why is this light on? Where is it from?"

"I don't know. Let me look." Jose moved closer to the panel and studied it. "Oh, that is the call button from the coach's office downstairs."

"Downstairs? I remember no downstairs to this building. Was it in the drawings you brought for me?"

"Maybe not," said the custodian. "You see, it's not much of a basement floor. Just a couple of rooms the Boosters added after the building was built, some offices for the coaches along with visitors' locker rooms."

"I do not remember this light from before. Is anyone down there?"

"Naw, I saw the Coach Baumer up with the others in the cafeteria," answered Jose.

"Then why is it on?" Yassim glared at the custodian.

Jose squirmed. "I don't know. The buttons are really sensitive. Probably, Coach just bumped eet on his way out. Didn't even know it." Two beads of perspiration appeared on Jose's forehead and slowly curled their way into his mustache.

"Did you search it?" Yassim barked.

"No-no-o," stuttered Jose. "You had me check out the other end of the building, the northeast end. These two rooms," Jose pointed to the lighted button and the next one, "are under the southeast section of the school."

"How do you get to these rooms?"

"There is a door in the gym at the south end of this hallway," Jose's bony finger pointed to the hallway outside the office, "that opens to steps to the lower floor."

Mustafa reappeared in the doorway. "They are all dead now, Yassim," he reported. "Only one lived through the explosion and my bullet sent him to Allah. There were twelve soldiers, all well armed. I relieved them, and put the weapons inside the building."

"Well done, my brother. Allah will reward you," said Yassim. "But there is no time to lose. I have another task for you." The cell leader turned to the custodian. "Jose, show Mustafa where these basement rooms are located," he said, pointing to the light on the panel. "Mustafa, search every space down there and make sure we have not overlooked anyone. Jose, take him to the stairs and then return here. I may have further need of your services."

"As you wish, leader." Mustafa turned his large form toward the door to the office.

"Wait!" directed the cell leader. "Leave that here," he said, pointing to the pack on the terrorist's back. Mustafa eased the knapsack off his back and set it gently on the countertop.

Jose shuffled his tall form across the office and met the terrorist just outside the doorway. "Eets this way," he said and both men headed down the hallway.

As Yassim listened to the echo of the footsteps decrease, he turned back to the fax. Hitting a key on the secretary's computer, he watched the screen come to life, as if resurrected by his touch. He sat at the keyboard and paused. "Perhaps, President Gregory is ready to discuss the future now," he said aloud.

Chapter 42

The building shuddered under the explosion, slamming my head against the wall of the closet. "What was that?"

"I believe our friends upstairs have just delivered a rude welcome to some visitors," explained Jerod as he sat up. He reached around in the dark, searching for his clothes. His hand landed on something else.

"Jerod! What do you mean?"

His hands continued their search and found a shirt. He moved himself to a sitting position and slid it over his head in the dark. "From the explosion, I'd venture that Jesus and his comrades must've rigged some charges."

"Do you think he's killing the kids?"

"I don't know, but I doubt it. Unless they moved them, the cafeteria is over there," he said, pointing in one direction. "From here, it sounded like it came from the front of the school." He pointed the other way. "I would suspect either someone tried to go out that way or, more likely, someone was tryin' to come in."

"Oh, God!"

"It's going to be okay," Jerod whispered. Then, in our private space, he kissed me and stood up, pants in hand. I lay, unmoving among the flattened sweat clothes that had been our bed and looked up at his handsome figure.

His head whipped around toward the crack between the two doors. "Someone's comin'!" He jammed one leg into the sweatpants and indicated for me to be quiet. His second leg stepped into the other side and he pulled the drawstring. He opened the door and stepped quickly into the room, his gaze darting toward the door of the office. He grabbed at some of the sweatshirts, pulling them from under me and whispered, "Quick! Get under these!"

His words were so intense, they galvanized my fear again and I scrambled, trying to burrow frantically into the smelly workout clothes like some cowardly mouse.

"Good. Now stay there till I come get ya."

Before I could object, he closed the closet door, returning me to relative blindness again. I strained to listen. I heard his bare feet scurrying across the linoleum and a door close. Suddenly, alone, without him, the cramped space became claustrophobic and I had the overwhelming urge to get out of that closet. Then I heard the voice.

"Like I said, there's notheeng down here, but some coaches' offices and a few locker rooms."

I'd recognize that voice anywhere and a wave of relief swept over me. I exhaled the breath I had been holding and sat up. Suddenly, I was glad that our crazy janitor never lost his accent. I sat up, ready to call out to him. What I heard next stopped me.

"There two's offices and two locker rooms down here," Jose was saying. "You go ahead and look, Mustafa, but you ain't going to find anyone. Sometime I hide out down here, when I wanna avoid work." The custodian laughed at his own joke. "The only one ever down here this time of the day is Coach Baumer and I saw heem in cafeteria."

"I will start with d' locker rooms," answered a second man with a thicker, Mideast accent.

The reality of Jose's involvement hit me and my heart hammered in my chest. I collapsed back onto the sweats, trying to burrow into the pile again. I squirmed to the bottom, feeling the cold vinyl against my flesh.

"O-key," Jose was saying, "I have to get back up to Yasseem."

I heard two sets of footsteps, each heading off in different directions. Oh God, someone's coming here. I knew it was just a matter of time and I panicked. I held my breath. Where the hell was Jerod? Breathe. Breathe.

Scooting down and flattening my breasts, I tried to bury myself deeper, knowing that if the searcher--what had Jose called him?--Mustafa?--bothered to check, it would do little good. I closed my eyes and held my breath again.

I heard the doors open and a harsh whisper. "Dee Dee?"

It took a moment for my brain to process and I didn't respond at first. "Dee Dee?" he repeated more urgently this time.

I turned my head slightly so I could answer and the sweats fell away, exposing my face. "Yeah, I'm here," I said, a squeak in my voice.

Kneeling down, he leaned his head close to the pile. "Listen, I've only got a second," he whispered, his head jerking back toward the hallway. He stopped and I held my breath. We both heard it. The footsteps grew louder and then receded again. "I've only got a second. He's searchin' the second locker room now." His head swiveled back toward the office door. "He's going to be here in a few minutes."

"Oh, Jerod!" I whimpered. "I'm terrified."

"I know. I know," Jerod said, but he didn't look at me, his head still turned toward the door. "I've got an idea. May not be a great one, but it's all I've got."

"What is it?"

"No time. Here's what I need ya to do," he said, suddenly breathless. His eyes were back on me, fear in the pupils. "When he comes into this room, stay huddled in the closet. But I want you to make some very quiet sounds, whimpering or somethin', got it?"

"What? What do you mean?" I protested.

"No time. Just do it!" he commanded in a whisper and shoved my head down, pulling sweat clothes back over my face.

Face down, I couldn't see but I heard the closet door close and the soft patter of his bare feet. I began to pray. Dear God, don't let me die. I'll come back to church. I'll call my mother every week. I'll--

Then I heard the slap of shoes--boots, I remember thinking--and I started to cry, murmuring in loud sobs there on the floor of the closet.

Chapter 43

Rashid stared with unbelieving eyes, squinting to peer into the semidarkness of the room. There, just on the fringe of the dim light he saw the two figures, a woman and a girl. Not much more than their silhouettes were visible, but he could have sworn, just for an instant, that he was watching his own mother and sister huddled there in the darkness. He knew the idea was ludicrous; he was in America and they were thousands of miles away, in the desolate Afghan desert. But something in the way the woman bent over the younger figure, her hands gently resting on the girl's shoulder, in the way the girl's diminutive body shook as she cried--called up the image of his family and his heart ached.

Rashid couldn't help it and was drawn to the pair. He hurried across the room to where they crouched. His abrupt appearance startled them both; the girl's sobbing increased as she cowered in front of him. Up close, it was obvious the woman was, of course, a teacher--a science teacher, he thought-- and he did not know the girl. She must have been a high school student, he reasoned, but she looked so small and helpless, it would have been easy to mistake her for ten, his sister's age. The two figures stared back in fear, clearly disturbed by his sudden intrusion into their intimacy, their eyes swollen red with crying. Rashid found himself apologizing quietly, as he backed away.

That was stupid, he chided himself. You are a soldier of Allah; do not forget your place. There was no room for weakness now! He reminded himself that his family is under the Sheik's protection and will be taken care of...as long as he did his part. About twenty feet from the pair, he stopped and looked back. They were watching him intently, fear obvious in both their faces, even at this distance in the dim light. He kept moving, but couldn't keep from glancing back. As he edged to the other side of the room, the image of the two again took on the eerie appearance of his mother and sister. As he walked, he shook his head, as if he could physically dislodge the image from his mind. You are here now, there is nothing you can do, he told himself. It is all in Allah's hands.

Shuffling his feet and keeping his eyes downcast, he wandered around the cafeteria, trying to blend in and look like one more frightened teen. Everywhere he looked, the students and teachers sat together, whispering in hushed tones, terrified eyes searching frantically for the next threat. As he moved among the knots of students and teachers, he was reminded that his earlier assessment was accurate. There were hundreds of teens scattered across the lunchroom, yet none challenged us, he thought. All held at bay by a few men. The Americans were, as he had been taught, selfish, spoiled and in the end, cowards.

Everywhere he moved in the large room, the scent of fear was overpowering, the odor of urine and excrement mixing with human sweat. He scanned the teens and adults as he shuffled quietly among them. He recognized the nervous actions of some as they stood and pranced, trying to control this function, and the resignation of others who had given up, no longer able to control themselves, and simply sat in their own waste. The smell assaulting his nostrils, he remembered his training on how hostages were to be denied such basic needs as going to the bathroom.

"This will humiliate those under your control and make them more willing to comply with your orders," the trainer had said. "Especially with the 'civilized' Americans," he had continued with disgust, "they consider this a great sign of weakness and this strategy will allow you to dominate them."

Now, in the midst of the stench, Rashid found himself questioning that idea. These are not fierce, fighting soldiers, he thought. They are mere frightened sheep. It hardly seemed necessary to strip these students and teachers of all dignity.

As he slowly moved about the room, he found himself back near the Journalism group again, the students Miss Sterber had intervened for, and it had cost her her life. Then he remembered his responsibility and he listened again for any hint of threats. He kept himself just to the side of one of the massive pillars that sprouted through the floor of the room like huge tree trunks. He could hear and observe them, but they couldn't see him.

"I can't believe Miss Sterber's gone," said the student called Goat, both hands bracing his chin as if cradling his small, angular beard.

"Well, she's dead all right," muttered Tess bitterly, "and it's all my fault!"

"Tess, you can't blame yourself," answered another. The black male put both arms on the shoulders of the editor Rashid had worked with on the interview. "It's that asshole of a terrorist that did that to her. Besides, I know you and your mouth. It'd probably be you at the bottom of the lake, if Miss Sterber hadn't stepped in front of you."

"Don't you get it!" Tess' voice was almost a whispered scream and she used both hands to knock off Tyrone's arms. "I wish it was me! I got her killed!" Then she started sobbing again, head buried in her own crossed arms.

Rashid felt her sorrow. Despite his efforts and training, he was not able to steel his heart completely. Maybe because he had worked with Tess at the prison or because he felt something for Miss Sterber, but as he heard the teen's weeping in that darkened space, he could not make himself feel triumph. Instead, he found himself again questioning the humiliation that Jesus had submitted Miss Sterber to before he executed her.

But he told himself he could not let it get to him and forced himself to move on, floating between groups until he was back at the front of the cafeteria. There his eyes met Yassim and his eyebrows went up, asking the unspoken question. There was the slightest nod from the cell leader and Rashid edged around the corner of the room and into the kitchen area. There, just inside the doorway, he saw the yellow 55-gallon drum marked "Cleaning Supplies." Rashid glanced back toward the doorway to make certain there were no eyes watching and he reached inside the huge container, his fingers exploring the contents in the near darkness of the small kitchen. It took a few seconds for his hand to probe through and beneath the soap granules and get to the bottom of the drum. Then he landed on what he needed. He grasped the plastic and pulled the package slowly out of the container. Although he couldn't make out the model in the darkness, from the meeting last week he knew what he held-- inside the sealed plastic bag was a nine-millimeter Glock handgun.

His eyes darted back to the door opening and then back to the gun in his hand inside the plastic. He took it out of the plastic bag and placed it in the pocket of the backpack.

Chapter 44

I squeezed my eyelids together so hard that my temples started to pound. Even with my eyes shut, I could tell that the lights in the office had been turned on. Someone else was in the small office with me. Where the hell was Jerod? My hands at my side, I tried to stay perfectly motionless, trying desperately to listen for the footsteps, but I could just barely hear them over the hammering of my heart in my chest. Then they stopped.

I held my breath and then I noticed something else. I could feel a slight breeze on the left side of my buttocks, the side facing the closet door. Panic shot through me. Some part of my body must have been exposed, the sweats dropped away, I thought with horror. The intruder will see me!

I didn't have time to decide what to do, and that probably saved me. The footsteps approached my hiding place and my fear froze me. Oh God, he's coming over here, I screamed inside my head and stifled a crying squeak. The footsteps stopped just outside. I heard the door swing open. I braced myself for a bullet.. I released an anguished cry, telling God I was sorry for everything I did. By this time, I couldn't tell if any of this was aloud or only in my head.

Then I heard a thump that sounded oddly like the home run hit by Hal Thompson in the faculty softball game. Within seconds, I felt this incredible weight land on my back. I squirmed, only to find myself trapped under an enormous burden. I gasped for air. Then, just as quickly, I felt the weight lifted off me and heard Jerod's voice.

"Dee Dee, are ya all right? Dee Dee?"

Jerod was kneeling over a body, bending his head down next to mine. The ceiling fluorescent light painted a bright halo around his face. "Yeah, I think so. What happened?"

"Well, this guy was the one searchin' the office," Jerod said, thumb gesturing to the prone figure on the floor at the foot of the closet, "and I gave him something to look at. "

"You what?"

"Well, I knew the only chance I had was t' catch him with his guard down. So I opened the one closet door and exposed a corner of your beautiful body," Jerod explained.

"You did what!"

"Yeah, well, I knew if he saw that pretty pink skin of yours on the floor of the closet, he'd have to come to investigate. So when he bent down to have a close look at your tush, I smacked him as hard as I could." Jerod brought a beaten aluminum bat into my focus and pounded the floor once with it. "He went down like a sack o' taters."

"Is he...dead?" I asked.

Jerod reached over and placed a finger on the neck of the lying figure. "Nope, but out good."

"Well, do you think, can I get out of this place now?"

"Sure," he said, standing up and taking a step back from the door to give me room to maneuver.

Bringing my legs to my chest, I tried to swing them out of the opening, all the time trying to avoid touching the body on the floor. Jerod stood a few feet off, watching me struggle and then extended a hand to help me rise. I needed it. My joints creaked as I tried to move and he ended up having to use both hands to help me get to a standing position. Getting out of the closet was such a physical ordeal, at first it didn't dawn on me that I was standing there naked until, uh--well, I was. Suddenly, modesty overcame me and I called to my rescuer, "Turn around!"

His eyes did a quick dance up and down my nude form--I swear men will never change--and replied, "I've pretty much seen everythin' you got up close, but okay."

Holding on to the closet for balance, I bent down to check the clothes, sending new streaks of pain slicing through my head. I rummaged quickly through the discarded sweats that had served as covers, trying to come up with something, anything that would work.

I grabbed any two pieces, just hoping that I had a top and bottom. Luckily, I did and slipped the one over my head and stepped warily into the other, needing to balance on the closet door to keep from falling. The clothes were dirty and smelly, but at least I was dry and covered.

"Okay, you can turn around," I said, looking around at our surroundings.

We were standing in a makeshift office with gray concrete block walls adorned with athletic motivation posters. The floor space was littered with football equipment and jerseys scattered around a table, a couple of filing cabinets, a beat-up desk and two closets. Then I looked at him again and said,

"Where'd you get that?" I noticed he was wearing new red and white jogging pants.

"Found it in the other cupboard," Jerod said, pointing to a small corner closet next to the desk and saw my face. Both closets, the one he was indicating and the one we had just crawled out of, were little more than plywood walls and doors, hastily thrown together. He quickly added, "It wouldn't fit ya anyway. And that's not all I found."

"What?"

"First things first," he said. "We gotta get this guy tied up. Help me look for some rope."

"I've got a better idea," I said and stepped around the body over to the desk. I pulled out the top drawer and sure enough, it was right there. Every coach I'd ever known had kept a roll or two of athletic tape in the top drawer of their desk. One coach I dated had put the tape to some interesting uses…well maybe I'll cover that later.

I pulled it out, walked back and handed it to Jerod. "How will this do?"

"That'll work fine," he said, taking the almost full roll of tape. "See if you can find a rag small enough to stuff into his mouth," he added, pointing to the heap of sweats I had huddled in.

I rummaged through the pile, but couldn't find anything small enough. I grabbed an old sweatshirt and, using my teeth, ripped off a piece. By the time I was finished, Jerod had rolled the body over and wrapped his hands together, and was working on his ankles. When he finished, he said, "Go ahead, stuff it in there but leave it a little loose so he can breathe."

As I bent over, I looked at the man for the first time. I hadn't noticed him before. How many were there? Our prisoner was a huge man with dark Arab features, broad shoulders, and hardly any neck. I had to use both hands to open his mouth and insert the ripped cloth and noticed that his nose was crooked. Then Jerod grabbed the head and began winding the tape around and across the large mouth like he was taping up a mummy. After a few trips around with the diminishing roll, he said, "That oughtta hold him." He patted down the pockets of the hog-tied figure and came up with a silver revolver. He slipped the gun in the back of his waistband and went on, "Now help me git him into our private space."

It took both of us to lift the heavy body, all dead weight now, and wedge him into the closet and close the doors. As Jerod walked away, I said, "Give me the tape, will you?" I wrapped it around the metal handles of the door, making an effective chain lock.

"Good idea. I guess you're not just another pretty face."

"Who is he?"

"Hell if I know. Just another of the terrorists, I guess," he said and stood an AK-47 up against the bank of lockers.

"Do you have any idea how many there are?"

"Not a clue."

"We can't just sit here. We've got to get the kids out." I pointed toward the ceiling.

"Dee Dee, I wanna help them as much as you. But until we have some idea what we're up against, we can't just go barrelin' up there."

I was still shaking and he stood there, hands on hips, the essence of calm. How did he do that?

"Well, at least we've got some weapons now," I said, motioning to the AK-47.

"Yeah, but if we go up those stairs at the end of the hall, we're li'ble to walk into a firestorm."

"Well, I don't want to just sit here. Any ideas?" I asked.

"We can't call out. They've disabled the phone system. I already tried. Oh, yeah. Com'on and I'll show ya what else I found," he exclaimed and opened the smaller closet in the office. "Take a gander at that."

On a small shelf in the closet was a new twenty-four inch computer screen. I immediately recognized the newest IMac computer.

I turned back to Jerod. "What's this doing here?" I said, even as I pulled the keyboard down, striking it to see it come to life. "We were told with all the cutbacks, there was no money for new computers."

"Easy girl! You're the one who told me the athletic department always seems to have money from the boosters or somebody. After all, we have to keep the coaches happy because we know what's important in school. Too bad the terrorists took the whole phone and data system off line or we might be able to use this to get a message out."

"You're right," I said, turning back to the screen. I began punching keys, trying to get the computer to access the network, even though I'd heard what the terrorist leader had said. I had no luck and stopped and turned to face Jerod. "How did the terrorists know so much about our school?"

"What do ya mean?"

"Well, they knew just what time to strike, when we'd all be around the cafeteria. And they seemed to know their way around the school," I said.

"Well, if I remember correctly, someone gave Jesus a guided tour of the school," Jerod said.

"Thanks for reminding me, but I didn't show Jesus this place. And how did they know how to shut down the phone and data network?"

"I dunno," he muttered, "I'd guess they got some expert on their team. Either that or they had somebody on the inside."

We both said, "Jose!" and Jerod added, "Shit!"

That's when I looked behind the monitor and saw the extra cable. My heart beat faster, but I didn't say anything else. I set it back on the small shelf and got on my knees, running my hand over the newly discovered cord. I followed it all the way to the wall and found the connection.

I got up and my fingers returned to the keyboard. "Bless those devious, athletic types!" I said, my right hand manipulating the small mouse.

"What is it?"

"Not only did the boosters get Coach Baumer a new computer, they got him his own outside line," I said, holding the telephone cable running from the back of the little box.

"Ya mean outside the system?"

"I think so," I said clicking on the telephone icon at the top of the screen. "That way there's no record if he ventures into, uh, should we say, inappropriate venues." We heard the unmistakable beep of a phone line making the connection. "Yes!" I called and hugged Jerod.

"Can we hook up a phone to that line?" he asked suddenly. "Then we could call somebody and git the cavalry out here."

"No go," I explained, looking at the phone on the desk. "These are all special phones that only work with our network system. But we can still call for help." I began to type, calling up Google.

When he saw the screen come up he caught on. "Okay, who d'ya think we should contact? How 'bout the police department?" Jerod suggested.

"Yeah, but we can get out to other sites." I studied the display, pondering. "With the explosion and everything, I suspect this has gotten a whole lot bigger than the Hammerville Police Department. Let's go to the top."

Jerod leaned in and squinted as I typed. "Department of Homeland Security?"

"Well, the Director of Homeland Security, uh, Harold Samson, visited the prison a few weeks ago, remember?"

"Yeah, I remember it was a big deal and most of the officers never even saw the guy."

"I guess you just had to know the right people. I was at the press conference." After a few more long seconds, it finished loading and the Homeland Security site was up.

"How do you know where to send your message?" Jerod was asking as I scrolled through menus.

I found the one marked "Contact Us" and clicked it. "I'm hoping there's a way to get a message to the director or someone close enough." This page didn't take so long to come up. "And I hope someone's monitoring it," I said as I scrolled through my options. "There it is!" I clicked on the link for "Office of the Director," and an email form appeared.

Of course, I knew Director Samson wouldn't be monitoring e-mails, but I hoped someone was who could get through to him. With Jerod hovering over my right shoulder, I began typing furiously, the clicking of the keys echoing in the small office.

Just then we both heard it; the clang of the door at the top of the stairs as it slammed shut. Someone else was coming.

Chapter 45

Yassim again adjusted the strap of the automatic weapon on his shoulder as he surveyed the entire darkened lunchroom. The dull light of the afternoon was dying, casting menacing shadows against the rear wall. The cell leader studied the right wall, pockmarked by the bullets from the earlier barrage, and was surprised that the digital clock, sitting in the middle, had somehow remained unscathed and continued to blink away. 4:18. Not long now, he thought. Either the president will take action to free Asad or we will all die. Either way Allah wins. He studied the frightened people scattered around him in the cafeteria. If it comes to that, these poor ones will become famous in their deaths, he thought. And I will join Fatima and Jamal in Allah's light..

His gaze swept to the clock on the damaged wall again. 4:24. Seeing the time pass, his glance darted around the room again. He observed the hostages and noticed a man making his way slowly, threading through the knots of students and teachers. After a few seconds, the name came to him, Thompson, the principal. Although the man stopped periodically to talk quietly to a few individuals, resting his hands on their shoulders, Yassim figured he was probably making his way to see him. Something in the man's bearing. Fear still, but something else...resolve maybe.

As he watched the tall figure move among the hostages, it struck him. Where was Mustafa?

He turned and yelled down the hallway behind him, "Jose!" A few students near him jumped at the noise.

The custodian sauntered down the side hall. "Si?" he asked.

"Was there anything out of place in the basement when you went with Mustafa?"

"Everytheeng looked fine to me."

"Go back down and check on him."

The custodian nodded and headed back down the dark hallway, heading toward the gym. Yassim watched him disappear back into the darkness and turned back. He had been right, the principal was standing in front of him. Automatically, Yassim's left hand went to the pistol in his belt.

"What are you going to do with us?" Thompson asked, his tone demanding.

Yassim didn't answer. He resisted the urge to remind the man who was in charge but instead just examined the tall figure standing before him. The plastic frames of his glasses had been broken and the crooked bifocals were perched precariously atop his nose, looking like they would fall off at the slightest sneeze. His scarce brown hair lay limp across his forehead and his underarms were stained with wide circles of perspiration.

"What was that explosion?"

"That," Yassim answered, deliberately stopping to let his gaze roam the room, making certain the principal's tactic wasn't one of distraction. "That was a foolhardy attempt to storm the building. The 'attack' resulted in the death of all the men who were sent to come to your rescue." Yassim smiled. "I suspect your leaders have learned their lesson and will not likely send the commandos in again so soon."

"What are you going to do with us? Kill us too?"

"That depends."

"On what?" Thompson asked.

The cell leader stared hard at the principal before he answered. "On your president, of course. Which reminds me." He turned his gaze from the man before him and called to the other side of the room. "Jesus, come here. Go to Mr. Thompson's office and check to see if the president has sent any further correspondence. Oh, and Jesus? Check to make sure we have no more visitors at the front door."

Yassim watched as his soldier skirted around the cafeteria and headed to the north end of the building. "We are not interested in killing anyone, Mr. Thompson."

"Well, your people have a funny way of showing it, you know, since they already killed three people."

The principal's response was a harsh chuckle as his head nodded to where several bodies lay bleeding along the sidewall.

"I apologize for the hasty actions of some of my comrades," the cell leader said. "We have all been chosen for this great Jihad and they overacted in their faith. Our task is merely to free Asad Akadi, the valiant soldier of Allah and then we will all leave here."

"Do you believe that they will simply give you Akadi?" Thompson asked. "You are fools then. Our government does not negotiate with terrorists."

"I know that is what they tell you, their public face. But you do not know about the secret negotiations your government conducted with our comrades in Iraq and Afganistan." Yassim *was pleased when surprise registered on Thompson's face.* *"Anyway, you had better hope that President Gregory is willing to negotiate with us."* He stared directly at the principal. *"Otherwise, when they execute Asad, he will be signing a death warrant for the 484 hostages left."*

"Do you hate us all so much?" Thompson called back.

"Mr. Thompson, you do not understand. We do not hate your country or your people. We are only at war with your evil government and their persecution of Muslims."

Thompson tried to object, but suddenly Yassim turned to his left and called, *"Fadi! Go to the gym and find the door to the basement,"* Yassim said, clearly unhappy. *"Go down the stairs and locate Mustafa. Tell him enough searching. What is he looking for, rats? Bring him and Jose back up here."*

"Yes," answered Fadi.

"Jose?" said Thompson.

Jesus turned his attention back to the principal. *"My advice to you, Mr. Thompson,"* said Yassim, his voice icy, *"is to go back and pray that your president is a sensible man. Or make certain you and your people are prepared to meet Allah. I assure you we are ready."*

Chapter 47

"Mr. President, I think we may have received a communication from someone inside the school," Harold Samson said.

As the door to the Situation Room slid closed behind him, he glanced around the table and studied the faces of each man. It was hard to believe he had left only an hour ago. The freshly pressed clothes of all four men were wrinkled, the shirts marked with ragged circles of perspiration. The crisis seemed to be eating away at the veneer of command and control these men put on with their suits.

The highly polished surface of the table was littered with gold-rimmed china plates containing unappealing remnants of tuna salad sandwiches and chips. His nose detected the lingering aroma of a wilted dill pickle.

Samson passed out copies of the communiqué, first to President Gregory and then to the others around the table. The four men snatched up the papers like starving men grabbing at morsels.

"We received this email four minutes ago. It came in through our contact link on the Department's webpage," he continued.

President Gregory read the email out loud.

"Mr. Samson,

My name is Dee Dee Sterber and I'm a teacher at Thurber High School. Around noon school was taken over by a group of armed Arab terrorists. They're holding almost five hundred students and teachers hostage. Have already killed some and injured others. Don't know how many. Writing this email from the basement where we're hiding. We overpowered one of the terrorists and captured him. Don't have much time and they--'

Is that it?"

"Yes, sir, that is all that was sent," said Samson.

"Are you sure this is legit?" asked CIA Director Garcia. "Maybe it's a ruse being used by the terrorists."

"It's possible, Jerry, but I don't think so. My people did some initial checking already. The email came in through a phone line at the high school, a line installed just four months ago by the athletic department, which is in the basement. Apparently this line is a separate POTS line, one not connected to the new phone system that the rest of the building uses. Also, it turns out that

Thurber has a teacher on staff named Danielle Sterber, nicknamed Dee Dee. Age 29, 5'4, 115 pounds, teaches English, been at Thurber four years."

"And you believe this 115-pound weakling overpowered an armed terrorist? Come on!" said Garcia, slapping the paper down on the polished surface.

"Obviously, we don't know," Samson conceded, "but the email says 'we.' Perhaps she's not alone."

"Did your research turn up any information on a military background on this Sterber?" asked Tom Dickson.

"My people are checking on her background now. I should have that information in a few minutes," answered Samson, refusing to be baited.

"What happened to the rest of the message?" asked Ryan Gregory.

"This is all we received, sir," Samson answered. "My IT people believe she may have been interrupted. We have been trying to send reply emails back, but so far no response."

"It's not much." The President's pen clicked away in his right hand.

"No, sir, it is not," agreed Samson, "but it's the first possible communication link inside the school and I thought you should know about it."

"Mr. President, it could also be a trap," Dean Settler said. "Perhaps, it's a ploy by the terrorists for us to let our guard down and let something slip."

The President narrowed his tired, azure eyes toward his Chief of Staff. "Dean, what would the terrorists have to gain by pretending they are some young teacher at the school? They already have five hundred hostages at gunpoint and the place booby trapped with explosives."

"Sir...sir, uh, I don't know," stuttered Settler, withering under his boss's wrath. "Perhaps...uh, they're going to try to get us to reveal our plans."

"Then I guess we won't do that, Mr. Settler," answered the President.

"Mr. President?" Dickson asked. President Ryan Gregory turned slowly in his seat, fixing his gaze upon the FBI Director. "Sir, we have a full SWAT and an HRT team ready to take the school. They are in position on the ground just beyond line of sight of the school, about two miles from the building. They are ready and awaiting orders, sir."

"What are you proposing, Tom?"

"Sir," Dickson hesitated before going on. "I am suggesting we launch a full out assault to capture the school."

"We already lost one team and you're anxious to sacrifice more. And what about the hostages?" snapped Gregory.

"They may already be dead, sir, for all we know," answered Dickson, but the conviction seemed to be slipping from his words.

"What about the email?"

"Sir, I'm inclined to agree with Dean. We don't know. It may just as well be a ruse, and even the writer says that some are already dead," Dickson responded, but with less certainty.

"Are you willing to bet on the lives of five hundred children and teachers?" snapped the President.

Dickson did not attempt an answer.

The silence was broken by the beep of the speakerphone. "President Ryan, it is Mr. Samson's secretary. She says she has another fax from the terrorists."

Chapter 48

When we heard the sound of the footsteps clanging on the steps, Jerod grabbed my shoulder. I clicked on the "send" icon. I knew I was in the middle of the email, but I was afraid I was about to run out of time. I was right. I just hope what I sent made some sense.

"Com'ere," Jerod said in a harsh whisper and pulled me away from the computer. His right hand shut the door on the small closet while his left steered me toward the open door to the office.

"Where are we going?" I whispered back.

His head jerked to the locker room across the hall. He snuck a glance around the corner of the doorway toward the stairs as we heard more footfalls on the metal stairs. His head popped back into the room.

Then I heard the unmistakable sound of Jose's off-key singing. "What was I-I-I theenk-ing? I know what I was fee--ling, but what was I theenk-ing?"

Options raced through my head almost as rapidly as my heart hammered in my chest. At least it wasn't another of the terrorists. I knew Jose; he was in my classroom everyday. He and I had talked about things, the school, his family, unfair administrators. Maybe I could get him to tell me exactly what was going on. I remembered talking to him a few weeks ago about Akadi. What was it he had said?

As these thoughts skidded through my brain, Jerod took the option out of my hands. He reached around to the back of his waistband, feeling for the pistol, and then seemed to think better of it. Placing both hands firmly on my shoulders, he shoved me back flush against the wall a few feet from the doorjamb. His mouth an inch from my right ear, his urgent whisper commanded, "Stay here by the wall. Make sure he can't see you. I don't want anythin' to happen to you."

"What are you going to--" I tried to say but his hand over my mouth silenced my words.

We both heard the footsteps approaching, coming down the hall. The nasal sound of Jose's voice echoed in the narrow confines. "Mustafa, hey-ey, where are you? You sleeping down here?"

Jerod's face opposite mine, his fierce blue eyes bored into mine--which I'm sure by now probably looked as wide as egg whites. Peering intently into those determined azure eyes for several long seconds, I could find no speck of fear and, I have to admit, that made me feel better. My heart slowed its frantic pace and I exhaled a long breath. Then he kissed me and moved to the doorway.

I pressed my body against the wall, flattening myself as much as possible. Glancing sideways, I tried to keep my eye on Jerod and the doorway. Perched there, just inches from the doorjamb, his strong body looked like a coiled spring. I watched him raise both hands even with his head and could see the muscles in his upper arms as he tensed. I held my breath as we listened to the footsteps slapping the concrete floor near our position.

I saw Jose stick his head through the door opening. "Musta--" was all he got out.

Jerod's reaction was so fast, his movements were a blur. Like any brave female, I shut my eyes and waited. All I heard was some scuffling and then Jose uttering.

"Hey, man!" Jose squealed and then coughed and choked.

I opened my eyes. Jerod's right arm was wrapped around the lanky custodian's neck and his left was reaching behind, grasping for the gun. Obviously it was no match. Jerod was much stronger, his sinews flexed as he tightened his grip around Jose's neck. But the custodian was taller and his wiry body writhed, his feet seeking leverage on the slick concrete, even as his arms fought vainly against Jerod's fierce grip. To hold him off, Jerod had to give up trying to get the gun. I heard Jose choking again, audibly struggling for breath and when his arms stopped grabbing at Jerod's hold, I thought he was about to collapse.

Then suddenly both arms of the janitor shot out and grabbed the doorway and yanked. Jerod must have been surprised by the move because he was caught off balance and was pulled into the hallway along with the taller custodian.

They disappeared from my view but I heard more scuffling and then the clattering of metal on the concrete floor. Jerod spat through gritted teeth, "Dammit, Jose, if you don't stop movin', I'm gonna tighten my grip till you can't breathe at all." Then nothing.

Encouraged by the silence, I inched toward the doorway and peered around the doorframe. A few feet down the hallway, Jerod held the taller custodian in a headlock. Jose was no longer moving. It looked as if Jose had tried to drag Jerod, vice grip and all, back toward the stairs he had just come down. Now the two stood, Jose facing the stairs and Jerod behind him, his right arm in a death grip around the custodian's neck. Several feet farther down the hallway lay the gun that must have fallen out in the struggle.

I edged around both men to get the gun and, as I came up alongside Jose, I noticed his face had lost all color, his skin turning blue. Under the clamp of Jerod's powerful arm, the custodian could not breathe. His brown eyes stared over at me, pleading, bug-eyed. Both arms hung limp at his side.

I turned back. "Jerod, you're going to strangle him." He did not ease his grip and I reached my hand to his arm. His muscles felt like a taut rope. "Jerod, we need to talk to him. Let up a little. Let him breathe." My fingers tapped his bulging forearm and I looked at his eyes.

Finally, I saw his muscles relax a bit and heard Jose's sudden intake of breath.

"Thanks, Mees Dee Dee," Jose wheezed. "I was just checking down here. There must be some meestake." His feet edged forward an inch on the concrete.

"Afraid not, Jose," I responded and I looked down at his feet, which immediately stopped moving.

"Mees, I would not hurt you," Jose said, pleading in his voice.

"Jose, we know about you and the terrorists," I said.

"Mees Dee Dee, I don't know what you talking ab--" was all he got out.

Jerod tightened his grip again, cutting off the airflow. He said, "Try again, Jose!"

"Jose, don't even bother," I said and rested my hand on Jerod's tightened grip. He eased up half an inch and Jose coughed and breathed in again. "We heard you down here before talking with the other terrorist."

"Where is he?" Jose said.

"We'll ask the questions," Jerod said, first tightening his grip and then he backed off a bit. "First of all, how do we get out of here without being seen?"

"I don't know what you mean. The stairs there lead up to the gym," Jose said, his head nodding toward the stairs he had just come down.

"I don't mean those stairs," Jerod said as he tightened his grip again. "I mean the other way out!"

"Jerod, what are you talking about?" Jose choked out.

"Jose, I saw ya come in down those stairs earlier," Jerod said, "and you never went out the same way."

"Oka-ay, okay. There is a set of fire stairs in the back of the locker room. Most people don't know about them. They come up in the kitchen behind the cafeteria."

"That's better," responded Jerod, easing his grip around the custodian's neck.

"What I want to know is where are they holding all the kids and the teachers?" I asked.

"I don't know, Mees Dee--" Jerod's grip cut him off again before he could finish.

I moved next to him, looked up into his face and threw my hard words like darts at his pinched features. "Jose, these criminals have already killed people and tried to kill me and Jerod. Either you help us or I'll let Jerod choke the rest of the life out of you."

I don't know if I would have let Jerod squeeze his neck till his eyes popped, but right then with my rage seething like an angry sea, it was an attractive prospect. My fury at what Jose and the terrorists had done to my school was unraveling whatever moral compunctions held such inhibitions at bay. I thought again of the blossoming red circle on Christie's white sweater and I wanted to choke this sniveling janitor with my own two hands. Perhaps Jose read the anger in my eyes. Either that or he couldn't breathe and was willing to do anything to get some air. He nodded his head and Jerod relaxed his arm.

After several loud breaths, Jose managed to get out, "Oka-ay. When I left to come down here, Yasseem had them in the cafeteria."

"Yassim?" I asked.

"Yes, he's the leader."

"How many are there?" I snapped back.

"I'm not sure," Jose started and when the grip started to tighten, his right arm came up to Jerod and tugged. "Let me feenish," he got out and then breathed again as Jerod relaxed his grip again. "I never saw all of them in one place, but I think there is only four."

"Four?" Jerod said. "Four terrorists holding five hundred? Come on, Jose?" He pulled his arm back toward him.

Jose clawed at the encroaching arm. "I tell you the truth," he gasped. "They keep the keeds in the lunchroom with two guns." Jerod let up as he listened. "You know those automatic guns?"

"You mean AK-47's?"

"Yes, I heard them say AK-47...and bombs."

"Bombs?" I said.

"Yes, they say Mustafa has booby trapped schools weeth--"

The staccato burst of gunfire erupted from the end of the hall, just in front of the stairs. Jose's body slumped beside me, his blood erupting in red jets onto me. I shot a glance down the narrow corridor. Another terrorist pointed an automatic rifle directly at me.

"Oh, God!" I screamed before he fired again.

Chapter 49

"Excuse me again for interrupting, Mr. President," petitioned the voice through the speakerphone, "but we've received another fax from the school."

"Send the fax through," commanded the President.

In a few seconds the fax machine whirred. Samson rose from the table, walked over to the machine and retrieved the single sheet of paper. Returning to the oval table, he laid the page in front of President Gregory, who read it aloud.

"TIME IS QUICKLY RUNNING OUT. MR. PRESIDENT. RELEASE OUR BROTHER ASAD AKADI. IF YOU DO NOT, YOU AND THE CHILDREN OF THURBER HIGH SCHOOL WILL SOON LEARN JUST HOW IMPOTENT YOU AND YOUR GOVERNMENT ARE. Pompous asshole!" Gregory slammed his palms on the table.

"Who do these people think they are?" snarled Dean Settler, pacing across the front of the room. His feet hammered the ceramic tiles on the floor. "We can't let them get away--" His complaint was interrupted by another beep of the speakerphone.

"Mr. President? Sir, you might want to turn on CNN in there."

"Thanks, MC," said President Gregory.

Closest to the bank of large screen televisions, Settler moved to the first and hit the power button. The huge picture sprang to life, showing a talking head with a picture of a second head to his right, the second one Arab. Settler reached up and turned up the sound.

"...and we have just learned that Al Jazeera network has broadcast what they claim is a fax from terrorists holding over five hundred children and adults hostage in a high school in rural Ohio," the talking head half spoke, half read.

"Oh shit!" snarled Tom Dickson. "The whole Goddamn world will know in about five minutes!"

The talking head on the screen continued while his foreign counterpart spoke in Arabic, holding a copy of the fax that lay on the cherry table. "According to the Al Jazeera report, these terrorists are holding the hostages in a demand for the release of Asad Akadi, the convicted member of Al Quaida held in a nearby prison. Akadi is scheduled to be executed by lethal injection at the prison in Hammerville, Ohio in less than ninety minutes from now, at six p.m."

As CNN carried a close up of the Al Jazeera camera shot of the fax, the reporter read it aloud for the audience. Settler reached up and turned down the volume.

"The whole Goddamn world already knows!" repeated the FBI Director.

"Okay, gentlemen, what do we do about it?" asked the President.

"Sir! This, this terrorist," stammered Settler, his face red and his slight tick returning to his eye, "this terrorist just called you 'impotent' in front of the entire world!"

"Mr. President, sir," added Dickson, "my SWAT and HRT teams are in place. Just say the word and they can neutralize this bastard."

"And the hostages?" asked the President.

"Sir, for the sake of the election and for the stature of our country, you cannot even appear to be impotent," said Settler.

"Well, Dean, I don't think it will do my election or the stature of our country any good if we end up killing hundreds of teenagers and adults," said the President.

"Sir, the terrorists may just kill them anyway," said Garcia. "That is how these terrorist groups work."

"Jerry, you're not saying we should give up Akadi, are you?" the President asked, facing him.

"No sir."

"Well, come down off that ivory tower intelligence mountain. What do you think we ought to do?"

"Sir, with the little 'intelligence' we have about what's going on, I'm inclined to agree with Tom. The worst thing would be to do nothing," Garcia said.

"Harold?"

Samson felt the stares of all four men on him again. "Well sir, I'm certainly no expert in interpreting these kinds of messages, but it looks to me like he's trying to goad you into rash action. Not only the rhetoric, but the fact that he released it to the Al Jazeera network." Harold's eyes roamed around the table, searching the face of each man. "I believe the email we received is legitimate, sir, and I believe we have a chance to save the hostages. If we rush the school, who's to say that the terrorists haven't laid another trap for our assault team, as well as the hostages?"

"That's exactly what these fanatics crave," the President said, "to go out in a blaze of glory on network TV." He went silent, his fingers drumming the top of the cherry table. For almost a minute, none of the other men interrupted or spoke.

Ryan Gregory finally looked up and turned to Dickson, "Tom, tell your troops that they need to move up to within a hundred yards of the school but hold their place. No one in or anywhere near that school yet, and that includes air as well. We can't have a news copter fly over the school and get shot down live on CNN."

"Yes, sir," replied Dickson, his thick shoulders straightening at the order.

"And Harold," Gregory turned back to Samson, the president's eyes the frozen blue of the sky on a frigid winter day, "get me some communication from that Dee Dee or whomever. We have to have some idea what's going on inside that school."

Chapter 50

For the second time in hours, I stared, helpless, into the specter of my own death. Down the hall, a gray-bearded Arab pointed the AK-47 directly at us. The barrel of the gun erupted again, spitting fire.

At the same instant, Jerod grabbed me with his left arm and pulled me behind him, as he backed up using Jose's body as a narrow shield. Another round of bullets hit the concrete where I had been standing a second before, blasting cement chips into my legs. The next volley slammed into the dead body of Jose, jerking it with each hit, like a gangly puppet on strings. Jerod tried to duck behind the thinner man, struggling to avoid the bullets. Then, with one arm, he threw me sideways through the open doorway into the locker room.

"Get the gun!" He yelled as he dropped Jose's bloodied body on the concrete and disappeared back into the small office across the hall.

The echo of the terrorist's boots bounced loudly off the walls in the narrow hallway sounding like the recent staccato of gunfire. For a second, I lay there, sprawled on the locker room floor, stunned.

Where was the gun? I looked frantically around the locker room. Four more hurried steps on the concrete floor outside the door. I scrambled to my feet, scanning the room, and tried to remember. I saw the gun and the intruder's shadow at the same time. I dove headlong under the bench in the back corner of the room, just as another burst of gunfire sprayed the room. The rounds exploded into the metal lockers in rapid succession. The stink of burning cordite mingled with the locker room smells.

"Hey, Ahab!" I heard Jerod scream from the office across the hall. Craning my neck around the wood of the bench, I dared a look back at the door and saw the barrel of the gun retreat back through the doorway. Jerod's yell distracted the terrorist. I heard him retreat into the hallway.

Jerod had no weapon. The handgun he had taken off the first terrorist was still lying on the concrete floor in the hall. I couldn't get to it without being seen. From my prone position, I studied the locker room. It was a good-sized room with blue and white lockers lining each wall and another group, back to back, forming a bay down the center of the room. I saw the automatic rifle across the room just beyond the corner of the center lockers, but I didn't know if I could work it. I'd never even held one before. In seconds, the intruder was surely going to spray the office where Jerod was.

I willed myself to move and pulled my body out from under the bench and scurried across the room to the other set of lockers. As I crossed the room to get to the gun, I had to go past the open door.

The terrorist was in the doorway across the hall with his back to me but he must've heard my footsteps. He turned back toward the locker room, and I saw the barrel of the AK-47 swing toward me.

"Our Father who art in heaven!" I whispered. Even as my hands reached the gun, I turned to see the ugly smirk of the brown jagged teeth staring at me as his finger moved to the trigger. I remember thinking I didn't have enough time. I can't get the gun raised up in time.

Jerod had somehow managed to grab onto the frame above the door and hoist himself up. He swung his body in a hard arc at the terrorist like some crazed acrobat. The Arab was concentrating on me, watching me fumble with the gun. He smiled, watching me squirm as he raised the automatic rifle at me. He never even saw it coming.

Jerod's two swinging feet slammed into his back so hard that the terrorist fell straight down. He struck the concrete floor of the hallway with such force that the crash knocked the AK-47 out of his grasp. I watched the gun slide left out of my view and heard it bang against the far wall. From the sound I guessed it was out of his reach and Jerod's as well.

Jerod dropped onto the floor and grabbed the Arab, who was momentarily dazed. But the terrorist uttered a guttural yell and turned even in Jerod's grasp. He lowered his shoulders into Jerod and drove hard. Both men staggered back through the doorway of the office, the Arab on top now. I raised the rifle and had to look down to find the safety and, after fumbling a bit, flipped it off. I didn't know what I was going to do. I didn't see how I could shoot the terrorist without hitting Jerod, but I had to do something.

When I looked back up, the two men were gone from my view. I heard an unintelligible word in Arabic and a crash from inside the room across the hallway. Gun raised, I edged out the door of the locker room across the hall toward the office. Just before I got to the door, I heard it. One shot exploded from inside the room. Then a scream.

Cradling the rifle with both hands, I stepped around Jose's bullet-riddled body and the ugly mud-red rivulets of blood and peered through the door into the office. There, on the cement floor lay the two men, the Arab still atop Jerod.

Neither was moving. I held the gun at the pair, not knowing what to do. Then I noticed the blood running over Jerod's sweatshirt and flooding onto the gray concrete. Tears poured down my face and I tried to aim the gun at the terrorist but my hand was shaking.

""You bastard!" I screamed through my tears and tightened my finger on the trigger.

Chapter 51

Rashid leaned against the huge pillar on the right side of the cafeteria and closed his eyes. Standing there out of view of the others, he tried again to call up the picture of his mother and sister again, but nothing came this time. Desperately, he willed his mind to produce their images, but all he could conjure up were indistinct silhouettes, all fog and hazy details. Except the eyes. He could see their brown eyes clearly, red-rimmed and haunted.

The words of the Sheik came back to him. "I will make it my personal responsibility to take care of them...while you serve our sacred cause. If you perform your duties well, I will make certain nothing happens to them." The Sheik did not need to say the rest.

Rashid wrestled his attention back and studied the room again. With the damaged, intermittent lighting, all he could catch were glimpses of faces and forms, the rest swallowed up by the darkened patches of the room. As his eyes swept the lunchroom, he saw no cause for concern. The faces he was able to make out were those of defeated adults and teens, clinging to each other, waiting to die. Many of the students huddled together, crying and praying quietly, desperately. As he listened, the voices of the students and teachers receded and merged to a single murmur that seemed to drift around the cafeteria from one group to another like some ominous cloud.

As his glance made the next sweep around the room, he caught a glimpse of a face. His eyes focused on her, a slim figure standing alone about twenty feet away. Like everyone else, she wore the mantle of fear, the features of her face pinched tightly, but beyond that, there was something more. He could not tear his gaze from her face, the shallow light from one of the working fixtures drew a line down the center of her face, leaving half in shadow. As Rashid stared across the dimly lit space, the half-lit face ignited another memory. Her skin was fairer, of course, and her nose smaller, more petite, but the resemblance was startling. Otherwise, he could have sworn that he had just seen Jabirah, the maiden who had attended him in the Cavern of Near Paradise. The same soft lips and the one eye visible, a piercing blue. It was not possible, he rationalized. She was thousands of miles away and this room was hardly the Cavern.

Then, the girl turned fully toward Rashid, the fluorescent bulb bathing the skin of her face in an alabaster sheen. The two blue eyes, deep in their saddened sockets, called to him, pleaded with him. Now, in full light, the lines of fear seemed to tighten around the mouth, forcing the imagined resemblance to fade. He saw her for who she was, just another terrified, helpless American teen. He glanced away.

When he looked at where the girl had been standing, he expected to see her gone, an apparition swallowed by the mist of the shadows in the room. But she was still there, still standing alone, still staring back at him. Even knowing this was no Jabirah, his gaze remained riveted on her and, as he watched, silent tears trickled down her whitened cheeks, glistening in the limited florescent light. Her quiet weeping served only to intensify his guilt.

Was this the Islam his Imam had dutifully taught him, reading each night from the Koran? Did Allah have no regard for these, for ones like the frail weeping young woman? he wanted to ask.

Even remembering the boasting of the Americans and the abuse he had taken, and recalling the tales he had been told in the camp, it was now hard to see these terrified teens as part of some powerful enemy of Islam. Glancing around at the huddled hostages, he pondered the unthinkable for a soldier of Allah: what would their certain deaths accomplish? What would his? He decided he needed to speak with Yassim.

Weaving between the knotted throngs of students, he made his way back up to the front of the room, where Yassim stood, automatic rifle in hand. With a wary look, the cell leader watched him approach.

"You have a question," Yassim said to the teen soldier, without even taking his eyes off the crowd. "I can see it in your face."

"Yes." Rashid stared at the cell leader, an intimidating figure with a pistol wedged into his belt and his arms gripping the AK-47. His resolve evaporated and he said, "The American president is not going to release our brother, Asad."

"Is that a question or a statement?" Yassim looked at Rashid for the first time. The teen fighter watched his fingers twitch slightly on the trigger.

"A question," Rashid said quietly.

"And a perceptive one." The cell leader peered again across the lunchroom. "In a few minutes, I will check the fax, but I do not expect any concessions. To answer your question, no, I do not think President Gregory is

interested in releasing Asad. No doubt, his political handlers tell him, it is bad for his image. But the Sheik knew that was a possibility from the beginning."

"What of these?" Rashid asked, his head nodding toward the crowd of huddled students and teachers behind him.

"The American president's actions simply prove what we have learned in the camps." Yassim again stared at his youngest team member, a small smile playing across his face. "He cares a great deal more for his political career than for several hundred American teenagers."

"And now?"

"Now I am concerned because Mustafa and Fadi have not returned. Perhaps someone remains downstairs. It is possible we may have more problems than we had planned for."

"Do you wish me to go search for them?"

"No, I cannot afford to lose any more of my soldiers. We will wait for our enemy to come to us." Yassim paused and looked directly at his younger partner. "It does not matter now."

"I do not understand, Yassim."

The cell leader glanced at his watch. "Asad is scheduled to be executed in less than an hour. And, if Mustafa did the rest of his work around the building as well as the front entrance, we will all be meeting Allah at that appointed hour."

"Is there nothing else to do?"

"Do not concern yourself, young soldier. Make your peace with Allah. The Sheik has arranged for our martyrdom to be witnessed around the world." The cell leader's eyes glowed at the prospect. "You are indeed fortunate. You are about to become a famous warrior of the Jihad. Generations of believers will sing songs to your bravery."

"Yes, Yassim."

Turning away from the face of the cell leader, it was only then the vision of his mother jumped into Rashid's mind. He saw her clearly now, her wispy brown hair pulled back and her small mouth turned down. In his mind's eye, she stared at him, shook her head slowly from side to side and began to cry.

Rashid moved away so Yassim would not see him, but he could not control himself. His own tears rolled silently down his face.

Chapter 52

"Hey, lit'l lady, ease up on that trigger finger!"

I was standing over the two sprawled figures on the floor of the office, the terrorist atop the blood-covered form of Jerod. I had figured Jerod was dead and my finger tensed, ready to fire. I was gripping the gun so hard my knuckles were white.

"Ya know, that rifle can put eight bullets in me in 1.6 seconds," Jerod said from beneath the terrorist, "and I'd rather you not."

"If you don't cut out the 'lit'l lady' stuff, I might just be tempted to," I said.

"Dee Dee, could you put that down and help get this guy off me? He weighs a ton."

I dropped the automatic weapon heavily on the cement floor. The arms of the Arab lying atop Jerod had flailed out, spread-eagle style, his body completely covering Jerod's body. I moved up beside the two and my right foot stepped into a pool of warm liquid. I looked down, seeing the blood, bright red against the gray concrete, oozing onto my bare foot, and I gagged.

"Hang in there, Dee Dee," said Jerod, "breathe through your mouth."

I did as he said, three long breaths.

"Ya goin' to be okay?" he asked from the floor.

I nodded my head slowly.

"Okay, grab his arm and see if you can flip him over."

I tried but couldn't budge him.

"This guy is heavy. We'll do it together," he said, seeing me struggle. "On three. One...two...three!"

I heaved and he pushed and, with our combined effort we rolled the body over with a thud onto the concrete floor. My glance traveled with the motion of the dead man and only then did I notice the hilt of a knife sticking out of the side of his chest, surrounded by a gaping red hole.

"Where'd that come from?" I asked, my eyes transfixed on the knife.

Jerod pushed himself up to a sitting position, his bare chest covered with streaks of the dead man's blood.

"After I kicked the gun outta his hands, he pulled that thing," he said. "I believe he intended to use it on me. It wasn't easy, but I got it away from him. Then all of a sudden, he charged me and I got the knife up just in time. He ran into it."

He looked over at me as I was staring at the blood covering his chest and running down the front of his pants. His eyes did a once-over of the blood splattered down his frame and then met mine. "Yeah, when I first felt the blood runnin' on me, I waddn't sure it weren't mine. When I realized it was his, I felt a mite better. That is, until I thought you was goin' shoot me."

"When I came in and saw all that blood, I--I--I thought it was yours. I thought you were dead," I blubbered.

"Glad to see ya still care," Jerod said and flashed that wonderful southern boy smile.

I was so glad to see that smile again, I almost bawled in front of him.

He got to his feet and walked quickly out the door. I heard his feet on the concrete pace into the locker room across the hall. When he returned, he was holding a grubby sweatshirt and used it to wipe off.

"We need to get outta here," he said. "When this guy dudn't come back," his hand jerked toward the dead man on the floor next to me, "his friends'll send somebody else to find him, not to mention snoozy there." Jerod's head jerked toward the closet where our first visitor lay, tied up and apparently still unconscious.

"How do they know we're down here?"

"I dunno," Jerod said, as he finished wiping the worst of the blood off his chest and pants. He slid another top over his head, covering up his red-smeared flesh. He had donned a soiled gray Notre Dame sweatshirt with the logo of the Irishman ready to pick a fight. "Or mebbe they just sent somebody down here to check things out and they ran into us. Either way, I don't think it matters."

"At least we know there's only two of them left."

"If Jose was tellin' the truth."

As I watched, he began searching the body with the practiced precision of a police officer, and I was suddenly reminded of his real job as a professional prison guard.

"How did you know to do all this?" I asked.

"What?"

"Where did you learn to handle these guys?"

"Oh, I did a stint as a Navy Seal in the Gulf. The skills come in handy every once in a while."

I shook my head and examined the face of the terrorist. I didn't recognize him at first. This wasn't the Arab who had been the one in charge of the cafeteria takeover, the guy Jose had called Yassim. The dead Arab was lying face up on the floor, his brown eyes wide open, as if staring at me, looking wild, even in death. The bottom of his face was edged with a scruffy, gray beard and the top by an unkempt sprout of hair of the same color. His features were ugly-- broken nose and scars beneath the mouth and running down the side of his head into the right ear--a face that looked fearsome, even in death. He was about six feet tall and I would've guessed weighed almost three hundred pounds. Seeing his size, I wondered how Jerod had been able to overpower him. Then my glance traveled up to his mouth again, and seeing the rotten teeth, it came back to me. I could still see the vision of him, leering at my naked body along with Jesus up on the deck. Suddenly I felt a primal thrill that he was dead. I wanted to kick the body.

Jerod's hands moved methodically over the body with little concern for the dead, exploring pockets and checking expertly for stashed weapons. Watching Jerod work, I realized it was no accident that he had saved my life twice already.

"Why would he lie?" I asked, when I could find my voice again.

"What?" He was still absorbed in his task.

"Why would Jose lie?"

"Why not?" Jerod said, completing the search. He had found nothing else. "He had thrown his lot in with the terrorists. Why would he tell us the truth?"

"I don't get it. Jose was a Mexican immigrant, who had been in this country for something like fifteen years. Why would he help a bunch of Arab terrorists?"

"I dunno," replied Jerod immediately, standing alongside of me. "Mebbe they were able to get to him because America had denied him the good life for all those years." He stopped and looked directly at me. "Or maybe, he just wanted the money. We learned the hard way in Iraq and Afganistan that a great many terrorists are motivated more by greed than by any religious causes."

I headed for the door, but his hand on my arm stopped me. The warmth of his hand on my skin was electric and comforting at the same time. I turned to look back at him

"Not that way, remember?" he said, smiling at me again. "We need t' use the back stairs Jose told us about."

I nodded my head up and down slowly, my gaze focused on his hand gently resting on my arm.

"And I believe I have a plan!" he added, his smile widening as we moved down the hallway.

Standing in the cramped office, he filled me in on his "grand plan" in less than two minutes. It was improbable at best, but it was a cinch I wasn't coming up with anything better, so I said, "Okay."

"Yeah, but first I think that ya need to contact your friend at Homeland Security and let 'em know what we know."

"You sure you don't want to do it?" I asked.

"Nope. We ain't got much time and you're a faster typist," Jerod said. "Besides that'll give me time to go up the stairs and reconnoiter. See if ole Jose was tellin' the truth. If everythin's okay, I'll be back to get you." When I didn't move right away, he said, "Get to it, lit'l lady. Ya got three minutes."

I moved back to the computer. I didn't know what I was going to say, but as soon as the computer was up and connected, my fingers were flying over the keys, spelling and grammar be damned.

Chapter 53

When he reentered the Situation Room, copies of the newest email in hand, Samson thought the President was in the worst shape he had ever seen. Gregory maintained his position at the head of the conference table, but nothing else about him looked the same. The expression he wore was one of defeat, and perhaps fear. His mouth drooped, reversing his charismatic smile into an oppressive frown. His right hand squeezed a blue pen, his fingertips white from exertion and his thumb tapped on the pen nonstop. His gaze was fixed on the widescreen TV's, on which the networks were maintaining continuous coverage of what the media had dubbed, "The Siege at Thurber."

"Sir, this just came in," began Samson. "It's from Dee Dee Sterber again at Thurber."

Without preamble, President Gregory began reading out loud again.

"Mr. Samson,

Interrupted by another intruder before. We've seen two more terrorists. Both dead now. Going upstars to get to the teachers and students. Jerod's gota plan and I only got a minute. Got from one of them before we killed him, there only be a few terrorists left upstairs, but not sure. None down here any more. Got to go now.

One more. Got out of him that the terrorists have booby-trapped all the school exits and rigged them to blow.

Dee Dee Sterber"

"Come on, Harold," blurted out Garcia, who had moved a few seats up to be closer to the President. "This sounds too good to be true. If I understand it, this teacher and this Jerod have killed three terrorists? Are we expected to believe this?"

"Who is Jerod?" The President's gaze alternated between Samson and the TV's.

"I'm sorry, sir, that's what took me a few minutes. All we got is a first name, so we're not sure, but we believe he is Jerod Thomas, a correctional officer employed by HBE. He also spent seven years as a Navy SEAL and served in the Iraq War."

"What's he doing at the high school?" asked Dickson, who had hung up the phone and had taken a chair near the end of the table by the President. Only

Settler remained where he had been, paper in hand, still pacing at the front of the room.

"Again, we can't be certain, but Jerod Thomas is registered as a volunteer mentor for some of Ms. Sterber's students," continued Harold. "We believe he may have just been in the building when the terrorists staged their takeover."

"Why wasn't he working at the prison?" Dickson asked, skepticism evident in his voice.

"According to Jim Cromer, he just came off a twelve-hour shift and left the prison around ten this morning," Samson explained. "He usually does his volunteer work right after he leaves HBE, so his showing up at Thurber makes sense."

"Really bad timing on his part," mused Gregory.

"Could just as easily be a set up," said a testy Garcia. "How do we know he's not working with the terrorists?"

"We don't know ANYTHING for sure, Jerry," said Samson, matching Garcia's tone briefly, "because we don't have anyone in that school."

"Well, I think we should send the HRT to take the school," said the FBI Director. "If there are only a few left, our trained men can overpower them and save some lives."

"How many lives?" the President asked.

"I don't know, sir. There are too many factors we don't know."

"What if it's a set up?" asked Garcia again. "We have no idea who this email came from," Garcia said. "It could just as easily come from one of the terrorists. Maybe they want us to think that there are only a few left." His gaze shifted from one man to the other and ended on Gregory. "Or maybe they want us to think the place is booby-trapped, so we don't come storming in. That's exactly the kind of disinformation our people have been trained to give in this kind of situation."

"Which is it?" asked President Gregory sharply.

"Sir?" said Garcia. "I don't understand."

"Are the terrorists telling us that they are down to a few men to *lure* us in or are they planting the story that the school is rigged to blow so we *don't* come? It can't be both."

"I-I-I don't know, sir," said Garcia.

Settler chose this moment to stop his pacing and stepped over to the end of the table. He stood next to Gregory and said, "Mr. President, I concur with Tom. I think we need to go in," Settler said.

"And why is that?" the President said with increasing impatience.

"Sir, I believe that no matter which way it turns out, it's important that we have to play this one right," said the Chief of Staff and hesitated and then added, "if you want to have any political future after this."

"What do you mean?"

"Well, sir, the most important thing is that you do not appear impotent." Settler paused briefly and then went on. "I'm afraid that is how we look right now."

"I'd think that the most important thing is saving students' lives," said Gregory.

Samson stared at the man hunched above the President. Dean Settler appeared even more gaunt than normal, the skin on his face hanging loose as if it could actually slide off.

"What if the building blows up and kills everyone?" Gregory asked.

"I'm not sure that matters, sir," said Settler. "In the public eye, you cannot be seen to be sitting on your hands. Americans want their President to take decisive action against these terrorists."

"Even if it costs innocent lives?"

"Even at the cost of innocent lives, sir. They want their leader to be strong and not concede."

Sitting to the side, Harold watched this exchange as the two men faced each other, ignoring the others in the room. Settler was in his element now. As he made his rational argument, a calm seemed to descend upon him. After the exchange, Harold thought Settler's face sagged less, as if air had been pumped into his features and brought them new life. Even after three years in this White House, Samson found it strange that when Settler plotted political strategy, he divorced himself from all other reality. When he was saving Ryan Gregory's presidency, nothing else mattered, not even the lives of innocent children.

"Go on," said Gregory, the impatience in his voice replaced by curiosity. "And what of the five hundred students and teachers?"

Settler finished. "For all we know they may die even if we do nothing. And if some die in the process, Americans will blame the terrorists, not you, sir."

Ryan Gregory sat and nodded slightly, still silent.

"Mr. President," Samson interrupted, "I realize that we cannot make deals with terrorists, but is it possible that we could postpone the execution? We have less than an hour. If we delayed Akadi's death, it might stall the terrorists and give us the time to put a stronger plan together."

Settler, still standing over the others, shook his head. "That would only make you look weak, sir," he said.

"My teams are ready now, Mr. President," announced Tom Dickson.

Gregory turned his gaze directly on the Director of Homeland Security. "Harold, do you think postponing the execution will cause them to do anything different?"

"It might buy us some time," Samson answered, "but no, sir. I now don't believe the terrorists counted on freeing Akadi. Oh, they wanted us to, but they knew, going in, we don't negotiate with terrorists. They probably made up their minds to be satisfied with the media coverage to show the world the true face of the Great Satan."

"And what about the students?" asked Gregory.

Samson sighed loudly and looked at the President. "My guess is that they are probably to be sacrificed on the terrorists' altar, along with the true disciples of Allah."

"Then we don't have much choice, do we?" said the President.

"I'm just suggesting we give Sterber and this Jerod a little more time, sir," responded Samson. "What do we have to lose?"

"Critical time!" screamed Dickson.

Just then the speakerphone beeped loudly. "Mr. President, I have a call for Mr. Samson from James Cromer at HBE."

"Harry?" said the voice through the speaker.

"Yes, Jim," answered Samson quickly.

"Are you with the President?" asked Cromer.

"Yes, Jim, go ahead," said Harold.

"Harry, I just thought you should know," began Cromer and then added, "And you too, Mr. President. The Fox News truck that was here covering the

execution just left the designated area and is supposed to be heading for
Thurber. According to the guard who cleared them to leave, the reporter,
Claudia somebody, said they just got a tip that there was going to be a lot bigger
story at the high school. According to the guard, some anonymous tip actually
said, 'A real explosive story.'"

"Okay, Jim, what about the other news crews?" asked Harold.

"They seemed to be staying put--at least for now. Harry, what the hell is
going on? We're a little busy around here but my guys heard about the threat on
TV? Is it for real?"

"Yes, Jim, it's very real," said Harold Samson.

"No shit," started Cromer and then corrected himself. "Excuse me, Mr.
President. Sir, do you want me to postpone the execution?"

"No, warden, I do not. Stay your course and we will be in touch." Ryan
Gregory pushed the disconnect button. Without waiting, he took one look at the
bank of TV monitors and turned to the FBI Director. "Dickson, move your team
outside the school. Get ready, but don't go in until I say so. I want them close
enough to be seen from the school, but I don't want some trigger happy kid to
go in blasting until I authorize it."

"Yes, sir, Mr. President," answered Tom Dickson. The former NFL
fullback stood and moved quickly to the phone he had been using at the other
end of the table. He grabbed up the receiver and his fat fingers started
hammering numbers.

Looking at the piece of paper, Samson whispered, "God help you, Dee Dee
Sterber."

Chapter 54

Before I was finished typing the email, Jerod was back. I keyed the last few words and hit the send button. "I just hope somebody gets these."

"I'm not sure it matters much. I figger we're pretty much on our own."

"That just fills me with confidence, you know."

I took the few steps over to him by the newly discovered door. It was just a single plywood panel in the wall with a recessed handle, not obvious to the untrained eye. I could see how we missed it before.

Standing next to me, Jerod leaned in close and kissed me.

"You goin' to be all right, Dee Dee?"

"I think so."

"Ya know what you gotta do?"

"Yeah," I answered, nodding my head slowly. "I'm to get to the kids and get them out."

"Okay, then, stay close behind me." Jerod kissed me again, a quick peck this time.

Before I could respond, he walked over to the desk and, in one move, grabbed the AK-47, slid the strap over his head, and stepped through the small doorway. I followed right behind. My legs felt heavy as if they had been nailed to their spot, but I forced them upward, taking the steps one at a time. The stairs were narrow, metal grilles, the ones you can see right through. I always had a sense of vertigo walking on see-through steps, and this was no exception. The telltale signs hit my head, the dizziness cascading across my skull in waves from front to back. I shook my head to clear it, but clarity was slow in coming, my head still reeling from the earlier concussion.

My eyes flitted from the darkened stairs to the figure ascending faster than I could keep up. What the hell, I thought and pushed ahead. Above me, Jerod's movements were fluid, purposeful, a man who knew what he was doing. How can he have such confidence? I drew a breath, tried to quiet my trembling and pumped my legs up the steps to try to keep pace with my partner.

"Com'on Dee Dee!"

I hurried up the last few steps. At the second to the last step, Jerod grabbed my hand and half-pulled, half-guided me up. As I stepped through the small doorway, I realized we had emerged near the rear of the cafeteria kitchen. Just beyond the doorway, we had to step around a 55-gallon drum that sat conspicuously in front of the door on the floor of the kitchen. I noted the yellow label along the side of the barrel, which read "Cleaning Supplies." As we edged around it, careful not to make a sound, I thought what a strange place to leave a drum.

The rest of the kitchen was all shadows and darkness with the only light seeping in through the grease-covered, slanted window above two huge stoves. As my eyes began to adjust, I could make out the shapes of the large stoves standing like hulking monsters against the right wall. Along the opposite wall were the doors of the huge walk-in refrigerator, their chrome handles and hinges barely reflected in the grayish light. A sheet with dollops of peanut butter cookie dough still sat atop the first oven, waiting to be baked, their shapes darkened teardrops caught amid fall. The cookie dough wasn't fragrant, but hadn't yet started to stink.

Jerod stepped up to one of the islands the cooks used to prepare the food and I came up alongside him. At the base of the island, I spotted a small paring knife lying on the floor. It lay like some forgotten child's toy, alone, ignored, the black handle and silver blade a sharp contrast against the white vinyl floor. Without thinking, I reached down and pocketed it. Leaning against the work island, Jerod swung the automatic rifle around and lifted the sling over his head. He brought the weapon around and rested it against the crook of his left arm.

The aluminum swing doors stood directly ahead of us, like silent, still sentries guarding passage into the cafeteria. Standing at the island, I studied the dim kitchen. The entire room had an eerie, deserted quality about it. It was hard to imagine that a few hours ago it had been bustling with action, preparing hundreds of lunches.

Jerod moved around the island and went through the doors and, in a few seconds, reemerged through the aluminum doors. I breathed an audible sigh at his reappearance.

"I've checked and the area in front of the doors is clear," Jerod whispered. "The terrorists must've taken out some more lights 'cause it's pretty dark out there." His face was turned toward me and he must've seen something he didn't like. "Dee Dee, ya all right? Your face is all white!"

I looked back and nodded. "Yeah, I'm okay. Just scared."

"At least one of the terrorists is at this end of the cafeteria, left out those doors. When I peeked out before I couldn't see him--couldn't see much from the doorway--but I could hear 'm pacing back and forth. At least, I figgered it was him. He's my job. Ya' give me a few seconds and you head out those doors and turn right." He nodded toward the pair of motionless aluminum doors.

I strained to listen from where we stood, but I couldn't hear anything from the cafeteria. It was hard to believe there were almost five hundred students and teachers out there and you couldn't hear a sound where we were. For a moment, I considered the unthinkable, that they were already dead. Jerod didn't let me ponder the possibility for more than a second.

"Ya understand, you need to get to the kids, while I'm, um, should we say, distractin' the terrorists," he said, still keeping his voice in an even whisper, the essence of calm. My insides were jumping.

"I know, I know," I whispered back. "I'm heading right and around the corner to the hallway and then to the side door to the cafeteria to where we think the first of the students and teachers are." I repeated my part of our plan to reassure myself as well as him.

"Give me a lit'l time," Jerod reminded me. "If they see ya first, you'll be in trouble."

"You be careful, Jerod," I pleaded, and without warning, tears began sliding down over my cheekbones.

"Don't worry about me, lit'l lady," he said in a poor imitation of the Duke and then he kissed me. It was a short, friendly kiss--all reassurance and no passion--and that worried me somehow.

At the kiss I closed my eyes briefly and by the time I opened them again, he was gone and the left aluminum door was swinging silently back. I urged my sluggish feet to move. By the time my hand gently pushed open the right door, I figured I was about ten seconds behind Jerod. As I exited, I looked to my left, to the direction Jerod had gone and thought I could see his shadow moving along the wall, but I couldn't be sure.

With Jerod gone, standing alone in the shroud of darkness outside the doors, a new wave of panic engulfed me. A temptation flitted through my brain. I knew my way around the building and I figured I could have easily kept going down the corridor past the cafeteria and been out of the building in less than a minute. I would be safe and alive and away from this madness.

My body began to tremble with indecision and I had to wrap both arms around my torso to stop the quivering. In my head, the siren of safety beckoned and involuntarily my foot took one step toward freedom. Then I heard her.

Somewhere, on the other side of the wall that shielded me, I heard a girl sobbing, her cries carrying through the plasterboard. She said, "I don't want to die."

That student, those words sealed it. If I hadn't heard that plea, who knows what I might've done. I may not even be here to tell you it all. I never did find out who the student was, but I'm so glad she was there. I started down the hall, searching in the darkness for the side door to the cafeteria just as we planned. I was amazed how quickly I reached it.

When I came up alongside the frame of the door, I stopped short. The door was shut and I brought my face up to the window in the door. Hands cupping my eyes, I peered through the glass panel, squinting into the darkened cafeteria. The room was a patchwork of ink and gray, with only the barest streaks of light filtering down from the few light fixtures still operating in the cafeteria. I had just enough light to make out some images and, as I squinted, the shadowy figures of teens and adults emerged from the darkness.

Everywhere I looked, they were huddled in small clusters, with the closest group to me fifteen feet from the door. Most were sitting, a few standing and pacing. In a few of the groups, I could see some of the students had lain down, their legs stretched out on the vinyl floor. I peered intently at the scene, trying desperately to locate students and teachers I recognized. I had more than a hundred students in my classes and knew every teacher by sight. I thought it would help steel my shaking resolve if I recognized some friendly faces, but the fates seemed intent on keeping me blind. No matter how hard I stared, it was no good. Almost all the students and teachers had their backs to my position and the patches of blackness that hung in the room conspired to hide faces.

From my vantage point at the door, I couldn't see either of the terrorists--or more if Jose had lied--and more importantly, I couldn't see Jerod. If he were able to sneak to where he figured he needed to be, he would be out of my view until I was inside the lunchroom, mixing with the students. I had not heard an ugly burst of gunfire, ripping the quiet stillness of the room of captives. I took that to be a good sign, so far. But I had to get out into the cafeteria if I was going to do any good--or get myself killed in the process, that voice in my head warned. I ignored the siren.

Instead I slowly opened the door and, crouching low, slipped into the lunchroom and tried to hide myself next to a table by the wall. From there I tried to half walk, half crouch to get to the nearest group of students. They were huddled together, their backs to me and did not see me approach. The first student I reached was a dark male, sitting on the ground, his head drooping in his hands. I tapped him gently on the shoulder and he lifted his dark face and turned to see who it was. As his gaze met mine, the fear that had initially ignited in his eyes melted quickly into relief. As recognition dawned on his features, a smile blossomed across his face.

"Ms. Sterber?!" he said, a little louder than I would have liked.

"Sh-sh-sh," I whispered, and then added, "Yeah, it's me and it's good to see you, Tyrone."

At the mention of his name, his smile widened. I had always loved to see that bright smile, flashing white against the brown skin and I couldn't remember a time when that sight was better. He turned abruptly away from me and stood up. Then he edged his way around three students and I saw him come up behind a girl sitting on the floor by herself and he put his hand on her shoulder. When she did not respond, he leaned over and whispered into her ear. Her head shot up like it had been pulled by a string and she turned in my direction. Even before she turned, I knew it was Tess. She stared back, wide-eyed behind those wonderful, brown horn-rimmed glasses. God, it was great to see that face! She jumped up and hurried over to my position.

In the few seconds it took her to reach me, my eyes briefly darted around the room. I located both terrorists, one at the front and the rear of the room, and studied them briefly. Neither one had seemed to notice me. It was obvious they were waiting, but they didn't look nervous. Both appeared calm as they surveyed the hostages spread out around them. I also couldn't see Jerod, but I figured that was good. He needed to stay hidden until he could reach the terrorist at the rear.

At the same time Tess reached me, calling my name aloud, I saw the figure and froze.

"Ms. S, I can't believe it!" Tess got out between flowing tears by the time she reached me. She grabbed me and hugged me, "I thought you were dead!"

My gaze drifted past her. When I didn't respond to her words, she tensed and asked, "What is it, Ms. S?" She followed my eyes and looked back where I was staring.

"Get behind me, Tess," I said.

Chapter 55

Rashid stared unbelieving at this newest apparition. First, my mother and sister and then Jabirah and now HER? It cannot be, he told himself.

He pushed himself away from the pillar he was using as support and stood up. Sliding the backpack off, he reached behind into the pocket, just to make sure the weapon was still there. Satisfied, he slid the pack on again and started walking toward her. With each step, he tried to make sense of it. It could not be. No longer bothering to blend in inconspicuously, he strode across the room. He bumped into several students, his shoulders roughly shoving them aside, ignoring their murmured protests. He kept his eyes trained on her, or the image, he still was not sure. He was aware of nothing else, of no one else in the room. In ten steps, he was standing in front of her. No, he thought, there can be no doubt.

"Ms. Sterber?" he asked, his voice a respectful whisper. "Is it truly you?" He noticed several students had gathered around her, their stances suddenly protective. His eyes darted to them and then back to her.

"Yes, Rashid, it is I," she responded with obvious confidence. "A little worse for the wear, perhaps."

"But--but I thought you were dead. I thought Jesus killed you."

"That seems to be the prevailing sentiment," she said and glanced at the students flanking her.

"I watched Jesus debase you and beat you unconscious and then knock you into the water," Rashid protested. He reached out his hand and touched her bare arm and then quickly withdrew his hand, as if her skin had been scalding to the touch.

"In the flesh." Miss Sterber smiled.

"But, b- but," he began, stuttering, "how can that be?"

She said, "To a man of faith like you, I would think the answer is obvious. It is not Allah's will that I die this day."

"I do not understand," Rashid said, shaking his head.

"Of course, you do, Rashid," she said quietly. "We are all subject to Allah's will. Jesus did all he could to humiliate me and tried his best to kill me, but Allah has other plans. Allah saved me in the water and he has brought me back to save these children."

Turmoil showed on Rashid's face.

Before he could decide what to do, he was distracted by a commotion in the rear of the cafeteria. Hypnotized by the appearance of Ms. Sterber, he had taken his attention off Yassim's position and now when he looked across the crowd, he could no longer see the leader. Drawn to the commotion, the students and teachers between him and Yassim stood up and blocked his view. He tried to move up closer, pushing his way around some students but there were too many standing now. He heard some scuffling noises and then the sounds of hundreds of teens and adults scrambling to their feet. He was trying to decide what to do when he heard a man yell across the room.

"Tell your men to come here and throw down their weapons!" the man screamed. The entire crowd went suddenly still. Then a murmur coursed through the hostages, like a giant wave coming to shore, realization rippling through the crowd.

The voice came from the rear about fifty feet away.

"I said tell your men to come here and throw down their weapons or I will kill you!" the voice repeated. "Now!"

Some of the teens had parted and turned to look at Jesus, who was stationed at the front of the room, at the opposite end of the lunchroom. From his vantage point, Rashid could see Jesus clearly now. Jesus did not move, except to raise the AK-47 and put his finger on the trigger. He waved the weapon from side to side and the hostages, who were standing, emboldened with new hope, cringed at the threat.

Rashid turned back to look at Ms. Sterber and noticed her gaze was also fixed on the confrontation at the rear. He moved again to try to see around the students and teachers and finally decided to use a chair. He pulled one from a table nearby and climbed atop it. He used the top of the plastic back to steady himself and stared toward the rear wall of the cafeteria. He saw Yassim in front of the glass doors with the deck and lake beyond. He was facing the hostages with another man's arm around his neck and a knife blade against his throat. Rashid noticed the cell leader did not have his weapon.

"This is the last time I'm going to ask," yelled the American and Rashid saw a jet of blood spurt from Yassim's neck. He flinched at the sight of his leader's wound and his hand went to the back pocket.

Then he heard Yassim call out through clenched teeth "إلى تعالوا ، يسوع؛ انه؛"

Chapter 56

I heard the terrorist yell in Arabic, "Jesus, come over here!" I still couldn't see Jerod or the cell leader--and I don't think they could see me and that was how we planned it. I guessed from the desperation in the shouted Arabic that Jerod had been able to surprise and get the upper hand on the terrorist.

When we had discussed the plan earlier, Jerod had decided he needed to use the knife to subdue the leader.

"But, now that we got an automatic rifle, wouldn't it make sense to use it on them?" I had asked. Even if it were only two to one--as Jose had said--I was scared of the odds and wanted to give Jerod any advantage we could.

"Sure, but we can't take the chance of hittin' some of the students and teachers," he had argued. "We know they sure as hell won't care if they have to take some of the students out. A gunfight at the OK Corral might just play right into their hands."

"But these guys are trained fighters," I raised, "how are you going to use a knife to overcome a guy with an AK-47?"

"Darlin', I'll just have t' be smarter than him. And remember I'm a SEAL."

And yet, when I moved to where I could get a look at them, there was Jerod, in control, the terrorist in a deadly headlock, the razor-sharp blade at Yassim's neck. When I heard the leader give the command to Jesus, I relaxed a bit. One more time, Jerod had beaten the odds. How long could his luck hold out?

In Jerod's grand plan, while he held the leader hostage and distracted the second terrorist, I was supposed to start getting the students out of the cafeteria by the side door. I glanced at the students around me, whose gazes darted from the rear where Jerod held Yassim and back to me. Their faces were expectant, waiting for me to tell them what to do next. But then there was Rashid. Downstairs, neither of us had factored him in and here he was blocking any quick exit.

I turned back to Rashid, who had been watching and listening to the terrorist leader, his attention riveted on the rear of the lunchroom. I sensed the delicate balance I had achieved with him was tipping. Studying his face, I thought he might come to his leader's rescue. I didn't know if he had a weapon, but I couldn't take a chance that he might try to use it against Jerod. I also figured he might interfere with the students I was going to try to slip out the side door. I had to engage him, to distract him if nothing else.

Suddenly, the students and teachers around me got deathly quiet. Both Rashid and I turned to see the source of the change. Jesus strode through the crowd. Both his hands still gripped the automatic rifle and he swerved it slowly back and forth as he walked. The students and teachers parted as he approached them, their brief hope teetering. I studied the terrorist's stride and something about it, about him, bothered me. I expected that he would at least be wary about the recent turn of events. But his gait and posture seemed wrong. Every step appeared too haughty, as if he, not Jerod, was in control. Like everyone else in the room, I watched the display of bravado unfold.

When Jesus was about twenty feet away from his leader, I heard Yassim begin shouting in Arabic. Within a few syllables, Jesus joined in and began reciting the verse with his leader. Their diction singsongy and strangely accented, I could only catch a few words and phrases.

المؤمنين بك يرجى نرحب. خطايانا لنا لي‌غفر. المتواضع فاسقين كنت ، "
في "مجدك."

"Allah help us.... forgive...please receive your believers..."

Jerod yelled, "What the hell are you saying?" He must have tightened his grip because the leader's words were suddenly cut off and Jesus ceased as well.

Then Jerod must have let up some, because I heard Yassim cough and say, "We are only asking for forgiveness."

"Good!" said Jerod, his one word conveying his growing confidence.

But something didn't feel right. I still didn't have a clear view of Jerod and Yassim. If I wanted to see clearly, I'd have to get up on a chair like Rashid, but that would call too much attention to me and mess up our plan. I was still hoping Jerod could hold them off so I could get the students and teachers out.

While I was trying desperately to figure out what to do, the words in Arabic I heard kept rolling around in my head. The recited words petitioned Allah for forgiveness, just as Yassim had claimed, but something was off. Then it came to me. Yassim and Jesus were reciting the ritual Islamic prayers for martyrs.

It made perfect sense. Jerod's plan had been a good one, but it had one fatal flaw. He had counted on a human being's most basic desire, that of self-preservation. What he and I had not considered was the rabid, suicidal lunacy of these men.

Jesus stopped walking and stood about ten feet in front of the two men. Jerod held Yassim, the knife at his neck, the terrorist's blood oozing, the crimson trickle like a slow, polluted stream down his gray sweatshirt. All the students and teachers moved well out of the way. Jesus stood ramrod straight, his back to me. His large body moved and blocked my view of Jerod and Yassim. At that moment I wish I had taken the gun Jerod wanted me to have downstairs, but had declined. If I had that gun, I would've walked up a few steps and emptied the chamber into Jesus with cold-blooded precision. How much I had changed.

I heard Jerod demand, "Tell Jesus to lay down his weapons or I will slit your throat in front of all of these children!" When Yassim said nothing, Jerod screamed "Now!"

Yassim nodded his head as if in agreement and began yelling quickly in Arabic, his words tumbling out one after the other. "يسوع ، ونحن جميعا أن مكرسة الجندي مثل أداء .الموت لمواجهة استعداد على وأنا .حال أية على قريبا يموت جميعا قتلهم ثم !الكافر هذا من والتخلص لمكافأة لي أرسل .كنت التي للإسلام ال تترك الطفل وراء!"

Jerod must have assumed that he was giving Jesus orders to lay down the weapons because he let him finish.

From the right side of the room, I listened, trying feverishly to translate the words in my head. As I translated idioms and rearranged the sentence structures, I grasped the meaning.

"Jesus, we are all to die soon anyway. I am ready to face my death. Perform like the dedicated soldier of Islam that you are. Send me to my reward and dispose of this infidel! Then kill them all! Leave no child behind!"

I took off at a run. My only hope was to reach Jesus in time and slam into him to force him to miss. I yelled at the top of my lungs, "Jerod, he's going to shoot! Move!"

Five steps away, my bare feet pounded on the linoleum as hard as I could. I bounced into students and shoved them out of the way. I heard Rashid running behind me but I ignored him and kept going. Everything seemed to flow in slow motion. I saw students staring at me, wide-mouthed, with frightened eyes. Two steps. I reached down for my last ounce of acceleration and sprung toward Jesus, bracing for the impact.

For a moment, Jesus hesitated and glanced over at me. Then he stepped sideways to dodge my rushing figure and flashed that arrogant smirk. I ran past him and stopped in two steps. Then Jesus turned back toward his target and calmly raised the weapon and fired. A volley of loud gunfire exploded in the hushed lunchroom. Teens and adults dove for cover under tables and chairs. The body of the terrorist leader jerked fiercely at the impact of the bullets, hurtling the full weight back upon my friend. As blood spurted from what looked like a hundred ruptures, both men collapsed onto the floor.

I ran over and fell on my knees between the smoking barrel of the AK-47 and the two bleeding men. I stared at the bloodied tangle of limbs and bodies and willed Jerod to be alive. Silence settled on the entire room. The pungent smell of gunpowder polluted the stuffy air.

Oblivious to anything else in the room, my gaze was riveted on the bleeding men, unbelieving. On the floor ahead, neither figure moved as the blood streamed from the bodies into a widening, red pool, flowing toward my exposed legs. I coughed and choked on my tears.

Beside me, I heard, "Well, well...Miss Sterber."

Chapter 57

I lowered my forehead to the linoleum, the vinyl surface cold against my skin. I pounded the unforgiving linoleum with my palms in futile protestation. Oh my God, Jerod! I couldn't hold back my tears and they ran in twin floods down my cheeks. Crouched to the floor, I coughed and felt I was going to vomit. I could not bring myself to raise my head to look at the two motionless bodies, a few inches away.

As I knelt there, collapsed, Jesus lowered his head beside me. I again smelled his putrid breath reeking of phlegm and garlic. "Dee Dee, you should not waste your tears," he spoke into my ear, his words edged with sarcasm. "Remember they are both with Allah now...that is, if you are a true believer."

Then he placed his hand on my back. My body cringed at his touch. Dazed and spiraling into shock, I tried to focus on Jerod, bleeding to death inches from me. Jesus' hand crawled from the small of my back around my rib cage to my left breast. It took me a few seconds, but when this latest violation registered through my shock, an uncontrolled rage erupted inside me, the molten lava of my anger seeking only revenge. I reacted on instinct, no longer rational. I guess some part of me realized Jesus still held the AK-47 and would gladly kill me. I simply no longer cared.

While still in the half-prone position, I raised my right hand off the floor and slipped it into my pocket, my fingers closing around the handle of the small knife I had found.

"What the matter?" taunted Jesus. "The insolent American woman has no response?"

Slowly I straightened and turned toward Jesus while he still tried to keep one palm on my breast. In one swift move, I pulled the paring knife from the pocket and plunged it fiercely into Jesus' arm. He staggered back, jerking his hand away from my body and dropping the automatic rifle on the floor. The metal clattered loudly on the vinyl, the sound reverberating in the now hushed lunchroom. Eyes wild with disbelief, Jesus brought his arm up and yanked out the small knife, the blood spurting from the gash just below the wrist.

"You bitch! You will pay for this!"

Slowly, I raised myself up and stood, facing our captor. I could see the rabid fury flashing behind the whites of his eyes. He looked at the AK-47 at his feet, then at his blood oozing from his skin and finally back at me. His left hand gripped the wound on his wrist, trying to stem the bleeding, the scarlet flow coursing through his fingers.

"Ms. Sterber," he growled, "for a mere woman, you have caused me too many problems. This time I think a bullet will send you to meet Allah!"

Jesus released his bleeding right hand and whipped it behind his back. When it reappeared a second later, it was holding a large silver handgun. The blood from the wound now poured over his brown skin and onto the white handle of the gun. He was standing six feet from me. I knew he could not miss and he was right: the bullet would quickly end my life. I'm not sure if it was shock or rage, but I stood unmoving, rooted to the spot. I stared at the blood-smeared silver pistol. I peered directly into the black hollow cylinder and then back up at Jesus. But I did not flinch. With all the defiance I could muster, I glared back at our captor and said nothing. My reaction must have surprised Jesus because he hesitated and lowered his arm slightly.

When I exhaled slightly, his hideous grin returned and his hand came back up. I watched his finger tense the trigger and started to pray silently.

During this whole exchange, Rashid had stood just off to the side watching this scene unfold. He called aloud in Arabic, "لا ، يسوع! انها ليست شيئة الله." "No, Jesus! It is not Allah's will."

Jesus turned to look at him, but kept his gun trained on my chest. He said nothing but his eyes questioned the teen soldier.

"You have already tried once to kill her and failed," Rashid responded. "Perhaps, Allah wants us to spare her."

The triumphant grin returned and Jesus said in English, "As the Americans say, 'Practice makes perfect!'" His head turned back toward me and I could see his eyes sighting down the barrel at me.

I hurriedly tried to finish my prayers. Our Father who art in heaven... I had much to repent and closed my eyes, waiting for the explosion.

Rashid screamed "NO!" I felt my body shoved roughly to the side and, at the same time heard the deafening report of the gun. As my body careened toward the floor, I jerked my eyes open, trying to catch myself. Deafened, I could make out no sounds and, by the time I realized I had not been hit, I saw Rashid lying on the linoleum, crumpled in front of me, blood pouring from a ragged hole in his shoulder.

"Oh, Rashid," I said but I couldn't hear anything, so I repeated his name, this time louder. The teen turned his head toward me and then closed his eyes in obvious pain.

"That was stupid, Rashid!" screamed Jesus. He stared down at the two of us on the floor. "That bullet was meant for Ms. Sterber. Praise Allah, I have more where that came from." Then he laughed, throwing his head back and cackling hysterically.

Pushing myself up, my glance went from the laughing Jesus back to Rashid. The teen lay sideways on the floor with his back to me, his figure lying between Jesus and me, like some final, protective barrier. When he hit the floor, the impact had jostled his backpack, forcing his rear pocket open. I looked inside the flap and saw the gun. Without thinking or planning, I pulled the pistol from the backpack and quickly released the safety.

Jesus must have sensed my movement because he ceased his laughing and turned back to me. I did not hesitate. Before he could even raise his arm, I aimed the gun up at the final terrorist. I pulled the trigger. Over and over again, I kept pulling the trigger until the chamber clicked empty.

Chapter 58

As the figure of Jesus collapsed in front of me, blood spewing from the bullet holes, I dropped the gun on the linoleum, the clang echoing in the stunned cafeteria. Then my whole body began shaking uncontrollably.

Next to me, Rashid stirred and I turned toward him. "Rashid? Why?" I stared down at the widening stain of red on his shoulder. "Rashid, I'm sorry," I said, as my tears dropped onto the floor. "Why did you do that?"

He coughed again, violently this time. "I thought Jesus might listen to me...."

I cradled his head and looked into his face. He closed his eyes and then slowly opened them again. "I will never forget what you did," I told him. "Is there anything I can do?"

"Do not tell th--" he mumbled and started coughing again.

"What?"

His lips moved, but I couldn't hear the words, so I leaned my ear close. "Do not...uh-huh...say anything, about what I did," he got out.

I moved my head so I was looking at him and wiped my tears with the sleeve of my sweatshirt. "I don't understand." I shook my head.

His mouth opened again and, not hearing anything, I leaned in close again. "They have...my mother and sister," I made out and then he drew in a sharp breath and cried in pain.

"Who?" I asked without moving.

He had trouble forming the two words but eventually whispered, "Al Quaida."

"What about your mother and sister?" I asked into his ear and then leaned to hear his response.

"My family..." he managed, his breathing getting more ragged. "They will kill them...if they find out I helped you." He closed his eyes again.

"Okay, Rashid," I said, the horror of the threat dawning on me. I sat back up and stared at his wounded body. "I will protect you and your family. Now just rest quiet till we can get you out of here."

He leaned his head back against my hand. I listened to the ragged breathing. Then, with obvious effort he raised his head up and his eyes popped open, alive with a question.

He tried to say something but all that came out were wisps. I leaned in, my ear almost on top of his mouth. "What time...is it?" he asked.

The question was so strange I thought he might be losing his mind.

Turning back to Rashid, I said, "I don't know. Sometime after five, I think."

"Ms. Sterber..." Cough, cough. "It is important," he mouthed, managing somehow to get some air and sound behind the syllables. He was agitated and tried to raise himself up, I guessed to check for himself, but the sharp pain forced him back to the floor.

Seeing his reaction, I patted his side and said, "Wait a second, Rashid." Then I turned to one of the students who had edged closer to us and called, "Does anybody have a watch? What time is it?"

At first, the students stared at me dumbstruck. Then a tall, redheaded guy, his hair plastered to his temple, said, "I have eleven minutes before six, Ms. Sterber."

"Rashid, did you hear?" I said, but didn't get a response. "You said you wanted to know what time it was. It's 5:49, eleven minutes before six."

His eyes popped open like a jolt of electricity had been plugged into his body. "Get them out!" he said, loud enough for me to hear.

"What? I don't understand," I said.

His mouth started moving and when I couldn't hear the words, I lowered my ear to his lips again.

"Mustafa has set ...explosions to go off at six."

When he said no more, I moved so I could look into his eyes. He closed his eyes and took in raspy breaths, one after another and tried again. I leaned my ear closer to his lips.

"You must...get everyone out," he got out and I heard the intake of ragged breath. "The explosions are set to go off at six o'clock."

I jerked my head back and looked him in his eyes. "The execution. The execution was scheduled for six o'clock."

With great effort, he nodded slightly.

"Oh, my God!"

"Ms. Sterber, I'm so glad you're okay," I heard a familiar voice say, but it did not penetrate the fog enveloping my brain, not at first. My head was reeling from the realization of what Rashid had told me and I stared at the teen and he held my gaze.

Then the deep, bass voice spoke again and cut through my thoughts. "Dee Dee, it's me, Hal Thompson." He reached down to me and I felt his hand brush my arm. "Are you okay?" I could hear him, but his voice was muffled.

I looked up at him and tried to reply. "Yeah, I'm all right."

Just then, Rashid cried at my feet. His warning suddenly came back to me.

"Hal! Right now we have to get everyone out of the school!"

"What?" he asked. "Why?"

"They've set explosives around the school and they're set to go off at six," I cried out.

"Are you sure?" he asked, his eyes searching the room.

"What do you mean, am I sure? Get these kids out of here. Now!"

"But the terrorists claimed all the exits were booby-trapped," Thompson said, his eyes getting very large. "What if we go through the door and it sets off the charge?"

"What if we stay here and the building blows up with us in it? We have to take that chance." The principal didn't move. "Hal, we have to hurry. Time is running out!"

"What about the other terrorists?" he protested, not moving.

"What other terrorists?"

"Jesus said there were terrorists guarding every exit!" he said.

"He was just bluffing," I tried to explain, hoping I was right. "Jose said that there were only the four."

"Jose?" the principal asked. "Where's Jose?"

"Later. I don't have the time to explain. Let's get these students out of here while we can." When he hesitated, I commanded. "Hal, you grab some of the staff and get the kids started and I'll bring up the rear with some of the other teachers. Don't let them panic and send them out the front doors, or what's left of them. Since the terrorists already used the explosives there, we should be safe."

He nodded, the sole black lock bobbing on his head, and he moved quickly through the crowd. Near the front of the lunchroom, he turned and faced the group. His large, bass voice boomed across the room. "Everyone listen up!" he called out. He waited a beat and heads turned toward him. "We want everyone to file out toward the front of the school. We need to do this quickly in an orderly fashion." His eyes searched around the cafeteria. "Teachers, take charge of students around you and get them in order out to the front exit. Students, help those who are injured. Help anyone around you, if they need it. Some of you guys," he pointed to some athletes nearby, "you go back and help Miss Sterber with the injured men in the back. Get going!" And with that he led the throng.

I watched him disappear around the corner of the lunchroom, and like the Pied Piper, students and teachers followed without question, their numbers soon clogging the doorways. I studied the body of Rashid, whose chest was still moving up and down. How much time had passed? I wasn't sure, but I thought less than two minutes since Rashid had told me. That gives us maybe nine minutes.

"What do you want us to do?" asked a voice, disturbing my calculations. I looked up to see Tyrone, his bright smile flashing. Other students came up behind him and I recognized Goat loping along with the small group.

"Hi, Miss S," Goat said. "Glad you're all right."

"Thanks," I said.

"How can we help?" He gestured to some friends standing behind him.

"A couple of guys grab Rashid and carry him out," I said. "Be careful. He's hurt pretty bad."

"Sure," said Goat. He turned to the tall guy next to him and said, "Clete, com'on."

The two boys lifted the body of Rashid and started toward the front of the building. I watched as they moved and joined the crowd queuing up to get out through the narrow doorway.

Another student, a black-haired boy with a pimply face, pointed to Jesus. "Should we get him?"

I bent down and felt his carotid artery; there was no pulse. I shook my head. Then I moved a few steps to where Yassim still lay atop Jerod. I repeated my inspection and again, no pulse.

I turned to Tyrone and pimple-face and, pointing to the dead terrorist leader, said, "Roll him off Mr. Thomas."

They reached down and clumsily flipped the limp body of Yassim off Jerod and the bloodied terrorist's body plopped onto his face with a clunk.

Terrified of what I would find, I placed my quivering fingertips on Jerod's neck. I eyed the right side of his body that was covered with blood, the gray sweatshirt sleeve completely drenched in red. At first, I thought I felt nothing, no pulse, just like the other two and my hopes plummeted. But then, just before I pulled my fingers off his neck, I felt it. A very weak pulse, but it was there. My heart leaped, even as I had to remind myself that the pulse was barely detectable. But it was there!

"Hurry, Tyrone and you, pick him up and carry him! Let's go!" I cried.

They needed no further encouragement. Tyrone grabbed Jerod's legs and the other student his arms. The two strong young men struggled at first--Jerod's unconscious body was so limp it was hard to handle--but then they got the hang of it and started walking quickly, his wounds bleeding between them as they stepped. I followed right behind.

I looked around the cafeteria and noticed that most of the students were around the corner and down the hallway. With Jerod in tow, we had to move more slowly and by the time we reached the front of the lunchroom, we were the last ones out.

The boys hesitated slightly as they tried to round a corner, having to maneuver Jerod through the doorway. I watched, agonizing, as Jerod's head lolled to one side or the other as the boys angled his body through the doorway. My heart prayed, demanded that he survive. The seconds ticked away in my head.

"You guys all right?" I asked, nervously.

"Yes, ma'am, we're okay," replied Tyrone, though a little out of breath.

"Let's keep going. We don't have much time," I said, trying to encourage them.

"Till what?" Tyrone had asked. He and his partner stopped to adjust their grip on Jerod.

"Never mind, guys. Let's just keep going," I added quickly.

My eyes moved to the floor and I watched Jerod bleeding, leaving a trail of red, oval drops on the white linoleum. I stayed to one side so I didn't step in the blood, as if that would somehow desecrate him. Not wanting to think about how much blood he was losing, I looked ahead.

We turned another corner and headed down the main hallway. I peered beyond them and could see the front foyer. Where the beautiful entryway had once stood, there were no glass doors or side panels anymore and the cold air blew in full on our faces. The expensive glass was fractured, scattered into millions of pieces lying like loose misshapened diamonds on the floor. The metal frames were twisted into grotesque shapes that looked remarkably like some exotic modern art sculpture. My bare feet exposed, I tried my best to avoid the broken glass, but it was no use. The sharp edges bit into my flesh, slicing across my soles. I looked down and saw my blood drops trailed beside the path of Jerod's blood.

Then I glanced ahead and caught sight of Hal Thompson. Standing in the space that had been the doorway, the principal was waving his long arms in exaggerated sweeps, beckoning us furiously. Then he pointed to a watch on his wrist.

My eyes darted from him to the two boys carrying Jerod. "You guys are doing great. Just a little bit more." I tried to keep the edge of panic out of my voice. "You can make it."

Just then, two dark figures brushed past Hal at the opening and another pulled him roughly away from the building. In a few seconds, the two men were beside us and were grabbing Jerod's body from Tyrone and his partner. I realized that the men were wearing dark-blue flak jackets and had the letters FBI stenciled across the back.

"We'll take him," the older one said. "We have to hurry and get out." With that, he took Jerod from the teens and hoisted the limp body on his shoulder, fireman style. He took off at a trot for the blasted-out exit, Jerod's body flopping on his shoulder. The second FBI agent grabbed the two teens and said, "Can you guys run?"

The two teens nodded in unison.

"Okay, as fast as you can, make for the outside," he directed. Now sensing the danger, the two boys sprinted for the opening, each one trying to best the other. Then he turned to me, "You, too, ma'am."

He grabbed my arm and propelled me, trotting the last hundred yards. My feet, riddled with lacerations from the glass, screamed in pain with every step. As the agent and I ran, his hand on my elbow, I glanced briefly across at him and noticed the side of his head. A long, old-fashioned sideburn--one they would have called muttonchops—bordered the side of his face and he was sweating profusely. I had just enough time to think, how odd. I glanced ahead again. Up to the doorway and through, we kept moving. The agent didn't relinquish his grip till we were out, twenty yards clear of the structure.

Standing there trying to catch my breath, my gaze swept left and right, taking in the scene in front of me. Husks of blackened school buses lay in contorted positions, like toys destroyed and discarded by some angry giant. Lined up behind the skeletons of the burned-out buses must have been fifty FBI agents, standing shoulder to shoulder, clad like the two that had come to escort us out of the high school. The agents formed a ring that encircled the entire front of the school and three other agents stood off to the side, talking with Hal Thompson and a handful of students. One of the students, an overweight, redhead girl, gestured toward me and the group turned in my direction. As I took in the scene, I watched, frozen to the spot, as a discarded, plastic Wal-Mart bag puffed up with air, pranced in the wind in front of me, rolling over like some brown cellophane tumbleweed. I studied the apparition for a few seconds, momentarily mesmerized by the strange dance. I stared down at my bleeding bare feet and the ground beneath and then finally started moving again. My feet protested anew with every step. After three uncertain steps, I brought my gaze up and saw as the line of agents, still thirty feet ahead of me, part and a gurney come through the opening and the agent lowered Jerod onto it. Four med techs surrounded him and were swallowed by the blue wave. Only then did I notice the flashing strobes of the ambulances and squad cars behind the agents.

Behind me I heard a slow rumble build and started to turn to see what was happening. A huge explosion rented the air behind me. A pressure wave of heat and wind slammed into my body with incredible force. Then, nothing.

Chapter 59

"Three minutes, Mr. President," the technician said to Ryan Gregory, who nodded behind the crew of make-up men.

Harold Samson gazed at the monitor and watched the president shoo away the TV men and focus his attention on the teleprompter, his eyes concentrating on the scrolling lines. He sat behind the desk in the Oval Office, looking regal and handsome and assured again. He had showered and dressed, once again resplendent in a navy suit with white shirt and red tie, a perfect patriotic symbol for the nation, thought Samson somewhat cynically. Yes, the President was ready to tell Americans what they wanted to hear.

"Mr. President, we want to do a final light check. If you'll look into number one camera?" the female director asked, somewhere off-camera.

Harold watched the screen as Gregory tried out a reassuring smile for the cameras.

"Great. Thank you, Mr. President. Ninety seconds, sir."

Samson stared down at his own clothes, tie askew, white shirt spotted with perspiration marks and stray food stains. He stood, with two other cabinet members, in the outside office, focused on the Chief Executive as he got ready to address the nation. Harold's eyes took in the figures of two other members of the team--Dickson and Garcia--also banished to the outer office. They too looked spent, their clothes equally disheveled. Only Chief of Staff, Dean Settler, remained in the inner sanctum, off to the side and out of view of the camera. Just far enough so the strings would still reach, thought Samson, cynicism in full throttle.

Samson shook his head and took another sip of his drink in his hand, a double Scotch and water. He figured he deserved it. Hell, he needed it. He thought about Settler, off in the wings. After the students and teachers had escaped and the school building had exploded, it had taken Settler only three minutes to pounce.

"Mr. President, now that the crisis has passed," he had begun. There hadn't even been an accurate body count yet. "We need to talk about your response."

Gregory had looked up with those tired, red eyes that seemed to have been bearing the pain of the nation. He had said nothing. Samson stared at the image of the President on the monitor, trying mentally to reconcile the image on the screen with the spent man he had witnessed two short hours ago. The face on the monitor looked perfect, no bloodshot eyes, no hint of fatigue. The marvels of modern medicine, Samson thought.

"Mr. President, the nation needs you right now," Settler had said. "We can't let the media run with this. We need to spin this in our direction."

"Dean?" Ryan Gregory had said.

"Sir, you are the president and right now three hundred million Americans want to be assured that their safety and security is not threatened. And hell, yes, it won't hurt your campaign any, sir."

No one else in the Situation Room said a word. The entire group was exhausted and stunned, except the Chief of Staff. He seemed to get more animated with "the opportunity," his scarecrow features swelling as if some plastic surgeon had injected collagen in the pores. Samson was once again amazed at the Chief of Staff's callous ability to use the tragedy to boost the President's ratings.

Settler continued, "Sir, you've had to give up almost twenty-fours hours of critical campaign time, holed up in this bunker," he argued. "What's wrong with spinning this in our favor to get some of that advantage back?"

"What do you have in mind?"

"We could talk about the U.S. standing up to terrorism. And you could salute the heroism of individual Americans."

"And you could talk about the deployment of the FBI as a strike force," Dickson had contributed, sensing the tide was shifting.

"No, not strike force," Settler had argued and Dickson had looked wounded. Then Settler corrected, "The FBI rescue force." Dickson smiled at the change and nodded. "We need to work up a full statement, Mr. President," he continued and then suddenly added, "For your approval, sir."

"I'll leave you to it then." Gregory had disappeared through the doorway.

"I'll make arrangements for the President to pre-empt prime time," Settler had said, as soon as the President was gone.

Samson had risen from the table. The other three men noted his move and stopped talking. "This is more your thing. I'll let you guys handle this. I need a drink."

The announcement on the TV brought Samson back to the present. A solemn voice declared, "The President of the United States."

The camera opened with a wide shot, showing Gregory behind the desk and the green carpet with the presidential seal on the floor in front. Then the camera moved in tightly on the President, sitting erect in the chair.

"My fellows Americans, as you have probably heard, a group of cowardly terrorists tried to strike at the heart of America, but they failed. Their target was a small high school in rural Ohio, Thurber High School in Hammerville, Ohio. At this high school, this band of ruthless terrorists held more than five hundred innocent students and teachers hostage for almost six hours in the school cafeteria. These terrorists had demanded the release of another Al Quaida terrorist, a convicted murderer named Asad Akadi, who had been slated to be executed for his crimes at six o'clock today."

He paused and stared into the camera, working the audience.

"I am pleased to tell you that we did not and will not, as long as I am President, negotiate with terrorists. Per the law of the land, and the determination of the court and a jury of his peers, Asad Akadi was executed at six o'clock p.m. He will terrorize America no more. And the terrorists' attempt to take control of the school was thwarted, all because of the courage and heroism of individuals at the high school, coordinated with the strategic tactics of our own FBI. The Department of Homeland Security was able to make secret contact with one of the hostages and, with her help, we were able to save nearly all the hostages. I can tell you now, my fellow Americans, that we have been in constant contact with the hostages and we provided hope and ultimately rescue to those caught in the maelstrom of this ordeal."

"All this was not without cost, though. Several of our fellow citizens lost their lives in this crisis and rescue, including some heroic teachers and brave members of the FBI. Many more were injured in the confrontation."

Gregory's face seemed to inch closer to the camera and Samson could have sworn he saw a tear in one eye. "Those injured includes one teacher who risked her own life and stood up to the terrorists. Her name is Dee Dee Sterber and tonight she lies, unconscious, in a hospital bed. Ms. Sterber, on behalf of the five hundred hostages and on behalf of Americans everywhere, our humble thanks for your unselfish heroism and courage. Our prayers are with you," he said quietly.

"My fellow Americans, we will never rest, as long as there are terrorists whose only desire is to destroy our cherished freedoms," President Gregory continued, once again adopting a presidential tone. "Once more, the enemies of these freedoms have been defeated and tonight we are sending a message to terrorists everywhere: we will not rest until these terrorists--these criminals--are dragged out of the burrows where they hide like cowards and brought to the light of justice..."

Samson turned away from the television. He scanned the room and noticed everyone's eyes were riveted on the screen. His glance came to rest on the drink in his hand, which was now empty. He looked up at the TV, but no longer heard the President's words. In disgust, he realized that Settler had been right: the whole thing was turning out to be a real PR coup for President Ryan Gregory.

Gazing back at his empty glass, he thought, I need another drink. He turned and walked out of the outer office. Tomorrow, he decided, he would draft his letter of resignation.

Chapter 60

I struggled to open my eyes, but my lids felt glued to my sockets. I took a full, deliberate breath, then tried again to slowly raise my eyelids, but they wouldn't budge. Unable to see anything, I tried to focus my attention on my other senses, but found my brain slow in cooperating.

Something soft cushioned the back of my head. And what was that smell, that odd mixture of garden scents and chemicals? I knew it, but couldn't place it. My ears picked up noises of someone beside me, not talking, just some movement along with some breathing. I sensed someone was there, hovering, and my paranoia kicked in. The vision of the metal barrel of a large pistol gripped in a bloody hand coalesced in my head, fractured piece by fractured piece, like some ugly, misshapen puzzle. Suddenly, I wasn't sure I had killed Jesus at all. The horrific image of the terrorist leapt into my mind, standing in front of me with that disgusting leer, waiting for me to look up at him, just before he pulled the trigger. I jolted my eyes open and uttered a squeal.

"Well...welcome back to the land of the living," said a voice beside me.

It was--not Jesus or Yassim--but a woman. I turned and studied the image beside me. Her figure seemed to be wrapped in layers of cotton and I blinked twice. It took several more seconds for my clouded vision to clear and for reality to register in my brain. I fought to concentrate but my senses were dulled, dimmed as if oozed through some barely permeable filter.

As the haze started to lift, I could make out that the woman was about my age, though slimmer. As she stood beside me, my gaze took in a white smock with flowers scattered across it, miniature smudges of tulips, daffodils, and lilacs. Her auburn hair was tied haphazardly in a ponytail, as if she had been in a hurry to put it up. She had an attractive face, sparkling green eyes above a petite nose with a scattering of freckles on her cheeks. She smiled warmly, her lips two thin pink lines bracketing white teeth.

"Good to see those eyes of yours," she said warmly. She checked and adjusted the feed on a tube that hooked into my arm from a translucent bag dangling below a metal stand. My gaze followed the path of the tube and I saw two other long tubes dangling down like the arms of some pale spider.

"Where am I?" My voice was so raspy that I didn't think it could be heard outside my head.

Why is it people always ask that? I mean, like, duh, I knew where I had to be, but I asked it anyway.

She reached across me and handed me a bottle of water with a stem. She squirted some into my mouth. "Why, honey, you're in Canfield Community Hospital." Then she added, "And my name is Dawn and I'm here to take care of you."

My glance wandered around the room and out the window. Beyond the green and yellow plaid curtains, I could see only a gray haziness. It was impossible to tell whether dawn or dusk was crowding the window, or whether the dim light was merely the paleness of another gray, cold day in northern Ohio. I saw no clock in the room and returned my gaze to my visitor.

I tried my voice again. "What..." I got out and then had to clear my throat. "Uh-huh, what time is it?"

Dawn must have heard the raspiness in my voice. She lifted the bottle of water to my lips again, as she answered my question. "Well, I don't know," she said and glanced at the watch on her wrist, "it's about 11:20." She gave my left arm an affectionate pat.

I reached up to take the glass and noticed for the first time that my right arm was held captive in a tight sling against my body. I switched to my left arm. I sucked through the straw and the water felt wonderfully cool on my throat. I drank greedily.

"Easy, Miss Sterber," said Nurse Dawn and her hand eased back the cup slightly. "Take it easy. You've gone through a lot. Just a little bit at a time, now."

I swallowed, and tried to register what she had said. It took a few moments for the meaning to sink in. I asked, "What day is it?"

"It's Saturday, hon." Her eyes met mine and softened. Then she must have read my mind, because she added, "You must've gone through quite an ordeal because you've been out for almost forty hours."

Her index finger and thumb pinched my wrist and her eyes glanced at her watch, checking my pulse.

"Forty hours?" My gaze traveled to the sling and then to the tubes snaking down to my body. "What happened? Am I going to be okay?" I said in a hoarse whisper.

The nurse smiled at me and said, "You're going to be just fine, don't you worry none. We're going to take good care of you and before you know it, you'll be good as new." She glanced back down at the chart she had picked up, suddenly avoiding my eyes.

I looked up at her and she brought her eyes to meet mine. She must've read something in my expression because she wrinkled her nose and said, "Let me get the doctor. She can answer your questions better than me." She patted my hand, turned and was out the door.

Even through the fog of drugs, I began to feel the dull throb of pain that seemed to radiate from different parts of my body. As consciousness slowly ebbed back, the aches began announcing themselves from my feet to my neck.

Left alone, fractured thoughts bombarded my brain. I tried to sift through the mental chaos, to think back. What was the last thing I remembered before? Before what? I rested my head back against the pillow and tried to concentrate. Despite the nurse's overly cheery manner, I felt, I knew something was wrong. It was not just the aches. I felt a hollowness, an emptiness inside, but try as I might, I couldn't get my mind to acknowledge the memory.

Then, in one blast, it all burst upon me--the wave, the heat, the explosion. As if suddenly reminded by the memory, my body's individual pains shot through me. A sharp ache ebbed and flowed from my right shoulder and, when I tried to move my arm a bit in the sling, the hurt went from a rumble to a scream. As I turned to glance toward the door, a sharp pain shot up my left side. My legs hurt too, but I couldn't quite figure out what was wrong. My eyes traveled down the white sheet and I traced the outline of my legs and feet. I raised my left arm to pull back the covers.

"Well, it's great to see you're up!" announced another visitor, this time in a polka-dot smock, as she rounded the doorway and strode into my room. "I'm Dr. Stevens, Emily Stevens. I'm the lead physician in the ICU."

"Intensive Care?" I croaked. "What's wrong with me?" I fought to keep the panic out.

"You're going to be fine," Dr. Stevens began. I noticed she had beautiful blond hair done in a smart pageboy and her eyes were sky blue. Her smile caused her features to wrinkle into easy creases, giving me the thought that she must have smiled a good deal. Her slender fingers gently touched the wrist of my right arm, just in front of the sling. I found her touch--like her smile--reassuring.

"You are far too important a patient for us to let anything happen to you. I'm not sure if I've ever had an honest-to-goodness hero for a patient before."

I looked back at her and realized, after a bit, she was serious. "A hero?" I said.

"Yes, ma'am," she answered. "They tell me you got every student out of the school alive...before the explosion. They said you saved hundreds of lives. I'd say that qualifies for hero status, if anything does."

Slowly, the series of events came back to me, snatches of scenes flashing in my head like some crudely edited video. Tyrone's grin, Tess's hug, Keith's head bleeding. Christie's crumpled form lying on the deck. Rashid falling. Oval drops of blood on the floor. The explosion.

"Are they okay?" I asked suddenly. "The students? What about Rashid?" Then the memories slammed me. I saw the shocked look on Christie's face when she realized she was shot. I saw Jerod on the floor, blood coursing from the side of his body. "Did they recover the bodies of the teachers who died...a teacher named Christie Ferguson. And what about Jerod?! Jerod Thomas? Did he make it?"

Dr. Stevens moved in closer and leaned over next to me. "I'm sure they're okay, but I can't tell you about anyone in particular. Dee Dee, you pulled off quite the hero act to get all those kids and teachers out. Right now you need to let us take care of you and let the medical staff take care of them. I've been swamped just concentrating on the few that are my patients. None of them had those names, though."

I must have looked confused so she pressed on.

"There were so many injuries we couldn't handle them all here. So some were flown to Canton Memorial. And others are here, on different floors and in whatever beds were available."

"Here," I said quickly and started to move, trying to sit up. With my slight attempt at movement, the pains that had been murmuring in different locations throughout my body began screaming. "Ow-ow-ow!" I gasped.

"Now, just hold on there," said Dr. Stevens. Her voice retained the same calm, soothing tone, but her petite hand was suddenly powerful, forcefully easing my body back down against the bed. "You're not going anywhere, at least not for a little while."

I winced as the pains sliced through my body. The doctor noticed and said, "You're going to be all right, but you're going to hurt for a while. It's just going to take some time."

I tried not to move, but stared at her face that hovered directly over mine. With a penlight, she checked my pupils and, bending over, examined both my ears. Then she announced, "Well, your eyes and ears appear to be in good shape. That's good."

I asked the question I had been dreading. "Why am I in ICU? What's wrong with me?"

"Nothing that won't heal in a little time."

I raised my head an inch off the pillow, sending jolts of pain down my neck. I took a deep breath. "Doc, I'm a big girl. I can take it. Be straight with me."

The smile returned to her face. "Yeah, well after what you've been through, I'm sure you can. You certainly got the badges of a hero." She reached down and placed her hand on my skull, her fingers rubbing gently on my hairline. "First of all, you've had a concussion...or maybe two. Must've taken some nasty lumps."

I managed a weak smile. "Yeah, courtesy of some very nasty terrorists."

"Then, according to the officers, you were the closest to the building when the bombs went off. The explosion picked you up and slammed you against the ground. That collision broke three ribs on your right side."

Her fingers moved to my side and indicated the area with the slightest of pressure. Even her tender touch ignited the pain.

"And the fall dislocated your shoulder on that side," she said, indicating the sling that held my right arm, "and it fractured your fibula."

"Oh, is that all?" I laughed without humor.

"And of course, your whole body has been bruised. But all that will heal in time," she said, still gentle but more serious.

"But there's more, isn't there? There's something you're not telling me?"

"Yes, a little more," she said, nodding. "Your lower legs and feet were burned pretty seriously from the explosion." Her hands gently lifted the white sheet. "Second and third degree burns on both feet and lower legs."

Without raising my head, I lowered my eyes to peer down the length of my body, taking in the red, exposed flesh of my legs. From my knees down, both legs looked to be covered in red and blue blisters, running in ugly, crooked lines down my scarred flesh, looking like some bizarre roadmap.

Horrified, I began to cry. "Will it..." I tried to get out.

"Heal?" the doctor finished for me. "Yes, I believe it will. We have one of the best burn specialists in this part of the state and he said it looks promising. Probably won't even need to do any skin grafts, he thinks."

I tried to nod, wanting to be braver than I felt.

Dr. Stevens took my free hand in hers. "In time, you're going to be able to run marathons or swim or bike or whatever you want. But you're probably not going to be able to enter any graceful legs competition, I'm afraid. But Jim-- that's the burn specialist--he thinks there won't even be that much scarring. For a while though, it's going to hurt like hell."

I was silent at first, staring at the ceiling and letting the news sink in. Dr. Stevens knew enough to let me be. Eventually, I was able to drag myself out of my self-pity and remembered the others.

"What about Jerod? And Christie? Rashid?" I asked quietly, turning my eyes to her.

Her hand moved to the valve on one of the hanging plastic bags, her two fingers twisting the valve a half turn.

"I'm going to increase your Demerol to ease the pain," she said softly. "Try to keep you a little more comfortable to get through the worst of it. It anesthetizes the pain pretty well, but you're going to sleep some more."

When I started to say something, she stopped me. "I'll check on those names and try to find out for you when you wake up."

My eyelids grew incredibly heavy again. I could hear myself breathing and noticed for the first time the beeping of a monitor.

"Right now, just rest," was the last thing I heard her say before the shroud of sleep engulfed me again.

In a barely conscious whisper, I cried, "Jerod...Christie...Rashid..."

Chapter 61

I don't know how long I lay there, slipping between hazy semi-consciousness and drugged slumber. When, at last, the effects of the drugs began to fade and sleep no longer held me prisoner, I stirred and tried to shake the tendrils of unconsciousness. I opened my eyes slowly and glanced around. In the room the darkness was gone, but the light slipping in through the panes did little to lift the oppressive weight of my grief. No matter how hard I tried, the deadly scenes re-ran relentlessly in my head, Christie collapsing onto the deck, her white sweater erupting in red, Rashid's eyes on mine as the life drained from them, my bare footprints in Jerod's blood dripping onto the floor.

"How is my favorite patient today?" I heard the light voice of Dr. Emily Stevens as she entered the room. She saw the tears flowing down my cheeks. "Are you in pain? Do you need me to increase your meds?"

I shook my head and tried to wipe the tears with my free arm. "No, that's not it. I have to find out about my friends."

"Yes, of course. I told you I'd check on them." Dr. Stevens looked down, refusing to meet my gaze. "I was just waiting till you came out of the drugs."

My heart plummeted and I slammed my head back against the pillows. "They're dead, aren't they?" I got out as the sobbing returned full bore.

"You asked about a Rashid, Rashid Hermani, I assume," the doctor said. "I'm afraid he died in the ambulance. Wasn't he one of the terrorists?"

I snatched a tissue and blew. My head nodded. "But he changed his mind and tried to save me. He sacrificed his life for mine." Then I remembered my promise to Rashid and my promise to protect his family. My flood of tears restarted in warm trickles on my cheeks. The doctor waited, giving me time.

"What about Christie?" I asked, already afraid of the answer.

"Christie Ferguson, one of the teachers?" Dr. Stevens asked and her eyes met mine now. I nodded again and swallowed hard. She went on. "I'm afraid she didn't make it. They got her out of the school and rushed her here, but she had lost too much blood." She shook her head slowly.

"Oh God!" I squealed. My mind conjured up the image of her laughing, hair shaking, beer bottle in hand. "Oh my God!"

I wept, salty tears running into my mouth. Dr. Emily just stayed by my bed and rested her small hand on my arms. She didn't speak and the only sounds in the room were the regular beeps of the monitor and my sobbing.

I could put it off no longer. I grabbed her hand and her gaze met mine. "Please tell me Jerod isn't dead!" I pleaded.

"No, he's alive," Dr. Stevens said, one tear sliding down her cheek, "but I don't have many details. He's not here. They lifeflighted him to Canton Memorial and he's listed in critical condition."

I tried to interrupt her to demand more but she stopped me.

"With HIPPA, they won't give me any more information officially, but I've got a good friend over there, Dr. Murphy. He said your friend is in a coma. I'm sorry, Dee Dee." One tear completed its journey down her chin and I watched it splash onto my bedsheet.

"Oh…God!" I whispered.

Dr. Stevens reached up and adjusted the dial on the IV feed. Slowly I let sleep swallow me again. I didn't want to ever wake up.

Chapter 62

I refused to accept the prognosis.

The ordeal had cost me too much already. Rashid sacrificed his life for mine. And Christie was dead. I trembled every time I thought of it, seeing again the bullet transform her smile into a shocked O. God, how I missed that smirk and those witty innuendos. I would not lose Jerod too. I could not.

All the doctors would say is that the trauma from the wounds and the loss of blood were so severe they didn't know what to expect. The tests showed that Jerod maintained minimal, but continuous brain activity. With each week that passed, though, their platitudes became a little weaker. As the coma dragged into its sixth week, they began to venture that "we should prepare ourselves for the possibility that he might not wake up." But I stubbornly refused to accept that. Crutches and all, each day I clumsily climbed into my car--my right leg had healed well enough and the doctors reluctantly allowed me to drive--and made the thirty-minute trip up the highway to the hospital in Canton.

In between my grueling physical therapy I spent hours in that sterile hospital room, meeting Jerod's family, what there was of it. Two fussy, spinster aunts who lived together and could finish each other's sentences and a gentle, gray-haired grandmother who was the closest thing he had to a parent. Right away, I liked them and I think they liked me.

We had tried to cheer each other up with hopeful promises and reassurances of his improvement. Together for much of the time, the four of us clung to each other and to the stubborn belief that he would soon wake up and, in inimical Jerod fashion, would start flirting with the nurses and complaining about the food.

But as the weeks dragged on, the optimism of Jerod's relatives had diminished, the smiles of the three ladies faded day by day like the dusk-erased sunlight on the western horizon. Eventually, the two aunts, Ferdie and Eloise, left Canton, saying they needed to return to their home and jobs in Stanley, more than an hour away.

"We really need to get back to our place," Ferdie had begun.

"Our cat will be going crazy now," Eloise had continued.

"Miss Larson only agreed to watch Snickers for a little while," Ferdie went on.

"And you know Snickers can be quite a handful," added Eloise.

I had nodded, as if I understood, but I recognized that they had given up. They had accepted the prognosis and were getting on with their lives--though they'd never say that out loud. The thought occurred to me that they might be the smart ones, but I just couldn't bring myself to do that.

His grandmother, an unpretentious woman with a face permanently creased into a sad smile and who insisted I call her Catherine, held on longer. Though she held it in well, I learned that her pain at watching Jerod in this state was deep and personal. She told me she had buried Jerod's mother, her daughter, and she wasn't about to watch them lower a casket with her favorite grandson into the cold earth.

"I guess this was my fault," Catherine, with her thinning gray hair pulled in a bun, blurted out one day when we were alone, sitting in the two chairs beside his bed. Her gray-green eyes stared at Jerod's still form on the bed, his only motion the slight rise and fall of his chest.

"Why would you say that?"

"Well, I'm the one who talked him into coming up here from Tennessee," she insisted and adjusted her bifocals atop a small nose.

"Yeah, he told me that you passed the info about the jobs at HBE to him," I answered. "But I think he would claim it was his idea to take that advice."

"I suppose you're right," she said, her wan smile returning.

"Besides, I'm the one who got him into the whole thing," I said, my own guilt suddenly fresh and raw. "If he hadn't tried to save me, he'd probably been safe."

Catherine took my hand in hers and, taking her eyes off the form on the bed, looked at me. "If I know my grandson, he could no more have done that than stop breathing."

I nodded.

"Coming into your classroom, seeing you and helping those kids, was--I mean, is the best part of his life," she said and squeezed my hand. "I can't tell you how many times he told me that, child. And I don't believe there isn't anything he wouldn't do to save your life."

I nodded again, this time tears starting at the corners of my eyes. "Thank you." I squeezed her small hand back.

At seventy-eight, the daily endurance of those unforgiving hospital chairs wreaked havoc on her back. Eventually her own doctor had insisted that she stay in her house. I promised to call her and I did, almost every day. Each day she would probe for any change, any new development, and each day I would give her the same answer.

"Catherine, he's pretty much the same today. I can't tell any difference, but I am praying for the best."

Against her doctor's orders, she came back and sat with me from time to time. "Them doctors don't know everything," she would say, smiling that sad smile, her parchment skin crinkling comfortably around her mouth.

On those waning days of her visits, sometimes we would talk and sometimes we'd just sit in the hospital room and hold hands, watching over Jerod together. She called us "his two guardian angels." As her visits became less and less frequent, at the unrelenting nagging of her physician, I came to believe it was her breaking heart as much as her ailing back that kept her away.

I had assured Catherine that hers would be the first call I'd make "as soon as he opened his eyes and started that southern drawl of his." With that she had agreed--at least temporarily--to accede to her doctor's wishes and stay home. By this time, I think she too had come to believe, but wouldn't voice, that her next trip into the hospital would be to claim Jerod's remains.

I still refused to admit defeat. My father had always said that blind obstinacy was either my worst quality or my best. Faced with the inevitable, I would not succumb to the morbid inevitability everyone else saw. Left to my own devices and with no one else for company, I began just to talk to Jerod.

When he didn't answer, I told myself he just wasn't paying attention, pretty much like most men. And then I'd cave in to babbling and crying.

Deep down inside, I believed he could hear me, could understand every word I said. I didn't know how to begin, so I started off telling him small, everyday details, details about my family, about what I had seen about the revitalization of Thurber. I shared my surprise at the plaque dedicated to Robert Holden at the school, "hero of the Thurber stand against the terrorists." The latest gossip in town gave me ample items to share.

I told him about the visit from none other than Harold Samson, Director of Homeland Security. As his last official act, he had come to notify me that I had been awarded the Presidential Medal of Valor. Oh, and I told him that the President had a medal for him as well. But he had to wake up first.

Several times during these one-way, rambling conversations, the nurses came in to check on their patient. Although no one ever said anything, I could read the signs of pity in their eyes. They probably thought I was crazy to hobble into the small hospital room and stay there day after day. I didn't care.

After a while, the small talk got old, even for me...and I don't normally have a problem carrying on a conversation, even a one-way one. Then, when I didn't know what else to do, I began speaking from my heart, thinking that if only I would tell Jerod how I felt, he would awaken and call me his "lit'l lady" again. I told him how much I liked his family, including his two crazy aunts. I shared the little I had learned about his life before and told him I wanted to know more, so much more. I believed, I felt in my heart he was listening-- though I never witnessed any physical change to attest to it. His eyes remained shut, his breathing steady while the monitors beeped on like blinking, uncaring sentries.

Then, when I could avoid it no longer, I said it, fully convinced my confession would have to elicit some reaction. "Jerod...Jerod, I miss you," I began haltingly. "You know, you have no right to leave me. Jerod, I love you," I managed, choking back tears.

I half expected to hear his smug, "Yeah, I know," or "Of course you do." But the only thing I heard was the sound of his even, unaltered pattern of respiration and that damn beep. My face in my hands, I sat in that hardened, plastic chair and cried till the flood of my tears had wet my sneakers. Everything that had happened surfaced in my memory again and I saw again the dying faces of Rashid and Jose, the red stain on Christie's sweater, Jerod's blood dripping onto the floor in front of me. I could keep it at bay no longer. I felt myself being pulled into an abyss of despair. I grabbed my crutches and threw them against the side of his bed, the collision with the metal frame incredibly loud in the quiet room.

Hearing the racket, Lindsay, the nurse on duty, hurried in to see what was wrong. Seeing my tear-covered face, she asked after me, but I waved her away.

"Maybe, you just need a break, hon," she said, moving closer to me. "You've been coming here every day for weeks now. It's only natural that sitting here day after day with no change, it would have to get to you." She patted me on the shoulder and I nodded. Then she left me alone again, staring at the man who had saved my life.

You can't quit on him, I told myself. It was just that I didn't know what else was left to do, to say. I stared absently down at the pile of books from my Lit class, stacked on the table next to me. I was slated to return to teaching in a few days, complete with crutches, and had brought some of the texts with me to bone up. In a momentary fit of inspiration or frenzy, I grabbed the book on top of the stack, opened the cover and started to read aloud the words on the page.

"Moby Dick. Chapter one. Loomings. Call me Ishmael. Some years ago--never mind how long precisely--having little or no money in my purse, and nothing particular to interest me on shore, I thought I would sail about a little and see the watery part of the world."

"That's…crap," a raspy voice said.

"It's not crap--"

I jumped up, knocking the book to the floor, and ran to the bed. Jerod's eyes were open, looking at me. I grabbed his hand, squeezed it and did a little hop.

"Lindsay!" I screamed. "He's awake! He's awake!" I tried to choke back my sobs, but it was no use. Tears were pouring out of my eyes so fast, I was having trouble seeing that damn smile. As I squeezed his hand, though, I saw it start and slowly spread across his mouth.

Before I could say anymore, Lindsay bounded into the room and edged me away from the bed. Another nurse and the doctor followed quickly behind and I had to move to the foot of the bed. I didn't care. They checked his vitals. Jerod seemed to take it all in and slowly his eyes found me. He smiled.

"Oh, Jerod, you're back," I managed between sobs. "I love you!"

"I know," he whispered, "I heard ya."

Chapter 63

Forty-five minutes earlier, Jerod had screeched to a halt in front of my apartment in his brand new red Ford Explorer. I eyed the new car, its metallic crimson coat glimmering in the summer sun. I examined him sitting there confidently behind the wheel, sunglasses donned and tanned arm extended. "I have to tell you. This," I gestured to the SUV, "is you!"

"You're right, a'course," he had agreed, all smiles. "Climb in, lit'l lady!"

I threw the small case in the back, set the Igloo cooler on the floor and climbed aboard.

While we rode, he said very little and turned the radio up, playing his favorite country music station. I tried to probe, but I couldn't get him to say anything more about our getaway--he had called it a "clandestine rendezvous." I needed it.

My body had healed well in the past eight months, the burn scars yielding to the treatment and shrinking to pink lines running down my legs. The scars on my heart and soul had not been so easy. I still had nightmares of the glinting steel of the AK-47 and the ugly blackness of the pistol barrel.

I had returned to school to much fanfare--though I wasn't comfortable with that--and had resumed teaching part time. Though the explosions had badly damaged parts of the school, President Ryan and the legislators couldn't move fast enough to allocate special funds to rebuild Thurber. The progress was amazing. Each day I passed the place in the cafeteria where Rashid had spilled his blood for me and I had shot Jesus. The red stain was long since gone, bleached out of the floor that had amazingly survived. Though I no longer shuddered when I crossed the spot on the tile, the deaths still gripped me.

I was working hard to regain my positive perspective on my life and my passion for teaching teenagers, but it was a daily struggle. Jerod was helping, though.

He had promised a scintillating time--I hadn't realized he even knew that word--but no matter how hard I pressed, he would answer none of my questions. He had asked me to pack a picnic lunch, so I selected some cold broiled chicken and a bottle of wine and both were nestled with the ice in the cooler. The weatherman had predicted a rather warm day, typical for July and I had picked out a turquoise tank top and jean cut offs. Jerod had the top down and the warm air blew hot onto my face and tugged at my hair, pulled tight into a ponytail that flapped crazily in the breeze. It felt wonderful. It seemed like I hadn't been able to get warm for months.

"I've got somethin' I want you to see," Jerod announced finally, interrupting my reverie.

He wheeled the Jeep off the main road and turned onto a small, gravel drive. The tires bounced madly over the stones and threw a cloud of dust in the air behind us. At the end of the drive sat a charming, rustic log cabin complete with Americana porch and rockers.

"Jerod, it's beautiful!" I cried, as I climbed out of the Jeep. "It's so Norman Rockwell. How did you find it?"

When I looked beyond the cabin, I saw the glistening water of a small quiet lake, its waves slowly lapping at the shore. Exploring, I took a few tentative steps, edging around the side of the cabin to inspect the rear, and was struck by an incredible view. This was the kind of secret, hidden place they profile on the Travel Channel.

A narrow inlet of water jutted toward the cabin, ending in a small brown sandy beach, and was surrounded on both sides with towering trees. I studied the scene, the rustic cabin, the forested surroundings and the placid water. Not a soul was visible. I watched a pair of birds flitting between two of the tallest pines, and my gaze returned to the lake.

My near drowning in Lake Harold had left me with a deathly fear of the water. In the months since, I had not even ventured out onto the deck at Thurber, much less put my toe in the water. As I stood there staring at the rippling waves, my fear of the water was re-ignited and I shivered involuntarily. I tried to smile, but it must've come out as a grimace.

Recognizing the rising panic in my eyes, Jerod tried to reassure me. "It's okay, Dee Dee. Just relax and breathe deep." He stared into my eyes and breathed with me. In. Out. In. Out. "I'll help ya'."

I continued to inhale and exhale slowly.

He smiled back with that drowsy smile I had come to love. He said, "We're the only ones out here. And this cabin and this beautiful spot is ours for the weekend. Just take your time." He draped his arm comfortably around my shoulders and stood beside me, the two of us gazing out at the scene. Then he leaned in and kissed me lightly. "The cabin comes equipped with some fishing poles and inner tubes and other fun toys. The way I look at it is, you can't stay afraid of the water forever."

"I hope you're right, Jerod." My glance went again to the lake, the water slowly rolling into the shore, and then back at my handsome companion. "I don't think it's going to be easy. I may need a little help."

"That's why I'm here. I have an idea that just might help take your mind off any fear of water," he said, his voice deadpan, as he stared straight ahead at the lake.

Then, looking at his stoic face next to mine, I got it. "But I didn't bring a swim suit."

His smile became a bit of a leer, but one I liked. "I told you that we were completely alone out here...and I won't tell."

"Are you sure you're healed enough?"

He touched his side and his smile turned to a grimace. "You'll just have to be gentle with me." Then another leer.

I kissed him, a kiss still tinged with some anxiety. Wrapping both arms around my middle, he hugged me tightly. He returned the kiss, his tongue briefly touching mine, setting off pleasant sensations rippling inside me. I began to forget about the water. I felt Jerod rise to meet me between my legs. I let my gaze travel down between us and said, "Not too gentle, I hope."

Using only his one good arm, he grabbed me around the waist and carried me to the edge of the water. "Better kick off those nice shoes if you don't want them to get wet," he said.

I kicked off my new leather Birkenstocks and let them drop on the sand. He carried me two steps out, kissed me again and gently lowered my legs into the water.

At first, the warm water lapping at my ankles startled me, but then, secure in his arms, I relaxed and enjoyed the refreshing sensation of the warm water on my bare feet and ankles. I put my arms around his neck and kissed him back, no hesitation this time and a little more passion in the effort. As our lips and tongues touched again, exploring, probing, I was enjoying the sensation. He lowered me gently and my footing settled on the sandy bottom, the water less than eight inches deep. When I realized I was standing, I pulled away briefly and looked down. My eyes came up to meet his and I smiled. He smirked back as if to say, "I told you so." I tightened my hold on his neck and kissed him again, my tongue on a quest for passion.

"You better be careful. You're giving me ideas," he said, his arms still securely around my waist.

"Go ahead," I responded, smiling, "I think it might be advisable to pursue some of those ideas."

"How about this one?" he asked. He grabbed the bottom of my tank top and, in one quick motion, pulled it over my head, my ponytail bouncing. His right hand tossed the turquoise top and we both watched it float to the sand, just out of reach of the lapping waves.

I stood there, the sun warming my bare skin and found that I was more than comfortable. Inexplicably, surrounded by this lake, I felt no fear of water, only the rush of passion and love for this incredible man. The pair of lovebirds-- that's what I decided they must've been--began singing to us. He leaned his head toward mine and kissed me again, but this time his lips didn't linger long. Instead they began a series of slow kisses that started at my neck and edged slowly southward.

I looked down toward his head, smiling. "I like where this is headed."

He returned my smile and continued his quest.

LEAVE NO CHILD BEHIND

READER'S GUIDE

- What is a hero? Do you believe everyday individuals can be regarded as heroes?

- Do you believe the character of Dee Dee Sterber is a hero? Is her commitment to and defense of her students, even at the risk of her own life, realistic and acceptable within the context of the story? Have you known teachers or worked with teachers, or have your children had teachers like Dee Dee who would be willing to sacrifice their lives for her students? Do you consider them heroes?

- There are some important time elements in the story. In the prologue, the terrorist, Asad Akadi, is given direction to explode his bomb at a specific time? Why is the selection of this moment important to Al Quaida? What is the significance in the story of the time showing on the clock on the book cover?

- The story is set largely in a high school in rural, small town America. Are the high school experiences captured in the story similar to your experiences as a student? a teacher? as a parent of a student? How does this geographical setting contribute to the tale? Could this story take place in other settings such as a suburban or urban high school?

- "Before you embark on a journey of revenge, dig two graves." --Confucius. Which of the characters in the story appear to be motivated largely by revenge? Why does this quote seem especially appropriate to these characters?

- Have you known teachers like Bob Holden in your experience as a student or teacher? How do you feel about what happens to this character? What do you think about the plaque dedicated to him in the newly rebuilt school?

- What message do you believe Rashid passed on to Asad Akadi during the interview in the HBE prison?

- The title is obviously a deliberate twist on the well-known and politically manipulated phrase, "No Child Left Behind." During the novel, the actual words of the title are used twice in the story by two different speakers. Which two characters speak these words and how are their meanings significant to the story?

- What are your impressions of the character of Harold Samson? Do you think he should have done more to influence the President with regards to the terrorist threat and the execution of Asad Akadi? Compare the novel's portrayal of decision-making within this bureaucracy to your own experiences or your perception of how this process functions in your organization.

- How well do you believe the character of Dean Settler captures the essence of the political element of American democratic leadership? How is the physical description an apt metaphor for his character. Given the current state of election politics in this country, are his political concerns out of place, or necessary in the crisis situation of the story?

- This story is in part about the transitions individuals go through, especially in crisis. The crises of the story cause significant changes in the belief systems of the central character, Dee Dee Sterber. Given the predicaments she encounters, is the transition of Dee Dee's character acceptable, from a tolerant individual willing to accept everyone to someone who could pull the trigger on another human being? What would it take for you to be willing to take another's life?

HARSH LESSONS

"All right, guys, it's 9:20 and almost time for lights out for all fifth graders," shouted a loud male voice over the din of voices and music in cabin number three.

"But Mr. Taylor, it's wa-a-y too early. We're not supposed to go to bed yet," James countered in his most unassuming voice. "I haven't been able to finish my daily journal entry and *I* wouldn't want to be late getting my work done for school." This was followed by a hail of laughter from the other fifteen boys in the cabin.

John Taylor, the father of one of the boys, knew this group well. He strode across the wooden cabin to the third upper bunk where a music player bellowed out the strained lyrics of some rap group, whose name he didn't know and didn't want to know. Studying the top of the Ipod player, he found what he wanted and with a flourish hit the stop button and immediately the music--though he wouldn't call it that--ceased. "Things are already quiet and dark in the other cabins. I'll give you ten minutes," he declared. "Hit the bathroom, get your teeth brushed, take your shower if you want, but in ten minutes, the lights go off and you're all going to bed." He walked quickly out through the doorway away from a quieted group of fifth grade boys, the frenzied cacophony reduced to mumbles and whispered protests.

"Guys, you heard what he said," James said with assumed authority.

"What?" Robert said, waddling over to him, "You're going to do what *he* said?"

"Guys, the man said we have to hit the hay, and that's what we're going to do," James answered loudly enough for all the boys to hear. Then, in a voice that only the two around him could make out, "Besides, we can't get the good stuff out until everyone is asleep and this place is quiet."

Chad and Robert nodded in hushed conspiracy. One of the other boys turned the player back on, but turned the volume down. As if on cue, all the boys in the cabin went about their preparations for bed, if somewhat begrudgingly. Crowding around the small, rustic sinks stained long ago with yellow-brown streaks, the boys hurriedly brushed their teeth. They waited their turns to use the two urinals and two toilets. One small boy with brown hair and croooked teeth, who had waited too long to go, bounced from one foot to the other, trying to hold it a little longer. Three of the boys decided to take quick showers. When they stepped out of the shower stalls, they dried off quickly, but not completely, and put their sweats on their still wet bodies, the cotton clothing clinging to their moist skin.

True to his word, Mr. Taylor returned and rousted the remaining stragglers into their beds. He walked the length of the small cabin, checking each of the eight pairs of bunk beds. Returning to the entrance, he put his hand up to the sole light switch. "Okay, gentlemen, the counselors tell me they have another big day planned for tomorrow," he said in this best parental voice. "Let's get to sleep so we're ready for it. Good night."

A chorus of reluctant "good nights" answered and he switched off the lights, waited for a while, and then walked back out through the only doorway.

As soon as he was out of earshot, the whispers began again. Waiting long enough to be sure Mr. Taylor would not return, pairs of students spoke of the day's events in hushed tones. One pair of boys plotted their great prank for tomorrow. Finally, Robert, who was in the top bunk in the far corner, leaned his bulk over the edge of the bed and squinted his face at his bunkmate, "Okay, James, now what?" he whispered.

"Now nothing, dumb ass!" James answered in a long, almost angry whisper.

"But, you said after they turned the lights off and we went to bed we would --" Robert began.

James cut him off. "We gotta wait till the others are asleep," he said through clenched teeth. "Be quiet and I'll call ya' when it's time." His tone left no quarter and Robert knew better than to argue with James anyway.

"Hey, don't forget about me!" hissed a third whining voice from the bunk next to Robert.

"I know, Chad. Just shut up!" James shot back.

It took almost an hour for the sixteen restless youths to settle down to silence. There were just too many tales of the day to rehash and the darkness of the primitive cabin provided a mantle of secrecy that added to the thrill of violating the camp rule of quiet at lights out. But, eventually, the strenuous exercise of the day's activities caught up with them, and most could hold sleep off no longer. Movement on the cots ceased. One by one, the whispers died away and were replaced with the slow, steady breathing of slumber.

Through it all, James listened and did not move. He could barely contain himself. He had been told that what he brought with him was an experience like he had never had. But he couldn't let anyone else know, except his buddies, Robert and Chad. He waited till he was sure that the rest of the cabin was asleep, then he kicked the upper bunk where Robert's head was.

"Hey!" Robert cried at the jab.

"Sh-h-h!" James hissed back. "It's party time. Come on down here."

Robert reached over and slapped Chad's arm that hung over the edge of the neighboring top bunk. The same sequence of cries and "sh's" followed and then Chad joined the other two boys in the darkness next to James' bed.

"Okay, where is this big deal?" Robert whispered impatiently.

"Not with my clothes, asshole," James shot back. "You can't keep this stuff with your clothes, my brother told me that. I've got it stashed in a loose board I found in the wall." He led the two over to a darkened corner, counted five boards up from the floor, and began probing with his fingers. "There!" he said, his voice filled with exhilaration, and pulled his hand out. All the other two could see was a closed fist around a plastic bag.

"Hey, what do you have there?" said a squeaky voice behind them. All three boys reeled in unison, James whipping his fist behind his back.

The three boys stood in the dark, facing the slightly gangly figure of another student staring at them. Knowing he couldn't possibly replace his cargo without being seen, James tried bravado. "Hey guys, it's the squeaky freak. Justin, shut up and get back in your bunk," he hissed.

The macho was lost on Justin. His brown eyes narrowed in determination. "Look, you guys are into something and I want in," he argued in a whisper, trying to sound just as tough. "Either I'm in or I'll get my father," he challenged, playing his trump card.

For a long moment the boys stood, silent, facing each other. Chad and Robert turned to look at James, who stared angrily at the intruder. They thought for a moment that James would hit Justin and start a fight in the dim corner of the cabin, but James knew better. Any fight, almost any noise, would screw up his plans for the night, and he wasn't about to let that happen. A new plan was taking shape in his mind, and he broke into a wide grin. Seeing his reaction, Chad and Robert immediately relaxed without really knowing why, but Justin remained tense, uncertain of what the change meant.

"Okay, you want in, huh?" hissed James with a smirk. "Well, it's gonna cost you."

"What?" was all Justin could squeal out.

"If you're going to join us, you gotta contribute." Before Justin could interrupt, James went on. "I want ya' to go get your dad's car keys."

"Why? Wh-wh-what do you want those for?" stammered Justin.

"Because I just got a great idea. We're goin' for a little ride out of here and take our party on the road," James said.

Justin's face turned white, evident even in the darkness. He didn't know what to do. He was scared at the prospect of answering to his father, but even more terrified of being embarrassed by James. Finally, he turned and padded noiselessly to the other end of the cabin where his father slept in the small adjacent bedroom.

"Have you ever driven a car?" asked Chad in a voice with equal parts of fear and excitement.

"Sure," James answered with false assurance. "I've driven my mom's old car plenty, at least in the driveway."

"This is gonna be fuckin'-A great," added Robert, trying to build up his confidence. He was alternately thrilled and terrified at the prospect of joy riding with James, but whenever these little battles raged inside him, he would always side with James.

Justin returned to the dark corner where the three boys were huddled and James didn't wait long before saying, "Well?" Justin's response was to raise his right hand slowly in front of the other boys and open his palm. There attached to a battered Budweiser key chain were the keys to a G.M. automobile. "What kind of car does your dad drive anyway?" James asked in a mean whisper.

"A Camaro Z-28," answered Justin, his voice an odd mixture of pride and anxiety.

"That ain't no piece of shit," said James, smiling broadly. "Okay, let's go."

At his command the other three boys moved quietly through the side door of the cabin. As they opened it, it squeaked, just a bare bleep of a noise, but loud enough to alarm Chad who was already halfway through the doorframe. Turning quickly to look into the darkened room, he saw a few of the boys roll over at the sound, but nothing else. He sighed in relief and continued out the door, holding it for the other three boys.

James took up his accustomed position at the front of the small group as they began threading their way through the woods surrounding the cabin. The four boys had to wind their way through the woods on a narrow trail, their only light from the full moon that danced from treetop to treetop. Intent, James pressed on and rounded the corners, his feet stepping faster as they moved away from the cabins and edged closer to his goal. The gravel lot where the cars were parked was more than a quarter mile from the cabins and by the time they had reached the clearing in the forest, all four boys were panting, out of breath and hot with anticipation. When they came out of the dense woods, they saw the sleek car sitting, darkly alone on the gravel lot as if awaiting their arrival. James stopped beside the car, admiring, and the other three halted abruptly beside him, asking no questions. Staring wide-eyed at the sports car, he examined it for a moment, as if inspecting an unexpected gift. In the dim light of the night forest, the car seemed to be a shimmering black, though it could have been any dark color. Even in the bare moonlight, it was obvious to James that the car was in mint condition, despite the years.

James approached the driver's side and ran his fingers over the smooth finish. He tried the handle and it opened easily to his touch, the metal door swinging out heavily. Excitedly, he climbed in behind the steering wheel and Chad, Robert, and Justin all climbed inside. The fabric on the seat was soft to his touch and reflected a red and gray pattern in the dim dome light. The boys closed the two doors, one after the other and at the clunk of the heavy doors, they glanced back toward the cabins. They waited and held their breath, but no lights came on in the cabins, so they exhaled loudly and laughed nervously.

James turned the key in the ignition and the engine coughed once quietly but nothing happened. Then James remembered in an older car he needed to press the accelerator to feed gas to the large engine. He repeated the process, this time depressing the gas pedal. The engine coughed twice more and then caught, with a low, throaty sound. "Yes!" called James a little too loudly and all four stole looks toward the cabins again, worried. Still, there was no sign of life and James figured they must be far enough away for the dense trees to swallow up the noises. He was grateful for the darkness of the woods. His hands sweat as he tried to grip the steering wheel and he tried to cover up so the others wouldn't notice. "Okay, let's get the hell out of here!" he squealed, laughing nervously. Then with the arrogance born of youth and folly, James plunged ahead with abandon. Into a deathtrap of his own making.

Hungry anticipation shining in his eyes, James put the car in reverse and began backing the car across the clearing, turning the wheel to angle it on the gravel. At the touch of his foot on the accelerator, the car responded more strongly than he expected and rolled quickly across the clearing, crunching the gravel under the tires. Hurriedly, James moved his foot from the accelerator to the brake pedal, but the seat was still too far back for him to reach. He had to stretch to reach the pedal. He extended his leg to jam on the petal but not in time as the back bumper of the car clunked a tree on the edge of the turnaround, echoing in the dark woods. At the noise, the other three boys dove into the seats, the three heads disappearing from the windows like small animals hiding in burrows, leaving James alone upright in the seat. Terrified, James turned his head slowly to look back toward the cabins, fully expecting to see Justin's father running down the path toward the car. Remarkably, he saw no one and noticed that the cabins remained the same--quiet, dark. He blurted something inaudible, laughing at the other three, put the car in drive and hit the accelerator. At first, the Z-28 didn't move, its tires only spinning wildly in the loose gravel, shooting the tiny stones in all directions. Then, suddenly, the wheels bit and the car barreled down the dark gravel road. James' fingers searched frantically and finally found the right switch and flipped on the headlights, illuminating the darkened surroundings. James couldn't contain himself. He let out a celebratory whoop, turning to look at his friends in triumph. The fellow conspirators were all smiles now, basking in the cocky assurance of their leader.

As James turned even briefly to look at the others, he did what the inexperienced driver often does. He turned the wheel slightly, his hands following his glance. The power steering of the powerful vehicle responded to the slight touch and suddenly James saw the car veering off the small road headed for the woods. He turned the wheel sharply back to the left and found the Camaro now careening off the other side of the road. He struggled several times, turning the wheel in opposite directions until he was able to get it centered back on the road. Exhaling audibly, he hit the brakes and turned around to look at the three other boys. Chad, Robert, and Justin were all various shades of ash, their knuckles white as they grabbed the armrests on the doors. It wasn't until James unleashed his challenge, "What a bunch of pussies! You chickenshits ain't afraid, are you?" that they let go of the armrests and pretended to relax.

"I think you guys need a little help and that's just what I got," James said as he patted the pocket of his bulky sweatshirt. Robert, who sat in the front seat beside his buddy, looked over and could just barely make out the edge of a plastic bag James had had earlier, sticking out of the pocket. "Let's get up here where I can pull this beast over."

He drove the car farther down the gravel lane. The others sat quietly, breathing heavily, anticipating the next thrill from their leader. Just before the lane turned to meet Highway 27, the camp road branched off to the left. James turned the car onto the fork, hit the brakes, put the car in park and killed the engine. He turned to look at his buddies and when he flipped on the interior light, the boys noticed his smile was broader than ever. He pulled out the plastic bag and, dangling it so the cellophane caught and bounced the dim light, brandished it in front of the others.

"These are what they call 'acid tattoos' and they are just what you need." As he spoke, he removed the small objects carefully from the zip lock bag, while the other three strained to see what he held in the dim light. What they saw looked to be brightly colored slips of paper, about two inches square. On the paper in brilliant hues of blue, white, and yellow was the clear image of a wolf's head. The boys were intrigued but not sure what to make of it.

"So, how does it work?" Chad was brave enough to ask.

"Gimme your arm and I'll show you," answered James as his hand beckoned like a carnival barker. Laying his arm over the worn headrest, Chad pulled up the sleeve of his shirt, exposing his bare arm. James took the first of the 'tattoos' off the pile and, holding it between his two fingers, carefully peeled off the backing. He gripped Chad's arm tightly and applied the patch to the bare arm just about halfway between the shoulder and elbow. Then, still gripping the arm, he held it up to the bare light bulb and examined his work. "That oughta do it," he proclaimed.

"Do what?" Chad asked.

"Just wait a bit," James answered. "My brother said it takes a few minutes before it hits you. Okay, who's next?"

"I'm game," piped up Robert and exposed his arm for the application. James repeated the same motions and soon they were staring at a second wolf's head image applied to Robert's arm.

"Well, Justin, you said you wanted in. Put up or shut up," challenged James, eyeing the small figure in the back seat.

"Wh-wh-what about you?" stammered back Justin, his voice squeaking, suddenly nervous at his decision to join the adventure.

"Oh, I'm going as soon as I take care of you guys. I wouldn't miss this ride for the world," James said. "You wouldn't be turning chicken on us now, would you, Justin?" At the mention of the word, both Robert and Chad began making loud clucking sounds at Justin.

Quickly, Justin thrust his arm at the larger boy in the driver's seat and said, "Here." In a few seconds, James had a third tattoo exposed and applied. With Justin's arm done, James rolled up his sleeve and, while Robert held back the shirt, he attached the patch carefully to his own arm. He sat back and released a satisfied sigh. He eased his body back, resting his shoulders against the door, and stretched his legs out across the seat toward Robert.

For a few moments, the car was quiet. The only sound, beyond those of nature at night, was the tense breathing of the four boys, the quiet before the storm.

It was Chad who first broke the silence. "Wow! Holy shit!" was what the other three boys heard.

"Tell us!" commanded James, still in charge.

"You won't believe it," began Chad again. "That light, it's not white anymore," he said, pointing at the car dome light. "It's.... it's.... it's split into a hundred goddamn colors. God, it's great. It looks like one of them tubes you look into with all them colored cubes that change when you turn it." His words came fast, hurriedly, rambling. He turned his head to look at the light sideways and repeated, "This is so great."

"Oh god, I see it," declared Robert. "They're like jumping out at me. I can almost grab them," and he reached his hands out toward the light. The movement of the tattooed arm sent more acid into his bloodstream and he reacted to it. "God, the colors are changing. Now they look sick."

"I don't know what you're talking about, but I can taste the colors." Inside James' head the colors danced. As he turned his head to look up at the single light, he watched as bright oranges, reds and blues darted past his face. He stuck out his tongue to try to catch them as they passed. He was successful with a few and he laughed as he ingested them, or thought he did. "The reds taste goddamn incredible and the blues, wow. My brother was right. This is one hell of a trip."

"I wish you guys could see how weird you look, right now," Justin announced in a taunting voice from the back seat, as he turned his head cockeyed at the other three. "I always thought you were a little strange, but now your faces look...weird like the green mask guy in that movie we saw on TV the other night, only butt uglier!" he laughed at the boy across the seat from him.

"Well you--" began Chad and then stopped mid-sentence, his arm stretched out menacingly toward Justin. "I'll be dammed. Look at my arm. It looks like it's...forever. I think I could stretch it to touch that tree trunk over there," he said pointing to a tree about twenty feet away. The other three boys stared wide-eyed in Chad's direction, but they were each lost in their own world. Then Chad said, "James, I never noticed your face looks like a huge banana!"

"Shut up, you dumb ass and listen," commanded James and he turned and rolled down the window. The cool night air oozed into the car along with the sounds of the forest at night. "Can't you hear that?" he demanded of the others and at his insistent voice, they all leaned toward him to listen. "Hey do-da-do-da-ach-ooh," he attempted to sing, rambling nonsense syllables and discordant notes together. "The forest is so great, it sings along with you," intoned the large fifth grader, singing far more loudly than he ever did with the Maestro in music class. James sang on in an incoherent babble, as the sounds of crickets and frogs were transformed into notes in his head and he sang to try to match them.

His stream of mixed up notes was cut off abruptly by Robert's hand on his shoulder. "Hey, James let's get outa here," Robert said in a voice suddenly laced with fear.

"Why?" James asked, his head back still bouncing to the unvoiced music in his head.

"I don't know," answered Robert, glancing out the windows anxiously. "I think we better just get the hell out of here."

"Sure, Robert, why not?" said James. "Let's go for another ride, out on the open road." He reached down for where the keys were supposed to be. As he stared at the ignition, he noticed the keys that hung there seemed to pulse in and out, receding every time he tried to reach for them. He tried three times, each time his fingers came away empty, grasping only air and for some reason he found his failures ridiculously funny. His laughed again and again, his whole body convulsing with spasms of laughter. Soon his three partners were chortling uncontrollably too, though they had no idea why. James took a deep breath and on the fourth try, he finally grabbed the dangling keys, turned the ignition, and the engine roared to life. The four boys made imitative engine sounds, laughing again at their own wonderful noises.

James flipped the headlights back on and backed the car onto the gravel. Turning to focus his eyes on the highway ahead, he saw no signs of any traffic. With drug-induced confidence he steered the heavy frame onto the asphalt road and down the black path, the lumbering weight of the car bearing down upon the blacktop. Since the camp was set so far out in the country, there were no other lights on the country road, the only illumination coming from the car's headlights. He drove on, feeling exhilarated and powerful and he stretched out his foot to press the accelerator further. The powerful engine responded with a surge. "Yeah!" James uttered triumphantly, laughing at the world.

"Hey, I want some more fresh air, so I can drink in this nature-loving shit," called Chad, mimicking the camp counselors. He rolled the window all the way down and pulled his body up to the edge of the frame. He sat with his torso out the window. "God, this is beautiful, James, just beautiful. Hey, Justin, get your ass up here, the weather's fine," and he threw his head back and laughed.

In the euphoric effect of the drug, Justin was less inhibited now, willing to try to be fearless. He followed Chad's lead and was soon perched, buttocks on the window frame, hands pounding on the roof of the car, slapping the metal crazily. Soon all four boys were laughing again fitfully, uncontrollably. As James moved the car around a wide turn, both Chad and Justin had to hold on as the car swayed and Justin yelled "Whoa, boy!" and they giggled again.

As they came out of the turn, the light came at them from the other end of the now straight stretch of highway. As it approached and grew brighter, it struck their fractured sense of sight. The kaleidoscope effect they had experienced earlier returned, splintering the white headlights into brilliant, dashing blues, reds, oranges, yellows and purples. All four boys were mesmerized by the vision, their brains seduced by the fractured light and they drank it in hungrily. James sat back, let go of the wheel, and muttered, "Isn't that smooth?"

As he relaxed his grip of the steering wheel, the car began to swerve to the right, pulled by the unaligned front right side. Enraptured by the drug-induced vision, the boys didn't notice as the right side of the car bumped off the pavement onto the gravel of the narrow shoulder. The right tires bit into the soft earth off the road and pulled the car farther to the right. Even though James had eased his foot off the accelerator, the car continued at too fast a speed, carried by the weight. The front right tire hit a large rock in the gully and the car bounced over it, angling the big frame towards the woods. There was still time now, but James, the steering wheel before him, was caught up in his own psychedelic world. The vehicle now moved on its own as if it were some evil predator, bouncing over the edge of the roadway into the woods.

To the four boys, it was vision- and sound-laden, almost in slow motion, though it was over in mere seconds. As the car came off the road, the front end dove into the woods. The front of the Camaro barreled down small saplings. The land beside the road dropped off quickly to a ravine, thirty feet below the paved surface. Without guidance, the car was propelled down the steep slope and careened down the hillside. In a matter of seconds, the auto hit the bottom of the ravine, the front fender slamming savagely into the rock ledge.

The impact of the crash was tremendous, throwing Chad and Justin fiercely from the car like huge rag dolls. Chad's body was hurled roughly against a large oak that grew out of the bottom of the ravine. The sound of cracking bones echoed through the forest as his small frame was wrapped around the large tree. On the other side Justin's small body was tossed out the open window onto a smaller tree nearby. The force was so great that his stomach was impaled on one of the thin branches. His blood spurted through the wound, splashing crimson over the side of the car. From the front seat Robert's big body was hurled at the windshield, which shattered on impact. The broken glass sliced his tender skin everywhere. Rivulets of red to streamed down every part of his exposed front, smearing the fractured windshield with a thin scarlet glaze.

In the same instant, James, in the driver's seat, was smashed against the steering wheel, the force so great that it instantly crushed his rib cage and collapsed his lungs. Just before he lost all consciousness, he thought he heard a car door and a voice calling.